George Bernard Shaw was born in Dublin, Ireland, on July 26, 1856. He attended four different schools but his real education came from a thorough grounding in music and painting, which he obtained at home. In 1871, he was apprenticed to a Dublin estate agent, and later he worked as a cashier. In 1876, Shaw joined his mother and sister in London, where he spent the next nine years in unrecognized struggle and genteel poverty.

From 1885 to 1898, he wrote for newspapers and magazines as critic of art, literature, music, and drama. But his main interest at this time was political propaganda, and, in 1884, he joined the Fabian Society. From 1893 to 1939, the most active period of his career, Shaw wrote 47 plays. By 1915, his international fame was firmly established and productions of *Candida*, *Man and Superman*, *Arms and the Man*, *The Devil's Disciple*, *Caesar and Cleopatra*, *Major Barbara*, and *The Doctor's Dilemma*, were being played in many countries of the world, from Britain to Japan. In 1925 the playwright was awarded the Nobel Prize for Literature. Between the ages of fifty-seven and sixty-seven, Shaw wrote such dramas as *Heartbreak House*, *Back to Methuselah*, *Androcles and the Lion*, *St. Joan*. During his lifetime he was besieged by offers to film his plays, but he accepted only a few, the most notable being *Caesar and Cleopatra*, *Major Barbara*, and *Pygmalion*, which was adapted (after his death) as the basis for the musical *My Fair Lady*. He died at the age of ninety-four at Ayot St. Lawrence, England, on November 2, 1950.

GEORGE BERNARD SHAW

Three Plays

MAJOR BARBARA

•

CAESAR and CLEOPATRA

•

THE DOCTOR'S DILEMMA

A SIGNET CLASSIC

NEW AMERICAN LIBRARY

NEW YORK AND SCARBOROUGH, ONTARIO

NAL BOOKS ARE AVAILABLE AT QUANTITY DISCOUNTS
WHEN USED TO PROMOTE PRODUCTS OR SERVICES.
FOR INFORMATION PLEASE WRITE TO PREMIUM MARKETING DIVISION.
NEW AMERICAN LIBRARY. 1633 BROADWAY.
NEW YORK. NEW YORK 10019.

Acknowledgment is made to The Society of Authors Ltd. London, England, on behalf of the Bernard Shaw Estate, for permission to reprint the Prologue to *Caesar and Cleopatra*.

SIGNET TRADEMARK REG. U.S. PAT. OFF. AND FOREIGN COUNTRIES
REGISTERED TRADEMARK—MARCA REGISTRADA
HECHO EN CHICAGO. U.S.A.

SIGNET, SIGNET CLASSIC, MENTOR, PLUME, MERIDIAN AND NAL BOOKS
are published by New American Library,
1633 Broadway, New York, New York 10019

First Signet Classic Printing, August, 1985

1 2 3 4 5 6 7 8 9

PRINTED IN THE UNITED STATES OF AMERICA

CONTENTS

Introduction
vii

A Note on Shaw's Spelling
xxx

Chronology
xxxi

MAJOR BARBARA
3

CAESAR AND CLEOPATRA
139

THE DOCTOR'S DILEMMA
257

INTRODUCTION

Bernard Shaw (1856–1950) wrote fifty-three plays, including several one-act plays. This body of work may not seem remarkably large for a man who lived more than ninety-four years, but plays were only a part of it. Shaw was a journalist (art criticism, music criticism, drama criticism); lecturer and writer on religion (he espoused an evolutionary religion whose equivalent of Providence was the Life Force); lecturer and writer on social topics (war, socialism, housing, prison reform, vivisection, education, spelling reform, and countless other subjects); unsuccessful novelist (five novels between 1876 and 1883); and, in a random sort of way, autobiographer. He was also actively engaged in staging his plays, at least ten of which remain staples of the English-language repertory. Only Shakespeare provides a larger number. If one thinks of the repertory, one thinks—putting aside Shakespeare—of a single play by Marlowe, perhaps two or three by Jonson, two by Congreve, one by Goldsmith, two by Sheridan, one or two by Wilde, one or two by Synge and by Yeats (it's interesting to notice how Irishmen keep turning up on the English stage), and perhaps three or four each by O'Neill, Miller, Williams, and Beckett, but time probably will winnow the works of these last writers. To note, then, that Shaw still lives on the stage with ten or perhaps even a dozen plays (say, *Mrs. Warren's Profession*, *Arms and the Man*, *Candida*, *The Doctor's Dilemma*, *Caesar and Cleopatra*, *Man and Superman, Major Barbara, Misalliance, Androcles and the Lion, Pygmalion, Heartbreak House,* and *Saint Joan*) is to call attention to an extraordinary achievement.

This volume contains the chief plays that Shaw wrote between 1898 and 1906, with the omission of *Man and Superman* (published in another Signet Classic volume) and of the underrated *John Bull's Other Island.* He had already written his "unpleasant" plays (*Widowers' Houses, The Philanderer, Mrs. Warren's Profession*) and also his "pleasant" plays (*Arms and the Man, Candida, The Man of Destiny, The Devil's Disciple*), which is to say that he was a mature dramatist at the height of his powers. And, as might be expected from a master playwright and a man of wide interests, each of our three plays is distinctive. *Caesar and Cleopatra* can be called a history play, *Major Barbara* a discussion play, the *The Doctor's Dilemma* a tragedy—although all of these terms will have to be modified, and we will in the end find that it is best simply to call all three plays Shavian.

Since Shaw was so ardent a pamphleteer, often equipping his published plays with long prefaces that were sometimes only loosely connected to issues in the plays, it is not surprising that writers on Shaw have given more attention to his ideas than to his artistry. Shaw himself said that he turned to the stage because he wanted to convey ideas effectively: "Fine art is the only teacher except torture. . . . You cannot listen to a lesson or a sermon unless the teacher or the preacher is an artist." Over and over again he insisted that he was a didactic writer, but because his theatrical sermons introduced new topics into drama, and because he espoused the drama of Ibsen—who in the nineties was not yet acceptable in the eyes of most British drama critics—Shaw was regarded as an utterly unconventional dramatist. In reply he often made the point that he learned his dramatic techniques not only from Ibsen but from the whole history of drama and of opera. Thus, he pointed out, the stage was used for didactic purposes by the ancient Greeks (Aristophanes did not hesitate to address the audience directly) and by the medieval church; and in the preface to his *Complete Plays* he said that his "business as a classic writer is 'to chasten morals with ridicule.' " Of course he sometimes emphasized his iconoclastic role, as in this statement:

> I am not an ordinary playwright in general practice. I am a specialist in immoral and heretical plays. My reputation has been gained by my persistent struggle to force the public to reconsider its morals. . . . I write plays with the deliberate object of converting the nation to my opinion in these matters.

At least as often, however, he insisted that he was pouring his new wine into old bottles:

> My stories are the old stories; my characters are the familiar harlequin and Columbine, clown and pantaloon. . . . My stage tricks and suspenses and thrills and jests are the ones in vogue when I was a boy, by which time my grandfather was tired of them.

And in the last year of his life, at the age of ninety-four, he said, "I was, and still am, the most old-fashioned playwright outside China and Japan." Something of this union of shocking ideas set forth by means of traditional dramatic techniques was foreshadowed in Shaw's activities when the critic William Archer first met him, before Shaw turned his hand to playwrighting. (It was Archer who later urged Shaw to write for the stage, and the two then collaborated on a play for a while, before Archer dropped it. Shaw later revised the work into his first play, *Widowers' Houses*.) Archer (to get back to their first meeting) encountered Shaw in the reading room of the British Museum, where Shaw was simultaneously reading Marx's *Capital* and the score of Wagner's *Tristan and Isolde*. Shaw had acquired an interest in economics more or less on his own, but he had inherited his interest in music from his mother, who was an opera singer and a teacher of music. He was later to find that drama, especially drama with what can be called operatic passages, could be the art that would enable him to preach effectively. "Opera," he wrote,

> taught me to shape my plays into recitatives, arias, duets, trios, ensemble finales, and bravura pieces to display the technical accomplishments of the executants, with the quaint result that the Times critic declared that they were not plays at all as plays had been defined for all times by Aristotle.

It would be an exaggeration to say that one has only to open this volume at random to see the truth of this remark, but it is no exaggeration to say that dozens of examples can be found. Here, for instance, is a duet from *Major Barbara*. Undershaft, the munitions manufacturer, has offered to take into his business Cusins, a professor of Greek. In the course of the bargaining Cusins demands, among other things, ten percent of the profit:

UNDERSHAFT (*taken aback*). Ten per cent! Why, man, do you know what my profits are?

CUSINS. Enormous, I hope: otherwise I shall require twenty-five per cent.

UNDERSHAFT. But, Mr. Cusins, this is a serious matter of business. You are not bringing any capital into the concern.

CUSINS. What! no capital! Is my mastery of Greek no capital? Is my access to the subtlest thought, the loftiest poetry yet attained by humanity, no capital? My character! my intellect! my life! my career! what Barbara calls my soul! are these no capital? Say another word; and I double my salary.

UNDERSHAFT. Be reasonable—

CUSINS (*peremptorily*). Mr. Undershaft: you have my terms. Take them or leave them.

UNDERSHAFT (*recovering himself*). Very well. I note your terms; and I offer you half.

CUSINS (*disgusted*). Half!

UNDERSHAFT (*firmly*). Half.

CUSINS. You call yourself a gentleman; and you offer me half!!

UNDERSHAFT. I do not call myself a gentleman; but I offer you half.

When Shaw says, however, that the operatic influence caused him to produce plays that "the Time's critic declared . . . were not plays at all as plays had been defined for all times by Aristotle," he is being mischievous. The accusations that he was not dramatic were based on his habit of including in his plays—which often follow the traditions of comedy, of melodrama, and sometimes even of tragedy—

serious, sustained discussions of pressing social issues. To the charge that his plays were all talk, he offered a witty answer: "It is quite true that my plays are all talk, just as Raphael's pictures are all paint, Michael Angelo's statues all marble, Beethoven's symphonies all noise." He went on to say that of course the talk has "ideas behind it," and that "the quality of a play is the quality of its ideas."

And here we get to something that, despite his frequent protestations that he is a traditional dramatist, sets him off from most of the dramatists who preceded Ibsen. In the essay that includes the last two quotations, Shaw goes on to say that it is not enough for a playwright merely to record the passing scene, to hold the mirror up to nature (Hamlet's words, echoing a passage attributed to Cicero on the function of comedy). The perceptive playwright is not a mere spectator but an interpreter; he is, of course, an entertainer too, but what makes him immortal is that he is "intensely didactic." Shaw had pointed out much earlier, in *The Quintessence of Ibsenism* (1891, revised 1913), that Ibsen introduced into drama "a new technical factor," a discussion. When Ibsen came to the stage, the chief form of drama was the so-called well-made play, really a melodrama in a contemporary middle-class setting, with an exposition, situation, and unraveling or denouement, a kind of plot that has been described as "Get your man up a tree, throw rocks at him, and then get him down from the tree." But Ibsen, Shaw explained, was not content with the well-made play. "Formerly," he said,

> you had in what was called a wellmade play an exposition in the first act, a situation in the second, and unravelling in the third. Now you have exposition, situation, and discussion; and the discussion is the test of the playwright. . . . The discussion conquered Europe in Ibsen's *Doll's House;* and now the serious playwright recognizes in the discussion not only the main test of his highest powers, but also the real centre of his play's interest.

Later, commenting on the drama after Ibsen, he returned to the topic:

> But the discussion, though at first it appears as a regularly placed feature at the end of the last act, and is initiated by the

> woman, as in *A Doll's House* and *Candida*, soon spreads itself over the whole play. Both authors and audiences realise more and more that the incidents and situations in a play are only pretences, and that what is interesting is the way we should feel and argue about them if they were real. . . . In *The Doctor's Dilemma* you have discussion producing action, and that action being finally discussed.

None of this could have been written, of course, if Ibsen's Nora, near the end of *A Doll's House*, had not said, "Sit down, Torvald; we have a lot to talk over," and then forced on Torvald the first serious talk in their eight years of married life. This all seems very familiar to us, but we should remember that the first English production of *A Doll's House*, in William Archer's translation, was given in 1889. In 1892 Shaw wrote *Widowers' Houses* in order to provide an English Ibsenite play for the English stage. He followed it with *The Philanderer* (1893) and *Mrs. Warren's Profession* (1893–94), thus producing three plays that he called "unpleasant" because they dealt with contemporary social issues that most Englishmen did not wish to discuss. We will talk more about the "discussion" play later, especially in connection with *Major Barbara*, but now it is time to look at the plays in this book.

The three "unpleasant" plays were followed by four "pleasant" plays written in 1894–96, and then by *The Devil's Disciple* (1897), a play that used the conventions of melodrama but used them to set forth a critique of modern Christianity. For Shaw, Christianity had ceased to be a religion of joy and love and had become irritable and selfish. Given this modern sort of Christianity, its foe—the devil's disciple—is of course not wicked but good; repressive bourgeois morality regards him as diabolic, but in fact he is the selfless man endowed with true religious energy, something Shaw called the Life Force and "the inner will of the world." The Life Force, Shaw explained in many writings, through an evolutionary process will in time produce a race of supermen. The artistic genius of the past and present is one form that the superman takes, but another form, one that especially interested Shaw, is the man of destiny, the political genius whose art, so to speak, expresses itself in action in the world. Such a man is an anticipation of a race that will be wiser and juster than most of the people of today. The Caesar whom Shaw set forth in his next play, *Caesar and Cleopatra*, is a clear example, though his appearance on the British stage was delayed. The play was written in 1898 but because it calls for a large cast and for expensive sets it was not produced professionally until 1906. And even then, since the play is long, the London production omitted the third act. For a production given in 1912 Shaw wrote a prologue, to be spoken by the hawk-headed god Ra, and the first scene of the first act was dropped (in later printed versions it was then called "An Alternative to the Prologue") but the third act was given. Our text gives the prologue of the 1912 production, and the entire text of the play as Shaw originally wrote it.

To understand and enjoy *Caesar and Cleopatra*, the first thing one must do is to forget Shakespeare's *Julius Caesar* and *Antony and Cleopatra*. Shaw of course was thoroughly aware of these and of Shakespeare's other plays: he had often commented on Shakespeare, usually, to put the matter briefly, seeing Shakespeare's plays as obstacles to the new, Ibsenite drama. The gist of the position is that Shakespeare is a great verbal musician and a keen psychologist (especially of neurotic lovers and murderers) but most of his heroes have rather vulgar concerns (Hamlet commits three murders and keeps apologizing for not committing a fourth). Shakespeare, in Shaw's view, is not much of a thinker when it comes to understanding the forces that have produced great statecraft, but so great is his rhetorical power, and so great is his reputation, that the British public can scarcely imagine a drama with serious ideas. In a letter written to the actress Ellen Terry in 1897 Shaw put it quite directly: "Shakespeare . . . is to me one of the towers of the Bastille, and down he must come." Many decades later he could reassure his audience that *Caesar and Cleopatra* is thoroughly in the tradition of Shakespeare's chronicle plays, but early in his career he felt that his drama could establish itself only if Shakespeare was put down. If Caesar is to be properly seen as a Shavian hero, a superman, we must (Shaw says) realize that Shakespeare misrepresented Caesar abominably. Shakespeare of course had great "power of language," but he was unable to "conceive high affairs of state," and he gave us a Caesar who was not wise but fatuous. A few months before Shaw started to write his own play about Caesar, he said of the hero of *Julius Caesar*, "It is impossible for even the most judicially minded critic to look without a revulsion of indignant contempt at this travestying of a great man as a silly braggart." A true hero, Shaw says, is a man not merely concerned with aggrandizing himself but is a man whose passions produce "the philosophy, the poetry, the art, and the statecraft of the world." Such a man is Shaw's Caesar.

In preparing to write *Caesar and Cleopatra*, Shaw consulted a fair number of historical sources, but his chief source was the German historian Theodor Mommsen. Mommsen was a liberal who in his *History of Rome* (1854–56) described a Caesar who was a champion of the populace against a selfish, entrenched elite. Shaw adopted this view of Caesar, and given his view of the nature of a true hero, found it easy to say that his own play "is the first and only adequate dramatization of the greatest man that ever lived. I want to revive . . . the projection on the stage of the hero in the big sense of the word."

Shaw's view of Caesar of course required him to gloss over certain matters; for example, Caesar's sexual exploits. Caesar was alleged to be guilty of debauchery, and he undoubtedly fathered one of Cleopatra's children. Though in historical fact Caesar brought Cleopatra back to Rome to live with him for a while, Shaw presents him as a man without interest in sex—and certainly without sexual interest in Cleopatra. This Caesar says in the prologue, speaking to the Sphinx, "I am he of whose genius you are the symbol: part brute, part woman, and part god—nothing of man in me at all." Or, to take an example from a later scene in the play, Shaw's rational Caesar explains to an Egyptian official that he bears no resentment toward Cleopatra even though she plans to betray him:

> O thou foolish Egyptian, what have I to do with resentment? Do I resent the wind when it chills me, or the night when it makes me stumble in the darkness? Shall I resent youth when it turns from age, and ambition when it turns from servitude?

> To tell me such a story as this is but to tell me that the sun will rise to-morrow.

What we have here, then, is the hero, the superman who, moving in lonely isolation and misunderstood by lesser people, is animated by the Life Force, the world-spirit that, working through individuals, strives to produce a higher society. In fact, the Life Force has worked to produce a mature Caesar who is morally superior to what Caesar was in his youth; in his youth, we learn, he believed that "duty," "statesmanship," and the "protection of the commonwealth" required him to murder Vercingetorix, but now he sees that these ideals were "follies and fictions ten times bloodier than honest vengeance." Still, whatever the relative ranking of "duty" and of "vengeance," both must be outgrown. "To the end of history, murder shall breed murder, always in the name of right and honor and peace, until the gods are tired of blood and create a new race that can understand." Caesar, the speaker of these lines, is a member of that new race.

Shaw's hero or superman of course does not *look* like a hero or wear an *S* on his chest; rather, he is for the most part ordinary. For instance, Shaw's Caesar nibbles on dates. This may seem a small thing, but how many earlier heroes on the stage eat snacks? (One is reminded of Shaw's own Captain Bluntschli in *Arms and the Man,* who keeps chocolate rather than ammunition on hand.) For Shaw, the true hero or superman is a man (or woman) like the rest of us in many ways but with greater insight into the goals of life. Shaw often wrote about the hero, and it would be easy but tiresome to quote him at length on this subject, yet one passage seems especially close to this Caesar who for the most part seems so humdrum:

> Our conception of heroism has changed of late years. . . . The demand now is for heroes in whom we can recognize our own humanity, and who, instead of walking, talking, eating, drinking, making love and fighting single combats in a monotonous ecstasy of continuous heroism, are heroic in the true human fashion: that is, touching the summits only at rare moments, and finding the proper level of all occasions, condescending with humour and good sense to the prosaic ones as

> well as rising to the noble ones, instead of ridiculously persisting in rising to them all on the principle that a hero must always soar, in season or out of season.

Thus, Caesar is bald, somewhat absentminded, and unable to pronounce Ftatateeta's name—but he is courageous and, more important, governed by an enlightened morality. He knows nothing of revenge, and if in Egypt (a land of mystery and artifice) he seems to be a commonplace fellow from a culture that seems to be unskilled in the arts, he reminds us that Rome excelled in the art of government: "What! Rome produce no art! Is not peace an art? is war not an art? is government not an art? is civilization not an art?"

Rufio and Britannus are devoted to him; we might say that he educates or civilizes them, at least to the degree that they are capable of, but he fails with Cleopatra, who at the end of the play is looking forward to the arrival of Mark Antony, he of the brawny arms, the traditional handsome hero who (we know from Shakespeare) will make such a mess of things. Nor is Shaw's Caesar, for all of his Shavian heroism, able to bring about the high civilization he sees without the aid of Rufio's sword, and even of Lucius's treachery. The time is some two thousand years ago, and although the Life Force produced a Caesar, Caesar's world was not yet fully ready for him. As Shaw was soon to write, "All progress is initiated by challenging current conceptions, and executed by supplanting existing institutions." The difficulty, of course, is that "current institutions" may pride themselves on their virtue and on their dedication to serving virtuous institutions—just as Shaw's youthful Caesar quite sincerely executed Vercingetorix in the name of "duty." In *Caesar and Cleopatra* the faithful Britannus insists on serving Caesar, but Britannus cannot understand that his own very British idea of "justice" is in Caesar's enlightened view mere retaliation. What for Britannus is civilization, for the hero is organized cruelty or imbecility, something that stands in the way of progress far more effectively than does unabashed barbarism. Shaw of course is not really writing about the past, but about the present. As he said in the preface (1907) to a reprint of "The Sanity of Art" (1895), "I deal with all periods; but I never study any period but the present. . . . The man who writes about himself and his own times is the only man who writes about all people and about all time."

In *Major Barbara* (1905) Shaw clearly writes about his own time. The play chiefly concerns power, the power of gunpowder of course, but especially the power of money. Shaw had already in *Widowers' Houses* and in *Mrs. Warren's Profession* addressed himself to slums and tainted money, but not before *Major Barbara* had he discussed them so extensively and so forcefully. *Discussed* is the right word. A few years after writing *Major Barbara*, which he originally subtitled "a discussion in three acts," Shaw subtitled *Misalliance* "A Debate," and a little later, in *Fanny's First Play* (1911) he spoofed his critics and himself by having a theater critic in *Fanny* indignantly reject argumentative "entertainments of this sort." "I am aware," the critic says,

> that one author, who is, I blush to say, a personal friend of mine, resorts freely to the dastardly subterfuge of calling them conversations, discussions, and so forth, with the express object of evading criticism. But I'm not to be disarmed by such tricks. I say they are not plays. Dialogues, if you will. Exhibitions of character, perhaps: especially the character of the author. Fictions, possibly. . . . But plays, no. I say NO. Not plays.

But of course *Major Barbara* is not all "discussion." There is plenty of action of the sort we expect in a play, for instance, in Barbara's fight for Bill Walker's soul, in Undershaft's fight for Barbara's, and in the fight between Undershaft and Cusins for supremacy in the munitions factory. Moreover, in the exchange between Undershaft and Cusins we have already seen that the play is not lacking in cut-and-thrust dialogue. In fact, in the first act of the play, set in the library of Lady Britomart's house, we are fairly close to the world of Oscar Wilde's *The Importance of Being Earnest* (1894), with its witty dialogue. But in Wilde social criticism flashes out only intermittently, and it is all but dissolved in the general play of wit, whereas in *Major Barbara*, even in the first act, social criticism is so continually evident that we strongly feel the dialogue exists not simply to entertain but to provoke thought and perhaps even to provoke action—action not from the characters but from the spectators. Unlike Wilde's characters, who seem only to *play* at being earnest, Shaw's characters argue in earnest, giving us the feeling that we are being presented with recognizable social types. These are not simply traditional comic types, it should be noted, but are types who stand for strongly held contemporary points of view. A comparison between Wilde's Lady Bracknell and Shaw's Lady Britomart will make the point clear. Lady Bracknell, conducting an interview with a potential son-in-law, asks the young man, "Do you smoke?" He uneasily replies, "Well, yes, I must admit I smoke," and she reassures him, "I am glad to hear it. A man should always have an occupation of some kind. There are far too many idle men in London as it is." On reflection we can of course find criticism here of the idle rich, but Wilde's preposterous dialogue exists chiefly for its exuberant comedy. Shaw's Lady Britomart doubtless is indebted to Wilde's fanciful Lady Bracknell, but she is far more believable. Lady Bracknell is one of the glories of the English stage, but we can scarcely take her seriously as representing the ideas of a social type, whereas Lady Britomart quite evidently stands for those autocratic women who claim to be helpless but who manipulate others and get what they want. Lady Britomart in fact was largely based on Lady Rosalind Francis, countess of Carlisle (and mother of Gilbert Murray, of whom more will be said later), a temperance reformer and a leader of the Woman's Liberal Federation. Although she was a Liberal, she did not hesitate to impose her aristocratic will on all whom she encountered. Similarly, Lady Britomart's fatuous son Stephen—though undeniably a comic figure—is, broadly speaking, a believable type. Stephen is scarcely able to engage in anything that can reasonably be called a discussion, but he certainly represents a point of view, let's say that of mindless conventional opinion.

The second act moves from the world of drawing-room comedy to the Salvation Army shelter at West Ham, that is, from the world of the rich to the world of the poor—or so it seems, until it is revealed that the rich in fact own the Salvation Army. Here we get additional contemporary types: Bill Walker, the defiant working man; Peter Shirley, the brainwashed worker who is cast off when he is of no further use to his employers; Snobby Price, the small-time cheat. There is still plenty of comedy, but the social criticism is stronger and the tone darkens almost to tragedy when Barbara sees that the Salvation Army can be bought by anyone who has enough money. The army can afford to reject a contribution of a pound from an immoral person, but it cannot afford to reject a contribution of five thousand pounds from anyone. To say that in this act the play moves toward tragedy is not to overstate the matter. When Barbara's recognition (or *anagnorisis*, to use the term often used for the recognition scene in a tragedy) causes her faith in the army to melt, she reminds us of all of those tragic figures—let's say Othello or Lear—who find themselves betrayed (or seemingly so) by those to whom they granted infinite trust. The tragic figure sees his world dissolve, and at this point nothing is left to him except his anguish. And just as this stripping from the hero of all that is most valuable is sometimes symbolized by literally stripping the hero of his garments (Lear, the Emperor Jones), so in *Major Barbara* we find Barbara removing from her collar the army "S" brooch, a symbol that no longer can give meaning to her life. Her equation of herself with the suffering Christ ("My God: why hast thou forsaken me?") is daring but, given the context, it is convincing and moving. The recognition forced on Stephen in Act I, that for all of his stuffy repudiation of Undershaft's money he has in fact been living on it, is comic because Stephen's feelings have no depth, but Barbara's recognition—her perception that all that she has worked for has been undone—is the material of tragedy. Later, in the second scene of the third act, Undershaft will dissipate the tragedy ("Come, come, my daughter! don't make too much of your little tinpot tragedy") and return the play to comedy in the broadest sense, that is, to a play not simply with laughs but also with a happy ending. Probably no tragic figure, and no tragedy, could quite stand up to Undershaft's words, and from here on we are, so to speak, on the way up, moving out of hell and purgatory and into a world of light and joy.

Even before Barbara's desolating recognition—indeed, contributing to it—we hear the Dionysian strain in Cusins's ecstatic remarks about playing the bass drum in the Salvation Army band's rendition of a wedding march from Donizetti; and of course ecstasy (literally being outside of oneself) is what comedy is about, symbolized by the general joy at the end and by the marriage (a giving of oneself) that usually concludes a comedy. Guided by Undershaft ("You have made for yourself something that you call a morality or a religion or what not. It doesn't fit the facts. Well, scrap it. Scrap it and get one that does fit"), Barbara moves to a quest and a joy that far exceed her earlier ideals. The ideals of the past, Shaw suggests, are scarcely worth mourning over; they are to be tossed out when they are worn out. This point had already been made in *Caesar and Cleopatra*, when Caesar received with equanimity the news that the great library at Alexandria was burning. To Theodotus's report that "What is burning there is the memory of mankind," Caesar replies, "A shameful memory. Let it burn." And to Theodotus's amazed question, "Will you destroy the past?" Caesar replies, "Ay, and build the future with its ruins." *Major Barbara* follows the traditional comic formula of freeing individuals from false ideals, and it even includes that venerable comic motif of the foundling (Cusins) discovered, but we should note in passing one unusual departure from comic tradition. Ordinarily in comedy the resilient young lovers outwit and displace the old repressive figures, giving (so to speak) a new birth to society, but in both *Caesar and Cleopatra* and *Major Barbara* the old instruct the young. Shaw's faith, so to speak, was in clear thinking rather than in romantic love.

Undershaft had promised to visit Barbara's headquarters in West Ham if she would then visit him at Perivale St. Andrews. The second part of the third act is accordingly set there, and it is there that most of the serious discussion in the play takes place. But to say "serious" is to be a trifle misleading, for the discussion at Perivale St. Andrews is witty, exuberant, energetic, not solemn. Shaw had a good deal of trouble in writing this scene, as the manuscripts and his correspondence show. Gilbert Murray, the classicist who was the chief model for Shaw's Adolphus Cusins, reported that Shaw said he was "quite desperate" because he didn't "know how to end the thing," and in a letter to Murray he said, "I must simply rewrite it." A few days later he wrote to another correspondent that this was "the first time I have ever had to do such a thing," and although many of Shaw's earlier manuscripts show substantial rewriting, it is obvious that the second part of this act of *Major Barbara* caused him exceptional difficulty.

Much of the difficulty probably was caused by the fact that Shaw used Undershaft as a mouthpiece for his arguments on the importance of eliminating poverty. By using a munitions manufacturer, i.e., a capitalist of a singularly shocking sort, he could goad his bourgeois audience, telling them that *this* is what capitalism essentially is. And by having his munitions manufacturer utter Marxist ideas about religion, poverty, and the state, Shaw could goad his Socialist friends. Yet Shaw the Socialist could hardly be happy with a capitalist—even one who talks like a Marxist—triumphant at the end of his comedy. But of course Undershaft is not a wicked man. Even Lady Britomart, in a Wildean passage, says that she cannot forgive Undershaft for preaching immorality while practicing morality, and we recognize in Undershaft a Shavian version of the devil's disciple, that is, a man who seems diabolic (Cusins calls him Mephistopheles and the Prince of Darkness) but only because his ideas oppose conventional (and, for Shaw, corrupt or dead) morality. Still, having committed himself to the choice of a spokesman whose profession would shock, and whose commitment is to materialism, Shaw found that he did not know how to resolve the play satisfactorily. Murray advised Shaw to strengthen Barbara and Cusins in the last scene, especially by having Barbara recover from her defeat and having Barbara and Cusins embrace Undershaft's principles "with a view of destroying them or subduing them" for their own ends. Shaw initially rejected the idea, writing to Murray that Barbara and Cusins are "very ignorant of the world'' and are unable to deal with Undershaft (we notice again Shaw's emphasis on mature thinking), but in fact when Shaw returned to the play he took Murray's advice; Barbara and Cusins accept Undershaft's invitation to join him, but they will do so on their own terms, and it is clear that they have in mind intellectual and spiritual goals that are not part of Undershaft's creed. Thus, where Undershaft insists that an armorer must sell weapons to all who can pay for them, Cusins insists that he will sell to whomever he chooses. Responding to Undershaft's challenge, ''Dare you make war on war?,'' Cusins announces that as a teacher of Greek he gave to the governing class intellectual weapons that could be used against the common people, but now, as a manufacturer of munitions, he will give to the common people weapons that can be used against those who govern—the intellectuals, the politicians, the professionals, all those who, holding power, operate society for their own good rather than for the common good. Thus, in the finished version, but not in the earlier draft, Cusins eloquently sets forth a goal different from Undershaft's. Undershaft, we recall, is committed to a valueless capitalism, for he will ''give arms to all men who offer an honest price for them, without respect of persons or principles: to aristocrat and republican, to Nihilist and Tsar.'' But Cusins says he will enunciate and follow his own principle—written in Greek, which Undershaft can't understand. The suggestion is that Cusins's principles are incomprehensible to Undershaft, not simply because they are written in Greek but because they represent a view as far in advance of Undershaft's thinking as Undershaft's thinking is in advance of most of the thought of the day. Cusins will ''sell cannons to whom I please.'' As we have seen, Shaw often liked to show the old educating the young, but in *Major Barbara* he allows Cusins to teach Undershaft a thing or two.

Even after revising the text Shaw continued to tinker with the scene, adding further revisions in the prompt book. One of them (picking up a hint that Murray had offered) was this passage: ''Society cannot be saved until either the Professors of Greek take to making gunpowder, or else the makers of gunpowder become Professors of Greek.'' Although spoken by Undershaft, this speech serves to enhance Cusins, suggesting that Cusins will conduct the business on moral principles superior to those of Undershaft. And a moment later Undershaft challenges Cusins with a line we have already noted: "Dare you make war on war? Here are the means." True, Undershaft expresses some skepticism, arguing (presumably drawing on his own experience) that once Cusins is in the job he will find that he will never again be able to do what he pleases, but Cusins replies that he is not to be judged by Undershaft: "I have more power than you, more will." So the play is not simply about the power of money and of explosives but also about the power of will, the power of the Life Force, the Dionysian energy that surges through Undershaft and through the professor of Greek. Undershaft, for all his energy, wit, and awareness that the factory and the community around it are driven by "a will of which I am a part," seems to realize that he needs to add Cusins's power to his own; he even seems to realize that his own creed, the amoral capitalism of the armorer's faith, needs to be superseded: "Come and make explosives with me. Whatever can blow men up can blow society up." Undershaft inspires Cusins, but Cusins, once inspired, goes beyond Undershaft.

And so, of course, does Barbara. As we have seen, Undershaft educates Barbara, first by showing her the inadequacy of her beliefs as a worker for the Salvation Army, then by dismissing her "tinpot tragedy" (strong words, not only for her but for us, because she has won our sympathy) and by urging her to develop a creed that fits the facts. Undershaft speaks tellingly of the seven deadly sins, not the Christian ones of pride, envy, wrath, sloth, avarice, gluttony, and lechery, but the Socialist ones of food, clothing, firing, rent, taxes, respectability, and children, explaining to Barbara that "nothing can lift those seven millstones from Man's neck but money; and the spirit cannot soar until the millstones are lifted." But Undershaft's vision of utopia seems to be limited to a healthy, prosperous society. He is quite content with the snobbery that animates his workers at Perivale St. Andrews: "The men snub the boys and order them about; the carmen snub the sweepers; the artisans snub the unskilled laborers;

the foremen drive and bully both the laborers and artisans," and so on. The result, he mischievously announces, "is a colossal profit, which comes to me." It is these well-fed but spiritually starved persons that Undershaft invites Barbara to convert to spirituality ("Try your hand on *my* men—Their souls are hungry because their bodies are full"), and Barbara, after a little further education by Undershaft, ecstatically accepts the challenge. True, Undershaft has most of the exciting lines in the play, but the title of the play directs us toward its real point. The play is not called *Andrew Undershaft's Profession*, a title that crossed Shaw's mind; rather, it is called *Major Barbara* because Shaw's final vision in this play is of a world that may be transformed by Barbara's spiritual power. How successful will Barbara be? We cannot tell, of course, but Shaw occasionally gives us a hint in a stage direction, when he reminds us that Barbara is very much her mother's daughter. The implication is that nothing can stop Barbara. Notice that Lady Britomart has a way of getting her way.

To understand and enjoy *The Doctor's Dilemma: A Tragedy* (1906), the first thing we have to do is to get rid of our veneration of doctors. Given all the medical heroes on soap operas this may be difficult to do, but we should recall that not until the later nineteenth century did the doctor become a heroic figure. Earlier he was often a figure of fun in satiric drama. Such satire can be seen briefly in Shakespeare's Doctor Pinch in *The Comedy of Errors*, and more pervasively in the *commedia dell'arte* and in the plays of Molière, where doctors are ridiculed for their ignorance and their hypocrisy. But Shaw was not simply writing in a tradition; he was writing out of a conviction, a conviction that, as he puts it in the play, "All professions are conspiracies against the laity." He had touched on this point in *Major Barbara*, when Cusins remarks that he wants to arm the common people "against the lawyer, the doctor, the priest, the literary man, the professor, the artist, and the politician, who, once in authority, are the most dangerous, disastrous and tyrannical of all the fools, rascals, and impostors." And again we are reminded of Caesar's willingness to let the library of Alexandria burn, to let all of its dead ideas—including its pernicious ideas of justice—go up in smoke. For Shaw, medical men no less than other professionals are obstructionists, indeed perhaps more so than most other professionals, because medical men are reductive, seeing human beings as mere machines. But Shaw's doctors, we should note, at least are not dishonest, like, say, the doctors in Robin Cook's *Coma*, who comatize otherwise healthy patients in order to sell their organs at a great profit. In *The Doctor's Dilemma* we are not back in the realm of Shaw's "unpleasant" plays, concerned with an immoral society; rather, for the most part we are in the world of sincere quacks, people who are stupid but not villainous.

The word *dilemma* in the title alerts us to the fact that this may be a "discussion" play, and indeed the play turns out to be largely on the issue of who is more valuable, a parasitic genius or a decent nonentity. This question, however, is never resolved. Along with the discussion of the dilemma we get Shaw's versions of two other dramatic forms, tragedy (announced in the subtitle) and comedy, the comedy being of two sorts: satire of doctors, and domestic comedy somewhat along the lines of *Candida* (1894–95), though in *The Doctor's Dilemma* the artist is not the would-be lover as in *Candida* but is the husband, and the doctor is the would-be lover.

The deepest origins of the play are of course in the venerable dramatic traditions, in Shaw's philosophic views, and in his understanding of the world around him, but the play was triggered by several more or less chance remarks. When Ibsen died in 1906, Shaw published an appreciative essay on him, but in the course of it he commented unfavorably on the suicides and accidental deaths in some of Ibsen's plays, remarking that Ibsen

> seems to have succumbed without a struggle to the old notion that a play is not really a play unless it contains a murder, a suicide, or something else out of the *Police Gazette*. . . . The Brand infant and Little Eyolf are as tremendously effective as a blow below the belt; but they are dishonorable as artistic devices, because they depend on a morbid horror of death and a morbid enjoyment of horror.

William Archer replied that Shaw was merely justifying his own practice of avoiding tragedy. "The profounder revelations of character," Archer went on to say, "come only in crises of tragic circumstance. [Shaw] shrinks from that affirmation and consummation of destiny which only death can bring. . . . If, in Mr. Shaw's own phrase, 'the illumination of life' is the main purpose of drama, what illuminant, we may ask, can be more powerful than death?" We have, of course, already seen in *Major Barbara* that Shaw's view was essentially untragic; for him, a devastating experience should lead not to lamentation but to a more sensible way of living. Three weeks after Archer's reply, Shaw published a notice that "Mr. Shaw is writing a play all about Death, which he declares will be the most amusing play he has ever written." (The play, begun in early August and completed in early October 1906, opened in November.) Also part of the origin of the play was a comment by Sir Almroth Wright, the model for Shaw's Ridgeon. When Wright was asked to add a tuberculosis patient to the list of those to whom he was administering his new opsonic treatment, he inquired, "Is he worth it?" A third ingredient was a discussion between Shaw's wife and a friend, the playwright, actor, and producer Harley Granville Barker (Barker soon played the artist in *The Doctor's Dilemma*) about the trouble doctors take to keep worthless people alive. And there was yet a further contemporary source: for the scoundrel Dubedat, Shaw drew in part on Edward Aveling, the (for a while) common-law husband of Karl Marx's daughter Eleanor. Shaw had acted with Edward and Eleanor in an amateur production of a play, and as a religious and social reformer he was well aware of Aveling's atheism and socialism, as well as of Aveling's willingness to use women and to take money on false pretenses. Out of such stuff came *The Doctor's Dilemma*.

A dilemma can of course be the material of tragedy: if Hamlet does not act, he neglects his father's command; but if he does act he may act unjustly, and in any case the action of killing Claudius will not return Hamlet, Senior, to life, nor will it obliterate Gertrude's shameful act of marrying Claudius. But for Shaw a dilemma is the material not for tragedy but for discussion. Ibsen, we have seen, prepared the way.

And we have noticed Shaw's remark that "In *A Doll's House* and *Candida* you have action producing discussion; in *The Doctor's Dilemma* you have discussion producing action, and that action being finally discussed." What is discussed in *The Doctor's Dilemma* is how a human being ought to act. Sir Patrick near the end of Act II says the dilemma is "a plain choice between a man and a lot of pictures," but this choice is never made. We know from Shaw's other writings, especially the preface (1907) to a new edition of "The Sanity of Art," where Shaw comments on *The Doctor's Dilemma*, that Shaw did not believe immorality can be overlooked just because the offender is a genius. And we know that Shaw considered morality inseparable from his own art, but we know too that despite his self-confessed "puritan" temperament he saw the true artist as the enemy of bourgeois values. Shaw himself offered an approving, if qualified, comment on the deathbed speech of his scoundrel-artist Dubedat. First, here is the speech:

> I'm not afraid, and not ashamed. *(Reflectively, puzzling it out for himself weakly)* I know that in an accidental sort of way, struggling through the unreal part of life, I havnt always been able to live up to my ideal. But in my own real world I have never done anything wrong, never denied my faith, never been untrue to myself. Ive been threatened and blackmailed and insulted and starved. But Ive played the game. Ive fought the good fight. And now it's all over, theres an indescribable peace. *(He feebly folds his hands and utters his creed.)* I believe in Michael Angelo, Velasquez, and Rembrandt; in the might of design, the mystery of color, the redemption of all things by Beauty everlasting, and the message of Art that has made these hands blessed. Amen. Amen. *(He closes his eyes and lies still.)*

And now here is a comment Shaw later made, in *Sixteen Self Sketches*, about this death scene:

> When Dubedat says on his deathbed that he has fought the good fight, he is quite serious. He means that he has not painted little girls playing with fox terriers to be exhibited and sold at the Royal Academy, instead of doing the best he could do in his art. . . . He had his faith, and upheld it.

What Shaw is doing, of course, is changing the grounds of the usual argument about the relation of art to morality. The artist must be moral, he says, in that the artist must be true to his vision of art, but this has nothing to do with the artist's doings in other matters. And this has nothing to tell us about how the doctor in the play should act in order to solve the moral dilemma.

In fact, the dilemma becomes somewhat obscured in the play; when Ridgeon acts—he hands Dubedat over to an incompetent doctor—he acts not on the basis of having made a choice between immoral genius and commonplace decency, but on the basis of love for Jennifer, the artist's wife. Even here there is some ambiguity in his motive. We know that he hopes to marry Jennifer, and thus in a sense he murders Dubedat by allowing an incompetent colleague to treat him, but he gives another motive too: he says that he allowed Dubedat to die in order to let Jennifer preserve her illusions about her scoundrelly genius-husband. It turns out, in fact, that Jennifer cannot conceive of marrying Ridgeon, and, further, she is quite aware of Dubedat's faults but nevertheless reveres him. In short, perhaps Ridgeon's motive is selfish (he wants Jennifer), or perhaps he is unselfish (he wishes to preserve Jennifer's illusions), or perhaps he is utterly self-deceived (he acts selfishly but deludes himself into thinking he acts for Jennifer's good), but whatever motive prompts him to send Dubedat to death, it ignores the dilemma that is set forth in the play.

Since Ridgeon's action does not produce the end he desires, it is ironic, and to say that his action proves to be ironic is to say that the play has some affinity with tragedy. Ridgeon can be regarded as hubristic (he thinks Jennifer will marry him, or he thinks that he is needed to protect Jennifer from disillusionment, or both); this pride leads him, in effect, to commit a deed of horror (murder, though a legally sanctioned one since the killing is done by the well-intended medical treatment of a licensed physician), and the deed fails to bring about the good that he envisions. The "tragedy" of the subtitle can be said to be not the death of Dubedat but the mistaken decision of Ridgeon.

Only three of Shaw's plays can be said to be tragic, or to

approach tragedy: *Mrs. Warren's Profession*, *The Doctor's Dilemma*, and *Saint Joan*. In discussing *Major Barbara* something has already been said about Shaw's aversion to tragedy, and here we can add that Dubedat dies with such satisfaction, and Jennifer goes on living with such satisfaction, that despite the death and despite the irony of Ridgeon's action the play is pretty far removed from what we usually think of as tragedy. Ridgeon says that "The most tragic thing in the world is a man of genius who is not also a man of honor," and Shaw later quoted the line in defending the subtitle of the play, but this view, too, that Dubedat's life rather than his death is tragic does not bring the play into the fold of tragedy. Shaw made yet a further comment on *The Doctor's Dilemma* and tragedy. Explaining that, like Ibsen in *The Wild Duck*, he fuses comedy with tragedy, he said: "The comedy of the medical profession as at present organized in England, is a tragic comedy, with death conducting the orchestra."

This is not quite the note on which to leave Shaw, since his work as a whole is concerned with life rather than with death, but of course we are not leaving him on this note. The plays are here to be read.

Sylvan Barnet
Tufts University

A NOTE ON SHAW'S SPELLING

Shaw was much concerned with spelling, a concern seen most obviously in his refusal to use the apostrophe where conventional English requires it. Thus, for instance, he wrote "dont" instead of "don't." He did, however, use the apostrophe when it served to distinguish one word from another, as in the contraction "it's," which without an apostrophe might be confused with the possessive pronoun "its."

A somewhat related point: because Shaw used italics for stage directions, he did not use them for emphasis, preferring to space out the letters of a word that he wanted to emphasize, thus: y o u (rather than *you*). This device has some merit, for it slows down the word, as in speech. But since "I" cannot be spaced out, Shaw does italicize "I" when he means to emphasize it.

CHRONOLOGY

Shaw lived for almost a century. The following chronology lists only events in his own life, but something of the surrounding context can be suggested by a few additional dates. When Shaw was born in 1856, Queen Victoria was in the twentieth year of her reign; she celebrated her Golden Jubilee in 1887, when Shaw was thirty-one, and she died in 1902, when Shaw was forty-six. Another way of emphasizing the fact that although Shaw lived until late in 1950 he was largely an author of the nineteenth century is to recall that he was born in the same year that Wilde was born, and four years earlier than Chekhov. Wilde died in 1900, Chekhov in 1904.

1856 Shaw born in Dublin, 26 July, of a middle-class Irish Protestant family. His father is an unsuccessful merchant given to drinking; his mother, a resourceful woman who teaches singing, is the chief support of the family.

1871 Shaw leaves school at age fifteen, to work as a clerk in a real estate office.

1872 Shaw's mother moves to London, where she supports herself by giving music lessons and by singing.

1876 Shaw leaves Dublin, to join his mother in London.

1879–83	Completes his first novel, *Immaturity*, in 1879 but it is not published until 1930. The next four novels (1880–83) are rejected by publishers but are serialized in magazines edited by friends, and later are published as books. In 1882 he hears a lecture in London by Henry George, an American economist, and he becomes converted to socialism.
1885	Begins his first play, *Widowers' Houses*, but does not complete it until 1892.
1885–98	Writes journalism, beginning with book reviews and then criticism of art, music, and drama.
1891	*The Quintessence of Ibsenism.*
1892–95	*Widowers' Houses* completed and produced in 1892, and published in 1893; *Mrs. Warren's Profession* written 1893–94; *Arms and the Man* written and produced 1894; *Candida* written 1894–95, produced 1895.
1898	Marries Charlotte Payne-Townshend, a fellow Socialist. Writes *Caesar and Cleopatra*. Publishes his first collection of plays, the two-volume *Plays, Pleasant and Unpleasant*.
1901–4	Writes *Man and Superman* 1901–3 (produced 1905). In 1904 writes *John Bull's Other Island*, which is produced later in the year.
1905	*Major Barbara* written and produced.
1906	*The Doctor's Dilemma* written and produced.
1912	*Pygmalion* (produced 1913).
1914	*Common Sense about the War*, a long pamphlet.
1916–17	*Heartbreak House* (published 1919, produced 1920).
1918–20	*Back to Methuselah* (produced 1922), a five-part play on creative evolution.
1923	*Saint Joan* written and produced; published 1924.

1925	Receives Nobel Prize for Literature.
1928	*The Intelligent Woman's Guide to Socialism and Capitalism*, Shaw's fullest exposition of economic systems.
1939	*In Good King Charles's Golden Days*, Shaw's last important play.
1943	Death of Charlotte Shaw.
1950	Dies, 2 November, in his ninety-fifth year.

MAJOR BARBARA

PREFACE TO MAJOR BARBARA

FIRST AID TO CRITICS

BEFORE dealing with the deeper aspects of Major Barbara, let me, for the credit of English literature, make a protest against an unpatriotic habit into which many of my critics have fallen. Whenever my view strikes them as being at all outside the range of, say, an ordinary suburban churchwarden, they conclude that I am echoing Schopenhauer, Nietzsche, Ibsen, Strindberg, Tolstoy, or some other heresiarch in northern or eastern Europe.

I confess there is something flattering in this simple faith in my accomplishment as a linguist and my erudition as a philosopher. But I cannot tolerate the assumption that life and literature is so poor in these islands that we must go abroad for all dramatic material that is not common and all ideas that are not superficial. I therefore venture to put my critics in possession of certain facts concerning my contact with modern ideas.

About half a century ago, an Irish novelist, Charles Lever, wrote a story entitled A Day's Ride: A Life's Romance. It was published by Charles Dickens in Household Words, and proved so strange to the public taste that Dickens pressed Lever to make short work of it. I read scraps of this novel when I was a child; and it made an enduring impression on me. The hero was a very romantic hero, trying to live bravely, chivalrously, and powerfully by dint of mere romance-fed imagination, without courage, without means, without knowledge, without skill, without anything real except his bodily appetites. Even in my childhood I found in this poor devil's unsuccessful encounters with the facts of life, a poignant quality that romantic fiction lacked. The book, in spite of its first failure, is not dead: I saw its title the other day in the catalogue of Tauchnitz.

Now why is it that when I also deal in the tragi-comic irony of the conflict between real life and the romantic imagination, no critic ever affiliates me to my countryman and immediate forerunner, Charles Lever, whilst they confidently derive me from a Norwegian author of whose language I do not know three words, and of whom I knew nothing until years after the Shavian *Anschauung* was already unequivocally declared in books full of what came, ten years later, to be perfunctorily labelled Ibsenism. I was not Ibsenist even at second hand; for Lever, though he may have read Henri Beyle, *alias* Stendhal, certainly never read Ibsen. Of the books that made Lever popular, such as Charles O'Malley and Harry Lorrequer, I know nothing but the names and some of the illustrations. But the story of the day's ride and life's romance of Potts (claiming alliance with Pozzo di Borgo) caught me and fascinated me as something strange and significant, though I already knew all about Alnaschar and Don Quixote and Simon Tappertit and many another romantic hero mocked by reality. From the plays of Aristophanes to the tales of Stevenson that mockery has been made familiar to all who are properly saturated with letters.

Where, then, was the novelty in Lever's tale? Partly, I think, in a new seriousness in dealing with Potts's disease. Formerly, the contrast between madness and sanity was deemed comic: Hogarth shews us how fashionable people went in parties to Bedlam to laugh at the lunatics. I myself have had a village idiot exhibited to me as something irresistibly funny. On the stage the madman was once a regular comic figure: that was how Hamlet got his opportunity before Shakespear touched him. The originality of Shakespear's version lay in his taking the lunatic sympathetically and seriously, and thereby making an advance towards the eastern consciousness of the fact that lunacy may be inspiration in disguise, since a man who has more brains than his fellows necessarily appears as mad to them as one who has less. But Shakespear did not do for Pistol and Parolles what he did for Hamlet. The particular sort of madman they represented, the romantic make-believer, lay outside the pale of sympathy in literature: he was pitilessly despised and ridiculed here as he was in the east under the name of Alnaschar, and was doomed to be, centuries later, under the name of Simon Tappertit. When Cervantes relented over Don Quixote, and Dickens relented over Pickwick, they did not become impartial: they simply changed sides, and became friends and apologists where they had formerly been mockers.

In Lever's story there is a real change of attitude. There is no relenting towards Potts: he never gains our affections like Don Quixote and Pickwick: he has not even the infatuate courage of Tappertit. But we dare not laugh at him, because, somehow, we recognize ourselves in Potts. We may, some of us, have enough nerve, enough muscle, enough luck, enough tact or skill or address or knowledge to carry things off better than he did; to impose on the people who saw through him; to fascinate Katinka (who cut Potts so ruthlessly at the end of the story); but for all that, we know that Potts plays an enormous part in ourselves and in the world, and that the social problem is not a problem of storybook heroes of the older pattern, but a problem of Pottses, and of how to make men of them. To fall back on my old phrase, we have the feeling—one that Alnaschar, Pistol, Parolles, and Tappertit never gave us—that Potts is a piece of really scientific natural history as distinguished from comic story telling. His author is not throwing a stone at a creature of another and inferior order, but making a confession, with the effect that the stone hits everybody full in the conscience and causes their self-esteem to smart very sorely. Hence the failure of Lever's book to please the readers of Household Words. That pain in the self-esteem nowadays causes critics to raise a cry of Ibsenism. I therefore assure them that the sensation first came to me from Lever and may have come to him from Beyle, or at least out of the Stendhalian atmosphere. I exclude the hypothesis of complete originality on Lever's part, because a man can no more be completely original in that sense than a tree can grow out of air.

Another mistake as to my literary ancestry is made whenever I violate the romantic convention that all women are angels when they are not devils; that they are better looking than men; that their part in courtship is entirely passive; and that the human female form is the most beautiful object in nature. Schopenhauer wrote a splenetic essay which, as it is neither polite nor profound, was probably intended to knock this nonsense violently on the head. A sentence denouncing the idolized form as ugly has been largely quoted. The English critics have read that sentence; and I must here affirm, with as much gentleness as the implication will bear, that it has yet to be proved that they have dipped any deeper. At all events, whenever an English playwright represents a young and marriageable woman as being anything but a romantic heroine, he is disposed of without further thought as an echo of Schopenhauer. My own case is a specially hard one, because, when I implore the critics who are obsessed with the Schopenhaurian formula to remember that playwrights, like sculptors, study their figures from life, and not from philosophic essays, they reply passionately that I am not a playwright and that my stage figures do not live. But even so, I may and do ask them why, if they must give the credit of my plays to a philosopher, they do not give it to an English philosopher? Long before I ever read a word by Schopenhauer, or even knew whether he was a philosopher or a chemist, the Socialist revival of the eighteen-eighties brought me into contact, both literary and personal, with Mr. Ernest Belfort Bax, an English Socialist and philosophic essayist, whose handling of modern feminism would provoke romantic protests from Schopenhauer himself, or even Strindberg. As a matter of fact I hardly noticed Schopenhauer's disparagements of women when they came under my notice later on, so thoroughly had Mr. Bax familiarized me with the homoist attitude, and forced me to recognize the extent to which public opinion, and consequently legislation and jurisprudence, is corrupted by feminist sentiment.

But Mr. Bax's essays were not confined to the Feminist question. He was a ruthless critic of current morality. Other writers have gained sympathy for dramatic criminals by eliciting the alleged "soul of goodness in things evil"; but Mr.

Bax would propound some quite undramatic and apparently shabby violation of our commercial law and morality, and not merely defend it with the most disconcerting ingenuity, but actually prove it to be a positive duty that nothing but the certainty of police persecution should prevent every right-minded man from at once doing on principle. The Socialists were naturally shocked, being for the most part morbidly moral people; but at all events they were saved later on from the delusion that nobody but Nietzsche had ever challenged our mercanto-Christian morality. I first heard the name of Nietzsche from a German mathematician, Miss Borchardt, who had read my Quintessence of Ibsenism, and told me that she saw what I had been reading: namely, Nietzsche's Jenseits von Gut und Böse. Which I protest I had never seen, and could not have read with any comfort, for want of the necessary German, if I had seen it.

Nietzsche, like Schopenhauer, is the victim in England of a single much quoted sentence containing the phrase "big blonde beast." On the strength of this alliteration it is assumed that Nietzsche gained his European reputation by a senseless glorification of selfish bullying as the rule of life, just as it is assumed, on the strength of the single word Superman (Übermensch) borrowed by me from Nietzsche, that I look for the salvation of society to the despotism of a single Napoleonic Superman, in spite of my careful demonstration of the folly of that outworn infatuation. But even the less recklessly superficial critics seem to believe that the modern objection to Christianity as a pernicious slave-morality was first put forward by Nietzsche. It was familiar to me before I ever heard of Nietzsche. The late Captain Wilson, author of several queer pamphlets, propagandist of a metaphysical system called Comprehensionism, and inventor of the term "Crosstianity" to distinguish the retrograde element in Christendom, was wont thirty years ago, in the discussions of the Dialectical Society, to protest earnestly against the beatitudes of the Sermon on the Mount as excuses for cowardice and servility, as destructive of our will, and consequently of our honor and manhood. Now it is true that Captain Wilson's moral criticism of Christianity was not a historical theory of it, like Nietzsche's; but this objection cannot be made to Mr.

Stuart-Glennie, the successor of Buckle as a philosophic historian, who has devoted his life to the elaboration and propagation of his theory that Christianity is part of an epoch (or rather an aberration, since it began as recently as 6000 B.C. and is already collapsing) produced by the necessity in which the numerically inferior white races found themselves to impose their domination on the colored races by priestcraft, making a virtue and a popular religion of drudgery and submissiveness in this world not only as a means of achieving saintliness of character but of securing a reward in heaven. Here you have the slave-morality view formulated by a Scotch philosopher long before English writers began chattering about Nietzsche.

As Mr. Stuart-Glennie traced the evolution of society to the conflict of races, his theory made some sensation among Socialists—that is, among the only people who were seriously thinking about historical evolution at all—by its collision with the class-conflict theory of Karl Marx. Nietzsche, as I gather, regarded the slave-morality as having been invented and imposed on the world by slaves making a virtue of necessity and a religion of their servitude. Mr. Stuart-Glennie regards the slave-morality as an invention of the superior white race to subjugate the minds of the inferior races whom they wished to exploit, and who would have destroyed them by force of numbers if their minds had not been subjugated. As this process is in operation still, and can be studied at first hand not only in our Church schools and in the struggle between our modern proprietary classes and the proletariat, but in the part played by Christian missionaries in reconciling the black races of Africa to their subjugation by European Capitalism, we can judge for ourselves whether the initiative came from above or below. My object here is not to argue the historical point, but simply to make our theatre critics ashamed of their habit of treating Britain as an intellectual void, and assuming that every philosophical idea, every historic theory, every criticism of our moral, religious and juridical institutions, must necessarily be either imported from abroad, or else a fantastic sally (in rather questionable taste) totally unrelated to the existing body of thought. I urge them to remember that this body of thought is the slowest of growths and the rarest of blossomings, and that if there is such a thing on the philosophic plane as a matter of course, it is that no individual can make more than a minute contribution to it. In fact, their conception of clever persons parthenogenetically bringing forth complete original cosmogonies by dint of sheer "brilliancy" is part of that ignorant credulity which is the despair of the honest philosopher, and the opportunity of the religious impostor.

THE GOSPEL OF ST. ANDREW UNDERSHAFT.

It is this credulity that drives me to help my critics out with Major Barbara by telling them what to say about it. In the millionaire Undershaft I have represented a man who has become intellectually and spiritually as well as practically conscious of the irresistible natural truth which we all abhor and repudiate: to wit, that the greatest of evils and the worst of crimes is poverty, and that our first duty—a duty to which every other consideration should be sacrificed—is not to be poor. "Poor but honest," "the respectable poor," and such phrases are as intolerable and as immoral as "drunken but amiable," "fraudulent but a good after-dinner speaker," "splendidly criminal," or the like. Security, the chief pretence of civilization, cannot exist where the worst of dangers, the danger of poverty, hangs over everyone's head, and where the alleged protection of our persons from violence is only an accidental result of the existence of a police force whose real business is to force the poor man to see his children starve whilst idle people overfeed pet dogs with the money that might feed and clothe them.

It is exceedingly difficult to make people realize that an evil is an evil. For instance, we seize a man and deliberately do him a malicious injury: say, imprison him for years. One would not suppose that it needed any exceptional clearness of wit to recognize in this an act of diabolical cruelty. But in England such a recognition provokes a stare of surprise, followed by an explanation that the outrage is punishment or justice or something else that is all right, or perhaps by a heated attempt to argue that we should all be robbed and murdered in our beds if such senseless villainies as sentences of imprisonment were not committed daily. It is useless to argue that even if this were true, which it is not, the alternative to adding crimes of our own to the crimes from which we suffer is not helpless submission. Chickenpox is an evil; but if I were to declare that we must either submit to it or else repress it sternly by seizing everyone who suffers from it and punishing them by inoculation with smallpox, I should be laughed at; for though nobody could deny that the result would be to prevent chickenpox to some extent by making people avoid it much more carefully, and to effect a further apparent prevention by making them conceal it very anxiously, yet people would have sense enough to see that the deliberate propagation of smallpox was a creation of evil, and must therefore be ruled out in favor of purely humane and hygienic measures. Yet in the precisely parallel case of a man breaking into my house and stealing my wife's diamonds I am expected as a matter of course to steal ten years of his life, torturing him all the time. If he tries to defeat that monstrous retaliation by shooting me, my survivors hang him. The net result suggested by the police statistics is that we inflict atrocious injuries on the burglars we catch in order to make the rest take effectual precautions against detection; so that instead of saving our wives' diamonds from burglary we only greatly decrease our chances of ever getting them back, and increase our chances of being shot by the robber if we are unlucky enough to disturb him at his work.

But the thoughtless wickedness with which we scatter sentences of imprisonment, torture in the solitary cell and on the plank bed, and flogging, on moral invalids and energetic rebels, is as nothing compared to the stupid levity with which we tolerate poverty as if it were either a wholesome tonic for lazy people or else a virtue to be embraced as St. Francis embraced it. If a man is indolent, let him be poor. If he is drunken, let him be poor. If he is not a gentleman, let him be poor. If he is addicted to the fine arts or to pure science instead of to trade and finance, let him be poor. If he chooses to spend his urban eighteen shillings a week or his agricultural thirteen shillings a week on his beer and his family instead of saving it up for his old age, let him be poor. Let nothing be done for "the undeserving": let him be poor.

Serve him right! Also—somewhat inconsistently—blessed are the poor!

Now what does this Let Him Be Poor mean? It means let him be weak. Let him be ignorant. Let him become a nucleus of disease. Let him be a standing exhibition and example of ugliness and dirt. Let him have rickety children. Let him be cheap and let him drag his fellows down to his price by selling himself to do their work. Let his habitations turn our cities into poisonous congeries of slums. Let his daughters infect our young men with the diseases of the streets and his sons revenge him by turning the nation's manhood into scrofula, cowardice, cruelty, hypocrisy, political imbecility, and all the other fruits of oppression and malnutrition. Let the undeserving become still less deserving; and let the deserving lay up for himself, not treasures in heaven, but horrors in hell upon earth. This being so, is it really wise to let him be poor? Would he not do ten times less harm as a prosperous burglar, incendiary, ravisher or murderer, to the utmost limits of humanity's comparatively negligible impulses in these directions? Suppose we were to abolish all penalties for such activities, and decide that poverty is the one thing we will not tolerate—that every adult with less than, say, £365 a year, shall be painlessly but inexorably killed, and every hungry half naked child forcibly fattened and clothed, would not that be an enormous improvement on our existing system, which has already destroyed so many civilizations, and is visibly destroying ours in the same way?

Is there any radicle of such legislation in our parliamentary system? Well, there are two measures just sprouting in the political soil, which may conceivably grow to something valuable. One is the institution of a Legal Minimum Wage. The other, Old Age Pensions. But there is a better plan than either of these. Some time ago I mentioned the subject of Universal Old Age Pensions to my fellow Socialist Mr. Cobden-Sanderson, famous as an artist-craftsman in bookbinding and printing. "Why not Universal Pensions for Life?" said Cobden-Sanderson. In saying this, he solved the industrial problem at a stroke. At present we say callously to each citizen: "If you want money, earn it," as if his having or not having it were a matter that concerned himself alone. We do not even secure for him the opportunity of earning it: on the contrary, we allow our industry to be organized in open dependence on the maintenance of "a reserve army of unemployed" for the sake of "elasticity." The sensible course would be Cobden-Sanderson's: that is, to give every man enough to live well on, so as to guarantee the community against the possibility of a case of the malignant disease of poverty, and then (necessarily) to see that he earned it.

Undershaft, the hero of Major Barbara, is simply a man who, having grasped the fact that poverty is a crime, knows that when society offered him the alternative of poverty or a lucrative trade in death and destruction, it offered him, not a choice between opulent villainy and humble virtue, but between energetic enterprise and cowardly imfamy. His conduct stands the Kantian test, which Peter Shirley's does not. Peter Shirley is what we call the honest poor man. Undershaft is what we call the wicked rich one: Shirley is Lazarus, Undershaft Dives. Well, the misery of the world is due to the fact that the great mass of men act and believe as Peter Shirley acts and believes. If they acted and believed as Undershaft acts and believes, the immediate result would be a revolution of incalculable beneficence. To be wealthy, says Undershaft, is with me a point of honor for which I am prepared to kill at the risk of my own life. This preparedness is, as he says, the final test of sincerity. Like Froissart's medieval hero, who saw that "to rob and pill was a good life," he is not the dupe of that public sentiment against killing which is propagated and endowed by people who would otherwise be killed themselves, or of the mouth-honor paid to poverty and obedience by rich and insubordinate do-nothings who want to rob the poor without courage and command them without superiority. Froissart's knight, in placing the achievement of a good life before all the other duties—which indeed are not duties at all when they conflict with it, but plain wickednesses—behaved bravely, admirably, and, in the final analysis, public-spiritedly. Medieval society, on the other hand, behaved very badly indeed in organizing itself so stupidly that a good life could be achieved by robbing and pilling. If the knight's contemporaries had been all as resolute as he, robbing and pilling would have been the shortest way to the gallows, just as, if we were all as resolute and clearsighted as Undershaft, an attempt to live by means of what is called "an independent income" would be the shortest way to the lethal chamber. But as, thanks to our political imbecility and personal cowardice (fruits of poverty, both), the best imitation of a good life now procurable is life on an independent income, all sensible people aim at securing such an income, and are, of course, careful to legalize and moralize both it and all the actions and sentiments which lead to it and support it as an institution. What else can they do? They know, of course, that they are rich because others are poor. But they cannot help that: it is for the poor to repudiate poverty when they have had enough of it. The thing can be done easily enough: the demonstrations to the contrary made by the economists, jurists, moralists and sentimentalists hired by the rich to defend them, or even doing the work gratuitously out of sheer folly and abjectness, impose only on the hirers.

The reason why the independent income-tax payers are not solid in defence of their position is that since we are not medieval rovers through a sparsely populated country, the poverty of those we rob prevents our having the good life for which we sacrifice them. Rich men or aristocrats with a developed sense of life—men like Ruskin and William Morris and Kropotkin—have enormous social appetites and very fastidious personal ones. They are not content with handsome houses: they want handsome cities. They are not content with be-diamonded wives and blooming daughters: they complain because the charwoman is badly dressed, because the laundress smells of gin, because the sempstress is anemic, because every man they meet is not a friend and every woman not a romance. They turn up their noses at their neighbors' drains, and are made ill by the architecture of their neighbors' houses. Trade patterns made to suit vulgar people do not please them (and they can get nothing else): they cannot sleep nor sit at ease upon "slaughtered" cabinet makers' furniture. The very air is not good enough for them: there is too much factory smoke in it. They even demand abstract conditions: justice, honor, a noble moral atmosphere, a mystic nexus to replace the cash nexus. Finally they declare that though to rob and pill with your own hand on horseback and in steel coat may have been a good life, to rob and pill by the hands of the policeman, the bailiff, and the soldier, and to underpay them meanly for doing it, is not a good life, but rather fatal to all possibility of even a tolerable one. They call on the poor to revolt, and, finding the poor shocked at their ungentlemanliness, despairingly revile the proletariat for its ''damned wantlessness'' (*verdammte Bedürfnislosigkeit*).

So far, however, their attack on society has lacked simplicity. The poor do not share their tastes nor understand their art-criticisms. They do not want the simple life, nor the esthetic life; on the contrary, they want very much to wallow in all the costly vulgarities from which the elect souls among the rich turn away with loathing. It is by surfeit and not by abstinence that they will be cured of their hankering after unwholesome sweets. What they do dislike and despise and are ashamed of is poverty. To ask them to fight for the difference between the Christmas number of the Illustrated London News and the Kelmscott Chaucer is silly: they prefer the News. The difference between a stockbroker's cheap and dirty starched white shirt and collar and the comparatively costly and carefully dyed blue shirt of William Morris is a difference so disgraceful to Morris in their eyes that if they fought on the subject at all, they would fight in defence of the starch. ''Cease to be slaves, in order that you may become cranks'' is not a very inspiring call to arms; nor is it really improved by substituting saints for cranks. Both terms denote men of genius; and the common man does not want to live the life of a man of genius: he would much rather live the life of a pet collie if that were the only alternative. But he does want more money. Whatever else he may be vague about, he is clear about that. He may or may not prefer Major Barbara to the Drury Lane pantomime; but he always prefers five hundred pounds to five hundred shillings.

Now to deplore this preference as sordid, and teach children that it is sinful to desire money, is to strain towards the extreme possible limit of impudence in lying, and corruption in hypocrisy. The universal regard for money is the one hopeful fact in our civilization, the one sound spot in our social conscience. Money is the most important thing in the world. It represents health, strength, honor, generosity and beauty as conspicuously and undeniably as the want of it represents illness, weakness, disgrace, meanness and ugliness. Not the least of its virtues is that it destroys base people as certainly as it fortifies and dignifies noble people. It is only when it is cheapened to worthlessness for some, and made impossibly dear to others, that it becomes a curse. In short, it is a curse only in such foolish social conditions that life itself is a curse. For the two things are inseparable: money is the counter that enables life to be distributed socially: it *is* life as truly as sovereigns and bank notes are money. The first duty of every citizen is to insist on having money on reasonable terms; and this demand is not complied with by giving four men three shillings each for ten or twelve hours' drudgery and one man a thousand pounds for nothing. The crying need of the nation is not for better morals, cheaper bread, temperance, liberty, culture, redemption of fallen sisters and erring brothers, nor the grace, love and fellowship of the Trinity, but simply for enough money. And the evil to be attacked is not sin, suffering, greed, priestcraft, kingcraft, demagogy, monopoly, ignorance, drink, war, pestilence, nor any other of the scapegoats which reformers sacrifice, but simply poverty.

Once take your eyes from the ends of the earth and fix them on this truth just under your nose; and Andrew Undershaft's views will not perplex you in the least. Unless indeed his constant sense that he is only the instrument of a Will or Life Force which uses him for purposes wider than his own, may puzzle you. If so, that is because you are walking either in artificial Darwinian darkness, or in mere stupidity. All genuinely religious people have that consciousness. To them Undershaft the Mystic will be quite intelligible, and his perfect comprehension of his daughter the Salvationist and her lover the Euripidean republican natural and inevitable. That, however, is not new, even on the stage. What is new, as far as I know, is that article in Undershaft's religion which recognizes in Money the first need and in poverty the vilest sin of man and society.

This dramatic conception has not, of course, been attained

per saltum. Nor has it been borrowed from Nietzsche or from any man born beyond the Channel. The late Samuel Butler, in his own department the greatest English writer of the latter half of the XIX century, steadily inculcated the necessity and morality of a conscientious Laodiceanism in religion and of an earnest and constant sense of the importance of money. It drives one almost to despair of English literature when one sees so extraordinary a study of English life as Butler's posthumous Way of All Flesh making so little impression that when, some years later, I produce plays in which Butler's extraordinarily fresh, free and future-piercing suggestions have an obvious share, I am met with nothing but vague cacklings about Ibsen and Nietzsche, and am only too thankful that they are not about Alfred de Musset and Georges Sand. Really, the English do not deserve to have great men. They allowed Butler to die practically unknown, whilst I, a comparatively insignificant Irish journalist, was leading them by the nose into an advertisement of me which has made my own life a burden. In Sicily there is a Via Samuele Butler. When an English tourist sees it, he either asks "Who the devil was Samuele Butler?" or wonders why the Sicilians should perpetuate the memory of the author of Hudibras.

Well, it cannot be denied that the English are only too anxious to recognize a man of genius if somebody will kindly point him out to them. Having pointed myself out in this manner with some success, I now point out Samuel Butler, and trust that in consequence I shall hear a little less in future of the novelty and foreign origin of the ideas which are now making their way into the English theatre through plays written by Socialists. There are living men whose originality and power are as obvious as Butler's; and when they die that fact will be discovered. Meanwhile I recommend them to insist on their own merits as an important part of their own business.

THE SALVATION ARMY.

When Major Barbara was produced in London, the second act was reported in an important northern newspaper as a withering attack on the Salvation Army, and the despairing ejaculation of Barbara deplored by a London daily as a tasteless blasphemy. And they were set right, not by the professed critics of the theatre, but by religious and philosophical publicists like Sir Oliver Lodge and Dr. Stanton Coit, and strenuous Nonconformist journalists like Mr. William Stead, who not only understand the act as well as the Salvationists themselves, but also saw it in its relation to the religious life of the nation, a life which seems to lie not only outside the sympathy of many of our theatre critics, but actually outside their knowledge of society. Indeed nothing could be more ironically curious than the confrontation Major Barbara effected of the theatre enthusiasts with the religious enthusiasts. On the one hand was the playgoer, always seeking pleasure, paying exorbitantly for it, suffering unbearable discomforts for it, and hardly ever getting it. On the other hand was the Salvationist, repudiating gaiety and courting effort and sacrifice, yet always in the wildest spirits, laughing, joking, singing, rejoicing, drumming, and tambourining: his life flying by in a flash of excitement, and his death arriving as a climax of triumph. And, if you please, the playgoer despising the Salvationist as a joyless person, shut out from the heaven of the theatre, self-condemned to a life of hideous gloom; and the Salvationist mourning over the playgoer as over a prodigal with vine leaves in his hair, careering outrageously to hell amid the popping of champagne corks and the ribald laughter of sirens! Could misunderstanding be more complete, or sympathy worse misplaced?

Fortunately, the Salvationists are more accessible to the religious character of the drama than the playgoers to the gay energy and artistic fertility of religion. They can see, when it is pointed out to them, that a theatre, as a place where two or three are gathered together, takes from that divine presence an inalienable sanctity of which the grossest and profanest farce can no more deprive it than a hypocritical sermon by a snobbish bishop can desecrate Westminster Abbey. But in our professional playgoers this indispensable preliminary conception of sanctity seems wanting. They talk of actors as mimes and mummers, and, I fear, think of dramatic authors as liars and pandars, whose main business is the voluptuous soothing of the tired city speculator when what he calls the serious business of the day is over. Passion, the life of drama, means nothing to them but primitive sexual excitement: such phrases as "impassioned poetry" or "passionate love of truth" have fallen quite out of their vocabulary and been replaced by "passional crime" and the like. They assume, as far as I can gather, that people in whom passion has a larger scope are passionless and therefore uninteresting. Consequently they come to think of religious people as people who are not interesting and not amusing. And so, when Barbara cuts the regular Salvation Army jokes, and snatches a kiss from her lover across his drum, the devotees of the theatre think they ought to appear shocked, and conclude that the whole play is an elaborate mockery of the Army. And then either hypocritically rebuke me for mocking, or foolishly take part in the supposed mockery!

Even the handful of mentally competent critics got into difficulties over my demonstration of the economic deadlock in which the Salvation Army finds itself. Some of them thought that the Army would not have taken money from a distiller and a cannon founder: others thought it should not have taken it: all assumed more or less definitely that it reduced itself to absurdity or hypocrisy by taking it. On the first point the reply of the Army itself was prompt and conclusive. As one of its officers said, they would take money from the devil himself and be only too glad to get it out of his hands and into God's. They gratefully acknowledged that publicans not only give them money but allow them to collect it in the bar—sometimes even when there is a Salvation meeting outside preaching teetotalism. In fact, they questioned the verisimilitude of the play, not because Mrs. Baines took the money, but because Barbara refused it.

On the point that the Army ought not to take such money, its justification is obvious. It must take the money because it cannot exist without money, and there is no other money to be had. Practically all the spare money in the country consists of a mass of rent, interest, and profit, every penny of which is bound up with crime, drink, prostitution, disease, and all the evil fruits of poverty, as inextricably as with enterprise, wealth, commercial probity, and national prosperity. The notion that you can earmark certain coins as tainted is an unpractical individualist superstition. None the less the fact that all our money is tainted gives a very severe shock to earnest young souls when some dramatic instance of the taint first makes them conscious of it. When an enthusiastic young clergyman of the Established Church first realizes that the Ecclesiastical Commissioners receive the rents of sporting public houses, brothels, and sweating dens; or that the most generous contributor at his last charity sermon was an employer trading in female labor cheapened by prostitution as unscrupulously as a hotel keeper trades in waiters' labor cheapened by tips, or commissionaire's labor cheapened by pensions; or that the only patron who can afford to rebuild his church or his schools or give his boys' brigade a gymnasium or a library is the son-in-law of a Chicago meat King, that young clergyman has, like Barbara, a very bad quarter hour. But he cannot help himself by refusing to accept money from anybody except sweet old ladies with independent incomes and gentle and lovely ways of life. He has only to follow up the income of the sweet ladies to its industrial source, and there he will find Mrs. Warren's profession and the poisonous canned meat and all the rest of it. His own stipend has the same root. He must either share the world's guilt or go to another planet. He must save the world's honor if he is to save his own. This is what all the Churches find just as the Salvation Army and Barbara find it in the play. Her discovery that she is her father's accomplice; that the Salvation Army is the accomplice of the distiller and the dynamite maker; that they can no more escape one another than they can escape the air they breathe; that there is no salvation for them through personal righteousness, but only through the redemption of the whole nation from its vicious, lazy, competitive anarchy: this discovery has been made by everyone except the Pharisees and (apparently) the professional playgoers, who still wear their Tom Hood shirts and underpay their washerwomen without the slightest misgiving as to the elevation of their private characters, the purity of their private atmospheres, and their right to repudiate as foreign to themselves the coarse depravity of the garret and the slum. Not that they mean any harm: they only desire to be, in their little private way, what they call gentlemen. They do not understand Barbara's lesson because they have not, like her, learnt it by taking their part in the larger life of the nation.

Barbara's Return to the Colors.

Barbara's return to the colors may yet provide a subject for the dramatic historian of the future. To go back to the Salvation Army with the knowledge that even the Salvationists themselves are not saved yet; that poverty is not blessed, but a most damnable sin; and that when General Booth chose Blood and Fire for the emblem of Salvation instead of the Cross, he was perhaps better inspired than he knew: such knowledge, for the daughter of Andrew Undershaft, will clearly lead to something hopefuller than distributing bread and treacle at the expense of Bodger.

It is a very significant thing, this instinctive choice of the military form of organization, this substitution of the drum for the organ, by the Salvation Army. Does it not suggest that the Salvationists divine that they must actually fight the devil instead of merely praying at him? At present, it is true, they have not quite ascertained his correct address. When they do, they may give a very rude shock to that sense of security which he has gained from his experience of the fact that hard words, even when uttered by eloquent essayists and lecturers, or carried unanimously at enthusiastic public meetings on the motion of eminent reformers, break no bones. It has been said that the French Revolution was the work of Voltaire, Rousseau and the Encyclopedists. It seems to me to have been the work of men who had observed that virtuous indignation, caustic criticism, conclusive argument and instructive pamphleteering, even when done by the most earnest and witty literary geniuses, were as useless as praying, things going steadily from bad to worse whilst the Social Contract and the pamphlets of Voltaire were at the height of their vogue. Eventually, as we know, perfectly respectable citizens and earnest philanthropists connived at the September massacres because hard experience had convinced them that if they contented themselves with appeals to humanity and patriotism, the aristocracy, though it would read their appeals with the greatest enjoyment and appreciation, flattering and admiring the writers, would none the less continue to conspire with foreign monarchists to undo the revolution and restore the old system with every circumstance of savage vengeance and ruthless repression of popular liberties.

The nineteenth century saw the same lesson repeated in England. It had its Utilitarians, its Christian Socialists, its Fabians (still extant): it had Bentham, Mill, Dickens, Ruskin, Carlyle, Butler, Henry George, and Morris. And the end of all their efforts is the Chicago described by Mr. Upton Sinclair, and the London in which the people who pay to be amused by my dramatic representation of Peter Shirley turned out to starve at forty because there are younger slaves to be had for his wages, do not take, and have not the slightest intention of taking, any effective step to organize society in such a way as to make that everyday infamy impossible. I, who have preached and pamphleteered like any Encyclopedist, have to confess that my methods are no use, and would be no use if I were Voltaire, Rousseau, Bentham, Mill, Dickens, Carlyle, Ruskin, George, Butler, and Morris all rolled into one, with Euripides, More, Molière, Shakespear, Beaumarchais, Swift, Goethe, Ibsen, Tolstoy, Moses and the prophets all thrown in (as indeed in some sort I actually am, standing as I do on all their shoulders). The problem being to make heroes out of cowards, we paper apostles and artist-magicians have succeeded only in giving cowards all the sensations of heroes whilst they tolerate every abomination, accept every plunder, and submit to every oppression. Christianity, in making a merit of such submission, has marked only that depth in the abyss at which the very sense of shame is lost. The Christian has been like Dickens' doctor in the debtor's prison, who tells the newcomer of its ineffable peace and security: no duns; no tyrannical collectors of rates, taxes, and rent; no importunate hopes nor exacting duties; nothing but the rest and safety of having no further to fall.

Yet in the poorest corner of this soul-destroying Christendom vitality suddenly begins to germinate again. Joyousness, a sacred gift long dethroned by the hellish laughter of derision and obscenity, rises like a flood miraculously out of the fetid dust and mud of the slums; rousing marches and impetuous dithyrambs rise to the heavens from people among whom the depressing noise called "sacred music" is a standing joke; a flag with Blood and Fire on it is unfurled, not in murderous rancor, but because fire is beautiful and blood a vital and splendid red; Fear, which we flatter by calling Self, vanishes; and transfigured men and women carry their gospel through a transfigured world, calling their leader General, themselves captains and brigadiers, and their whole body an Army: praying, but praying only for refreshment, for strength to fight, and for needful MONEY (a notable sign, that); preaching, but not preaching submission; daring ill-usage and abuse, but not putting up with more of it than is inevitable; and practising what the world will let them practise, including soap and water, color and music. There is danger in such activity; and where there is danger there is hope. Our present security is nothing, and can be nothing, but evil made irresistible.

WEAKNESS OF THE SALVATION ARMY.

For the present, however, it is not my business to flatter the Salvation Army. Rather must I point out to it that it has almost as many weaknesses as the Church of England itself. It is building up a business organization which will compel it eventually to see that its present staff of enthusiast-commanders shall be succeeded by a bureaucracy of men of business who will be no better than bishops, and perhaps a good deal more unscrupulous. That has always happened sooner or later to great orders founded by saints; and the order founded by St. William Booth is not exempt from the same danger. It is even more dependent than the Church on rich people who would cut off supplies at once if it began to preach that indispensable revolt against poverty which must also be a revolt against riches. It is hampered by a heavy contingent of pious elders who are not really Salvationists at all, but Evangelicals of the old school. It still, as Commissioner Howard affirms, "sticks to Moses," which is flat nonsense at this time of day if the Commissioner means, as I am afraid he does, that the Book of Genesis contains a trustworthy scientific account of the origin of species, and that the god to whom Jephthah sacrificed his daughter is any less obviously a tribal idol than Dagon or Chemosh.

Further, there is still too much other-worldliness about the Army. Like Frederick's grenadier, the Salvationist wants to live for ever (the most monstrous way of crying for the moon); and though it is evident to anyone who has ever heard General Booth and his best officers that they would work as hard for human salvation as they do at present if they believed that death would be the end of them individually, they and their followers have a bad habit of talking as if the Salvationists were heroically enduring a very bad time on earth as an investment which will bring them in dividends later on in the form, not of a better life to come for the whole world, but of an eternity spent by themselves personally in a sort of bliss which would bore any active person to a second death. Surely the truth is that the Salvationists are unusually happy people. And is it not the very diagnostic of true salvation that it shall overcome the fear of death? Now the man who has come to believe that there is no such thing as death, the change so called being merely the transition to an exquisitely happy and utterly careless life, has not overcome the fear of death at all: on the contrary, it has overcome him so completely that he refuses to die on any terms whatever. I do not call a Salvationist really saved until he is ready to lie down cheerfully on the scrap heap, having paid scot and lot and something over, and let his eternal life pass on to renew its youth in the battalions of the future.

Then there is the nasty lying habit called confession, which the Army encourages because it lends itself to dramatic oratory, with plenty of thrilling incident. For my part, when I hear a convert relating the violences and oaths and blasphemies he was guilty of before he was saved, making out that he was a very terrible fellow then and is the most contrite and chastened of Christians now, I believe him no more than I believe the millionaire who says he came up to London or Chicago as a boy with only three halfpence in his pocket. Salvationists have said to me that Barbara in my play would never have been taken in by so transparent a humbug as Snobby Price; and certainly I do not think Snobby could have taken in any experienced Salvationist on a point on which the

Salvationist did not wish to be taken in. But on the point of conversion all Salvationists wish to be taken in; for the more obvious the sinner the more obvious the miracle of his conversion. When you advertize a converted burglar or reclaimed drunkard as one of the attractions at an experience meeting, your burglar can hardly have been too burglarious or your drunkard too drunken. As long as such attractions are relied on, you will have your Snobbies claiming to have beaten their mothers when they were as a matter of prosaic fact habitually beaten by them, and your Rummies of the tamest respectability pretending to a past of reckless and dazzling vice. Even when confessions are sincerely autobiographic there is no reason to assume at once that the impulse to make them is pious or the interest of the hearers wholesome. It might as well be assumed that the poor people who insist on shewing appalling ulcers to district visitors are convinced hygienists, or that the curiosity which sometimes welcomes such exhibitions is a pleasant and creditable one. One is often tempted to suggest that those who pester our police superintendents with confessions of murder might very wisely be taken at their word and executed, except in the few cases in which a real murderer is seeking to be relieved of his guilt by confession and expiation. For though I am not, I hope, an unmerciful person, I do not think that the inexorability of the deed once done should be disguised by any ritual, whether in the confessional or on the scaffold.

And here my disagreement with the Salvation Army, and with all propagandists of the Cross (to which I object as I object to all gibbets) becomes deep indeed. Forgiveness, absolution, atonement, are figments: punishment is only a pretence of cancelling one crime by another; and you can no more have forgiveness without vindictiveness than you can have a cure without a disease. You will never get a high morality from people who conceive that their misdeeds are revocable and pardonable, or in a society where absolution and expiation are officially provided for us all. The demand may be very real; but the supply is spurious. Thus Bill Walker, in my play, having assaulted the Salvation Lass, presently finds himself overwhelmed with an intolerable conviction of sin under the skilled treatment of Barbara. Straightway he begins to try to unassault the lass and deruffianize his deed, first by getting punished for it in kind, and, when that relief is denied him, by fining himself a pound to compensate the girl. He is foiled both ways. He finds the Salvation Army as inexorable as fact itself. It will not punish him: it will not take his money. It will not tolerate a redeemed ruffian: it leaves him no means of salvation except ceasing to be a ruffian. In doing this, the Salvation Army instinctively grasps the central truth of Christianity and discards its central superstition: that central truth being the vanity of revenge and punishment, and that central superstition the salvation of the world by the gibbet.

For, be it noted, Bill has assaulted an old and starving woman also; and for this worse offence he feels no remorse whatever, because she makes it clear that her malice is as great as his own. "Let her have the law of me, as she said she would," says Bill: "what I done to her is no more on what you might call my conscience than sticking a pig." This shews a perfectly natural and wholesome state of mind on his part. The old woman, like the law she threatens him with, is perfectly ready to play the game of retaliation with him: to rob him if he steals, to flog him if he strikes, to murder him if he kills. By example and precept the law and public opinion teach him to impose his will on others by anger, violence, and cruelty, and to wipe off the moral score by punishment. That is sound Crosstianity. But this Crosstianity has got entangled with something which Barbara calls Christianity, and which unexpectedly causes her to refuse to play the hangman's game of Satan casting out Satan. She refuses to prosecute a drunken ruffian; she converses on equal terms with a blackguard whom no lady could be seen speaking to in the public street: in short, she behaves as illegally and unbecomingly as possible under the circumstances. Bill's conscience reacts to this just as naturally as it does to the old woman's threats. He is placed in a position of unbearable moral inferiority, and strives by every means in his power to escape from it, whilst he is still quite ready to meet the abuse of the old woman by attempting to smash a mug on her face. And that is the triumphant justification of Barbara's Christianity as against our system of judicial punishment and the vindictive villain-thrashings and "poetic justice" of the romantic stage.

For the credit of literature it must be pointed out that the situation is only partly novel. Victor Hugo long ago gave us the epic of the convict and the bishop's candlesticks, of the Crosstian policeman annihilated by his encounter with the Christian Valjean. But Bill Walker is not, like Valjean, romantically changed from a demon into an angel. There are millions of Bill Walkers in all classes of society to-day; and the point which I, as a professor of natural psychology, desire to demonstrate, is that Bill, without any change in his character whatsoever, will react one way to one sort of treatment and another way to another.

In proof I might point to the sensational object lesson provided by our commercial millionaires to-day. They begin as brigands: merciless, unscrupulous, dealing out ruin and death and slavery to their competitors and employees, and facing desperately the worst that their competitors can do to them. The history of the English factories, the American trusts, the exploitation of African gold, diamonds, ivory and rubber, outdoes in villainy the worst that has ever been imagined of the buccaneers of the Spanish Main. Captain Kidd would have marooned a modern Trust magnate for conduct unworthy of a gentleman of fortune. The law everyday seizes on unsuccessful scoundrels of this type and punishes them with a cruelty worse than their own, with the result that they come out of the torture house more dangerous than they went in, and renew their evil doing (nobody will employ them at anything else) until they are again seized, again tormented, and again let loose, with the same result.

But the successful scoundrel is dealt with very differently, and very Christianly. He is not only forgiven: he is idolized, respected, made much of, all but worshipped. Society returns him good for evil in the most extravagant overmeasure. And with what result? He begins to idolize himself, to respect himself, to live up to the treatment he receives. He preaches sermons; he writes books of the most edifying advice to young men, and actually persuades himself that he got on by taking his own advice; he endows educational institutions; he supports charities; he dies finally in the odor of sanctity, leaving a will which is a monument of public spirit and bounty. And all this without any change in his character. The spots of the leopard and the stripes of the tiger are as brilliant as ever; but the conduct of the world towards him has changed; and his conduct has changed accordingly. You have only to reverse your attitude towards him—to lay hands on his property, revile him, assault him, and he will be a brigand again in a moment, as ready to crush you as you are to crush him, and quite as full of pretentious moral reasons for doing it.

In short, when Major Barbara says that there are no scoundrels, she is right: there are no absolute scoundrels, though there are impracticable people of whom I shall treat presently. Every practicable man (and woman) is a potential scoundrel and a potential good citizen. What a man is depends on his character; but what he does, and what we think of what he does, depends on his circumstances. The characteristics that ruin a man in one class make him eminent in another. The characters that behave differently in different circumstances behave alike in similar circumstances. Take a common English character like that of Bill Walker. We meet Bill everywhere: on the judicial bench, on the episcopal bench, in the Privy Council, at the War Office and Admiralty, as well as in the Old Bailey dock or in the ranks of casual unskilled labor. And the morality of Bill's characteristics varies with these various circumstances. The faults of the burglar are the qualities of the financier: the manners and habits of a duke would cost a city clerk his situation. In short, though character is independent of circumstances, conduct is not; and our moral judgments of character are not: both are circumstantial. Take any condition of life in which the circumstances are for a mass of men practically alike: felony, the House of Lords, the factory, the stables, the gipsy encampment or where you please! In spite of diversity of character and temperament, the conduct and morals of the individuals in each group are as predicable and as alike in the main as if they were a flock of sheep, morals being mostly only social habits and circumstantial necessities. Strong people know this and count upon it. In nothing have the master-minds of the world been distinguished from the ordinary suburban season-ticket holder more than in their straight-forward perception of the fact that mankind is practically a single species, and not a menagerie of gentlemen and bounders, villains and heroes, cowards and daredevils, peers and peasants, grocers and aristocrats, artisans and laborers, washerwomen and duchesses, in which all the grades of income and caste represent distinct animals who must not be introduced to one another or intermarry. Napoleon constructing a galaxy of generals and courtiers, and even of monarchs, out of his collection of social nobodies; Julius Cæsar appointing as governor of Egypt the son of a freedman—one who but a short time before would have been legally disqualified for the post even of a private soldier in the Roman army; Louis XI. making his barber his privy councillor: all these had in their different ways a firm hold of the scientific fact of human equality, expressed by Barbara in the Christian formula that all men are children of one father. A man who believes that men are naturally divided into upper and lower and middle classes morally is making exactly the same mistake as the man who believes that they are naturally divided in the same way socially. And just as our persistent attempts to found political institutions on a basis of social inequality have always produced long periods of destructive friction relieved from time to time by violent explosions of revolution; so the attempt—will Americans please note—to found moral institutions on a basis of moral inequality can lead to nothing but unnatural Reigns of the Saints relieved by licentious Restorations; to Americans who have made divorce a public institution turning the face of Europe into one huge sardonic smile by refusing to stay in the same hotel with a Russian man of genius who has changed wives without the sanction of South Dakota; to grotesque hypocrisy, cruel persecution, and final utter confusion of conventions and compliances with benevolence and respectability. It is quite useless to declare that all men are born free if you deny that they are born good. Guarantee a man's goodness and his liberty will take care of itself. To guarantee his freedom on condition that you approve of his moral character is formally to abolish all freedom whatsoever, as every man's liberty is at the mercy of a moral indictment, which any fool can trump up against everyone who violates custom, whether as a prophet or as a rascal. This is the lesson Democracy has to learn before it can become anything but the most oppressive of all the priesthoods.

Let us now return to Bill Walker and his case of conscience against the Salvation Army. Major Barbara, not being a modern Tetzel, or the treasurer of a hospital, refuses to sell Bill absolution for a sovereign. Unfortunately, what the Army can afford to refuse in the case of Bill Walker, it cannot refuse in the case of Bodger. Bodger is master of the situation because he holds the purse strings. "Strive as you will," says Bodger, in effect: "me you cannot do without. You cannot save Bill Walker without my money." And the Army answers, quite rightly under the circumstances, "We will take money from the devil himself sooner than abandon the work of Salvation." So Bodger pays his conscience-money and gets the absolution that is refused to Bill. In real life Bill would perhaps never know this. But I, the dramatist, whose business it is to shew the connexion between things that seem apart and unrelated in the haphazard order of events in real life, have contrived to make it known to Bill, with the result that the Salvation Army loses its hold of him at once.

But Bill may not be lost, for all that. He is still in the grip of the facts and of his own conscience, and may find his taste for blackguardism permanently spoiled. Still, I cannot guarantee that happy ending. Let anyone walk through the poorer quarters of our cities when the men are not working, but resting and chewing the cud of their reflections; and he will find that there is one expression on every mature face: the expression of cynicism. The discovery made by Bill Walker about the Salvation Army has been made by everyone of them. They have found that every man has his price; and they have been foolishly or corruptly taught to mistrust and despise him for that necessary and salutary condition of social existence. When they learn that General Booth, too, has his price, they do not admire him because it is a high one, and admit the need of organizing society so that he shall get it in an honorable way: they conclude that his character is unsound and that all religious men are hypocrites and allies of their sweaters and oppressors. They know that the large subscriptions which help to support the Army are endowments, not of religion, but of the wicked doctrine of docility in poverty and humility under oppression; and they are rent by the most agonizing of all the doubts of the soul, the doubt whether their true salvation must not come from their most abhorrent passions, from murder, envy, greed, stubbornness, rage, and terrorism, rather than from public spirit, reasonableness, humanity, generosity, tenderness, delicacy, pity and kindness. The confirmation of that doubt, at which our newspapers have been working so hard for years past, is the morality of militarism; and the justification of militarism is that circumstances may at any time make it the true morality of the moment. It is by producing such moments that we produce violent and sanguinary revolutions, such as the one now in progress in Russia and the one which Capitalism in England and America is daily and diligently provoking.

At such moments it becomes the duty of the Churches to evoke all the powers of destruction against the existing order. But if they do this, the existing order must forcibly suppress them. Churches are suffered to exist only on condition that they preach submission to the State as at present capitalistically organized. The Church of England itself is compelled to add to the thirty-six articles in which it formulates its religious tenets, three more in which it apologetically protests that the moment any of these articles comes in conflict with the State it is to be entirely renounced, abjured, violated, abrogated and abhorred, the policeman being a much more important person than any of the Persons of the Trinity. And this is why no tolerated Church nor Salvation Army can ever win the entire confidence of the poor. It must be on the side of the police and the military, no matter what it believes or disbelieves; and as the police and the military are the instruments by which the rich rob and oppress the poor (on legal and moral principles made for the purpose), it is not possible to be on the side of the poor and of the police at the same time. Indeed the religious bodies, as the almoners of the rich, become a sort of auxiliary police, taking off the insurrectionary edge of poverty with coals and blankets, bread and treacle, and soothing and cheering the victims with hopes of immense and inexpensive happiness in another world when the process of working them to premature death in the service of the rich is complete in this.

CHRISTIANITY AND ANARCHISM.

Such is the false position from which neither the Salvation Army nor the Church of England nor any other religious organization whatever can escape except through a reconstitution of society. Nor can they merely endure the State passively, washing their hands of its sins. The State is constantly forcing the consciences of men by violence and cruelty. Not content with exacting money from us for the maintenance of its soldiers and policemen, its gaolers and executioners, it forces us to take an active personal part in its proceedings on pain of becoming ourselves the victims of its violence. As I write these lines, a sensational example is given to the world. A royal marriage has been celebrated, first by sacrament in a cathedral, and then by a bullfight having for its main amusement the spectacle of horses gored and disembowelled by the bull, after which when the bull is so exhausted as to be no longer dangerous, he is killed by a cautious matador. But the ironic contrast between the bull fight and the sacrament of marriage does not move anyone. Another contrast—that between the splendor, the happiness, the atmosphere of kindly admiration surrounding the young couple, and the price paid for it under our abominable social arrangements in the misery, squalor and degradation of millions of other young couples—is drawn at the same moment by a novelist, Mr. Upton Sinclair, who chips a corner of the veneering from the huge meat packing industries of Chicago, and shews it to us as a sample of what is going on all over the world underneath the top layer of prosperous plutocracy. One man is sufficiently moved by that contrast to pay his own life as the price of one terrible blow at the responsible parties. Unhappily his poverty leaves him also ignorant enough to be duped by the pretence that the innocent young bride and bridegroom, put forth and crowned by plutocracy as the heads of a State in which they have less personal power than any policeman, and less influence than any chairman of a trust, are responsible. At them accordingly he launches his sixpennorth of fulminate, missing his mark, but scattering the bowels of as many horses as any bull in the arena, and slaying twenty-three persons, besides wounding ninetynine. And of all these, the horses alone are innocent of the guilt he is avenging: had he blown all Madrid to atoms with every adult person in it, not one could have escaped the charge of being an accessory, before, at, and after the fact, to poverty and prostitution, to such wholesale massacre of infants as Herod never dreamt of, to plague, pestilence and famine, battle, murder and lingering death—perhaps not one who had not helped, through example, precept, connivance, and even clamor, to teach the dynamiter his well-learnt gospel of hatred and vengeance, by approving every day of sentences of years of imprisonment so infernal in its unnatural stupidity and panic-stricken cruelty, that their advocates can disavow neither the dagger nor the bomb without stripping the mask of justice and humanity from themselves also.

Be it noted that at this very moment there appears the biography of one of our dukes, who, being Scotch, could argue about politics, and therefore stood out as a great brain among our aristocrats. And what, if you please, was his grace's favorite historical episode, which he declared he never read without intense satisfaction? Why, the young General Bonapart's pounding of the Paris mob to pieces in 1795, called in playful approval by our respectable classes "the whiff of grapeshot," though Napoleon, to do him justice, took a deeper view of it, and would fain have had it forgotten. And since the Duke of Argyll was not a demon, but a man of like passions with ourselves, by no means rancorous or cruel as men go, who can doubt that all over the world proletarians of the ducal kidney are now revelling in "the whiff of dynamite" (the flavor of the joke seems to evaporate a little, does it not?) because it was aimed at the class they hate even as our argute duke hated what he called the mob.

In such an atmosphere there can be only one sequel to the Madrid explosion. All Europe burns to emulate it. Vengeance! More blood! Tear "the Anarchist beast" to shreds. Drag him to the scaffold. Imprison him for life. Let all civilized States band together to drive his like off the face of the earth; and if any State refuses to join, make war on it. This time the leading London newspaper, anti-Liberal and therefore anti-Russian in politics, does not say "Serve you right" to the victims, as it did, in effect, when Bobrikoff, and De Plehve, and Grand Duke Sergius, were in the same manner unofficially fulminated into fragments. No: fulminate our rivals in Asia by all means, ye brave Russian revolutionaries; but to aim at an English princess—monstrous! hideous! hound down the wretch to his doom; and observe, please, that we are a civilized and merciful people, and, however much we may regret it, must not treat him as Ravaillac and Damiens were treated. And meanwhile, since we have not yet caught him, let us soothe our quivering nerves with the bullfight, and comment in a courtly way on the unfailing tact and good taste of the ladies of our royal houses, who, though presumably of full normal natural tenderness, have been so effectually broken in to fashionable routine that they can be taken to see the horses slaughtered as helplessly as they could no doubt be taken to a gladiator show, if that happened to be the mode just now.

Strangely enough, in the midst of this raging fire of malice, the one man who still has faith in the kindness and intelligence of human nature is the fulminator, now a hunted wretch, with nothing, apparently, to secure his triumph over all the prisons and scaffolds of infuriate Europe except the revolver in his pocket and his readiness to discharge it at a moment's notice into his own or any other head. Think of him setting out to find a gentleman and a Christian in the multitude of human wolves howling for his blood. Think also of this: that at the very first essay he finds what he seeks, a veritable grandee of Spain, a noble, high-thinking, unterrified, malice-void soul, in the guise—of all masquerades in the world!—of a modern editor. The Anarchist wolf, flying from the wolves of plutocracy, throws himself on the honor of the man. The man, not being a wolf (nor a London editor), and therefore not having enough sympathy with his exploit to be made bloodthirsty by it, does not throw him back to the pursuing wolves—gives him, instead, what help he can to escape, and sends him off acquainted at last with a force that goes deeper than dynamite, though you cannot make so much of it for sixpence. That righteous and honorable high human deed is not wasted on Europe, let us hope, though it benefits the fugitive wolf only for a moment. The plutocratic wolves presently smell him out. The fugitive shoots the unlucky wolf whose nose is nearest; shoots himself; and then convinces the world, by his photograph, that he was no monstrous freak of reversion to the tiger, but a good looking young man with nothing abnormal about him except his appalling courage and resolution (that is why the terrified shriek Coward at him): one to whom murdering a happy young couple on their wedding morning would have been an unthinkably unnatural abomination under rational and kindly human circumstances.

Then comes the climax of irony and blind stupidity. The wolves, balked of their meal of fellow-wolf, turn on the man, and proceed to torture him, after their manner, by imprisonment, for refusing to fasten his teeth in the throat of the dynamiter and hold him down until they came to finish him.

Thus, you see, a man may not be a gentleman nowadays even if he wishes to. As to being a Christian, he is allowed some latitude in that matter, because, I repeat, Christianity has two faces. Popular Christianity has for its emblem a gibbet, for its chief sensation a sanguinary execution after torture, for its central mystery an insane vengeance bought off by a trumpery expiation. But there is a nobler and profounder Christianity which affirms the sacred mystery of Equality, and forbids the glaring futility and folly of vengeance, often politely called punishment or justice. The gibbet part of Christianity is tolerated. The other is criminal felony. Connoisseurs in irony are well aware of the fact that the only editor in England who denounces punishment as radically wrong, also repudiates Christianity; calls his paper The Freethinker; and has been imprisoned for two years for blasphemy.

SANE CONCLUSIONS.

And now I must ask the excited reader not to lose his head on one side or the other, but to draw a sane moral from these grim absurdities. It is not good sense to propose that laws against crime should apply to principals only and not to accessories whose consent, counsel, or silence may secure impunity to the principal. If you institute punishment as part of the law, you must punish people for refusing to punish. If you have a police, part of its duty must be to compel everybody to assist the police. No doubt if your laws are unjust, and your policemen agents of oppression, the result will be an unbearable violation of the private consciences of citizens. But that cannot be helped: the remedy is, not to license everybody to thwart the law if they please, but to make laws that will command the public assent, and not to deal cruelly and stupidly with lawbreakers. Everybody disapproves of burglars; but the modern burglar, when caught and overpowered by a householder, usually appeals, and often, let us hope, with success, to his captor not to deliver him over to the useless horrors of penal servitude. In other cases the lawbreaker escapes because those who could give him up do not consider his breach of the law a guilty action. Sometimes, even, private tribunals are formed in opposition to the official tribunals; and these private tribunals employ assassins as executioners, as was done, for example, by Mahomet before he had established his power officially, and by the Ribbon lodges of Ireland in their long struggle with the landlords. Under such circumstances, the assassin goes free although everybody in the district knows who he is and what he has done. They do not betray him, partly because they justify him exactly as the regular Government justifies its official executioner, and partly because they would themselves be assassinated if they betrayed him: another method learnt from the official government. Given a tribunal, employing a slayer who has no personal quarrel with the slain; and there is clearly no moral difference between official and unofficial killing.

In short, all men are anarchists with regard to laws which are against their consciences, either in the preamble or in the penalty. In London our worst anarchists are the magistrates, because many of them are so old and ignorant that when they are called upon to administer any law that is based on ideas or knowledge less than half a century old, they disagree with it, and being mere ordinary homebred private Englishmen without any respect for law in the abstract, naïvely set the example of violating it. In this instance the man lags behind the law; but when the law lags behind the man, he becomes equally an anarchist. When some huge change in social conditions, such as the industrial revolution of the eighteenth and nineteenth centuries, throws our legal and industrial institutions out of date, Anarchism becomes almost a religion. The whole force of the most energetic geniuses of the time in philosophy, economics, and art, concentrates itself on demonstrations and reminders that morality and law are only conventions, fallible and continually obsolescing. Tragedies in which the heroes are bandits, and comedies in which law-abiding and conventionally moral folk are compelled to satirize themselves by outraging the conscience of the spectators every time they do their duty, appear simultaneously with economic treatises entitled "What is Property? Theft!" and with histories of "The Conflict between Religion and Science."

Now this is not a healthy state of things. The advantages of living in society are proportionate, not to the freedom of the individual from a code, but to the complexity and subtlety of the code he is prepared not only to accept but to uphold as a matter of such vital importance that a lawbreaker at large is hardly to be tolerated on any plea. Such an attitude becomes impossible when the only men who can make themselves heard and remembered throughout the world spend all their energy in raising our gorge against current law, current morality, current respectability, and legal property. The ordinary man, uneducated in social theory even when he is schooled in Latin verse, cannot be set against all the laws of his country and yet persuaded to regard law in the abstract as vitally necessary to society. Once he is brought to repudiate the laws and institutions he knows, he will repudiate the very conception of law and the very groundwork of institutions, ridiculing human rights, extolling brainless methods as "historical," and tolerating nothing except pure empiricism in conduct, with dynamite as the basis of politics and vivisection as the basis of science. That is hideous; but what is to be done? Here am I, for instance, by class a respectable man, by common sense a hater of waste and disorder, by intellectual constitution legally minded to the verge of pedantry, and by temperament apprehensive and economically disposed to the limit of old-maidishness; yet I am, and have always been, and shall now always be, a revolutionary writer, because our laws make law impossible; our liberties destroy all freedom; our property is organized robbery; our morality is an impudent hypocrisy; our wisdom is administered by inexperienced or malexperienced dupes, our power wielded by cowards and weaklings, and our honor false in all its points. I am an enemy of the existing order for good reasons; but that does not make my attacks any less encouraging or helpful to people who are its enemies for bad reasons. The existing order may shriek that if I tell the truth about it, some foolish person may drive it to become still worse by trying to assassinate it. I cannot help that, even if I could see what worse it could do than it is already doing. And the disadvantage of that worst even from its own point of view is that society, with all its prisons and bayonets and whips and ostracisms and starvations, is powerless in the face of the Anarchist who is prepared to sacrifice his own life in the battle with it. Our natural safety from the cheap and devastating explosives which every Russian student can make, and every Russian grenadier has learnt to handle in Manchuria, lies in the fact that brave and resolute men, when they are rascals, will not risk their skins for the good of humanity, and, when they are sympathetic enough to care for humanity, abhor murder, and never commit it until their consciences are outraged beyond endurance. The remedy is, then, simply not to outrage their consciences.

Do not be afraid that they will not make allowances. All men make very large allowances indeed before they stake their own lives in a war to the death with society. Nobody demands or expects the millennium. But there are two things that must be set right, or we shall perish, like Rome, of soul atrophy disguised as empire.

The first is, that the daily ceremony of dividing the wealth of the country among its inhabitants shall be so conducted that no crumb shall go to any able-bodied adults who are not producing by their personal exertions not only a full equivalent for what they take, but a surplus sufficient to provide for their superannuation and pay back the debt due for their nurture.

The second is that the deliberate infliction of malicious injuries which now goes on under the name of punishment be abandoned; so that the thief, the ruffian, the gambler, and the beggar, may without inhumanity be handed over to the law, and made to understand that a State which is too humane to punish will also be too thrifty to waste the life of honest men in watching or restraining dishonest ones. That is why we do not imprison dogs. We even take our chance of their first bite. But if a dog delights to bark and bite, it goes to the lethal chamber. That seems to me sensible. To allow the dog to expiate his bite by a period of torment, and then let him loose in a much more savage condition (for the chain makes a dog savage) to bite again and expiate again, having meanwhile spent a great deal of human life and happiness in the task of chaining and feeding and tormenting him, seems to me idiotic and superstitious. Yet that is what we do to men who bark and bite and steal. It would be far more sensible to put up with their vices, as we put up with their illnesses, until they give more trouble than they are worth, at which point we should, with many apologies and expressions of sympathy, and some generosity in complying with their last wishes, place them in the lethal chamber and get rid of them. Under no circumstances should they be allowed to expiate their misdeeds by a manufactured penalty, to subscribe to a charity, or to compensate the victims. If there is to be no punishment there can be no forgiveness. We shall never have real moral responsibility until everyone knows that his deeds are irrevocable, and that his life depends on his usefulness. Hitherto, alas! humanity has never dared face these hard facts. We frantically scatter conscience money and invent systems of conscience banking, with expiatory penalties, atonements, redemptions, salvations, hospital subscription lists and what not, to enable us to contract-out of the moral code. Not content with the old scapegoat and sacrificial lamb, we deify human saviors, and pray to miraculous virgin intercessors. We attribute mercy to the inexorable; soothe our consciences after committing murder by throwing ourselves on the bosom of divine love; and shrink even from our own gallows because we are forced to admit that it, at least, is irrevocable—as if one hour of imprisonment were not as irrevocable as any execution!

If a man cannot look evil in the face without illusion, he will never know what it really is, or combat it effectually. The few men who have been able (relatively) to do this have been called cynics, and have sometimes had an abnormal share of evil in themselves, corresponding to the abnormal strength of their minds; but they have never done mischief unless they intended to do it. That is why great scoundrels have been beneficent rulers whilst amiable and privately harmless monarchs have ruined their countries by trusting to the hocus-pocus of innocence and guilt, reward and punishment, virtuous indignation and pardon, instead of standing up to the facts without either malice or mercy. Major Barbara stands up to Bill Walker in that way, with the result that the ruffian who cannot get hated, has to hate himself. To relieve this agony he tries to get punished; but the Salvationist whom he tries to provoke is as merciless as Barbara, and only prays for him. Then he tries to pay, but can get nobody to take his money. His doom is the doom of Cain, who, failing to find either a savior, a policeman, or an almoner to help him to pretend that his brother's blood no longer cried from the ground, had to live and die a murderer. Cain took care not to commit another murder, unlike our railway shareholders (I am one) who kill and maim shunters by hundreds to save the cost of automatic couplings, and make atonement by annual subscriptions to deserving charities. Had Cain been allowed to pay off his score, he might possibly have killed Adam and Eve for the mere sake of a second luxurious reconciliation with God afterwards. Bodger, you may depend on it, will go on to the end of his life poisoning people with bad whisky, because he can always depend on the Salvation Army or the Church of England to negotiate a redemption for him in consideration of a trifling percentage of his profits.

There is a third condition too, which must be fulfilled before the great teachers of the world will cease to scoff at its religions. Creeds must become intellectually honest. At present there is not a single credible established religion in the world. That is perhaps the most stupendous fact in the whole world-situation. This play of mine, Major Barbara, is, I hope, both true and inspired; but whoever says that it all happened, and that faith in it and understanding of it consist in believing that it is a record of an actual occurrence, is, to speak according to Scripture, a fool and a liar, and is hereby solemnly denounced and cursed as such by me, the author, to all posterity.

London, June 1906.

ACT I

It is after dinner on a January night, in the library in Lady Britomart Undershaft's house in Wilton Crescent. A large and comfortable settee is in the middle of the room, upholstered in dark leather. A person sitting on it (it is vacant at present) would have, on his right, Lady Britomart's writing-table, with the lady herself busy at it; a smaller writing-table behind him on his left; the door behind him on Lady Britomart's side; and a window with a window-seat directly on his left. Near the window is an armchair.

Lady Britomart is a woman of fifty or thereabouts, well dressed and yet careless of her dress, well bred and quite reckless of her breeding, well mannered and yet appallingly outspoken and indifferent to the opinion of her interlocutors, amiable and yet peremptory, arbitrary, and high-tempered to the last bearable degree, and withal a very typical managing matron of the upper class, treated as a naughty child until she grew into a scolding mother, and finally settling down with plenty of practical ability and worldly experience, limited in the oddest way with domestic and class limitations, conceiving the universe exactly as if it were a large house in Wilton Crescent, though handling her corner of it very effectively on that assumption, and being quite enlightened and liberal as to the books in the library, the pictures on the walls, the music in the portfolios, and the articles in the papers.

Her son, Stephen, comes in. He is a gravely correct young man under 25, taking himself very seriously, but still in some awe of his mother, from childish habit and bachelor shyness rather than from any weakness of character.

STEPHEN. Whats the matter?

LADY BRITOMART. Presently, Stephen.

(*Stephen submissively walks to the settee and sits down. He takes up The Speaker.*)

LADY BRITOMART. Don't begin to read, Stephen. I shall require all your attention.

STEPHEN. It was only while I was waiting—

LADY BRITOMART. Dont make excuses, Stephen. (*He puts down The Speaker.*) Now! (*She finishes her writing; rises; and comes to the settee.*) I have not kept you waiting v e r y long, I think.

STEPHEN. Not at all, mother.

LADY BRITOMART. Bring me my cushion. (*He takes the cushion from the chair at the desk and arranges it for her as she sits down on the settee.*) Sit down. (*He sits down and fingers his tie nervously.*) Dont fiddle with your tie, Stephen: there is nothing the matter with it.

STEPHEN. I beg your pardon. (*He fiddles with his watch chain instead.*)

LADY BRITOMART. Now are you attending to me, Stephen?

STEPHEN. Of course, mother.

LADY BRITOMART. No: it's n o t of course. I want something much more than your everyday matter-of-course attention. I am going to speak to you very seriously, Stephen. I wish you would let that chain alone.

STEPHEN (*hastily relinquishing the chain*). Have I done anything to annoy you, mother? If so, it was quite unintentional.

LADY BRITOMART (*astonished*). Nonsense! (*With some remorse*) My poor boy, did you think I was angry with you?

STEPHEN. What is it, then, mother? You are making me very uneasy.

LADY BRITOMART (*squaring herself at him rather aggres sively*). Stephen: may I ask how soon you intend to realize that you are a grown-up man, and that I am only a woman?

STEPHEN (*amazed*). Only a—

LADY BRITOMART. Dont repeat my words, please: it is a

most aggravating habit. You must learn to face life seriously, Stephen. I really cannot bear the whole burden of our family affairs any longer. You must advise me: you must assume the responsibility.

STEPHEN. I!

LADY BRITOMART. Yes, you, of course. You were 24 last June. Youve been at Harrow and Cambridge. Youve been to India and Japan. You must know a lot of things, now; unless you have wasted your time most scandalously. Well, a d v i s e me.

STEPHEN (*much perplexed*). You know I have never interfered in the household—

LADY BRITOMART. No: I should think not. I dont want you to order the dinner.

STEPHEN. I mean in our family affairs.

LADY BRITOMART. Well, you must interfere now; for they are getting quite beyond me.

STEPHEN (*troubled*). I have thought sometimes that perhaps I ought; but really, mother, I know so little about them; and what I do know is so painful—it is so impossible to mention some things to you—(*He stops, ashamed.*)

LADY BRITOMART. I suppose you mean your father.

STEPHEN (*almost inaudibly*). Yes.

LADY BRITOMART. My dear: we cant go on all our lives not mentioning him. Of course you were quite right not to open the subject until I asked you to; but you are old enough now to be taken into my confidence, and to help me to deal with him about the girls.

STEPHEN. But the girls are all right. They are engaged.

LADY BRITOMART (*complacently*). Yes: I have made a very good match for Sarah. Charles Lomax will be a millionaire at 35. But that is ten years ahead; and in the meantime his trustees cannot under the terms of his father's will allow him more than £800 a year.

STEPHEN. But the will says also that if he increases his income by his own exertions, they may double the increase.

LADY BRITOMART. Charles Lomax's exertions are much more likely to decrease his income than to increase it. Sarah will have to find at least another £800 a year for the next ten years; and even then they will be as poor as church mice. And what about Barbara? I thought Barbara was going to make the most brilliant career of all of you. And what does she do? Joins the Salvation Army; discharges her maid; lives on a pound a week; and walks in one evening with a professor of Greek whom she has picked up in the street, and who pretends to be a Salvationist, and actually plays the big drum for her in public because he has fallen head over ears in love with her.

STEPHEN. I was certainly rather taken aback when I heard they were engaged. Cusins is a very nice fellow, certainly: nobody would ever guess that he was born in Australia; but—

LADY BRITOMART. Oh, Adolphus Cusins will make a very good husband. After all, nobody can say a word against Greek: it stamps a man at once as an educated gentleman. And my family, thank Heaven, is not a pig-headed Tory one. We are Whigs, and believe in liberty. Let snobbish people say what they please: Barbara shall marry, not the man they like, but the man *I* like.

STEPHEN. Of course I was thinking only of his income. However, he is not likely to be extravagant.

LADY BRITOMART. Dont be too sure of that, Stephen. I know your quiet, simple, refined, poetic people like Adolphus—quite content with the best of everything! They cost more than your extravagant people, who are always as mean as they are second rate. No: Barbara will need at least £2000 a year. You see it means two additional households. Besides, my dear, you must marry soon. I dont approve of the present fashion of philandering bachelors and late marriages; and I am trying to arrange something for you.

STEPHEN. It's very good of you, mother; but perhaps I had better arrange that for myself.

LADY BRITOMART. Nonsense! you are much too young to begin matchmaking: you would be taken in by some pretty little nobody. Of course I dont mean that you are not to be consulted: you know that as well as I do. (*Stephen closes his lips and is silent.*) Now dont sulk, Stephen.

STEPHEN. I am not sulking, mother. What has all this got to do with—with—with my father?

LADY BRITOMART. My dear Stephen: where is the money to come from? It is easy enough for you and the other children to live on my income as long as we are in the same house; but

I cant keep four families in four separate houses. You know how poor my father is: he has barely seven thousand a year now; and really, if he were not the Earl of Stevenage, he would have to give up society. He can do nothing for us. He says, naturally enough, that it is absurd that he should be asked to provide for the children of a man who is rolling in money. You see, Stephen, your father must be fabulously wealthy, because there is always a war going on somewhere.

STEPHEN. You need not remind me of that, mother. I have hardly ever opened a newspaper in my life without seeing our name in it. The Undershaft torpedo! The Undershaft quick firers! The Undershaft ten inch! the Undershaft disappearing rampart gun! the Undershaft submarine! and now the Undershaft aerial battleship! At Harrow they called me the Woolwich Infant. At Cambridge it was the same. A little brute at King's who was always trying to get up revivals, spoilt my Bible—your first birthday present to me—by writing under my name, "Son and heir to Undershaft and Lazarus, Death and Destruction Dealers: address, Christendom and Judea." But that was not so bad as the way I was kowtowed to everywhere because my father was making millions by selling cannons.

LADY BRITOMART. It is not only the cannons, but the war loans that Lazarus arranges under cover of giving credit for the cannons. You know, Stephen, it's perfectly scandalous. Those two men, Andrew Undershaft and Lazarus, positively have Europe under their thumbs. That is why your father is able to behave as he does. He is above the law. Do you think Bismarck or Gladstone or Disraeli could have openly defied every social and moral obligation all their lives as your father has? They simply wouldnt have dared. I asked Gladstone to take it up. I asked The Times to take it up. I asked the Lord Chamberlain to take it up. But it was just like asking them to declare war on the Sultan. They wouldnt. They said they couldnt touch him. I believe they were afraid.

STEPHEN. What could they do? He does not actually break the law.

LADY BRITOMART. Not break the law! He is always breaking the law. He broke the law when he was born: his parents were not married.

STEPHEN. Mother! Is that true?

LADY BRITOMART. Of course it's true: that was why we separated.

STEPHEN. He married without letting you know this!

LADY BRITOMART (*rather taken aback by this inference*). Oh no. To do Andrew justice, that was not the sort of thing he did. Besides, you know the Undershaft motto: Unashamed. Everybody knew.

STEPHEN. But you said that was why you separated.

LADY BRITOMART. Yes, because he was not content with being a foundling himself: he wanted to disinherit you for another foundling. That was what I couldnt stand.

STEPHEN (*ashamed*). Do you mean for—for—for—

LADY BRITOMART. Dont stammer, Stephen. Speak distinctly.

STEPHEN. But this is so frightful to me, mother. To have to speak to you about such things!

LADY BRITOMART. It's not pleasant for me, either, especially if you are still so childish that you must make it worse by a display of embarrassment. It is only in the middle classes, Stephen, that people get into a state of dumb helpless horror when they find that there are wicked people in the world. In our class, we have to decide what is to be done with wicked people; and nothing should disturb our self-possession. Now ask your question properly.

STEPHEN. Mother: you have no consideration for me. For Heaven's sake either treat me as a child, as you always do, and tell me nothing at all; or tell me everything and let me take it as best I can.

LADY BRITOMART. Treat you as a child! What do you mean? It is most unkind and ungrateful of you to say such a thing. You know I have never treated any of you as children. I have always made you my companions and friends, and allowed you perfect freedom to do and say whatever you liked, so long as you liked what I could approve of.

STEPHEN (*desperately*). I daresay we have been the very imperfect children of a very perfect mother; but I do beg you to let me alone for once, and tell me about this horrible business of my father wanting to set me aside for another son.

LADY BRITOMART (*amazed*). Another son! I never said anything of the kind. I never dreamt of such a thing. This is what comes of interrupting me.

STEPHEN. But you said—

LADY BRITOMART (*cutting him short*). Now be a good boy, Stephen, and listen to me patiently. The Undershafts are descended from a foundling in the parish of St. Andrew Undershaft in the city. That was long ago, in the reign of James the First. Well, this foundling was adopted by an armorer and gun-maker. In the course of time the foundling succeeded to the business; and from some notion of gratitude, or some vow or something, he adopted another foundling, and left the business to him. And that foundling did the same. Ever since that, the cannon business has always been left to an adopted foundling named Andrew Undershaft.

STEPHEN. But did they never marry? Were there no legitimate sons?

LADY BRITOMART. Oh yes: they married just as your father did; and they were rich enough to buy land for their own children and leave them well provided for. But they always adopted and trained some foundling to succeed them in the business; and of course they always quarrelled with their wives furiously over it. Your father was adopted in that way; and he pretends to consider himself bound to keep up the tradition and adopt somebody to leave the business to. Of course I was not going to stand that. There may have been some reason for it when the Undershafts could only marry women in their own class, whose sons were not fit to govern great estates. But there could be no excuse for passing over m y son.

STEPHEN (*dubiously*). I am afraid I should make a poor hand of managing a cannon foundry.

LADY BRITOMART. Nonsense! you could easily get a manager and pay him a salary.

STEPHEN. My father evidently had no great opinion of my capacity.

LADY BRITOMART. Stuff, child! you were only a baby: it had nothing to do with your capacity. Andrew did it on principle, just as he did every perverse and wicked thing on principle. When my father remonstrated, Andrew actually told him to his face that history tells us of only two successful institutions: one the Undershaft firm, and the other the Roman Empire under the Antonines. That was because the

Antonine emperors all adopted their successors. Such rubbish! The Stevenages are as good as the Antonines, I hope; and you are a Stevenage. But that was Andrew all over. There you have the man! Always clever and unanswerable when he was defending nonsense and wickedness: always awkward and sullen when he had to behave sensibly and decently!

STEPHEN. Then it was on my account that your home life was broken up, mother. I am sorry.

LADY BRITOMART. Well, dear, there were other differences. I really cannot bear an immoral man. I am not a Pharisee, I hope; and I should not have minded his merely d o i n g wrong things: we are none of us perfect. But your father didnt exactly d o wrong things: he said them and thought them: that was what was so dreadful. He really had a sort of religion of wrongness. Just as one doesnt mind men practising immorality so long as they own that they are in the wrong by preaching morality; so I couldnt forgive Andrew for preaching immorality while he practised morality. You would all have grown up without principles, without any knowledge of right and wrong, if he had been in the house. You know, my dear, your father was a very attractive man in some ways. Children did not dislike him; and he took advantage of it to put the wickedest ideas into their heads, and make them quite unmanageable. I did not dislike him myself: very far from it; but nothing can bridge over moral disagreement.

STEPHEN. All this simply bewilders me, mother. People may differ about matters of opinion, or even about religion; but how can they differ about right and wrong? Right is right; and wrong is wrong; and if a man cannot distinguish them properly, he is either a fool or a rascal: thats all.

LADY BRITOMART (*touched*). Thats my own boy! (*She pats his cheek.*) Your father never could answer that: he used to laugh and get out of it under cover of some affectionate nonsense. And now that you understand the situation, what do you advise me to do?

STEPHEN. Well, what c a n you do?

LADY BRITOMART. I must get the money somehow.

STEPHEN. We cannot take money from him. I had rather go

and live in some cheap place like Bedford Square or even Hampstead than take a farthing of his money.

LADY BRITOMART. But after all, Stephen, our present income comes from Andrew.

STEPHEN (*shocked*). I never knew that.

LADY BRITOMART. Well, you surely didnt suppose your grandfather had anything to give me. The Stevenages could not do everything for you. We gave you social position. Andrew had to contribute s o m e t h i n g. He had a very good bargain, I think.

STEPHEN (*bitterly*). We are utterly dependent on him and his cannons, then?

LADY BRITOMART. Certainly not: the money is settled. But he provided it. So you see it is not a question of taking money from him or not: it is simply a question of how much. I dont want any more for myself.

STEPHEN. Nor do I.

LADY BRITOMART. But Sarah does; and Barbara does. That is, Charles Lomax and Adolphus Cusins will cost them more. So I must put my pride in my pocket and ask for it, I suppose. That is your advice, Stephen, is it not?

STEPHEN. No.

LADY BRITOMART (*sharply*). Stephen!

STEPHEN. Of course if you are determined—

LADY BRITOMART. I am not determined: I ask your advice; and I am waiting for it. I will not have all the responsibility thrown on my shoulders.

STEPHEN (*obstinately*). I would die sooner than ask him for another penny.

LADY BRITOMART (*resignedly*). You mean that *I* must ask him. Very well, Stephen: it shall be as you wish. You will be glad to know that your grandfather concurs. But he thinks I ought to ask Andrew to come here and see the girls. After all, he must have some natural affection for them.

STEPHEN. Ask him here!!!

LADY BRITOMART. Do n o t repeat my words, Stephen. Where else can I ask him?

STEPHEN. I never expected you to ask him at all.

LADY BRITOMART. Now dont tease, Stephen. Come! you see that it is necessary that he should pay us a visit, dont you?

STEPHEN (*reluctantly*). I suppose so, if the girls cannot do without his money.

LADY BRITOMART. Thank you, Stephen: I knew you would give me the right advice when it was properly explained to you. I have asked your father to come this evening. (*Stephen bounds from his seat.*) Dont jump, Stephen: it fidgets me.

STEPHEN (*in utter consternation*). Do you mean to say that my father is coming here to-night—that he may be here at any moment?

LADY BRITOMART (*looking at her watch*). I said nine. (*He gasps. She rises.*) Ring the bell, please. (*Stephen goes to the smaller writing-table; presses a button on it; and sits at it with his elbows on the table and his head in his hands, outwitted and overwhelmed.*) It is ten minutes to nine yet; and I have to prepare the girls. I asked Charles Lomax and Adolphus to dinner on purpose that they might be here. Andrew had better see them in case he should cherish any delusions as to their being capable of supporting their wives. (*The butler enters: Lady Britomart goes behind the settee to speak to him.*) Morrison: go up to the drawingroom and tell everybody to come down here at once. (*Morrison withdraws. Lady Britomart turns to Stephen.*) Now remember, Stephen: I shall need all your countenance and authority. (*He rises and tries to recover some vestige of these attributes.*) Give me a chair, dear. (*He pushes a chair forward from the wall to where she stands, near the smaller writing-table. She sits down; and he goes to the arm-chair, into which he throws himself.*) I dont know how Barbara will take it. Ever since they made her a major in the Salvation Army she has developed a propensity to have her own way and order people about which quite cows me sometimes. It's not ladylike: I'm sure I dont know where she picked it up. Anyhow, Barbara shant bully m e; but still it's just as well that your father should be here before she has time to refuse to meet him or make a fuss. Dont look nervous, Stephen; it will only encourage Barbara to make difficulties. *I* am nervous enough, goodness knows; but I dont shew it.

Sarah and Barbara come in with their respective young men, Charles Lomax and Adolphus Cusins. Sarah is slender, bored, and mundane. Barbara is robuster, jollier, much more energetic. Sarah is fashionably dressed: Barbara is in Salvation Army uniform. Lomax, a young man about town, is like many other young men about town. He is afflicted with a frivolous sense of humor which plunges him at the most inopportune moments into paroxysms of imperfectly suppressed laughter. Cusins is a spectacled student, slight, thin haired, and sweet voiced, with a more complex form of Lomax's complaint. His sense of humor is intellectual and subtle, and is complicated by an appalling temper. The life-long struggle of a benevolent temperament and a high conscience against impulses of inhuman ridicule and fierce impatience has set up a chronic strain which has visibly wrecked his constitution. He is a most implacable, determined, tenacious, intolerant person who by mere force of character presents himself as—and indeed actually is—considerate, gentle, explanatory, even mild and apologetic, capable possibly of murder, but not of cruelty or coarseness. By the operation of some instinct which is not merciful enough to blind him with the illusions of love, he is obstinately bent on marrying Barbara. Lomax likes Sarah and thinks it will be rather a lark to marry her. Consequently he has not attempted to resist Lady Britomart's arrangements to that end.

All four look as if they had been having a good deal of fun in the drawingroom. The girls enter first, leaving the swains outside. Sarah comes to the settee. Barbara comes in after her and stops at the door.

BARBARA. Are Cholly and Dolly to come in?

LADY BRITOMART (*forcibly*). Barbara: I will not have Charles called Cholly: the vulgarity of it positively makes me ill.

BARBARA. It's all right, mother. Cholly is quite correct nowadays. Are they to come in?

LADY BRITOMART. Yes, if they will behave themselves.

BARBARA (*through the door*). Come in, Dolly, and behave yourself.

Barbara comes to her mother's writing-table. Cusins enters smiling, and wanders towards Lady Britomart.

SARAH (*calling*). Come in, Cholly. (*Lomax enters, controlling his features very imperfectly, and places himself vaguely between Sarah and Barbara.*)

LADY BRITOMART (*peremptorily*). Sit down, all of you.

(They sit. Cusins crosses to the window and seats himself there. Lomax takes a chair. Barbara sits at the writing-table and Sarah on the settee.) I dont in the least know what you are laughing at, Adolphus. I am surprised at you, though I expected nothing better from Charles Lomax.

CUSINS *(in a remarkably gentle voice)*. Barbara has been trying to teach me the West Ham Salvation March.

LADY BRITOMART. I see nothing to laugh at in that; nor should you if you are really converted.

CUSINS *(sweetly)*. You were not present. It was really funny, I believe.

LOMAX. Ripping.

LADY BRITOMART. Be quiet, Charles. Now listen to me, children. Your father is coming here this evening. *(General stupefaction.)*

LOMAX *(remonstrating)*. Oh I say!

LADY BRITOMART. You are not called on to say anything, Charles.

SARAH. Are you serious, mother?

LADY BRITOMART. Of course I am serious. It is on your account, Sarah, and also on Charles's. *(Silence. Charles looks painfully unworthy.)* I hope you are not going to object, Barbara.

BARBARA. I! why should I? My father has a soul to be saved like anybody else. Hes quite welcome as far as I am concerned.

LOMAX *(still remonstrant)*. But really, dont you know! Oh I say!

LADY BRITOMART *(frigidly)*. What do you wish to convey, Charles?

LOMAX. Well, you must admit that this is a bit thick.

LADY BRITOMART *(turning with ominous suavity to Cusins)*. Adolphus: you are a professor of Greek. Can you translate Charles Lomax's remarks into reputable English for us?

CUSINS *(cautiously)*. If I may say so, Lady Brit, I think Charles has rather happily expressed what we all feel. Homer, speaking of Autolycus, uses the same phrase. πυκι νὸν δόμον ελθ εῖν means a bit thick.

LOMAX (*handsomely*). Not that I mind, you know, if Sarah dont.

LADY BRITOMART (*crushingly*). Thank you. Have I y o u r permission, Adolphus, to invite my own husband to my own house?

CUSINS (*gallantly*). You have my unhesitating support in everything you do.

LADY BRITOMART. Sarah: have you nothing to say?

SARAH. Do you mean that he is coming regularly to live here?

LADY BRITOMART. Certainly not. The spare room is ready for him if he likes to stay for a day or two and see a little more of you; but there are limits.

SARAH. Well, he cant eat us, I suppose. *I* dont mind.

LOMAX (*chuckling*). I wonder how the old man will take it.

LADY BRITOMART. Much as the old woman will, no doubt, Charles.

LOMAX (*abashed*). I didnt mean—at least—

LADY BRITOMART. You didnt t h i n k, Charles. You never do; and the result is, you never mean anything. And now please attend to me, children. Your father will be quite a stranger to us.

LOMAX. I suppose he hasnt seen Sarah since she was a little kid.

LADY BRITOMART. Not since she was a little kid, Charles, as you express it with that elegance of diction and refinement of thought that seem never to desert you. Accordingly—er—(*impatiently*) Now I have forgotten what I was going to say. That comes of your provoking me to be sarcastic, Charles. Adolphus: will you kindly tell me where I was.

CUSINS (*sweetly*). You were saying that as Mr. Undershaft has not seen his children since they were babies, he will form his opinion of the way you have brought them up from their behavior to-night, and that therefore you wish us all to be particularly careful to conduct ourselves well, especially Charles.

LOMAX. Look here: Lady Brit didnt say that.

LADY BRITOMART (*vehemently*). I did, Charles. Adolphus's recollection is perfectly correct. It is most important that you should be good; and I do beg you for once not to pair off into opposite corners and giggle and whisper while I am speaking to your father.

BARBARA. All right, mother. We'll do you credit.

LADY BRITOMART. Remember, Charles, that Sarah will want to feel proud of you instead of ashamed of you.

LOMAX. Oh I say! theres nothing to be exactly proud of, dont you know.

LADY BRITOMART. Well, try and look as if there was.

Morrison, pale and dismayed, breaks into the room in unconcealed disorder.

MORRISON. Might I speak a word to you, my lady?

LADY BRITOMART. Nonsense! Shew him up.

MORRISON. Yes, my lady. (*He goes.*)

LOMAX. Does Morrison know who it is?

LADY BRITOMART. Of course. Morrison has always been with us.

LOMAX. It must be a regular corker for him, dont you know.

LADY BRITOMART. Is this a moment to get on my nerves, Charles, with your outrageous expressions?

LOMAX. But this is something out of the ordinary, really—

MORRISON (*at the door*). The—er—Mr. Undershaft. (*He retreats in confusion.*)

Andrew Undershaft comes in. All rise. Lady Britomart meets him in the middle of the room behind the settee.

Andrew is, on the surface, a stoutish, easygoing elderly man, with kindly patient manners, and an engaging simplicity of character. But he has a watchful, deliberate, waiting, listening face, and formidable reserves of power, both bodily and mental, in his capacious chest and long head. His gentleness is partly that of a strong man who has learnt by experience that his natural grip hurts ordinary people unless he handles them very carefully, and partly the mellowness of age and success. He is also a little shy in his present very delicate situation.

LADY BRITOMART. Good evening, Andrew.

UNDERSHAFT. How d'ye do, my dear.

LADY BRITOMART. You look a good deal older.

UNDERSHAFT (*apologetically*). I a m somewhat older. (*With a touch of courtship*) Time has stood still with you.

LADY BRITOMART (*promptly*). Rubbish! This is your family.

UNDERSHAFT (*surprised*). Is it so large? I am sorry to say my memory is failing very badly in some things. (*He offers his hand with paternal kindness to Lomax.*)

LOMAX (*jerkily shaking his hand*). Ahdedoo.

UNDERSHAFT. I can see you are my eldest. I am very glad to meet you again, my boy.

LOMAX (*remonstrating*). No but look here dont you know— (*Overcome*) Oh I say!

LADY BRITOMART (*recovering from momentary speechlessness*). Andrew: do you mean to say that you dont remember how many children you have?

UNDERSHAFT. Well, I am afraid I—. They have grown so much—er. Am I making any ridiculous mistake? I may as well confess: I recollect only one son. But so many things have happened since, of course—er—

LADY BRITOMART (*decisively*). Andrew: you are talking nonsense. Of course you have only one son.

UNDERSHAFT. Perhaps you will be good enough to introduce me, my dear.

LADY BRITOMART. That is Charles Lomax, who is engaged to Sarah.

UNDERSHAFT. My dear sir, I beg your pardon.

LOMAX. Notatall. Delighted, I assure you.

LADY BRITOMART. This is Stephen.

UNDERSHAFT (*bowing*). Happy to make your acquaintance, Mr. Stephen. Then (*going to Cusins*) you must be my son. (*Taking Cusins' hands in his*) How are you, my young friend? (*To Lady Britomart*) He is very like you, my love.

CUSINS. You flatter me, Mr. Undershaft. My name is Cusins: engaged to Barbara. (*Very explicitly*) That is Major Barbara Undershaft, of the Salvation Army. That is Sarah, your second daughter. This is Stephen Undershaft, your son.

UNDERSHAFT. My dear Stephen, I b e g your pardon.

STEPHEN. Not at all.

UNDERSHAFT. Mr. Cusins: I am much indebted to you for explaining so precisely. (*Turning to Sarah*) Barbara, my dear—

SARAH (*prompting him*). Sarah.

UNDERSHAFT. Sarah, of course. (*They shake hands. He goes over to Barbara.*) Barbara—I am right this time, I hope.

BARBARA. Quite right. (*They shake hands.*)

LADY BRITOMART (*resuming command*). Sit down, all of you. Sit down, Andrew. (*She comes forward and sits on the settee. Cusins also brings his chair forward on her left. Barbara and Stephen resume their seats. Lomax gives his chair to Sarah and goes for another.*)

UNDERSHAFT. Thank you, my love.

LOMAX (*conversationally, as he brings a chair forward between the writing-table and the settee, and offers it to Undershaft*). Takes you some time to find out exactly where you are, dont it?

UNDERSHAFT (*accepting the chair*). That is not what embarrasses me, Mr. Lomax. My difficulty is that if I play the part of a father, I shall produce the effect of an intrusive stranger; and if I play the part of a discreet stranger, I may appear a callous father.

LADY BRITOMART. There is no need for you to play any part at all, Andrew. You had much better be sincere and natural.

UNDERSHAFT (*submissively*). Yes, my dear: I daresay that will be best. (*Making himself comfortable.*) Well, here I am. Now what can I do for you all?

LADY BRITOMART. You need not do anything, Andrew. You are one of the family. You can sit with us and enjoy yourself.

Lomax's too long suppressed mirth explodes in agonized neighings.

LADY BRITOMART (*outraged*). Charles Lomax: if you can behave yourself, behave yourself. If not, leave the room.

LOMAX. I'm awfully sorry, Lady Brit; but really, you know, upon my soul! (*He sits on the settee between Lady Britomart and Undershaft, quite overcome.*)

BARBARA. Why dont you laugh if you want to, Cholly? It's good for your inside.

LADY BRITOMART. Barbara: you have had the education of a lady. Please let your father see that; and dont talk like a street girl.

UNDERSHAFT. Never mind me, my dear. As you know, I am not a gentleman; and I was never educated.

LOMAX (*encouragingly*). Nobody'd know it, I assure you. You look all right, you know.

CUSINS. Let me advise you to study Greek, Mr. Undershaft. Greek scholars are privileged men. Few of them know Greek; and none of them know anything else; but their position is unchallengeable. Other languages are the qualifications of waiters and commercial travellers: Greek is to a man of position what the hallmark is to silver.

BARBARA. Dolly: dont be insincere. Cholly: fetch your concertina and play something for us.

LOMAX (*doubtfully to Undershaft*). Perhaps that sort of thing isnt in your line, eh?

UNDERSHAFT. I am particularly fond of music.

LOMAX (*delighted*). Are you? Then I'll get it. (*He goes upstairs for the instrument.*)

UNDERSHAFT. Do you play, Barbara?

BARBARA. Only the tambourine. But Cholly's teaching me the concertina.

UNDERSHAFT. Is Cholly also a member of the Salvation Army?

BARBARA. No: he says it's bad form to be a dissenter. But I dont despair of Cholly. I made him come yesterday to a meeting at the dock gates, and took the collection in his hat.

LADY BRITOMART. It is not my doing, Andrew. Barbara is old enough to take her own way. She has no father to advise her.

BARBARA. Oh yes she has. There are no orphans in the Salvation Army.

UNDERSHAFT. Your father there has a great many children and plenty of experience, eh?

BARBARA (*looking at him with quick interest and nodding*). Just so. How did y o u come to understand that? (*Lomax is heard at the door trying the concertina.*)

LADY BRITOMART. Come in, Charles. Play us something at once.

LOMAX. Righto! (*He sits down in his former place, and preludes.*)

UNDERSHAFT. One moment, Mr. Lomax. I am rather interested in the Salvation Army. Its motto might be my own: Blood and Fire.

LOMAX (*shocked*). But not your sort of blood and fire, you know.

UNDERSHAFT. My sort of blood cleanses: my sort of fire purifies.

BARBARA. So do ours. Come down to-morrow to my shelter—the West Ham shelter—and see what we're doing. We're going to march to a great meeting in the Assembly Hall at Mile End. Come and see the shelter and then march with us: it will do you a lot of good. Can you play anything?

UNDERSHAFT. In my youth I earned pennies, and even shillings occasionally, in the streets and in public house parlors by my natural talent for stepdancing. Later on, I became a member of the Undershaft orchestral society, and performed passably on the tenor trombone.

LOMAX (*scandalized*). Oh I say!

BARBARA. Many a sinner has played himself into heaven on the trombone, thanks to the Army.

LOMAX (*to Barbara, still rather shocked*). Yes; but what about the cannon business, dont you know? (*To Undershaft*) Getting into heaven is not exactly in your line, is it?

LADY BRITOMART. Charles!!!

LOMAX. Well; but it stands to reason, dont it? The cannon business may be necessary and all that: we cant get on without cannons; but it isnt right, you know. On the other hand, there may be a certain amount of tosh about the Salvation Army—I belong to the Established Church myself—but still you cant deny that it's religion; and you cant go against religion, can you? At least unless youre downright immoral, dont you know.

UNDERSHAFT. You hardly appreciate my position, Mr. Lomax—

LOMAX (*hastily*). I'm not saying anything against you personally, you know.

UNDERSHAFT. Quite so, quite so. But consider for a moment. Here I am, a manufacturer of mutilation and murder. I find myself in a specially amiable humor just now because, this morning, down at the foundry, we blew twenty-seven dummy soldiers into fragments with a gun which formerly destroyed only thirteen.

LOMAX (*leniently*). Well, the more destructive war becomes, the sooner it will be abolished, eh?

UNDERSHAFT. Not at all. The more destructive war becomes the more fascinating we find it. No, Mr. Lomax: I am obliged to you for making the usual excuse for my trade; but I am not ashamed of it. I am not one of those men who keep their morals and their business in watertight compartments. All the spare money my trade rivals spend on hospitals, cathedrals and other receptacles for conscience money, I devote to experiments and researches in improved methods of destroying life and property. I have always done so; and I always shall. Therefore your Christmas card moralities of peace on earth and goodwill among men are of no use to me. Your Christianity, which enjoins you to resist not evil, and to turn the other cheek, would make me a bankrupt. M y morality—m y religion—must have a place for cannons and torpedoes in it.

STEPHEN (*coldly—almost sullenly*). You speak as if there were half a dozen moralities and religions to choose from, instead of one true morality and one true religion.

UNDERSHAFT. For me there is only one true morality; but it might not fit you, as you do not manufacture aerial battleships. There is only one true morality for every man; but every man has not the same true morality.

LOMAX (*overtaxed*). Would you mind saying that again? I didnt quite follow it.

CUSINS. It's quite simple. As Euripides says, one man's meat is another man's poison morally as well as physically.

UNDERSHAFT. Precisely.

LOMAX. Oh, t h a t. Yes, yes, yes. True. True.

STEPHEN. In other words, some men are honest and some are scoundrels.

BARBARA. Bosh. There are no scoundrels.

UNDERSHAFT. Indeed? Are there any good men?

BARBARA. No. Not one. There are neither good men nor scoundrels: there are just children of one Father; and the sooner they stop calling one another names the better. You neednt talk to me: I know them. Ive had scores of them through my hands: scoundrels, criminals, infidels, philanthropists, missionaries, county councillors, all sorts. Theyre all just the same sort of sinner; and theres the same salvation ready for them all.

UNDERSHAFT. May I ask have you ever saved a maker of cannons?

BARBARA. No. Will you let me try?

UNDERSHAFT. Well, I will make a bargain with you. If I go to see you to-morrow in your Salvation Shelter, will you come the day after to see me in my cannon works?

BARBARA. Take care. It may end in your giving up the cannons for the sake of the Salvation Army.

UNDERSHAFT. Are you sure it will not end in your giving up the Salvation Army for the sake of the cannons?

BARBARA. I will take my chance of that.

UNDERSHAFT. And I will take my chance of the other. (*They shake hands on it.*) Where is your shelter?

BARBARA. In West Ham. At the sign of the cross. Ask anybody in Canning Town. Where are your works?

UNDERSHAFT. In Perivale St. Andrews. At the sign of the sword. Ask anybody in Europe.

LOMAX. Hadnt I better play something?

BARBARA. Yes. Give us Onward, Christian Soldiers.

LOMAX. Well, thats rather a strong order to begin with, dont you know. Suppose I sing Thourt passing hence, my brother. It's much the same tune.

BARBARA. It's too melancholy. You get saved, Cholly; and youll pass hence, my brother, without making such a fuss about it.

LADY BRITOMART. Really, Barbara, you go on as if religion were a pleasant subject. Do have some sense of propriety.

UNDERSHAFT. I do not find it an unpleasant subject, my dear. It is the only one that capable people really care for.

LADY BRITOMART (*looking at her watch*). Well, if you are determined to have it, I insist on having it in a proper and respectable way. Charles: ring for prayers. (*General amazement. Stephen rises in dismay.*)

LOMAX (*rising*). Oh I say!

UNDERSHAFT (*rising*). I am afraid I must be going.

LADY BRITOMART. You cannot go now, Andrew: it would be most improper. Sit down. What will the servants think?

UNDERSHAFT. My dear: I have conscientious scruples. May

I suggest a compromise? If Barbara will conduct a little service in the drawingroom, with Mr. Lomax as organist, I will attend it willingly. I will even take part, if a trombone can be procured.

LADY BRITOMART. Dont mock, Andrew.

UNDERSHAFT (*shocked—to Barbara*). You dont think I am mocking, my love, I hope.

BARBARA. No, of course not; and it wouldnt matter if you were: half the Army came to their first meeting for a lark. (*Rising.*) Come along. Come, Dolly, Come, Cholly. (*She goes out with Undershaft, who opens the door for her. Cusins rises.*)

LADY BRITOMART. I will not be disobeyed by everybody. Adolphus: sit down. Charles: you may go. You are not fit for prayers: you cannot keep your countenance.

LOMAX. Oh I say! (*He goes out.*)

LADY BRITOMART (*continuing*). But you, Adolphus, can behave yourself if you choose to. I insist on your staying.

CUSINS. My dear Lady Brit: there are things in the family prayer book that I couldnt bear to hear you say.

LADY BRITOMART. What things, pray?

CUSINS. Well, you would have to say before all the servants that we have done things we ought not to have done, and left undone things we ought to have done, and that there is no health in us. I cannot bear to hear you doing yourself such an injustice, and Barbara such an injustice. As for myself, I flatly deny it: I have done my best. I shouldnt dare to marry Barbara—I couldnt look you in the face—if it were true. So I must go to the drawingroom.

LADY BRITOMART (*offended*). Well, go. (*He starts for the door.*) And remember this, Adolphus: (*He turns to listen.*) I have a very strong suspicion that you went to the Salvation Army to worship Barbara and nothing else. And I quite appreciate the very clever way in which you systematically humbug me. I have found you out. Take care Barbara doesnt. Thats all.

CUSINS (*with unruffled sweetness*). Dont tell on me. (*He goes out.*)

LADY BRITOMART. Sarah: if you want to go, go. Anything's better than to sit there as if you wished you were a thousand miles away.

SARAH (*languidly*). Very well, mamma. (*She goes.*)

Lady Britomart, with a sudden flounce, gives way to a little gust of tears.

STEPHEN (*going to her*). Mother: whats the matter?

LADY BRITOMART (*swishing away her tears with her handkerchief*). Nothing. Foolishness. You can go with him, too, if you like, and leave me with the servants.

STEPHEN. Oh, you mustnt think that, mother. I—I dont like him.

LADY BRITOMART. The others do. That is the injustice of a woman's lot. A woman has to bring up her children; and that means to restrain them, to deny them things they want, to set them tasks, to punish them when they do wrong, to do all the unpleasant things. And then the father, who has nothing to do but pet them and spoil them, comes in when all her work is done and steals their affection from her.

STEPHEN. He has not stolen our affection from you. It is only curiosity.

LADY BRITOMART (*violently*). I wont be consoled, Stephen. There is nothing the matter with me. (*She rises and goes towards the door.*)

STEPHEN. Where are you going, mother?

LADY BRITOMART. To the drawingroom, of course. (*She goes out. Onward, Christian Soldiers, on the concertina, with tambourine accompaniment, is heard when the door opens.*) Are you coming, Stephen?

STEPHEN. No. Certainly not. (*She goes. He sits down on the settee, with compressed lips and an expression of strong dislike.*)

END OF ACT I.

ACT II

The yard of the West Ham shelter of the Salvation Army is a cold place on a January morning. The building itself, an old warehouse, is newly whitewashed. Its gabled end projects into the yard in the middle, with a door on the ground floor, and another in the loft above it without any balcony or ladder, but with a pulley rigged over it for hoisting sacks. Those who come from this central gable end into the yard have the gateway leading to the street on their left, with a stone horse-trough just beyond it, and, on the right, a penthouse shielding a table from the weather. There are forms at the table; and on them are seated a man and a woman, both much down on their luck, finishing a meal of bread (one thick slice each, with margarine and golden syrup) and diluted milk.

The man, a workman out of employment, is young, agile, a talker, a poser, sharp enough to be capable of anything in reason except honesty or altruistic considerations of any kind. The woman is a commonplace old bundle of poverty and hard-worn humanity. She looks sixty and probably is forty-five. If they were rich people, gloved and muffed and well wrapped up in furs and overcoats, they would be numbed and miserable; for it is a grindingly cold, raw, January day; and a glance at the background of grimy warehouses and leaden sky visible over the whitewashed walls of the yard would drive any idle rich person straight to the Mediterra-

nean. But these two, being no more troubled with visions of the Mediterranean than of the moon, and being compelled to keep more of their clothes in the pawnshop, and less on their persons, in winter than in summer, are not depressed by the cold: rather are they stung into vivacity, to which their meal has just now given an almost jolly turn. The man takes a pull at his mug, and then gets up and moves about the yard with his hands deep in his pockets, occasionally breaking into a stepdance.

THE WOMAN. Feel better arter your meal, sir?

THE MAN. No. Call that a meal! Good enough for you, praps; but wot is it to me, an intelligent workin man.

THE WOMAN. Workin man! Wot are you?

THE MAN. Painter.

THE WOMAN (*sceptically*). Yus, I dessay.

THE MAN. Yus, you dessay! I know. Every loafer that cant do nothink calls isself a painter. Well, I'm a real painter: grainer, finisher, thirty-eight bob a week when I can get it.

THE WOMAN. Then why dont you go and get it?

THE MAN. I'll tell you why. Fust: I'm intelligent—fffff! it's rotten cold here (*He dances a step or two.*)—yes: intelligent beyond the station o life into which it has pleased the capitalists to call me; and they dont like a man that sees through em. Second, an intelligent bein needs a doo share of appiness; so I drink somethink cruel when I get the chawnce. Third, I stand by my class and do as little as I can so's to leave arf the job for me fellow workers. Fourth, I'm fly enough to know wots inside the law and wots outside it; and inside it I do as the capitalists do: pinch wot I can lay me ands on. In a proper state of society I am sober, industrious and honest: in Rome, so to speak, I do as the Romans do. Wots the consequence? When trade is bad—and it's rotten bad just now—and the employers az to sack arf their men, they generally start on me.

THE WOMAN. Whats your name?

THE MAN. Price. Bronterre O'Brien Price. Usually called Snobby Price, for short.

THE WOMAN. Snobby's a carpenter, aint it? You said you was a painter.

PRICE. Not that kind of snob, but the genteel sort. I'm too uppish, owing to my intelligence, and my father being a Chartist and a reading, thinking man: a stationer, too. I'm none of your common hewers of wood and drawers of water; and dont you forget it. (*He returns to his seat at the table, and takes up his mug.*) Wots y o u r name?

THE WOMAN. Rummy Mitchens, sir.

PRICE (*quaffing the remains of his milk to her*). Your elth, Miss Mitchens.

RUMMY (*correcting him*). Missis Mitchens.

PRICE. Wot! Oh Rummy, Rummy! Respectable married woman, Rummy, gittin rescued by the Salvation Army by pretendin to be a bad un. Same old game!

RUMMY. What am I to do? I cant starve. Them Salvation lasses is dear good girls; but the better you are, the worse they likes to think you were before they rescued you. Why shouldnt they av a bit o credit, poor loves? theyre worn to rags by their work. And where would they get the money to rescue us if we was to let on we're no worse than other people? You know what ladies and gentlemen are.

PRICE. Thievin swine! Wish I ad their job, Rummy, all the same. Wot does Rummy stand for? Pet name praps?

RUMMY. Short for Romola.

PRICE. For wot!?

RUMMY. Romola. It was out of a new book. Somebody me mother wanted me to grow up like.

PRICE. We're companions in misfortune, Rummy. Both on us got names that nobody cawnt pronounce. Consequently I'm Snobby and youre Rummy because Bill and Sally wasnt good enough for our parents. Such is life!

RUMMY. Who saved you, Mr. Price? Was it Major Barbara?

PRICE. No: I come here on my own. I'm goin to be Bronterre O'Brien Price, the converted painter. I know wot they like. I'll tell em how I blasphemed and gambled and wopped my poor old mother—

RUMMY (*shocked*). Used you to beat your mother?

PRICE. Not likely. She used to beat me. No matter: you come and listen to the converted painter, and youll hear how she was a pious woman that taught me me prayers at er knee, an how I used to come home drunk and drag her out o bed be er snow white airs, an lam into er with the poker.

RUMMY. Thats whats so unfair to us women. Your confessions is just as big lies as ours: you dont tell what you really done no more than us; but you men can tell your lies right out at the meetins and be made much of for it; while the sort o confessions we az to make az to be whispered to one lady at a time. It aint right, spite of all their piety.

PRICE. Right! Do you spose the Army 'd be allowed if it went and did right? Not much. It combs our air and makes us good little blokes to be robbed and put upon. But I'll play the game as good as any of em. I'll see somebody struck by lightnin, or hear a voice sayin "Snobby Price: where will you spend eternity?" I'll ave a time of it, I tell you.

RUMMY. You wont be let drink, though.

PRICE. I'll take it out in gorspellin, then. I dont want to drink if I can get fun enough any other way.

Jenny Hill, a pale, overwrought, pretty Salvation lass of 18, *comes in through the yard gate, leading Peter Shirley, a half hardened, half worn-out elderly man, weak with hunger.*

JENNY (*supporting him*). Come! pluck up. I'll get you something to eat. Youll be all right then.

PRICE (*rising and hurrying officiously to take the old man off Jenny's hands*). Poor old man! Cheer up, brother: youll find rest and peace and appiness ere. Hurry up with the food, miss: e's fair done. (*Jenny hurries into the shelter.*) Ere, buck up, daddy! shes fetchin y'a thick slice o breadn treacle, an a mug o sky-blue. (*He seats him at the corner of the table.*)

RUMMY (*gaily*). Keep up your old art! Never say die!

SHIRLEY. I'm not an old man. I'm only 46. I'm as good as ever I was. The grey patch come in my hair before I was thirty. All it wants is three pennorth o hair dye: am I to be turned on the streets to starve for it? Holy God! I've worked ten to twelve hours a day since I was thirteen, and paid my way all through; and now am I to be thrown into the gutter and my job given to a young man that can do it no better than me because Ive black hair that goes white at the first change?

PRICE (*cheerfully*). No good jawrin about it. Youre ony a jumped-up, jerked-off, orspittle-turned-out incurable of an ole workin man: who cares about you? Eh? Make the thievin swine give you a meal: theyve stole many a one from you. Get a bit o your own back. (*Jenny returns with the usual meal.*) There you are, brother. Awsk a blessin an tuck that into you.

SHIRLEY (*looking at it ravenously but not touching it, and crying like a child*). I never took anything before.

JENNY (*petting him*). Come, come! the Lord sends it to you: he wasnt above taking bread from his friends; and why should you be? Besides, when we find you a job you can pay us for it if you like.

SHIRLEY (*eagerly*). Yes, yes: thats true. I can pay you back: it's only a loan. (*Shivering.*) Oh Lord! oh Lord! (*He turns to the table and attacks the meal ravenously.*)

JENNY. Well, Rummy, are you more comfortable now?

RUMMY. God bless you, lovey! youve fed my body and saved my soul, havent you? (*Jenny, touched, kisses her.*) Sit down and rest a bit: you must be ready to drop.

JENNY. Ive been going hard since morning. But theres more work than we can do. I mustnt stop.

RUMMY. Try a prayer for just two minutes. Youll work all the better after.

JENNY (*her eyes lighting up*). Oh isnt it wonderful how a few minutes prayer revives you! I was quite lightheaded at twelve o'clock, I was so tired; but Major Barbara just sent me to prayer for five minutes; and I was able to go on as if I had only just begun. (*To Price.*) Did you have a piece of bread?

PRICE (*with unction*). Yes, miss; but Ive got the piece that I value more; and thats the peace that passeth hall hannerstennin.

RUMMY (*fervently*). Glory Hallelujah!

Bill Walker, a rough customer of about 25, appears at the yard gate and looks malevolently at Jenny.

JENNY. That makes me so happy. When you say that, I feel wicked for loitering here. I must get to work again.

She is hurrying to the shelter, when the new-comer moves quickly up to the door and intercepts her. His manner is so threatening that she retreats as he comes at her truculently, driving her down the yard.

BILL. I know you. Youre the one that took away my girl. Youre the one that set er agen me. Well, I'm goin to av er out. Not that I care a curse for her or you: see? But I'll let er know; and I'll let you know. I'm goin to give er a doin thatll teach er to cut away from me. Now in with you and tell er to come out afore I come in and kick er out. Tell er Bill Walker wants er. She'll know what that means; and if she keeps me waitin itll be worse. You stop to jaw back at me; and I'll start on you: d'ye hear? Theres your way. In you go. (*He takes her by the arm and slings her towards the door of the shelter. She falls on her hand and knee. Rummy helps her up again.*)

PRICE (*rising, and venturing irresolutely towards Bill*). Easy there, mate. She aint doin you no arm.

BILL. Who are you callin mate? (*Standing over him threateningly*) Youre goin to stand up for her, are you? Put up your ands.

RUMMY (*running indignantly to him to scold him*). Oh, you great brute— (*He instantly swings his left hand back against her face. She screams and reels back to the trough, where she sits down, covering her bruised face with her hands and rocking herself and moaning with pain.*)

JENNY (*going to her*). Oh God forgive you! How could you strike an old woman like that?

BILL (*seizing her by the hair so violently that she also screams, and tearing her away from the old woman*). You Gawd forgive me again and I'll Gawd forgive you one on the jaw thatll stop you prayin for a week. (*Holding her and turning fiercely on Price*) Av you anything to say agen it? Eh?

PRICE (*intimidated*). No, matey: she aint anything to do with me.

BILL. Good job for you! I'd put two meals into you and fight you with one finger after, you starved cur. (*To Jenny*) Now are you goin to fetch out Mog Habbijam; or am I to knock your face off you and fetch her myself?

JENNY (*writhing in his grasp*). Oh please someone go in and tell Major Barbara—(*She screams again as he wrenches her head down; and Price and Rummy flee into the shelter.*)

BILL. You want to go in and tell your Major of me, do you?

JENNY. Oh please dont drag my hair. Let me go.

BILL. Do you or dont you? (*She stifles a scream.*) Yes or no.

JENNY. God give me strength—

BILL (*striking her with his fist in the face*). Go and shew her that, and tell her if she wants one like it to come and interfere with me. (*Jenny, crying with pain, goes into the shed. He goes to the form and addresses the old man.*) Here: finish your mess; and get out o my way.

SHIRLEY (*springing up and facing him fiercely, with the mug in his hand*). You take a liberty with me, and I'll smash you over the face with the mug and cut your eye out. Aint you satisfied—young whelps like you—with takin the bread out o the mouths of your elders that have brought you up and slaved for you, but you must come shovin and cheekin and bullyin in here, where the bread o charity is sickenin in our stummicks?

BILL (*contemptuously, but backing a little*). Wot good are you, you old palsy mug? Wot good are you?

SHIRLEY. As good as you and better. I'll do a day's work agen you or any fat young soaker of your age. Go and take my job at Horrockses, where I worked for ten year. They want young men there: they cant afford to keep men over forty-five. Theyre very sorry—give you a character and happy to help you to get anything suited to your years—sure a steady man wont be long out of a job. Well, let em try y o u. Theyll find the differ. What do y o u know? Not as much as how to beeyave yourself—layin your dirty fist across the mouth of a respectable woman!

BILL. Dont provoke me to lay it acrost yours: d'ye hear?

SHIRLEY (*with blighting contempt*). Yes: you like an old man to hit, dont you, when youve finished with the women. I aint seen you hit a young one yet.

BILL (*stung*). You lie, you old soupkitchener, you. There was a young man here. Did I offer to hit him or did I not?

SHIRLEY. Was he starvin or was he not? Was he a man or only a crosseyed thief an a loafer? Would you hit my son-in-law's brother?

BILL. Who's he?

SHIRLEY. Todger Fairmile o Balls Pond. Him that won £20 off the Japanese wrastler at the music hall by standin out 17 minutes 4 seconds agen him.

BILL (*sullenly*). I'm no music hall wrastler. Can he box?

SHIRLEY. Yes: an you cant.

BILL. Wot! I cant, cant I? Wots that you say (*threatening him*)?

SHIRLEY (*not budging an inch*). Will you box Todger Fairmile if I put him on to you? Say the word.

BILL (*subsiding with a slouch*). I'll stand up to any man alive, if he was ten Todger Fairmiles. But I dont set up to be a perfessional.

SHIRLEY (*looking down on him with unfathomable disdain*). Y o u box! Slap an old woman with the back o your hand! You hadnt even the sense to hit her where a magistrate couldnt see the mark of it, you silly young lump of conceit and ignorance. Hit a girl in the jaw and ony make her cry! If Todger Fairmile'd done it, she wouldnt a got up inside o ten minutes, no more than you would if he got on to you. Yah! I'd set about you myself if I had a week's feedin in me instead o two months starvation. (*He returns to the table to finish his meal.*)

BILL (*following him and stooping over him to drive the taunt in*). You lie! you have the bread and treacle in you that you come here to beg.

SHIRLEY (*bursting into tears*). Oh God! it's true: I'm only an old pauper on the scrap heap. (*Furiously*) But youll come to it yourself; and then youll know. Youll come to it sooner than a teetotaller like me, fillin yourself with gin at this hour o the mornin!

BILL. I'm no gin drinker, you old liar; but when I want to give my girl a bloomin good idin I like to av a bit o devil in me: see? An here I am, talkin to a rotten old blighter like you sted o givin her wot for. (*Working himself into a rage*) I'm goin in there to fetch her out. (*He makes vengefully for the shelter door.*)

SHIRLEY. Youre goin to the station on the stretcher, more likely; and theyll take the gin and the devil out of you there when they get you inside. You mind what youre about: the major here is the Earl o Stevenage's granddaughter.

BILL (*checked*). Garn!

SHIRLEY. Youll see.

BILL (*his resolution oozing*). Well, I aint done nothing to er.

SHIRLEY. Spose she said you did! who'd believe you?

BILL (*very uneasy, skulking back to the corner of the penthouse*). Gawd! theres no jastice in this country. To think wot them people can do! I'm as good as er.

SHIRLEY. Tell her so. It's just what a fool like you would do.

Barbara, brisk and businesslike, comes from the shelter with a note book, and addresses herself to Shirley. Bill, cowed, sits down in the corner on a form, and turns his back on them.

BARBARA. Good morning.

SHIRLEY (*standing up and taking off his hat*). Good morning, miss.

BARBARA. Sit down: make yourself at home. (*He hesitates; but she puts a friendly hand on his shoulder and makes him obey.*) Now then! since youve made friends with us, we want to know all about you. Names and addresses and trades.

SHIRLEY. Peter Shirley. Fitter. Chucked out two months ago because I was too old.

BARBARA (*not at all surprised*). Youd pass still. Why didnt you dye your hair?

SHIRLEY. I did. Me age come out at a coroner's inquest on me daughter.

BARBARA. Steady?

SHIRLEY. Teetotaller. Never out of a job before. Good worker. And sent to the knackers like an old horse!

BARBARA. No matter: if you did your part God will do his.

SHIRLEY (*suddenly stubborn*). My religion's no concern of anybody but myself.

BARBARA (*guessing*). I know. Secularist?

SHIRLEY (*hotly*). Did I offer to deny it?

BARBARA. Why should you? My own father's a Secularist, I think. Our Father—yours and mine—fulfils himself in many ways; and I daresay he knew what he was about when he made a Secularist of you. So buck up, Peter! we can always find a job for a steady man like you. (*Shirley, disarmed, touches his hat. She turns from him to Bill.*) Whats y o u r name?

BILL (*insolently.*) Wots that to you?

BARBARA (*calmly making a note*). Afraid to give his name. Any trade?

BILL. Who's afraid to give his name? (*Doggedly, with a sense of heroically defying the House of Lords in the person of Lord Stevenage.*) If you want to bring a charge agen me, bring it. (*She waits, unruffled.*) My name's Bill Walker.

BARBARA (*as if the name were familiar: trying to remember how*). Bill Walker? (*Recollecting*) Oh, I know: youre the man that Jenny Hill was praying for inside just now. (*She enters his name in her note book.*)

BILL. Who's Jenny Hill? And what call has she to pray for me?

BARBARA. I dont know. Perhaps it was you that cut her lip.

BILL (*defiantly*). Yes, it w a s me that cut her lip. I aint afraid o y o u.

BARBARA. How could you be, since youre not afraid of God? Youre a brave man, Mr. Walker. It takes some pluck to do our work here; but none of us dare lift our hand against a girl like that, for fear of her father in heaven.

BILL (*sullenly*). I want none o your cantin jaw. I suppose you think I come here to beg from you, like this damaged lot here. Not me. I dont want your bread and scrape and catlap. I dont believe in your Gawd, no more than you do yourself.

BARBARA (*sunnily apologetic and ladylike, as on a new footing with him*). Oh, I beg your pardon for putting your name down, Mr. Walker. I didnt understand. I'll strike it out.

BILL (*taking this as a slight, and deeply wounded by it*). Eah! you let my name alone. Aint it good enough to be in your book?

BARBARA (*considering*). Well, you see, theres no use putting down your name unless I can do something for you, is there? Whats your trade?

BILL (*still smarting*). Thats no concern o yours.

BARBARA. Just so. (*Very businesslike*) I'll put you down as (*writing*) the man who—struck—poor little Jenny Hill—in the mouth.

BILL (*rising threateningly*). See here. Ive ad enough o this.

BARBARA (*quite sunny and fearless*). What did you come to us for?

BILL. I come for my girl, see? I come to take her out o this and to break er jawr for her.

BARBARA (*complacently*). You see I was right about your trade. (*Bill, on the point of retorting furiously, finds himself, to his great shame and terror, in danger of crying instead. He sits down again suddenly.*) Whats her name?

BILL (*dogged*). Er name's Mog Abbijam: thats wot her name is.

BARBARA. Oh, she's gone to Canning Town, to our barracks there.

BILL (*fortified by his resentment of Mog's perfidy*). Is she? (*Vindictively*) Then I'm goin to Kennintahn arter her. (*He crosses to the gate; hesitates; finally comes back to Barbara.*) Are you lyin to me to get shut o me?

BARBARA. I dont want to get shut of you. I want to keep you here and save your soul. Youd better stay: youre going to have a bad time today, Bill.

BILL. Who's goin to give it to me? Y o u, praps.

BARBARA. Someone you dont believe in. But youll be glad afterwards.

BILL (*slinking off*). I'll go to Kennintahn to be out o the reach o your tongue. (*Suddenly turning on her with intense malice*) And if I dont find Mog there, I'll come back and do two years for you, selp me Gawd if I don't!

BARBARA (*a shade kindlier, if possible*). It's no use, Bill. Shes got another bloke.

BILL. Wot!

BARBARA. One of her own converts. He fell in love with her when he saw her with her soul saved, and her face clean, and her hair washed.

BILL (*surprised*). Wottud she wash it for, the carroty slut? It's red.

BARBARA. It's quite lovely now, because she wears a new look in her eyes with it. It's a pity youre too late. The new bloke has put your nose out of joint, Bill.

BILL. I'll put his nose out o joint for him. Not that I care a curse for her, mind that. But I'll teach her to drop me as if I was dirt. And I'll teach him to meddle with my judy. Wots iz bleedin name?

BARBARA. Sergeant Todger Fairmile.

SHIRLEY (*rising with grim joy*). I'll go with him, miss. I want to see them two meet. I'll take him to the infirmary when it's over.

BILL (*to Shirley, with undissembled misgiving*). Is that im you was speakin on?

SHIRLEY. Thats him.

BILL. Im that wrastled in the music all?

SHIRLEY. The competitions at the National Sportin Club was worth nigh a hundred a year to him. Hes gev em up now for religion; so hes a bit fresh for want of the exercise he was accustomed to. Hell be glad to see you. Come along.

BILL. Wots is weight?

SHIRLEY. Thirteen four. (*Bill's last hope expires.*)

BARBARA. Go and talk to him, Bill. He'll convert you.

SHIRLEY. He'll convert your head into a mashed potato.

BILL (*sullenly*). I aint afraid of him. I aint afraid of ennybody. But he can lick me. Shes done me. (*He sits down moodily on the edge of the horse-trough.*)

SHIRLEY. You aint goin. I thought not. (*He resumes his seat.*)

BARBARA (*calling*). Jenny!

JENNY (*appearing at the shelter door with a plaster on the corner of her mouth*). Yes, Major.

BARBARA. Send Rummy Mitchens out to clear away here.

JENNY. I think shes afraid.

BARBARA (*her resemblance to her mother flashing out for a moment*). Nonsense! she must do as shes told.

JENNY (*calling into the shelter*). Rummy: the Major says you must come.

Jenny comes to Barbara, purposely keeping on the side next Bill, lest he should suppose that she shrank from him or bore malice.

BARBARA. Poor little Jenny! Are you tired? (*Looking at the wounded cheek.*) Does it hurt?

JENNY No: it's all right now. It was nothing.

BARBARA (*critically*). It was as hard as he could hit, I expect. Poor Bill! You dont feel angry with him, do you?

JENNY. Oh no, no, no: indeed I dont, Major, bless his poor heart! (*Barbara kisses her; and she runs away merrily into the shelter. Bill writhes with an agonizing return of his new and alarming symptoms, but says nothing. Rummy Mitchens comes from the shelter.*)

BARBARA (*going to meet Rummy*). Now Rummy, bustle. Take in those mugs and plates to be washed; and throw the crumbs about for the birds.

Rummy takes the three plates and mugs; but Shirley takes back his mug from her, as there is still some milk left in it.

RUMMY. There aint any crumbs. This aint a time to waste good bread on birds.

PRICE (*appearing at the shelter door*). Gentleman come to see the shelter, Major. Says hes your father.

BARBARA. All right. Coming. (*Snobby goes back into the shelter, followed by Barbara.*)

RUMMY (*stealing across to Bill and addressing him in a subdued voice, but with intense conviction*). I'd av the lor of you, you flat eared pignosed potwalloper, if she'd let me. Youre no gentleman, to hit a lady in the face. (*Bill, with greater things moving in him, takes no notice.*)

SHIRLEY (*following her*). Here! in with you and dont get yourself into more trouble by talking.

RUMMY (*with hauteur*). I aint ad the pleasure o being hintroduced to you, as I can remember. (*She goes into the shelter with the plates.*)

SHIRLEY. Thats the—

BILL (*savagely*). Dont you talk to me, d'ye hear. You lea me alone, or I'll do you a mischief. I'm not dirt under y o u r feet, anyway.

SHIRLEY (*calmly*). Dont you be afeered. You aint such prime company that you need expect to be sought after. (*He is about to go into the shelter when Barbara comes out, with Undershaft on her right.*)

BARBARA. Oh there you are, Mr. Shirley! (*Between them*) This is my father: I told you he was a Secularist, didnt I? Perhaps youll be able to comfort one another.

UNDERSHAFT (*startled*). A Secularist! Not the least in the world: on the contrary, a confirmed mystic.

BARBARA. Sorry, I'm sure. By the way, papa, what is your religion—in case I have to introduce you again?

UNDERSHAFT. My religion? Well, my dear, I am a Millionaire. That is my religion.

BARBARA. Then I'm afraid you and Mr. Shirley wont be able to comfort one another after all. Youre not a Millionaire, are you, Peter?

SHIRLEY. No; and proud of it.

UNDERSHAFT (*gravely*). Poverty, my friend, is not a thing to be proud of.

SHIRLEY (*angrily*). Who made your millions for you? Me and my like. Whats kep us poor? Keepin you rich. I wouldnt have your conscience, not for all your income.

UNDERSHAFT. I wouldnt have your income, not for all your conscience, Mr. Shirley. (*He goes to the penthouse and sits down on a form.*)

BARBARA (*stopping Shirley adroitly as he is about to retort*). You wouldnt think he was my father, would you, Peter? Will you go into the shelter and lend the lasses a hand for a while: we're worked off our feet.

SHIRLEY (*bitterly*). Yes: I'm in their debt for a meal, aint I?

BARBARA. Oh, not because youre in their debt; but for love of them, Peter, for love of them. (*He cannot understand, and is rather scandalized.*) There! dont stare at me. In with you; and give that conscience of yours a holiday (*bustling him into the shelter*).

SHIRLEY (*as he goes in*). Ah! it's a pity you never was trained to use your reason, miss. Youd have been a very taking lecturer on Secularism.

Barbara turns to her father.

UNDERSHAFT. Never mind me, my dear. Go about your work; and let me watch it for a while.

BARBARA. All right.

UNDERSHAFT. For instance, whats the matter with that outpatient over there?

BARBARA (*looking at Bill, whose attitude has never changed, and whose expression of brooding wrath has deepened*). Oh, we shall cure him in no time. Just watch. (*She goes over to Bill and waits. He glances up at her and casts his eyes down again, uneasy, but grimmer than ever.*) It w o u l d be nice to just stamp on Mog Habbijam's face, wouldnt it, Bill?

BILL (*starting up from the trough in consternation*). It's a lie: I never said so. (*She shakes her head.*) Who told you wot was in my mind?

BARBARA. Only your new friend.

BILL. Wot new friend?

BARBARA. The devil, Bill. When he gets round people they get miserable, just like you.

BILL (*with a heartbreaking attempt at devil-may-care cheerfulness*). I aint miserable. (*He sits down again, and stretches his legs in an attempt to seem indifferent.*)

BARBARA. Well, if youre happy, why dont you look happy, as we do?

BILL (*his legs curling back in spite of him*). I'm appy enough, I tell you. Why dont you lea me alown? Wot av I done to y o u? I aint smashed y o u r face, av I?

BARBARA (*softly: wooing his soul*). It's not me thats getting at you, Bill.

BILL. Who else is it?

BARBARA. Somebody that doesnt intend you to smash women's faces, I suppose. Somebody or something that wants to make a man of you.

BILL (*blustering*). Make a man o me! Aint I a man? eh? aint I a man? Who sez I'm not a man?

BARBARA. Theres a man in you somewhere, I suppose. But why did he let you hit poor little Jenny Hill? That wasnt very manly of him, was it?

BILL (*tormented*). Av done with it, I tell you. Chack it. I'm sick of your Jenny Ill and er silly little face.

BARBARA. Then why do you keep thinking about it? Why does it keep coming up against you in your mind? Youre not getting converted, are you?

BILL (*with conviction*). Not ME. Not likely. Not arf.

BARBARA. Thats right, Bill. Hold out against it. Put out your strength. Dont lets get you cheap. Todger Fairmile said he wrestled for three nights against his salvation harder than he ever wrestled with the Jap at the music hall. He gave in to the Jap when his arm was going to break. But he didnt give in to his salvation until his heart was going to break. Perhaps youll escape that. You havnt any heart, have you?

BILL. Wot d'ye mean? Wy aint I got a art the same as ennybody else?

BARBARA. A man with a heart wouldnt have bashed poor little Jenny's face, would he?

BILL (*almost crying*). Ow, w i l l you lea me alown? Av I ever offered to meddle with y o u, that you come naggin and provowkin me lawk this? (*He writhes convulsively from his eyes to his toes.*)

BARBARA (*with a steady soothing hand on his arm and a gentle voice that never lets him go*). It's your soul thats hurting you, Bill, and not me. Weve been through it all ourselves. Come with us, Bill. (*He looks wildly round.*) To brave manhood on earth and eternal glory in heaven. (*He is on the point of breaking down.*) Come. (*A drum is heard in the shelter; and Bill, with a gasp, escapes from the spell as Barbara turns quickly. Adolphus enters from the shelter with a big drum.*) Oh! there you are, Dolly. Let me introduce a new friend of mine, Mr. Bill Walker. This is my bloke, Bill: Mr. Cusins. (*Cusins salutes with his drumstick.*)

BILL. Goin to marry im?

BARBARA. Yes.

BILL (*fervently*). Gord elp im! Gawd elp im!

BARBARA. Why? Do you think he wont be happy with me?

BILL. Ive only ad to stand it for a mornin: e'll av to stand it for a lifetime.

CUSINS. That is a frightful reflection, Mr. Walker. But I cant tear myself away from her.

BILL. Well, I can. (*To Barbara*) Eah! do you know where I'm going to, and wot I'm goin to do?

BARBARA. Yes: youre going to heaven; and youre coming back here before the week's out to tell me so.

BILL. You lie. I'm goin to Kennintahn, to spit in Todger Fairmile's eye. I bashed Jenny Ill's face; and now I'll get me own face bashed and come back and shew it to er. E'll it me ardern I it e r. Thatll make us square. (*To Adolphus*) Is that fair or is it not? Youre a genlman: you oughter know.

BARBARA. Two black eyes wont make one white one, Bill.

BILL. I didnt ast y o u. Cawnt you never keep your mahth shut? I ast the genlman.

CUSINS (*reflectively*). Yes: I think youre right, Mr. Walker. Yes: I should do it. It's curious: it's exactly what an ancient Greek would have done.

BARBARA. But what good will it do?

CUSINS. Well, it will give Mr. Fairmile some exercise; and it will satisfy Mr. Walker's soul.

BILL. Rot! there aint no sach a thing as a soul. Ah kin you tell wether Ive a soul or not? You never seen it.

BARBARA. Ive seen it hurting you when you went against it.

BILL (*with compressed aggravation*). If you was my girl and took the word out o me mahth lawk thet, I'd give you suthink youd feel urtin, so I would. (*To Adolphus*) You take my tip, mate. Stop er jawr; or youll die afore your time. (*With intense expression*) Wore aht: thets wot youll be: wore aht. (*He goes away through the gate.*)

CUSINS (*looking after him*). I wonder!

BARBARA. Dolly! (*indignant, in her mother's manner*).

CUSINS. Yes, my dear, it's very wearing to be in love with you. If it lasts, I quite think I shall die young.

BARBARA. Should you mind?

CUSINS. Not at all. (*He is suddenly softened, and kisses her over the drum, evidently not for the first time, as people cannot kiss over a big drum without practice. Undershaft coughs.*)

BARBARA. It's all right, papa, weve not forgotten you. Dolly: explain the place to papa: I havnt time. (*She goes busily into the shelter.*)

Undershaft and Adolphus now have the yard to themselves. Undershaft, seated on a form, and still keenly attentive, looks hard at Adolphus. Adolphus looks hard at him.

UNDERSHAFT. I fancy you guess something of what is in my mind, Mr. Cusins. (*Cusins flourishes his drumstick as if in the act of beating a lively rataplan, but makes no sound.*) Exactly so. But suppose Barbara finds you out!

CUSINS. You know, I do not admit that I am imposing on Barbara. I am quite genuinely interested in the views of the Salvation Army. The fact is, I am a sort of collector of religions; and the curious thing is that I find I can believe them all. By the way, have you any religion?

UNDERSHAFT. Yes.

CUSINS. Anything out of the common?

UNDERSHAFT. Only that there are two things necessary to Salvation.

CUSINS (*disappointed, but polite*). Ah, the Church Catechism. Charles Lomax also belongs to the Established Church.

UNDERSHAFT. The two things are—

CUSINS. Baptism and—

UNDERSHAFT. No. Money and gunpowder.

CUSINS (*surprised, but interested*). That is the general opinion of our governing classes. The novelty is in hearing any man confess it.

UNDERSHAFT. Just so.

CUSINS. Excuse me: is there any place in your religion for honor, justice, truth, love, mercy and so forth?

UNDERSHAFT. Yes: they are the graces and luxuries of a rich, strong, and safe life.

CUSINS. Suppose one is forced to choose between them and money or gunpowder?

UNDERSHAFT. Choose money a n d gunpowder; for without enough of both you cannot afford the others.

CUSINS. That is your religion?

UNDERSHAFT. Yes.

The cadence of this reply makes a full close in the conversation. Cusins twists his face dubiously and contemplates Undershaft. Undershaft contemplates him.

CUSINS. Barbara wont stand that. You will have to choose between your religion and Barbara.

UNDERSHAFT. So will you, my friend. She will find out that that drum of yours is hollow.

CUSINS. Father Undershaft: you are mistaken: I am a sincere Salvationist. You do not understand the Salvation Army. It is the army of joy, of love, of courage: it has banished the fear and remorse and despair of the old hell-ridden evangelical sects: it marches to fight the devil with trumpet and drum, with music and dancing, with banner and palm, as becomes a sally from heaven by its happy garrison. It picks the waster out of the public house and makes a man of him: it finds a worm wriggling in a back kitchen, and lo! a woman! Men and women of rank too, sons and daughters of the Highest. It takes the poor professor of Greek, the most artificial and self-suppressed of human creatures, from his meal of roots, and lets loose the rhapsodist in him; reveals the true worship of Dionysos to him; sends him down the public street drumming dithyrambs. (*He plays a thundering flourish on the drum.*)

UNDERSHAFT. You will alarm the shelter.

CUSINS. Oh, they are accustomed to these sudden ecstasies of piety. However, if the drum worries you—(*He pockets the drumsticks; unhooks the drum; and stands it on the ground opposite the gateway.*)

UNDERSHAFT. Thank you.

CUSINS. You remember what Euripides says about your money and gunpowder?

UNDERSHAFT. No.

CUSINS (*declaiming*).

One and another
In money and guns may outpass his brother;
And men in their millions float and flow
And seethe with a million hopes as leaven;
And they win their will; or they miss their will;
And their hopes are dead or are pined for still;
But whoe'er can know
As the long days go
That to live is happy, has found h i s heaven.

My translation: what do you think of it?

UNDERSHAFT. I think, my friend, that if you wish to know, as the long days go, that to live is happy, you must first acquire money enough for a decent life, and power enough to be your own master.

CUSINS. You are damnably discouraging. (*He resumes his declamation.*)

Is it so hard a thing to see
That the spirit of God—whate'er it be—
The Law that abides and changes not, ages long,
The Eternal and Nature-born: t h e s e things be strong?
What else is Wisdom? What of Man's endeavor,
Or God's high grace so lovely and so great?
To stand from fear set free? to breathe and wait?
To hold a hand uplifted over Fate?
And shall not Barbara be loved for ever?

UNDERSHAFT. Euripides mentions Barbara, does he?

CUSINS. It is a fair translation. The word means Loveliness.

UNDERSHAFT. May I ask—as Barbara's father—how much a year she is to be loved for ever on?

CUSINS. As Barbara's father, that is more your affair than mine. I can feed her by teaching Greek: that is about all.

UNDERSHAFT. Do you consider it a good match for her?

CUSINS (*with polite obstinacy*). Mr. Undershaft: I am in many ways a weak, timid, ineffectual person; and my health is far from satisfactory. But whenever I feel that I must have anything, I get it, sooner or later. I feel that way about Barbara. I dont like marriage: I feel intensely afraid of it; and I dont know what I shall do with Barbara or what she will do with me. But I feel that I and nobody else must marry her. Please regard that as settled.—Not that I wish to be arbitrary; but why should I waste your time in discussing what is inevitable?

UNDERSHAFT. You mean that you will stick at nothing: not even the conversion of the Salvation Army to the worship of Dionysos.

CUSINS. The business of the Salvation Army is to save, not to wrangle about the name of the pathfinder. Dionysos or another: what does it matter?

UNDERSHAFT (*rising and approaching him*). Professor Cusins: you are a young man after my own heart.

CUSINS. Mr. Undershaft: you are, as far as I am able to gather, a most infernal old rascal; but you appeal very strongly to my sense of ironic humor.

Undershaft mutely offers his hand. They shake.

UNDERSHAFT (*suddenly concentrating himself*). And now to business.

CUSINS. Pardon me. We were discussing religion. Why go back to such an uninteresting and unimportant subject as business?

UNDERSHAFT. Religion is our business at present, because it is through religion alone that we can win Barbara.

CUSINS. Have you, too, fallen in love with Barbara?

UNDERSHAFT. Yes, with a father's love.

CUSINS. A father's love for a grown-up daughter is the most dangerous of all infatuations. I apologize for mentioning my own pale, coy, mistrustful fancy in the same breath with it.

UNDERSHAFT. Keep to the point. We have to win her; and we are neither of us Methodists.

CUSINS. That doesnt matter. The power Barbara wields here—the power that wields Barbara herself—is not Calvinism, not Presbyterianism, not Methodism—

UNDERSHAFT. Not Greek Paganism either, eh?

CUSINS. I admit that. Barbara is quite original in her religion.

UNDERSHAFT (*triumphantly*). Aha! Barbara Undershaft would be. Her inspiration comes from within herself.

CUSINS. How do you suppose it got there?

UNDERSHAFT (*in towering excitement*). It is the Undershaft inheritance. I shall hand on my torch to my daughter. She shall make my converts and preach my gospel—

CUSINS. What! Money and gunpowder!

UNDERSHAFT. Yes, money and gunpowder; freedom and power; command of life and command of death.

CUSINS (*urbanely: trying to bring him down to earth*). This is extremely interesting, Mr. Undershaft. Of course you know that you are mad.

UNDERSHAFT (*with redoubled force*). And you?

CUSINS. Oh, mad as a hatter. You are welcome to my secret since I have discovered yours. But I am astonished. Can a madman make cannons?

UNDERSHAFT. Would anyone else than a madman make them? And now (*with surging energy*) question for question. Can a sane man translate Euripides?

CUSINS. No.

UNDERSHAFT (*seizing him by the shoulder*). Can a sane woman make a man of a waster or a woman of a worm?

CUSINS (*reeling before the storm*). Father Colossus—Mammoth Millionaire—

UNDERSHAFT (*pressing him*). Are there two mad people or three in this Salvation shelter to-day?

CUSINS. You mean Barbara is as mad as we are!

UNDERSHAFT (*pushing him lightly off and resuming his equanimity suddenly and completely*). Pooh, Professor! let us call things by their proper names. I am a millionaire; you are a poet; Barbara is a savior of souls. What have we three to do with the common mob of slaves and idolaters? (*He sits down again with a shrug of contempt for the mob.*)

CUSINS. Take care! Barbara is in love with the common people. So am I. Have you never felt the romance of that love?

UNDERSHAFT (*cold and sardonic*). Have you ever been in love with Poverty, like St. Francis? Have you ever been in love with Dirt, like St. Simeon? Have you ever been in love with disease and suffering, like our nurses and philanthropists? Such passions are not virtues, but the most unnatural of all the vices. This love of the common people may please an earl's granddaughter and a university professor; but I have been a common man and a poor man; and it has no romance for me. Leave it to the poor to pretend that poverty is a blessing: leave it to the coward to make a religion of his cowardice by preaching humility: we know better than that. We three must stand together above the common people: how else can we help their children to climb up beside us? Barbara must belong to us, not to the Salvation Army.

CUSINS. Well, I can only say that if you think you will get her away from the Salvation Army by talking to her as you have been talking to me, you dont know Barbara.

UNDERSHAFT. My friend: I never ask for what I can buy.

CUSINS (*in a white fury*). Do I understand you to imply that you can buy Barbara?

UNDERSHAFT. No; but I can buy the Salvation Army.

CUSINS. Quite impossible.

UNDERSHAFT. You shall see. All religious organizations exist by selling themselves to the rich.

CUSINS. Not the Army. That is the Church of the poor.

UNDERSHAFT. All the more reason for buying it.

CUSINS. I dont think you quite know what the Army does for the poor.

UNDERSHAFT. Oh yes I do. It draws their teeth: that is enough for me—as a man of business—

CUSINS. Nonsense. It makes them sober—

UNDERSHAFT. I prefer sober workmen. The profits are larger.

CUSINS. —honest—

UNDERSHAFT. Honest workmen are the most economical.

CUSINS. —attached to their homes—

UNDERSHAFT. So much the better: they will put up with anything sooner than change their shop.

CUSINS. —happy—

UNDERSHAFT. An invaluable safeguard against revolution.

CUSINS. —unselfish—

UNDERSHAFT. Indifferent to their own interests, which suits me exactly.

CUSINS. —with their thoughts on heavenly things—

UNDERSHAFT (*rising*). And not on Trade Unionism nor Socialism. Excellent.

CUSINS (*revolted*). You really are an infernal old rascal.

UNDERSHAFT (*indicating Peter Shirley, who has just come from the shelter and strolled dejectedly down the yard between them*). And this is an honest man!

SHIRLEY. Yes; and what av I got by it? (*He passes on bitterly and sits on the form, in the corner of the penthouse.*)

Snobby Price, beaming sanctimoniously, and Jenny Hill, with a tambourine full of coppers, come from the shelter and go to the drum, on which Jenny begins to count the money.

UNDERSHAFT (*replying to Shirley*). Oh, your employers must have got a good deal by it from first to last. (*He sits on the table, with one foot on the side form. Cusins, overwhelmed, sits down on the same form nearer the shelter. Barbara comes from the shelter to the middle of the yard. She is excited and a little overwrought.*)

BARBARA. Weve just had a splendid experience meeting at the other gate in Cripps's lane. Ive hardly ever seen them so much moved as they were by your confession, Mr. Price.

PRICE. I could almost be glad of my past wickedness if I could believe that it would elp to keep hathers stright.

BARBARA. So it will, Snobby. How much, Jenny?

JENNY. Four and tenpence, Major.

BARBARA. Oh Snobby, if you had given your poor mother just one more kick, we should have got the whole five shillings!

PRICE. If she heard you say that, miss, she'd be sorry I didnt. But I'm glad. Oh what a joy it will be to her when she hears I'm saved!

UNDERSHAFT. Shall I contribute the odd twopence, Barbara? The millionaire's mite, eh? (*He takes a couple of pennies from his pocket.*)

BARBARA. How did you make that twopence?

UNDERSHAFT. As usual. By selling cannons, torpedoes, submarines, and my new patent Grand Duke hand grenade.

BARBARA. Put it back in your pocket. You cant buy your Salvation here for twopence: you must work it out.

UNDERSHAFT. Is twopence not enough? I can afford a little more, if you press me.

BARBARA. Two million millions would not be enough. There is bad blood on your hands; and nothing but good blood can cleanse them. Money is no use. Take it away. (*She turns to Cusins.*) Dolly: you must write another letter for me to the papers. (*He makes a wry face.*) Yes: I know you dont like it; but it must be done. The starvation this winter is beating us: everybody is unemployed. The General says we must close this shelter if we cant get more money. I force the collections at the meetings until I am ashamed: dont I, Snobby?

PRICE. It's a fair treat to see you work it, miss. The way you got them up from three-and-six to four-and-ten with that hymn, penny by penny and verse by verse, was a caution. Not a Cheap Jack on Mile End Waste could touch you at it.

BARBARA. Yes; but I wish we could do without it. I am getting at last to think more of the collection than of the people's souls. And what are those hatfuls of pence and halfpence? We want thousands! tens of thousands! hundreds of thousands! I want to convert people, not to be always begging for the Army in a way I'd die sooner than beg for myself.

UNDERSHAFT (*in profound irony*). Genuine unselfishness is capable of anything, my dear.

BARBARA (*unsuspectingly, as she turns away to take the money from the drum and put it in a cash bag she carries*). Yes, isnt it? (*Undershaft looks sardonically at Cusins.*)

CUSINS (*aside to Undershaft*). Mephistopheles! Machiavelli!

BARBARA (*tears coming into her eyes as she ties the bag and pockets it*). How are we to feed them? I cant talk religion to a man with bodily hunger in his eyes. (*Almost breaking down*) It's frightful.

JENNY (*running to her*). Major, dear—

BARBARA (*rebounding*). No, dont comfort me. It will be all right. We shall get the money.

UNDERSHAFT. How?

JENNY. By praying for it, of course. Mrs. Baines says she prayed for it last night; and she has never prayed for it in vain: never once. (*She goes to the gate and looks out into the street.*)

BARBARA (*who has dried her eyes and regained her composure*). By the way, dad, Mrs. Baines has come to march with us to our big meeting this afternoon; and she is very anxious to meet you, for some reason or other. Perhaps she'll convert you.

UNDERSHAFT. I shall be delighted, my dear.

JENNY (*at the gate: excitedly*). Major! Major! heres that man back again.

BARBARA. What man?

JENNY. The man that hit me. Oh, I hope hes coming back to join us.

Bill Walker, with frost on his jacket, comes through the gate, his hands deep in his pockets and his chin sunk between his shoulders, like a cleaned-out gambler. He halts between Barbara and the drum.

BARBARA. Hullo, Bill! Back already!

BILL (*nagging at her*). Bin talkin ever sence, av you?

BARBARA. Pretty nearly. Well, has Todger paid you out for poor Jenny's jaw?

BILL. No he aint.

BARBARA. I thought your jacket looked a bit snowy.

BILL. So it is snowy. You want to know where the snow come from, dont you?

BARBARA. Yes.

BILL. Well, it come from off the ground in Parkinses Corner in Kennintahn. It got rubbed off be my shoulders: see?

BARBARA. Pity you didnt rub some off with your knees, Bill! That would have done you a lot of good.

BILL (*with sour mirthless humor*). I was saving another man's knees at the time. E was kneelin on my ed, so e was.

JENNY. Who was kneeling on your head?

BILL. Todger was. E was prayin for me: prayin comfortable with me as a carpet. So was Mog. So was the old bloomin meetin. Mog she sez, "O Lord break is stubborn spirit; but dont urt is dear art." That was wot she said. "Dont urt is dear art"! An er bloke—thirteen stun four!—kneelin wiv all is weight on me. Funny, aint it?

JENNY. Oh no. We're so sorry, Mr. Walker.

BARBARA (*enjoying it frankly*). Nonsense! of course it's funny. Served you right, Bill! You must have done something to him first.

BILL (*doggedly*). I did wot I said I'd do. I spit in is eye. E looks up at the sky and sez, "O that I should be fahnd worthy to be spit upon for the gospel's sake!" e sez; an Mog sez, "Glory Allelloolier!"; and then e called me Brother, an dahned me as if I was a kid and e was me mother washin me a Setterda nawt. I adnt just no show wiv im at all. Arf the street prayed; an the tother arf larfed fit to split theirselves. (*To Barbara*) There! are you settisfawd nah?

BARBARA (*her eyes dancing*). Wish I'd been there, Bill.

BILL. Yes: youd a got in a hextra bit o talk on me, wouldnt you?

JENNY. I'm so sorry, Mr. Walker.

BILL (*fiercely*). Dont you go bein sorry for me: youve no call. Listen ere. I broke your jawr.

JENNY. No, it didnt hurt me: indeed it didnt, except for a moment. It was only that I was frightened.

BILL. I dont want to be forgive be you, or be ennybody. Wot I did I'll pay for. I tried to get me own jawr broke to settisfaw you—

JENNY (*distressed*). Oh no—

BILL (*impatiently*). Tell y'I did: cawnt you listen to wots bein told you? All I got be it was bein made a sight of in the public street for me pains. Well, if I cawnt settisfaw you one way, I can another. Listen ere! I ad two quid saved agen the frost; an Ive a pahnd of it left. A mate o mine last week ad words with the judy e's goin to marry. E give er wot-for; an e's bin fined fifteen bob. E ad a right to it er because they was goin to be marrid; but I adnt no right to it you; so put anather fawv bob on an call it a pahnd's worth. (*He produces a sovereign.*) Eres the money. Take it; and lets av no more o your forgivin an prayin and your Major jawrin me. Let wot I done be done and paid for; and let there be a end of it.

JENNY. Oh, I couldnt take it, Mr. Walker. But if you would

give a shilling or two to poor Rummy Mitchens! you really did hurt her; and shes old.

BILL (*contemptuously*). Not likely. I'd give her anather as soon as look at er. Let her av the lawr o me as she threatened! S h e aint forgiven me: not mach. Wot I done to er is not on me mawnd—wot she (*indicating Barbara*) might call on me conscience—no more than stickin a pig. It's this Christian game o yours that I wont av played agen me: this bloomin forgivin an naggin an jawrin that makes a man that sore that iz lawf's a burdn to im. I wont av it, I tell you; so take your money and stop throwin your silly bashed face hup agen me.

JENNY. Major: may I take a little of it for the Army?

BARBARA. No: the Army is not to be bought. We want your soul, Bill; and we'll take nothing else.

BILL (*bitterly*). I know. It aint enough. Me an me few shillins is not good enough for you. Youre a earl's grendorter, you are. Nothing less than a underd pahnd for you.

UNDERSHAFT. Come, Barbara! you could do a great deal of good with a hundred pounds. If you will set this gentleman's mind at ease by taking his pound, I will give the other ninety-nine. (*Bill, astounded by such opulence, instinctively touches his cap.*)

BARBARA. Oh, youre too extravagant, papa. Bill offers twenty pieces of silver. All you need offer is the other ten. That will make the standard price to buy anybody who's for sale. I'm not; and the Army's not. (*To Bill*) Youll never have another quiet moment, Bill, until you come round to us. You cant stand out against your salvation.

BILL (*sullenly*). I cawnt stend aht agen music-all wrastlers and artful tongued women. Ive offered to pay. I can do no more. Take it or leave it. There it is. (*He throws the sovereign on the drum, and sits down on the horse-trough. The coin fascinates Snobby Price, who takes an early opportunity of dropping his cap on it.*)

Mrs. Baines comes from the shelter. She is dressed as a Salvation Army Commissioner. She is an earnest looking woman of about 40, *with a caressing, urgent voice, and an appealing manner.*

BARBARA. This is my father, Mrs. Baines. (*Undershaft*

comes from the table, taking his hat off with marked civility.) Try what you can do with him. He wont listen to me, because he remembers what a fool I was when I was a baby. (*She leaves them together and chats with Jenny.*)

MRS. BAINES. Have you been shewn over the shelter, Mr. Undershaft? You know the work we're doing, of course.

UNDERSHAFT (*very civilly*). The whole nation knows it, Mrs. Baines.

MRS. BAINES. No, sir: the whole nation does not know it, or we should not be crippled as we are for want of money to carry our work through the length and breadth of the land. Let me tell you that there would have been rioting this winter in London but for us.

UNDERSHAFT. You really think so?

MRS. BAINES. I know it. I remember 1886, when you rich gentlemen hardened your hearts against the cry of the poor. They broke the windows of your clubs in Pall Mall.

UNDERSHAFT (*gleaming with approval of their method*). And the Mansion House Fund went up next day from thirty thousand pounds to seventy-nine thousand! I remember quite well.

MRS. BAINES. Well, wont you help me to get at the people? They wont break windows then. Come here, Price. Let me shew you to this gentleman (*Price comes to be inspected*). Do you remember the window breaking?

PRICE. My ole father thought it was the revolution, maam.

MRS. BAINES. Would you break windows now?

PRICE. Oh no maam. The windows of eaven av bin opened to me. I know now that the rich man is a sinner like myself.

RUMMY (*appearing above at the loft door*). Snobby Price!

SNOBBY. Wot is it?

RUMMY. Your mother's askin for you at the other gate in Crippses Lane. She's heard about your confession. (*Price turns pale.*)

MRS. BAINES. Go, Mr. Price; and pray with her.

JENNY. You can go through the shelter, Snobby.

PRICE (*to Mrs. Baines*). I couldnt face her now, maam, with all the weight of my sins fresh on me. Tell her she'll find her son at ome, waitin for her in prayer. (*He skulks off through the gate, incidentally stealing the sovereign on his way out by picking up his cap from the drum.*)

MRS. BAINES (*with swimming eyes*). You see how we take the anger and the bitterness against you out of their hearts, Mr. Undershaft.

UNDERSHAFT. It is certainly most convenient and gratifying to all large employers of labor, Mrs. Baines.

MRS. BAINES. Barbara: Jenny: I have good news: most wonderful news. (*Jenny runs to her.*) My prayers have been answered. I told you they would, Jenny, didn't I?

JENNY. Yes, yes.

BARBARA (*moving nearer to the drum*). Have we got money enough to keep the shelter open?

MRS. BAINES. I hope we shall have enough to keep all the shelters open. Lord Saxmundham has promised us five thousand pounds—

BARBARA. Horray!

JENNY. Glory!

MRS. BAINES. —if—

BARBARA. "If!" If what?

MRS. BAINES. —if five other gentlemen will give a thousand each to make it up to ten thousand.

BARBARA. Who is Lord Saxmundham? I never heard of him.

UNDERSHAFT (*who has pricked up his ears at the peer's name, and is now watching Barbara curiously*). A new creation, my dear. You have heard of Sir Horace Bodger?

BARBARA. Bodger! Do you mean the distiller? Bodger's whisky!

UNDERSHAFT. That is the man. He is one of the greatest of our public benefactors. He restored the cathedral at Hakington. They made him a baronet for that. He gave half a million to the funds of his party: they made him a baron for that.

SHIRLEY. What will they give him for the five thousand?

UNDERSHAFT. There is nothing left to give him. So the five thousand, I should think, is to save his soul.

MRS. BAINES. Heaven grant it may! Oh Mr. Undershaft, you have some very rich friends. Cant you help us towards the other five thousand! We are going to hold a great meeting this afternoon at the Assembly Hall in the Mile End Road. If I could only announce that one gentleman had come forward to support Lord Saxmundham, others would follow. Dont you know somebody? couldnt you? wouldnt you? (*Her eyes fill with tears*) oh, think of those poor people, Mr. Undershaft: think of how much it means to them, and how little to a great man like you.

UNDERSHAFT (*sardonically gallant*). Mrs. Baines: you are irresistible. I cant disappoint you; and I cant deny myself the satisfaction of making Bodger pay up. You shall have your five thousand pounds.

MRS. BAINES. Thank God!

UNDERSHAFT. You dont thank m e?

MRS. BAINES. Oh sir, dont try to be cynical: dont be ashamed of being a good man. The Lord will bless you abundantly; and our prayers will be like a strong fortification round you all the days of your life. (*With a touch of caution*) You will let me have the cheque to shew at the meeting, wont you? Jenny: go in and fetch a pen and ink. (*Jenny runs to the shelter door.*)

UNDERSHAFT. Do not disturb Miss Hill: I have a fountain pen. (*Jenny halts. He sits at the table and writes the cheque. Cusins rises to make more room for him. They all watch him silently.*)

BILL (*cynically, aside to Barbara, his voice and accent horribly debased*). Wot prawce Selvytion nah?

BARBARA. Stop. (*Undershaft stops writing: they all turn to her in surprise.*) Mrs. Baines: are you really going to take this money?

MRS. BAINES (*astonished*). Why not, dear?

BARBARA. Why not! Do you know what my father is? Have you forgotten that Lord Saxmundham is Bodger the whisky man? Do you remember how we implored the County Council to stop him from writing Bodger's Whisky in letters of fire against the sky; so that the poor drink-ruined creatures on the embankment could not wake up from their snatches of sleep without being reminded of their deadly thirst by that wicked sky sign? Do you know that the worst thing I have had to fight here is not the devil, but Bodger, Bodger, Bodger, with his whisky, his distilleries, and his tied houses? Are you going to make our shelter another tied house for him, and ask me to keep it?

BILL. Rotten drunken whisky it is too.

MRS. BAINES. Dear Barbara: Lord Saxmundham has a soul to be saved like any of us. If heaven has found the way to make a good use of his money, are we to set ourselves up against the answer to our prayers?

BARBARA. I know he has a soul to be saved. Let him come down here; and I'll do my best to help him to his salvation. But he wants to send his cheque down to buy us, and go on being as wicked as ever.

UNDERSHAFT (*with a reasonableness which Cusins alone perceives to be ironical*). My dear Barbara: alcohol is a very necessary article. It heals the sick—

BARBARA. It does nothing of the sort.

UNDERSHAFT. Well, it assists the doctor: that is perhaps a less questionable way of putting it. It makes life bearable to millions of people who could not endure their existence if they were quite sober. It enables Parliament to do things at eleven at night that no sane person would do at eleven in the morning. Is it Bodger's fault that this inestimable gift is deplorably abused by less than one percent of the poor? (*He turns again to the table; signs the cheque; and crosses it.*)

MRS. BAINES. Barbara: will there be less drinking or more if all those poor souls we are saving come tomorrow and find the doors of our shelters shut in their faces? Lord Saxmundham gives us the money to stop drinking—to take his own business from him.

CUSINS (*impishly*). Pure self-sacrifice on Bodger's part, clearly! Bless dear Bodger! (*Barbara almost breaks down as Adolphus, too, fails her.*)

UNDERSHAFT (*tearing out the cheque and pocketing the book as he rises and goes past Cusins to Mrs. Baines*). I also, Mrs. Baines, may claim a little disinterestedness. Think of my business! think of the widows and orphans! the men and lads torn to pieces with shrapnel and poisoned with lyddite! (*Mrs. Baines shrinks; but he goes on remorselessly*) the oceans of blood, not one drop of which is shed in a really just cause! the ravaged crops! the peaceful peasants forced, women and men, to till their fields under the fire of opposing armies on pain of starvation! the bad blood of the fierce little cowards at home who egg on others to fight for the gratification of their national vanity! All this makes money for me: I am never richer, never busier than when the papers are full of it. Well, it is your work to preach peace on earth and goodwill to men. (*Mrs. Baines's face lights up again.*) Every convert you make is a vote against war. (*Her lips move in prayer.*) Yet I give you this money to help you to hasten my own commercial ruin. (*He gives her the cheque.*)

CUSINS (*mounting the form in an ecstasy of mischief*). The millennium will be inaugurated by the unselfishness of Undershaft and Bodger. Oh be joyful! (*He takes the drumsticks from his pockets and flourishes them.*)

MRS. BAINES (*taking the cheque*). The longer I live the more proof I see that there is an Infinite Goodness that turns everything to the work of salvation sooner or later. Who would have thought that any good could have come out of war and drink? And yet their profits are brought today to the feet of salvation to do its blessed work. (*She is affected to tears.*)

JENNY (*running to Mrs. Baines and throwing her arms round her*). Oh dear! how blessed, how glorious it all is!

CUSINS (*in a convulsion of irony*). Let us seize this unspeakable moment. Let us march to the great meeting at once. Excuse me just an instant. (*He rushes into the shelter. Jenny takes her tambourine from the drum head.*)

MRS. BAINES. Mr. Undershaft: have you ever seen a thousand people fall on their knees with one impulse and pray? Come with us to the meeting. Barbara shall tell them that the Army is saved, and saved through you.

CUSINS (*returning impetuously from the shelter with a flag and a trombone, and coming between Mrs. Baines and Undershaft*). You shall carry the flag down the first street, Mrs. Baines. (*He gives her the flag.*) Mr. Undershaft is a gifted trombonist: he shall intone an Olympian diapason to the the West Ham Salvation March. (*Aside to Undershaft, as he forces the trombone on him*) Blow, Machiavelli, blow.

UNDERSHAFT (*aside to him, as he takes the trombone*). The trumpet in Zion! (*Cusins rushes to the drum, which he takes *up and puts on. Undershaft continues, aloud*) I will do my best. I could vamp a bass if I knew the tune.

CUSINS. It is a wedding chorus from one of Donizetti's operas; but we have converted it. We convert everything to good here, including Bodger. You remember the chorus. "For thee immense rejoicing—immenso giubilo—immenso giubilo." (*With drum obbligato*) Rum tum ti tum tum, tum tum ti ta—

BARBARA. Dolly: you are breaking my heart.

CUSINS. What is a broken heart more or less here? Dionysos Undershaft has descended. I am possessed.

MRS. BAINES. Come, Barbara: I must have my dear Major to carry the flag with me.

JENNY. Yes, yes, Major darling.

CUSINS (*snatches the tambourine out of Jenny's hand and mutely offers it to Barbara*).

BARBARA (*coming forward a little as she puts the offer behind her with a shudder, whilst Cusins recklessly tosses the tambourine back to Jenny and goes to the gate*). I cant come.

JENNY. Not come!

MRS. BAINES (*with tears in her eyes*). Barbara: do you think I am wrong to take the money?

BARBARA (*impulsively going to her and kissing her*). No, no: God help you, dear, you must: you are saving the Army. Go; and may you have a great meeting!

JENNY. But arnt you coming?

BARBARA. No. (*She begins taking off the silver S brooch from her collar.*)

MRS. BAINES. Barbara: what are you doing?

JENNY. Why are you taking your badge off? You cant be going to leave us, Major.

BARBARA (*quietly*). Father: come here.

UNDERSHAFT (*coming to her*). My dear! (*Seeing that she is going to pin the badge on his collar, he retreats to the penthouse in some alarm.*)

BARBARA (*following him*). Dont be frightened. (*She pins the badge on the steps back towards the table, shewing him to the others.*) There! It's not much for £5000, is it?

MRS. BAINES. Barbara: if you wont come and pray with us, promise me you will pray for us.

BARBARA. I cant pray now. Perhaps I shall never pray again.

MRS. BAINES. Barbara!

JENNY. Major!

BARBARA (*almost delirious*). I cant bear any more. Quick march!

CUSINS (*calling to the procession in the street outside*). Off we go. Play up, there! I m m e n s o g i u b i l o. (*He gives the time with his drum; and the band strikes up the march, which rapidly becomes more distant as the procession moves briskly away.*)

MRS. BAINES. I must go, dear. Youre overworked: you will be all right tomorrow. We'll never lose you. Now Jenny: step out with the old flag. Blood and Fire! (*She marches out through the gate with her flag.*)

JENNY. Glory Hallelujah! (*flourishing her tambourine and marching*).

UNDERSHAFT (*to Cusins, as he marches out past him easing the slide of his trombone*). "My ducats and my daughter"!

CUSINS (*following him out*). Money and gunpowder!

BARBARA. Drunkenness and Murder! My God: why hast thou forsaken me?

She sinks on the form with her face buried in her hands. The march passes away into silence. Bill Walker steals across to her.

BILL (*taunting*). Wot prawce Selvytion nah?

SHIRLEY. Dont you hit her when shes down.

BILL. She it me wen aw wiz dahn. Waw shouldnt I git a bit o me own back?

BARBARA (*raising her head*). I didnt take your money, Bill. (*She crosses the yard to the gate and turns her back on the two men to hide her face from them.*)

BILL (*sneering after her*). Naow, it warnt enough for you. (*Turning to the drum, he misses the money.*) Ellow! If you aint took it summun else az. Weres it gorn? Blame me if Jenny Ill didnt take it arter all!

RUMMY (*screaming at him from the loft*). You lie, you dirty blackguard! Snobby Price pinched it off the drum wen e took ap iz cap. I was ap ere all the time an see im do it.

BILL. Wot! Stowl maw money! Waw didnt you call thief on him, you silly old mucker you?

RUMMY. To serve you aht for ittin me acrost the fice. It's cost y'pahnd, that az. (*Raising a pæan of squalid triumph*) I done you. I'm even with you. Ive ad it aht o y— (*Bill snatches up Shirley's mug and hurls it at her. She slams the loft door and vanishes. The mug smashes against the door and falls in fragments.*)

BILL (*beginning to chuckle*). Tell us, ole man, wot o'clock this mornin was it wen im as they call Snobby Prawce was sived?

BARBARA (*turning to him more composedly, and with unspoiled sweetness*). About half past twelve, Bill. And he pinched your pound at a quarter to two. *I* know. Well, you cant afford to lose it. I'll send it to you.

BILL (*his voice and accent suddenly improving*). Not if I was to starve for it. *I* aint to be bought.

SHIRLEY. Aint you? Youd sell yourself to the devil for a pint o beer; ony there aint no devil to make the offer.

BILL (*unshamed*). So I would, mate, and often av, cheerful. But s h e cawnt buy me. (*Approaching Barbara*) You wanted my soul, did you? Well, you aint got it.

BARBARA. I nearly got it, Bill. But weve sold it back to you for ten thousand pounds.

SHIRLEY. And dear at the money!

BARBARA. No, Peter: it was worth more than money.

BILL (*salvationproof*). It's no good: you cawnt get rahnd me nah. I dont blieve in it; and Ive seen today that I was right. (*Going*) So long, old soupkitchener! Ta, ta, Major Earl's Grendorter! (*Turning at the gate*) Wot prawce Selvytion nah? Snobby Prawce! Ha! ha!

BARBARA (*offering her hand*). Goodbye, Bill.

BILL (*taken aback, half plucks his cap off; then shoves it on again defiantly*). Git aht. (*Barbara drops her hand, discouraged. He has a twinge of remorse.*) But thets aw rawt, you knaow. Nathink pasnl. Naow mellice. So long, Judy. (*He goes.*)

BARBARA. No malice. So long, Bill.

SHIRLEY (*shaking his head*). You make too much of him, Miss, in your innocence.

BARBARA (*going to him*). Peter: I'm like you now. Cleaned out, and lost my job.

SHIRLEY. Youve youth an hope. Thats two better than me.

BARBARA. I'll get you a job, Peter. Thats hope for you: the youth will have to be enough for me. (*She counts her money.*) I have just enough left for two teas at Lockharts, a Rowton doss for you, and my tram and bus home. (*He frowns and rises with offended pride. She takes his arm.*) Dont be proud, Peter: it's sharing between friends. And promise me youll talk to me and not let me cry. (*She draws him towards the gate.*)

SHIRLEY. Well, I'm not accustomed to talk to the like of you—

BARBARA (*urgently*). Yes, yes: you must talk to me. Tell me about Tom Paine's books and Bradlaugh's lectures. Come along.

SHIRLEY. Ah, if you would only read Tom Paine in the proper spirit, Miss! (*They go out through the gate together.*)

END OF ACT II.

ACT III

Next day after lunch Lady Britomart is writing in the library in Wilton Crescent. Sarah is reading in the armchair near the window. Barbara, in ordinary dress, pale and brooding, is on the settee. Charles Lomax enters. Coming forward between the settee and the writing-table, he starts on seeing Barbara fashionably attired and in low spirits.

LOMAX. Youve left off your uniform!

Barbara says nothing; but an expression of pain passes over her face.

LADY BRITOMART (*warning him in low tones to be careful*). Charles!

LOMAX (*much concerned, sitting down sympathetically on the settee beside Barbara*). I'm awfully sorry, Barbara. You know I helped you all I could with the concertina and so forth. (*Momentously*) Still, I have never shut my eyes to the fact that there is a certain amount of tosh about the Salvation Army. Now the claims of the Church of England—

LADY BRITOMART. Thats enough, Charles. Speak of something suited to your mental capacity.

LOMAX. But surely the Church of England is suited to all our capacities.

BARBARA (*pressing his hand*). Thank you for your sympathy, Cholly. Now go and spoon with Sarah.

LOMAX (*rising and going to Sarah*). How is my ownest today?

SARAH. I wish you wouldnt tell Cholly to do things, Barbara. He always comes straight and does them. Cholly: we're going to the works at Perivale St. Andrews this afternoon.

LOMAX. What works?

SARAH. The cannon works.

LOMAX. What! Your governor's shop!

SARAH. Yes.

LOMAX. Oh I say!

Cusins enters in poor condition. He also starts visibly when he sees Barbara without her uniform.

BARBARA. I expected you this morning, Dolly. Didnt you guess that?

CUSINS (*sitting down beside her*). I'm sorry. I have only just breakfasted.

SARAH. But weve just finished lunch.

BARBARA. Have you had one of your bad nights?

CUSINS. No: I had rather a good night: in fact, one of the most remarkable nights I have ever passed.

BARBARA. The meeting?

CUSINS. No: after the meeting.

LADY BRITOMART. You should have gone to bed after the meeting. What were you doing?

CUSINS. Drinking.

LADY BRITOMART.	Adolphus!
SARAH.	Dolly!
BARBARA.	Dolly!
LOMAX.	Oh I say!

LADY BRITOMART. What were you drinking, may I ask?

CUSINS. A most devilish kind of Spanish burgundy, warranted free from added alcohol: a Temperance burgundy in fact. Its richness in natural alcohol made any addition superfluous.

BARBARA. Are you joking, Dolly?

CUSINS (*patiently*). No. I have been making a night of it with the nominal head of this household: that is all.

LADY BRITOMART. Andrew made you drunk!

CUSINS. No: he only provided the wine. I think it was Dionysos who made me drunk. (*To Barbara*) I told you I was possessed.

LADY BRITOMART. Youre not sober yet. Go home to bed at once.

CUSINS. I have never before ventured to reproach you, Lady Brit; but how could you marry the Prince of Darkness?

LADY BRITOMART. It was much more excusable to marry him than to get drunk with him. That is a new accomplishment of Andrew's, by the way. He usent to drink.

CUSINS. He doesnt now. He only sat there and completed the wreck of my moral basis, the rout of my convictions, the purchase of my soul. He cares for you, Barbara. That is what makes him so dangerous to me.

BARBARA. That has nothing to do with it, Dolly. There are larger loves and diviner dreams than the fireside ones. You know that, dont you?

CUSINS. Yes: that is our understanding. I know it. I hold to it. Unless he can win me on that holier ground he may amuse me for a while; but he can get no deeper hold, strong as he is.

BARBARA. Keep to that; and the end will be right. Now tell me what happened at the meeting?

CUSINS. It was an amazing meeting. Mrs. Baines almost died of emotion. Jenny Hill went stark mad with hysteria. The Prince of Darkness played his trombone like a madman: its brazen roarings were like the laughter of the damned. 117 conversions took place then and there. They prayed with the most touching sincerity and gratitude for Bodger, and for the anonymous donor of the £5000. Your father would not let his name be given.

LOMAX. That was rather fine of the old man, you know. Most chaps would have wanted the advertisement.

CUSINS. He said all the charitable institutions would be down on him like kites on a battle field if he gave his name.

LADY BRITOMART. Thats Andrew all over. He never does a proper thing without giving an improper reason for it.

CUSINS. He convinced me that I have all my life been doing improper things for proper reasons.

LADY BRITOMART. Adolphus: now that Barbara has left the Salvation Army, you had better leave it too. I will not have you playing that drum in the streets.

CUSINS. Your orders are already obeyed, Lady Brit.

BARBARA. Dolly: were you ever really in earnest about it? Would you have joined if you had never seen me?

CUSINS (*disingenuously*). Well—er—well, possibly, as a collector of religions—

LOMAX (*cunningly*). Not as a drummer, though, you know. You are a very clearheaded brainy chap, Dolly; and it must have been apparent to you that there is a certain amount of tosh about—

LADY BRITOMART. Charles: if you must drivel, drivel like a grown-up man and not like a schoolboy.

LOMAX (*out of countenance*). Well, drivel is drivel, dont you know, whatever a man's age.

LADY BRITOMART. In good society in England, Charles, men drivel at all ages by repeating silly formulas with an air of wisdom. Schoolboys make their own formulas out of slang, like you. When they reach your age, and get political private secretaryships and things of that sort, they drop slang and get their formulas out of The Spectator or The Times. Y o u had better confine yourself to The Times. You will find that there is a certain amount of tosh about The Times; but at least its language is reputable.

LOMAX (*overwhelmed*). You are so awfully strong-minded, Lady Brit—

LADY BRITOMART. Rubbish! (*Morrison comes in.*) What is it?

MORRISON. If you please, my lady, Mr. Undershaft has just drove up to the door.

LADY BRITOMART. Well, let him in. (*Morrison hesitates.*) Whats the matter with you?

MORRISON. Shall I announce him, my lady; or is he at home here, so to speak, my lady?

LADY BRITOMART. Announce him.

MORRISON. Thank you, my lady. You wont mind my asking, I hope. The occasion is in a manner of speaking new to me.

LADY BRITOMART. Quite right. Go and let him in.

MORRISON. Thank you, my lady. (*He withdraws.*)

LADY BRITOMART. Children: go and get ready. (*Sarah and Barbara go upstairs for their out-of-door wraps.*) Charles: go and tell Stephen to come down here in five minutes: you will find him in the drawing room. (*Charles goes.*) Adolphus: tell them to send round the carriage in about fifteen minutes. (*Adolphus goes.*)

MORRISON (*at the door*). Mr. Undershaft.

Undershaft comes in. Morrison goes out.

UNDERSHAFT. Alone! How fortunate!

LADY BRITOMART (*rising*). Dont be sentimental, Andrew. Sit down. (*She sits on the settee; he sits beside her, on her left. She comes to the point before he has time to breathe.*) Sarah must have £800 a year until Charles Lomax comes into his property. Barbara will need more, and need it permanently, because Adolphus hasnt any property.

UNDERSHAFT (*resignedly*). Yes, my dear: I will see to it. Anything else? for yourself, for instance?

LADY BRITOMART. I want to talk to you about Stephen.

UNDERSHAFT (*rather wearily*). Dont, my dear. Stephen doesnt interest me.

LADY BRITOMART. He does interest me. He is our son.

UNDERSHAFT. Do you really think so? He has induced us to bring him into the world; but he chose his parents very incongruously, I think. I see nothing of myself in him, and less of you.

LADY BRITOMART. Andrew: Stephen is an excellent son, and a most steady, capable, highminded young man. You are simply trying to find an excuse for disinheriting him.

UNDERSHAFT. My dear Biddy: the Undershaft tradition disinherits him. It would be dishonest of me to leave the cannon foundry to my son.

LADY BRITOMART. It would be most unnatural and improper of you to leave it anyone else, Andrew. Do you suppose this wicked and immoral tradition can be kept up for ever? Do you pretend that Stephen could not carry on the foundry just as well as all the other sons of the big business houses?

UNDERSHAFT. Yes: he could learn the office routine without understanding the business, like all the other sons; and the firm would go on by its own momentum until the real Undershaft—probably an Italian or a German—would invent a new method and cut him out.

LADY BRITOMART. There is nothing that any Italian or German could do that Stephen could not do. And Stephen at least has breeding.

UNDERSHAFT. The son of a foundling! nonsense!

LADY BRITOMART. My son, Andrew! And even you may have good blood in your veins for all you know.

UNDERSHAFT. True. Probably I have. That is another argument in favor of a foundling.

LADY BRITOMART. Andrew: dont be aggravating. And dont be wicked. At present you are both.

UNDERSHAFT. This conversation is part of the Undershaft tradition, Biddy. Every Undershaft's wife has treated him to it ever since the house was founded. It is mere waste of breath. If the tradition be ever broken it will be for an abler man than Stephen.

LADY BRITOMART (*pouting*). Then go away.

UNDERSHAFT (*deprecatory*). Go away!

LADY BRITOMART. Yes: go away. If you will do nothing for Stephen, you are not wanted here. Go to your foundling, whoever he is; and look after him.

UNDERSHAFT. The fact is, Biddy—

LADY BRITOMART. Dont call me Biddy. I dont call you Andy.

UNDERSHAFT. I will not call my wife Britomart: it is not good sense. Seriously, my love, the Undershaft tradition has landed me in a difficulty. I am getting on in years; and my partner Lazarus has at last made a stand and insisted that the succession must be settled one way or the other; and of course he is quite right. You see, I havnt found a fit successor yet.

LADY BRITOMART (*obstinately*). There is Stephen.

UNDERSHAFT. Thats just it: all the foundlings I can find are exactly like Stephen.

LADY BRITOMART. Andrew!!

UNDERSHAFT. I want a man with no relations and no schooling: that is, a man who would be out of the running altogether if he were not a strong man. And I cant find him. Every blessed foundling nowadays is snapped up in his infancy by Barnardo homes, or School Board officers, or Boards of Guardians; and if he shews the least ability, he is fastened on by schoolmasters; trained to win scholarships like a racehorse; crammed with secondhand ideas; drilled and disciplined in docility and what they call good taste; and lamed for life so that he is fit for nothing but teaching. If you want to keep the foundry in the family, you had better find an eligible foundling and marry him to Barbara.

LADY BRITOMART. Ah! Barbara! Your pet! You would sacrifice Stephen to Barbara.

UNDERSHAFT. Cheerfully. And you, my dear, would boil Barbara to make soup for Stephen.

LADY BRITOMART. Andrew: this is not a question of our likings and dislikings: it is a question of duty. It is your duty to make Stephen your successor.

UNDERSHAFT. Just as much as it is your duty to submit to your husband. Come, Biddy! these tricks of the governing class are of no use with me. I am one of the governing class myself; and it is waste of time giving tracts to a missionary. I have the power in this matter; and I am not to be humbugged into using it for your purposes.

LADY BRITOMART. Andrew: you can talk my head off; but you cant change wrong into right. And your tie is all on one side. Put it straight.

UNDERSHAFT (*disconcerted*). It wont stay unless it's pinned —(*He fumbles at it with childish grimaces.*)

Stephen comes in.

STEPHEN (*at the door*). I beg your pardon (*about to retire*).

LADY BRITOMART. No: come in, Stephen. (*Stephen comes forward to his mother's writing-table.*)

UNDERSHAFT (*not very cordially*). Good afternoon.

STEPHEN (*coldly*). Good afternoon.

UNDERSHAFT (*to Lady Britomart*). He knows all about the tradition, I suppose?

LADY BRITOMART. Yes. (*To Stephen.*) It is what I told you last night, Stephen.

UNDERSHAFT (*sulkily*). I understand you want to come into the cannon business.

STEPHEN. *I* go into trade! Certainly not.

UNDERSHAFT (*opening his eyes, greatly eased in mind and manner*). Oh! in that case—!

LADY BRITOMART. Cannons are not trade, Stephen. They are enterprise.

STEPHEN. I have no intention of becoming a man of business in any sense. I have no capacity for business and no taste for it. I intend to devote myself to politics.

UNDERSHAFT (*rising*). My dear boy: this is an immense relief to me. And I trust it may prove an equally good thing for the country. I was afraid you would consider yourself disparaged and slighted. (*He moves towards Stephen as if to shake hands with him.*)

LADY BRITOMART (*rising and interposing*). Stephen: I cannot allow you to throw away an enormous property like this.

STEPHEN (*stiffly*). Mother: there must be an end of treating me as a child, if you please. (*Lady Britomart recoils, deeply wounded by his tone.*) Until last night I did not take your attitude seriously, because I did not think you meant it seriously. But I find now that you left me in the dark as to matters which you should have explained to me years ago. I am extremely hurt and offended. Any further discussion of my intentions had better take place with my father, as between one man and another.

LADY BRITOMART. Stephen! (*She sits down again; and her eyes fill with tears.*)

UNDERSHAFT (*with grave compassion*). You see, my dear, it is only the big men who can be treated as children.

STEPHEN. I am sorry, mother, that you have forced me—

UNDERSHAFT (*stopping him*). Yes, yes, yes, yes: thats all right, Stephen. She wont interfere with you any more: your independence is achieved: you have won your latchkey. Dont rub it in; and above all, dont apologize. (*He resumes his seat.*) Now what about your future, as between one man and another—I beg your pardon, Biddy: as between two men and a woman.

LADY BRITOMART (*who has pulled herself together strongly*). I quite understand, Stephen. By all means go your own way if you feel strong enough. (*Stephen sits down magisterially in the chair at the writing-table with an air of affirming his majority.*)

UNDERSHAFT. It is settled that you do not ask for the succession to the cannon business.

STEPHEN. I hope it is settled that I repudiate the cannon business.

UNDERSHAFT. Come, come! dont be so devilishly sulky: it's boyish. Freedom should be generous. Besides, I owe you a fair start in life in exchange for disinheriting you. You cant become prime minister all at once. Havnt you a turn for something? What about literature, art and so forth?

STEPHEN. I have nothing of the artist about me, either in faculty or character, thank Heaven!

UNDERSHAFT. A philosopher, perhaps? Eh?

STEPHEN. I make no such ridiculous pretension.

UNDERSHAFT. Just so. Well, there is the army, the navy, the Church, the Bar. The Bar requires some ability. What about the Bar?

STEPHEN. I have not studied law. And I am afraid I have not the necessary push—I believe that is the name barristers give to their vulgarity—for success in pleading.

UNDERSHAFT. Rather a difficult case, Stephen. Hardly anything left but the stage, is there? (*Stephen makes an impatient movement.*) Well, come! is there a n y t h i n g you know or care for?

STEPHEN (*rising and looking at him steadily*). I know the difference between right and wrong.

UNDERSHAFT (*hugely tickled*). You dont say so! What! no capacity for business, no knowledge of law, no sympathy with art, no pretension to philosophy; only a simple knowledge of the secret that has puzzled all the philosophers, baffled all the lawyers, muddled all the men of business, and ruined most of the artists: the secret of right and wrong. Why, man, youre a genius, a master of masters, a god! At twenty-four, too!

STEPHEN (*keeping his temper with difficulty*). You are pleased to be facetious. I pretend to nothing more than any honorable English gentleman claims as his birthright. (*He sits down angrily.*)

UNDERSHAFT. Oh, thats everybody's birthright. Look at poor little Jenny Hill, the Salvation lassie! she would think you were laughing at her if you asked her to stand up in the street and teach grammar or geography or mathematics or even drawingroom dancing; but it never occurs to her to doubt that she can teach morals and religion. You are all alike, you respectable people. You cant tell me the bursting strain of a ten-inch gun, which is a very simple matter; but you all think you can tell me the bursting strain of a man under temptation. You darent handle high explosives; but youre all ready to handle honesty and truth and justice and the whole duty of man, and kill one another at that game. What a country! what a world!

LADY BRITOMART (*uneasily*). What do you think he had better do, Andrew?

UNDERSHAFT. Oh, just what he wants to do. He knows nothing; and he thinks he knows everything. That points clearly to a political career. Get him a private secretaryship to someone who can get him an Under Secretaryship; and then leave him alone. He will find his natural and proper place in the end on the Treasury bench.

STEPHEN (*springing up again*). I am sorry, sir, that you force me to forget the respect due to you as my father. I am an Englishman; and I will not hear the Government of my country insulted. (*He thrusts his hands in his pockets, and walks angrily across to the window.*)

UNDERSHAFT (*with a touch of brutality*). The government of your country! *I* am the government of your country: I, and Lazarus. Do you suppose that you and half a dozen amateurs like you, sitting in a row in that foolish gabble shop, can govern Undershaft and Lazarus? No, my friend: you will do what pays u s. You will make war when it suits us, and keep peace when it doesnt. You will find out that trade requires certain measures when we have decided on those measures. When I want anything to keep my dividends up, you will discover that my want is a national need. When other people want something to keep my dividends down, you will call out the police and military. And in return you shall have the support and applause of my newspapers, and the delight of imagining that you are a great statesman. Government of your country! Be off with you, my boy, and play with your caucuses and leading articles and historic parties and great leaders and burning questions and the rest of your toys. *I* am going back to my counting house to pay the piper and call the tune.

STEPHEN (*actually smiling, and putting his hand on his father's shoulder with indulgent patronage*). Really, my dear father, it is impossible to be angry with you. You don't know how absurd all this sounds to me. You are very properly proud of having been industrious enough to make money; and it is greatly to your credit that you have made so much of it. But it has kept you in circles where you are valued for your money and deferred to for it, instead of in the doubtless very old-fashioned and behind-the-times public school and university where I formed my habits of mind. It is natural for you to think that money governs England; but you must allow me to think I know better.

UNDERSHAFT. And what d o e s govern England, pray?

STEPHEN. Character, father, character.

UNDERSHAFT. Whose character? Yours or mine?

STEPHEN. Neither yours nor mine, father, but the best elements in the English national character.

UNDERSHAFT. Stephen: Ive found your profession for you. Youre a born journalist. I'll start with a high-toned weekly review. There!

Stephen goes to the smaller writing-table and busies himself with his letters.

Sarah, Barbara, Lomax, and Cusins come in ready for walking. Barbara crosses the room to the window and looks out. Cusins drifts amiably to the armchair, and Lomax remains near the door, whilst Sarah comes to her mother.

SARAH. Go and get ready, mamma: the carriage is waiting. (*Lady Britomart leaves the room.*)

UNDERSHAFT (*to Sarah*). Good day, my dear. Good afternoon, Mr. Lomax.

LOMAX (*vaguely*). Ahdedoo.

UNDERSHAFT (*to Cusins*). Quite well after last night, Euripides, eh?

CUSINS. As well as can be expected.

UNDERSHAFT. Thats right. (*To Barbara*) So you are coming to see my death and devastation factory, Barbara?

BARBARA (*at the window*). You came yesterday to see my salvation factory. I promised you a return visit.

LOMAX (*coming forward between Sarah and Undershaft*). Youll find it awfully interesting. Ive been through the Woolwich Arsenal; and it gives you a ripping feeling of security, you know, to think of the lot of beggars we could kill if it came to fighting. (*To Undershaft, with sudden solemnity*) Still, it must be rather an awful reflection for you, from the religious point of view as it were. Youre getting on, you know, and all that.

SARAH. You dont mind Cholly's imbecility, papa, do you?

LOMAX (*much taken aback*). Oh I say!

UNDERSHAFT. Mr. Lomax looks at the matter in a very proper spirit, my dear.

LOMAX. Just so. Thats all I meant, I assure you.

SARAH. Are you coming, Stephen?

STEPHEN. Well, I am rather busy—er— (*Magnanimously*) Oh well, yes: I'll come. That is, if there is room for me.

UNDERSHAFT. I can take two with me in a little motor I am experimenting with for field use. You wont mind its being rather unfashionable. It's not painted yet; but it's bullet proof.

LOMAX (*appalled at the prospect of confronting Wilton Crescent in an unpainted motor*). Oh I s a y!

SARAH. The carriage for me, thank you. Barbara doesnt mind what shes seen in.

LOMAX. I say, Dolly old chap: do you really mind the car being a guy? Because of course if you do I'll go in it. Still—

CUSINS. I prefer it.

LOMAX. Thanks awfully, old man. Come, Sarah. (*He hurries out to secure his seat in the carriage. Sarah follows him.*)

CUSINS (*moodily walking across to Lady Britomart's writing-table*). Why are we two coming to this Works Department of Hell? that is what I ask myself.

BARBARA. I have always thought of it as a sort of pit where lost creatures with blackened faces stirred up smoky fires and were driven and tormented by my father? Is it like that, dad?

UNDERSHAFT (*scandalized*). My dear! It is a spotlessly clean and beautiful hillside town.

CUSINS. With a Methodist chapel? Oh do say theres a Methodist chapel.

UNDERSHAFT. There are two: a Primitive one and a sophisticated one. There is even an Ethical Society; but it is not much patronized, as my men are all strongly religious. In the High Explosives Sheds they object to the presence of Agnostics as unsafe.

CUSINS. And yet they dont object to you!

BARBARA. Do they obey all your orders?

UNDERSHAFT. I never give them any orders. When I speak to one of them it is "Well, Jones, is the baby doing well? and has Mrs. Jones made a good recovery?" "Nicely, thank you, sir." And thats all.

CUSINS. But Jones has to be kept in order. How do you maintain discipline among your men?

UNDERSHAFT. I dont. They do. You see, the one thing Jones wont stand is any rebellion from the man under him, or any assertion of social equality between the wife of the man with 4 shillings a week less than himself, and Mrs. Jones! Of course they all rebel against me, theoretically. Practically, every man of them keeps the man just below him in his place. I never meddle with them. I never bully them. I dont even bully Lazarus. I say that certain things are to be done; but I dont order anybody to do them. I dont say, mind you, that there is no ordering about and snubbing and even bullying. The men snub the boys and order them about; the carmen snub the sweepers; the artisans snub the unskilled laborers; the foremen drive and bully both the laborers and artisans; the assistant engineers find fault with the foremen; the chief engineers drop on the assistants; the departmental managers worry the chiefs; and the clerks have tall hats and hymnbooks and keep up the social tone by refusing to associate on equal terms with anybody. The result is a colossal profit, which comes to me.

CUSINS (*revolted*). You really are a—well, what I was saying yesterday.

BARBARA. What was he saying yesterday?

UNDERSHAFT. Never mind, my dear. He thinks I have made you unhappy. Have I?

BARBARA. Do you think I can be happy in this vulgar silly dress? I! who have worn the uniform. Do you understand what you have done to me? Yesterday I had a man's soul in my hand. I set him in the way of life with his face to salvation. But when we took your money he turned back to drunkenness and derision. (*With intense conviction*) I will never forgive you that. If I had a child, and you destroyed its body with your explosives—if you murdered Dolly with your horrible guns—I could forgive you if my forgiveness would open the gates of heaven to you. But to take a human soul from me, and turn it into the soul of a wolf! that is worse than any murder.

UNDERSHAFT. Does my daughter despair so easily? Can you strike a man to the heart and leave no mark on him?

BARBARA (*her face lighting up*). Oh, you are right: he can never be lost now: where was my faith?

CUSINS. Oh, clever clever devil!

BARBARA. You may be a devil; but God speaks through you sometimes. (*She takes her father's hands and kisses them.*) You have given me back my happiness: I feel it deep down now, though my spirit is troubled.

UNDERSHAFT. You have learnt something. That always feels at first as if you had lost something.

BARBARA. Well, take me to the factory of death, and let me learn something more. There must be some truth or other behind all this frightful irony. Come, Dolly. (*She goes out.*)

CUSINS. My guardian angel! (*To Undershaft*) Avaunt! (*He follows Barbara.*)

STEPHEN (*quietly, at the writing-table*). You must not mind Cusins, father. He is a very amiable good fellow; but he is a Greek scholar and naturally a little eccentric.

UNDERSHAFT. Ah, quite so. Thank you, Stephen. Thank you. (*He goes out.*)

Stephen smiles patronizingly; buttons his coat responsibly; and crosses the room to the door. Lady Britomart, dressed for out-of-doors, opens it before he reaches it. She looks round for the others; looks at Stephen; and turns to go without a word.

STEPHEN (*embarrassed*). Mother—

LADY BRITOMART. Dont be apologetic, Stephen. And dont forget that you have outgrown your mother. (*She goes out.*)

Perivale St. Andrews lies between two Middlesex hills, half climbing the northern one. It is an almost smokeless town of white walls, roofs of narrow green slates or red tiles, tall trees, domes, campaniles, and slender chimney shafts, beautifully situated and beautiful in itself. The best view of it is obtained from the crest of a slope about half a mile to the east, where the high explosives are dealt with. The foundry lies hidden in the depths between, the tops of its chimneys sprouting like huge skittles into the middle distance. Across the crest runs a platform of concrete, with a parapet which suggests a fortification, because there is a huge cannon of the obsolete Woolwich Infant pattern peering across it at the town. The cannon is mounted on an experimental gun carriage: possibly the original model of the Undershaft disappearing rampart gun alluded to by Stephen. The parapet has a high step inside which serves as a seat.

Barbara is leaning over the parapet, looking towards the town. On her right is the cannon; on her left the end of a shed raised on piles, with a ladder of three or four steps up to the door, which opens outwards and has a little wooden landing at the threshold, with a fire bucket in the corner of the landing. The parapet stops short of the shed, leaving a gap which is the beginning of the path down the hill through the foundry to the town. Behind the cannon is a trolley carrying a huge conical bombshell, with a red band painted on it. Further from the parapet, on the same side, is a deck chair, near the door of an office, which, like the sheds, is of the lightest possible construction.*

Cusins arrives by the path from the town.

BARBARA. Well?

CUSINS. Not a ray of hope. Everything perfect, wonderful, real. It only needs a cathedral to be a heavenly city instead of a hellish one.

BARBARA. Have you found out whether they have done anything for old Peter Shirley.

CUSINS. They have found him a job as gatekeeper and timekeeper. He's frightfully miserable. He calls the timekeeping brainwork, and says he isnt used to it; and his gate lodge is so splendid that hes ashamed to use the rooms, and skulks in the scullery.

BARBARA. Poor Peter!

---

*When *Major Barbara* was reprinted in Shaw's *Complete Plays* (1931), Shaw added at this point a comment to the effect that "several dummy soldiers, more or less mutilated," are partly visible under the landing, and additional dummies are near the shed and on the emplacement.

Stephen arrives from the town. He carries a fieldglass.

STEPHEN (*enthusiastically*). Have you two seen the place? Why did you leave us?

CUSINS. I wanted to see everything I was not intended to see; and Barbara wanted to make the men talk.

STEPHEN. Have you found anything discreditable?

CUSINS. No. They call him Dandy Andy and are proud of his being a cunning old rascal; but it's all horribly, frightfully, immorally, unanswerably perfect.

Sarah arrives.

SARAH. Heavens! what a place! (*She crosses the trolley.*) Did you see the nursing home!? (*She sits down on the shell.*)

STEPHEN. Did you see the libraries and schools!?

SARAH. Did you see the ball room and the banqueting chamber in the Town Hall!?

STEPHEN. Have you gone into the insurance fund, the pension fund, the building society, the various applications of co-operation!?

Undershaft comes from the office, with a sheaf of telegrams in his hands.

UNDERSHAFT. Well, have you seen everything? I'm sorry I was called away. (*Indicating the telegrams*) News from Manchuria.

STEPHEN. Good news, I hope.

UNDERSHAFT. Very.

STEPHEN. Another Japanese victory?

UNDERSHAFT. Oh, I dont know. Which side wins does not concern us here. No: the good news is that the aerial battleship is a tremendous success. At the first trial it has wiped out a fort with three hundred soldiers in it.

CUSINS (*from the platform*). Dummy soldiers?

UNDERSHAFT. No: the real thing. (*Cusins and Barbara exchange glances. Then Cusins sits on the step and buries his face in his hands. Barbara gravely lays her hand on his shoulder, and he looks up at her in a sort of whimsical desperation.*) Well, Stephen, what do you think of the place?

STEPHEN. Oh, magnificent. A perfect triumph of organization. Frankly, my dear father, I have been a fool: I had no idea of what it all meant—of the wonderful forethought, the power of organization, the administrative capacity, the financial genius, the colossal capital it represents. I have been repeating to myself as I came through your streets "Peace hath her victories no less renowned than War." I have only one misgiving about it all.

UNDERSHAFT. Out with it.

STEPHEN. Well, I cannot help thinking that all this provision for every want of your workmen may sap their independence and weaken their sense of responsibility. And greatly as we enjoyed our tea at that splendid restaurant—how they gave us all that luxury and cake and jam and cream for threepence I really cannot imagine!—still you must remember that restaurants break up home life. Look at the continent, for instance! Are you sure so much pampering is really good for the men's characters?

UNDERSHAFT. Well you see, my dear boy, when you are organizing civilization you have to make up your mind whether trouble and anxiety are good things or not. If you decide that they are, then, I take it, you simply dont organize civilization; and there you are, with trouble and anxiety enough to make us all angels! But if you decide the other way, you may as well go through with it. However, Stephen, our characters are safe here. A sufficient dose of anxiety is always provided by the fact that we may be blown to smithereens at any moment.

SARAH. By the way, papa, where do you make the explosives?

UNDERSHAFT. In separate little sheds, like that one. When one of them blows up, it costs very little; and only the people quite close to it are killed.

Stephen, who is quite close to it, looks at it rather scaredly, and moves away quickly to the cannon. At the same moment the door of the shed is thrown abruptly open; and a foreman in overalls and list slippers comes out on the little landing and holds the door open for Lomax, who appears in the doorway.

LOMAX (*with studied coolness*). My good fellow: you neednt get into a state of nerves. Nothing's going to happen to you; and I suppose it wouldnt be the end of the world if anything did. A little bit of British pluck is what y o u want, old chap. (*He descends and strolls across to Sarah.*)

UNDERSHAFT (*to the foreman*). Anything wrong, Bilton?

BILTON (*with ironic calm*). Gentleman walked into the high explosives shed and lit a cigaret, sir: thats all.

UNDERSHAFT. Ah, quite so. (*To Lomax*) Do you happen to remember what you did with the match?

LOMAX. Oh come! I'm not a fool. I took jolly good care to blow it out before I chucked it away.

BILTON. The top of it was red hot inside, sir.

LOMAX. Well, suppose it was! I didnt chuck it into any of y o u r messes.

UNDERSHAFT. Think no more of it, Mr. Lomax. By the way, would you mind lending me your matches?

LOMAX (*offering his box*). Certainly.

UNDERSHAFT. Thanks. (*He pockets the matches.*)

LOMAX (*lecturing to the company generally*). You know, these high explosives dont go off like gunpowder, except when theyre in a gun. When theyre spread loose, you can put a match to them without the least risk: they just burn quietly like a bit of paper. (*Warming to the scientific interest of the subject*) Did you know that, Undershaft? Have you ever tried?

UNDERSHAFT. Not on a large scale, Mr. Lomax. Bilton will give you a sample of guncotton when you are leaving if you ask him. You can experiment with it at home. (*Bilton looks puzzled.*)

SARAH. Bilton will do nothing of the sort, papa. I suppose it's your business to blow up the Russians and Japs; but you might really stop short of blowing up poor Cholly. (*Bilton gives it up and retires into the shed.*)

LOMAX. My ownest, there is no danger. (*He sits beside her on the shell.*)

Lady Britomart arrives from the town with a bouquet.

LADY BRITOMART (*coming impetuously between Undershaft and the deck chair*). Andrew: you shouldnt have let me see this place.

UNDERSHAFT. Why, my dear?

LADY BRITOMART. Never mind why: you shouldnt have: thats all. To think of all that (*indicating the town*) being yours! and that you have kept it to yourself all these years!

UNDERSHAFT. It does not belong to me. I belong to it. It is the Undershaft inheritance.

LADY BRITOMART. It is not. Your ridiculous cannons and that noisy banging foundry may be the Undershaft inheritance; but all that plate and linen, all that furniture and those houses and orchards and gardens belong to us. They belong to m e: they are not a man's business. I wont give them up. You must be out of your senses to throw them all away; and if you persist in such folly, I will call in a doctor.

UNDERSHAFT (*stooping to smell the bouquet*). Where did you get the flowers, my dear?

LADY BRITOMART. Your men presented them to me in your William Morris Labor Church.

CUSINS (*springing up*). Oh! It needed only that. A Labor Church!

LADY BRITOMART. Yes, with Morris's words in mosaic letters ten feet high round the dome. NO MAN IS GOOD ENOUGH TO BE ANOTHER MAN'S MASTER. The cynicism of it!

UNDERSHAFT. It shocked the men at first, I am afraid. But now they take no more notice of it than of the ten commandments in church.

LADY BRITOMART. Andrew: you are trying to put me off the subject of the inheritance by profane jokes. Well, you shant. I dont ask it any longer for Stephen: he has inherited far too much of your perversity to be fit for it. But Barbara has rights as well as Stephen. Why should not Adolphus succeed to the inheritance? I could manage the town for him; and he can look after the cannons, if they are really necessary.

UNDERSHAFT. I should ask nothing better if Adolphus were a foundling. He is exactly the sort of new blood that is wanted in English business. But hes not a foundling; and theres an end of it.

CUSINS (*diplomatically*). Not quite. (*They all turn and stare at him. He comes from the platform past the shed to Undershaft.*) I think— Mind! I am not committing myself in any way as to my future course—but I think the foundling difficulty can be got over.

UNDERSHAFT. What do you mean?

CUSINS. Well, I have something to say which is in the nature of a confession.

SARAH.
LADY BRITOMART.
BARBARA.
STEPHEN.
} Confession!

LOMAX. Oh I say!

CUSINS. Yes, a confession. Listen, all. Until I met Barbara I thought myself in the main an honorable, truthful man, because I wanted the approval of my conscience more than I wanted anything else. But the moment I saw Barbara, I wanted her far more than the approval of my conscience.

LADY BRITOMART. Adolphus!

CUSINS. It is true. You accused me yourself, Lady Brit, of joining the Army to worship Barbara; and so I did. She bought my soul like a flower at a street corner; but she bought it for herself.

UNDERSHAFT. What! Not for Dionysos or another?

CUSINS. Dionysos and all the others are in herself. I adored what was divine in her, and was therefore a true worshipper. But I was romantic about her too. I thought she was a woman of the people, and that a marriage with a professor of Greek would be far beyond the wildest social ambitions of her rank.

LADY BRITOMART. Adolphus!!

LOMAX. Oh I s a y!!!

CUSINS. When I learnt the horrible truth—

LADY BRITOMART. What do you mean by the horrible truth, pray?

CUSINS. That she was enormously rich; that her grandfather was an earl; that her father was the Prince of Darkness—

UNDERSHAFT. Chut!

CUSINS. —and that I was only an adventurer trying to catch a rich wife, then I stooped to deceive her about my birth.

BARBARA. Dolly!

LADY BRITOMART. Your birth! Now Adolphus, dont dare to make up a wicked story for the sake of these wretched cannons. Remember: I have seen photographs of your parents; and the Agent General for South Western Australia knows them personally and has assured me that they are most respectable married people.

CUSINS. So they are in Australia; but here they are outcasts. Their marriage is legal in Australia, but not in England. My mother is my father's deceased wife's sister; and in this island I am consequently a foundling. (*Sensation*) Is the subterfuge good enough, Machiavelli?

UNDERSHAFT (*thoughtfully*). Biddy: this may be a way out of the difficulty.

LADY BRITOMART. Stuff! A man cant make cannons any the better for being his own cousin instead of his proper self. (*She sits down in the deck chair with a bounce that expresses her downright contempt for their casuistry.*)

UNDERSHAFT (*to Cusins*). You are an educated man. That is against the tradition.

CUSINS. Once in ten thousand times it happens that the schoolboy is a born master of what they try to teach him. Greek has not destroyed my mind: it has nourished it. Besides, I did not learn it at an English public school.

UNDERSHAFT. Hm! Well, I cannot afford to be too particular: you have cornered the foundling market. Let it pass. You are eligible, Euripides: you are eligible.

BARBARA (*coming from the platform and interposing between Cusins and Undershaft*). Dolly: yesterday morning, when Stephen told us all about the tradition, you became very silent; and you have been strange and excited ever since. Were you thinking of your birth then?

CUSINS. When the finger of Destiny suddenly points at a man in the middle of his breakfast, it makes him thoughtful. (*Barbara turns away sadly and stands near her mother, listening perturbedly.*)

UNDERSHAFT. Aha! You have had your eye on the business, my young friend, have you?

CUSINS. Take care! There is an abyss of moral horror between me and your accursed aerial battleships.

UNDERSHAFT. Never mind the abyss for the present. Let us settle the practical details and leave your final decision open. You know that you will have to change your name. Do you object to that?

CUSINS. Would any man named Adolphus—any man called Dolly!—object to be called something else?

UNDERSHAFT. Good. Now, as to money! I propose to treat you handsomely from the beginning. You shall start at a thousand a year.

CUSINS (*with sudden heat, his spectacles twinkling with mischief*). A thousand! You dare offer a miserable thousand to the son-in-law of a millionaire! No, by Heavens, Machiavelli! you shall not cheat m e. You cannot do without me; and I can do without you. I must have two thousand five hundred a year for two years. At the end of that time, if I am a failure, I go. But if I am a success, and stay on, you must give me the other five thousand.

UNDERSHAFT. What other five thousand?

CUSINS. To make the two years up to five thousand a year. The two thousand five hundred is only half pay in case I should turn out a failure. The third year I must have ten per cent on the profits.

UNDERSHAFT (*taken aback*). Ten per cent! Why, man, do you know what my profits are?

CUSINS. Enormous, I hope: otherwise I shall require twenty-five per cent.

UNDERSHAFT. But, Mr. Cusins, this is a serious matter of business. You are not bringing any capital into the concern.

CUSINS. What! no capital! Is my mastery of Greek no capital? Is my access to the subtlest thought, the loftiest poetry yet attained by humanity, no capital? My character! my intellect! my life! my career! what Barbara calls my soul! are these no capital? Say another word; and I double my salary.

UNDERSHAFT. Be reasonable—

CUSINS (*peremptorily*). Mr. Undershaft: you have my terms. Take them or leave them.

UNDERSHAFT (*recovering himself*). Very well. I note your terms; and I offer you half.

CUSINS (*disgusted*). Half!

UNDERSHAFT (*firmly*). Half.

CUSINS. You call yourself a gentleman; and you offer me half!!

UNDERSHAFT. I do not call myself a gentleman; but I offer you half.

CUSINS. This to your future partner! your successor! your son-in-law!

BARBARA. You are selling your own soul, Dolly, not mine. Leave me out of the bargain, please.

UNDERSHAFT. Come! I will go a step further for Barbara's sake. I will give you three fifths; but that is my last word.

CUSINS. Done!

LOMAX. Done in the eye. Why, *I* only get eight hundred, you know.

CUSINS. By the way, Mac, I am a classical scholar, not an arithmetical one. Is three fifths more than half or less?

UNDERSHAFT. More, of course.

CUSINS. I would have taken two hundred and fifty. How you can succeed in business when you are willing to pay all that money to a University don who is obviously not worth a junior clerk's wages!—well! What will Lazarus say?

UNDERSHAFT. Lazarus is a gentle romantic Jew who cares for nothing but string quartets and stalls at fashionable theatres. He will get the credit of your rapacity in money matters, as he has hitherto had the credit of mine. You are a shark of the first order, Euripides. So much the better for the firm!

BARBARA. Is the bargain closed, Dolly? Does your soul belong to him now?

CUSINS. No: the price is settled: that is all. The real tug of war is still to come. What about the moral question?

LADY BRITOMART. There is no moral question in the matter at all, Adolphus. You must simply sell cannons and weapons to people whose cause is right and just, and refuse them to foreigners and criminals.

UNDERSHAFT (*determinedly*). No: none of that. You must keep the true faith of an Armorer, or you dont come in here.

CUSINS. What on earth is the true faith of an Armorer?

UNDERSHAFT. To give arms to all men who offer an honest price for them, without respect of persons or principles: to aristocrat and republican, to Nihilist and Tsar, to Capitalist and Socialist, to Protestant and Catholic, to burglar and policeman, to black man white man and yellow man, to all sorts and conditions, all nationalities, all faiths, all follies, all causes and all crimes. The first Undershaft wrote up in his shop IF GOD GAVE THE HAND, LET NOT MAN WITHHOLD THE SWORD. The second wrote up ALL HAVE THE RIGHT TO FIGHT: NONE HAVE THE RIGHT TO JUDGE. The third wrote up TO MAN THE WEAPON: TO HEAVEN THE VICTORY. The fourth had no literary turn; so he did not write up anything; but he sold cannons to Napoleon under the nose of George the Third. The fifth wrote up PEACE SHALL NOT PREVAIL SAVE WITH A SWORD IN HER HAND. The sixth, my master, was the best of all. He wrote up NOTHING IS EVER DONE IN THIS WORLD UNTIL MEN ARE PREPARED TO KILL ONE ANOTHER IF IT IS NOT DONE. After that, there was nothing left for the seventh to say. So he wrote up, simply, UNASHAMED.

CUSINS. My good Machiavelli, I shall certainly write something up on the wall; only, as I shall write it in Greek, you wont be able to read it. But as to your Armorer's faith, if I take my neck out of the noose of my own morality I am not going to put it into the noose of yours. I shall sell cannons to whom I please and refuse them to whom I please. So there!

UNDERSHAFT. From the moment when you become Andrew Undershaft, you will never do as you please again. Dont come here lusting for power, young man.

CUSINS. If power were my aim I should not come here for it. Y o u have no power.

UNDERSHAFT. None of my own, certainly.

CUSINS. I have more power than you, more will. You do not drive this place: it drives you. And what drives the place?

UNDERSHAFT (*enigmatically*). A will of which I am a part.

BARBARA (*startled*). Father! Do you know what you are saying; or are you laying a snare for my soul?

CUSINS. Dont listen to his metaphysics, Barbara. The place is driven by the most rascally part of society, the money hunters, the pleasure hunters, the military promotion hunters; and he is their slave.

UNDERSHAFT. Not necessarily. Remember the Armorer's Faith. I will take an order from a good man as cheerfully as from a bad one. If you good people prefer preaching and shirking to buying my weapons and fighting the rascals, dont blame me. I can make cannons: I cannot make courage and conviction. Bah! You tire me, Euripides, with your morality mongering. Ask Barbara: s h e understands. (*He suddenly takes Barbara's hands, and looks powerfully into her eyes.*) Tell him, my love, what power really means.

BARBARA (*hypnotized*). Before I joined the Salvation Army, I was in my own power; and the consequence was that I never knew what to do with myself. When I joined it, I had not time enough for all the things I had to do.

UNDERSHAFT (*approvingly*). Just so. And why was that, do you suppose?

BARBARA. Yesterday I should have said, because I was in the power of God. (*She resumes her self-possession, withdrawing her hands from his with a power equal to his own.*) But you came and shewed me that I was in the power of Bodger and Undershaft. Today I feel—oh! how can I put it into words? Sarah: do you remember the earthquake at Cannes, when we were little children?—how little the surprise of the first shock mattered compared to the dread and horror of waiting for the second? That is how I feel in this place today. I stood on the rock I thought eternal; and without a word of warning it reeled and crumbled under me. I was safe with an infinite wisdom watching me, an army marching to Salvation with me; and in a moment, at a stroke of your pen in a cheque book, I stood alone; and the heavens were empty. That was the first shock of the earthquake: I am waiting for the second.

UNDERSHAFT. Come, come, my daughter! dont make too much of your little tinpot tragedy. What do we do here when we spent years of work and thought and thousands of pounds of solid cash on a new gun or an aerial battleship that turns out just a hairsbreadth wrong after all? Scrap it. Scrap it without wasting another hour or another pound on it. Well, you have made for yourself something that you call a morality or a religion or what not. It doesnt fit the facts. Well, scrap it. Scrap it and get one that does fit. That is what is wrong with the world at present. It scraps its obsolete steam engines and dynamos; but it wont scrap its old prejudices and its old moralities and its old religions and its old political constitutions. Whats the result? In machinery it does very well; but in morals and religion and politics it is working at a loss that brings it nearer bankruptcy every year. Dont persist in that folly. If your old religion broke down yesterday, get a newer and a better one for tomorrow.

BARBARA. Oh how gladly I would take a better one to my soul! But you offer me a worse one. (*Turning on him with sudden vehemence*) Justify yourself: shew me some light through the darkness of this dreadful place, with its beautifully clean workshops, and respectable workmen, and model homes.

UNDERSHAFT. Cleanliness and respectability do not need justification, Barbara: they justify themselves. I see no darkness here, no dreadfulness. In your Salvation shelter I saw poverty, misery, cold and hunger. You gave them bread and treacle and dreams of heaven. I give from thirty shillings a week to twelve thousand a year. They find their own dreams; but I look after the drainage.

BARBARA. And their souls?

UNDERSHAFT. I save their souls just as I saved yours.

BARBARA (*revolted*). You saved my soul! What do you mean?

UNDERSHAFT. I fed you and clothed you and housed you. I took care that you should have money enough to live handsomely—more than enough; so that you could be wasteful, careless, generous. That saved your soul from the seven deadly sins.

BARBARA (*bewildered*). The seven deadly sins!

UNDERSHAFT. Yes, the deadly seven. (*Counting on his fingers*) Food, clothing, firing, rent, taxes, respectability and children. Nothing can lift those seven millstones from Man's neck but money; and the spirit cannot soar until the millstones are lifted. I lifted them from your spirit. I enabled Barbara to become Major Barbara; and I saved her from the crime of poverty.

CUSINS. Do you call poverty a crime?

UNDERSHAFT. The worst of crimes. All the other crimes are virtues beside it: all the other dishonors are chivalry itself by comparison. Poverty blights whole cities; spreads horrible pestilences; strikes dead the very souls of all who come within sight, sound or smell of it. What y o u call crime is nothing: a murder here and a theft there, a blow now and a curse then: what do they matter? they are only the accidents and illnesses of life: there are not fifty genuine professional criminals in London. But there are millions of poor people, abject people, dirty people, ill fed, ill clothed people. They poison us morally and physically: they kill the happiness of society: they force us to do away with our own liberties and to organize unnatural cruelties for fear they should rise against us and drag us down into their abyss. Only fools fear crime: we all fear poverty. Pah! (*turning on Barbara*) you talk of your half-saved ruffian in West Ham: you accuse me of dragging his soul back to perdition. Well, bring him to me here; and I will drag his soul back again to salvation for you. Not by words and dreams; but by thirty-eight shillings a week, a sound house in a handsome street, and a permanent job. In three weeks he will have a fancy waistcoat; in three months a tall hat and a chapel sitting; before the end of the year he will shake hands with a duchess at a Primrose League meeting, and join the Conservative Party.

BARBARA. And will he be the better for that?

UNDERSHAFT. You know he will. Dont be a hypocrite, Barbara. He will be better fed, better housed, better clothed, better behaved; and his children will be pounds heavier and bigger. That will be better than an American cloth mattress in a shelter, chopping firewood, eating bread and treacle, and being forced to kneel down from time to time to thank heaven for it: knee drill, I think you call it. It is cheap work converting starving men with a Bible in one hand and a slice of bread in the other. I will undertake to convert West Ham to Mahometanism on the same terms. Try your hand on my men: their souls are hungry because their bodies are full.

BARBARA. And leave the east end to starve?

UNDERSHAFT (*his energetic tone dropping into one of bitter and brooding remembrance*). *I* was an east ender. I moralized and starved until one day I swore that I would be a full-fed free man at all costs—that nothing should stop me except a bullet, neither reason nor morals nor the lives of other men. I said "Thou shalt starve ere I starve"; and with that word I became free and great. I was a dangerous man until I had my will: now I am a useful, beneficent, kindly person. That is the history of most self-made millionaires, I fancy. When it is the history of every Englishman we shall have an England worth living in.

LADY BRITOMART. Stop making speeches, Andrew. This is not the place for them.

UNDERSHAFT (*punctured*). My dear: I have no other means of conveying my ideas.

LADY BRITOMART. Your ideas are nonsense. You got on because you were selfish and unscrupulous.

UNDERSHAFT. Not at all. I had the strongest scruples about poverty and starvation. Your moralists are quite unscrupulous about both: they make virtues of them. I had rather be a thief than a pauper. I had rather be a murderer than a slave. I dont want to be either; but if you force the alternative on me, then, by Heaven, I'll choose the braver and more moral one. I hate poverty and slavery worse than any other crimes whatsoever. And let me tell you this. Poverty and slavery have stood up for centuries to your sermons and leading articles: they will not stand up to my machine guns. Dont preach at them: dont reason with them. Kill them.

BARBARA. Killing. Is that your remedy for everything?

UNDERSHAFT. It is the final test of conviction, the only lever strong enough to overturn a social system, the only way of saying Must. Let six hundred and seventy fools loose in the street; and three policemen can scatter them. But huddle them together in a certain house in Westminster; and let them go through certain ceremonies and call themselves certain names until at last they get the courage to kill; and your six hundred and seventy fools become a government. Your pious mob fills up ballot papers and imagines it is governing its masters; but the ballot paper that really governs is the paper that has a bullet wrapped up in it.

CUSINS. That is perhaps why, like most intelligent people, I never vote.

UNDERSHAFT. Vote! Bah! When you vote, you only change the names of the cabinet. When you shoot, you pull down governments, inaugurate new epochs, abolish old orders and set up new. Is that historically true, Mr. Learned Man, or is it not?

CUSINS. It is historically true. I loathe having to admit it. I repudiate your sentiments. I abhor your nature. I defy you in every possible way. Still, it is true. But it ought not to be true.

UNDERSHAFT. Ought, ought, ought, ought, ought! Are you going to spend your life saying ought, like the rest of our moralists? Turn your oughts into shalls, man. Come and make explosives with me. Whatever can blow men up can blow society up. The history of the world is the history of those who had courage enough to embrace this truth. Have you the courage to embrace it, Barbara?

LADY BRITOMART. Barbara, I positively forbid you to listen

to your father's abominable wickedness. And you, Adolphus, ought to know better than to go about saying that wrong things are true. What does it matter whether they are true if they are wrong?

UNDERSHAFT. What does it matter whether they are wrong if they are true?

LADY BRITOMART (*rising*). Children: come home instantly. Andrew: I am exceedingly sorry I allowed you to call on us. You are wickeder than ever. Come at once.

BARBARA (*shaking her head*). It's no use running away from wicked people, mamma.

LADY BRITOMART. It is every use. It shews your disapprobation of them.

BARBARA. It does not save them.

LADY BRITOMART. I can see that you are going to disobey me. Sarah: are you coming home or are you not?

SARAH. I daresay it's very wicked of papa to make cannons; but I dont think I shall cut him on that account.

LOMAX (*pouring oil on the troubled waters*). The fact is, you know, there is a certain amount of tosh about this notion of wickedness. It doesnt work. You must look at facts. Not that I would say a word in favor of anything wrong; but then, you see, all sorts of chaps are always doing all sorts of things; and we have to fit them in somehow, dont you know. What I mean is that you cant go cutting everybody; and thats about what it comes to. (*Their rapt attention to his eloquence makes him nervous.*) Perhaps I dont make myself clear.

LADY BRITOMART. You are lucidity itself, Charles. Because Andrew is successful and has plenty of money to give to Sarah, you will flatter him and encourage him in his wickedness.

LOMAX (*unruffled*). Well, where the carcase is, there will the eagles be gathered, dont you know. (*To Undershaft*) Eh? What?

UNDERSHAFT. Precisely. By the way, may I call you Charles?

LOMAX. Delighted. Cholly is the usual ticket.

UNDERSHAFT (*to Lady Britomart*). Biddy—

LADY BRITOMART (*violently*). Dont dare call me Biddy. Charles Lomax: you are a fool. Adolphus Cusins: you are a Jesuit. Stephen: you are a prig. Barbara: you are a lunatic. Andrew: you are a vulgar tradesman. Now you all know my opinion; and m y conscience is clear, at all events. (*She sits down again with a vehemence that almost wrecks the chair.)

UNDERSHAFT. My dear: you are the incarnation of morality. (*She snorts.*) Your conscience is clear and your duty done when you have called everybody names. Come, Euripides! it is getting late; and we all want to get home. Make up your mind.

CUSINS. Understand this, you old demon—

LADY BRITOMART. Adolphus!

UNDERSHAFT. Let him alone, Biddy. Proceed, Euripides.

CUSINS. You have me in a horrible dilemma. I want Barbara.

UNDERSHAFT. Like all young men, you greatly exaggerate the difference between one young woman and another.

BARBARA. Quite true, Dolly.

CUSINS. I also want to avoid being a rascal.

UNDERSHAFT (*with biting contempt*). You lust for personal righteousness, for self-approval, for what you call a good conscience, for what Barbara calls salvation, for what I call patronizing people who are not so lucky as yourself.

CUSINS. I do not: all the poet in me recoils from being a good man. But there are things in me that I must reckon with: pity—

UNDERSHAFT. Pity! The scavenger of misery.

CUSINS. Well, love.

UNDERSHAFT. I know. You love the needy and the outcast: you love the oppressed races, the negro, the Indian ryot, the Pole, the Irishman. Do you love the Japanese? Do you love the Germans? Do you love the English?

CUSINS. No. Every true Englishman detests the English. We are the wickedest nation on earth; and our success is a moral horror.

UNDERSHAFT. That is what comes of your gospel of love, is it?

CUSINS. May I not love even my father-in-law?

UNDERSHAFT. Who wants your love, man? By what right do you take the liberty of offering it to me? I will have your due heed and respect, or I will kill you. But your love. Damn your impertinence!

CUSINS (*grinning*). I may not be able to control my affections, Mac.

UNDERSHAFT. You are fencing, Euripides. You are weakening: your grip is slipping. Come! try your last weapon. Pity and love have broken in your hand: forgiveness is still left.

CUSINS. No: forgiveness is a beggar's refuge. I am with you there: we must pay our debts.

UNDERSHAFT. Well said. Come! you will suit me. Remember the words of Plato.

CUSINS (*starting*). Plato! Y o u dare quote Plato to m e!

UNDERSHAFT. Plato says, my friend, that society cannot be saved until either the Professors of Greek take to making gunpowder, or else the makers of gunpowder become Professors of Greek.

CUSINS. Oh, tempter, cunning tempter!

UNDERSHAFT. Come! choose, man, choose.

CUSINS. But perhaps Barbara will not marry me if I make the wrong choice.

BARBARA. Perhaps not.

CUSINS (*desperately perplexed*). You hear!

BARBARA. Father: do you love nobody?

UNDERSHAFT. I love my best friend.

LADY BRITOMART. And who is that, pray?

UNDERSHAFT. My bravest enemy. That is the man who keeps me up to the mark.

CUSINS. You know, the creature is really a sort of poet in his way. Suppose he is a great man, after all!

UNDERSHAFT. Suppose you stop talking and make up your mind, my young friend.

CUSINS. But you are driving me against my nature. I hate war.

UNDERSHAFT. Hatred is the coward's revenge for being intimidated. Dare you make war on war? Here are the means: my friend Mr. Lomax is sitting on them.

LOMAX (*springing up*). Oh I say! You dont mean that this thing is loaded, do you? My ownest: come off it.

SARAH (*sitting placidly on the shell*). If I am to be blown up, the more thoroughly it is done the better. Dont fuss, Cholly.

LOMAX (*to Undershaft, strongly remonstrant*). Your own daughter, you know.

UNDERSHAFT. So I see. (*To Cusins*) Well, my friend, may we expect you here at six tomorrow morning?

CUSINS (*firmly*). Not on any account. I will see the whole establishment blown up with its own dynamite before I will get up at five. My hours are healthy, rational hours: eleven to five.

UNDERSHAFT. Come when you please: before a week you will come at six and stay until I turn you out for the sake of your health. (*Calling*) Bilton! (*He turns to Lady Britomart, who rises.*) My dear: let us leave these two young people to themselves for a moment. (*Bilton comes from the shed.*) I am going to take you through the guncotton shed.

BILTON (*barring the way*). You cant take anything explosive in here, sir.

LADY BRITOMART. What do you mean? Are you alluding to me?

BILTON (*unmoved*). No, maam. Mr. Undershaft has the other gentleman's matches in his pocket.

LADY BRITOMART (*abruptly*). Oh! I beg your pardon. (*She goes into the shed.*)

UNDERSHAFT. Quite right, Bilton, quite right: here you are. (*He gives Bilton the box of matches.*) Come, Stephen. Come, Charles. Bring Sarah. (*He passes into the shed.*)

Bilton opens the box and deliberately drops the matches into the fire-bucket.

LOMAX. Oh I say! (*Bilton stolidly hands him the empty box.*) Infernal nonsense! Pure scientific ignorance! (*He goes in.*)

SARAH. Am I all right, Bilton?

BILTON. Youll have to put on list slippers, miss: thats all. Weve got em inside. (*She goes in.*)

STEPHEN (*very seriously to Cusins*). Dolly, old fellow, think. Think before you decide. Do you feel that you are a sufficiently practical man? It is a huge undertaking, an enormous responsibility. All this mass of business will be Greek to you.

CUSINS. Oh, I think it will be much less difficult than Greek.

STEPHEN. Well, I just want to say this before I leave you to yourselves. Dont let anything I have said about right and wrong prejudice you against this great chance in life. I have satisfied myself that the business is one of the highest character and a credit to our country. (*Emotionally*) I am very proud of my father. I—(*Unable to proceed, he presses Cusins' hand and goes hastily into the shed, followed by Bilton.*)

Barbara and Cusins, left alone together, look at one another silently.

CUSINS. Barbara: I am going to accept this offer.

BARBARA. I thought you would.

CUSINS. You understand, dont you, that I had to decide without consulting you. If I had thrown the burden of the choice on you, you would sooner or later have despised me for it.

BARBARA. Yes: I did not want you to sell your soul for me any more than for this inheritance.

CUSINS. It is not the sale of my soul that troubles me: I have sold it too often to care about that. I have sold it for a professorship. I have sold it for an income. I have sold it to escape being imprisoned for refusing to pay taxes for hangmen's ropes and unjust wars and things that I abhor. What is all human conduct but the daily and hourly sale of our souls for trifles? What I am now selling it for is neither money nor position nor comfort, but for reality and for power.

BARBARA. You know that you will have no power, and that he has none.

CUSINS. I know. It is not for myself alone. I want to make power for the world.

BARBARA. I want to make power for the world too; but it must be spiritual power.

CUSINS. I think all power is spiritual: these cannons will not go off by themselves. I have tried to make spiritual power by teaching Greek. But the world can never be really touched by a dead language and a dead civilization. The people must have power; and the people cannot have Greek. Now the power that is made here can be wielded by all men.

BARBARA. Power to burn women's houses down and kill their sons and tear their husbands to pieces.

CUSINS. You cannot have power for good without having power for evil too. Even mother's milk nourishes murderers as well as heroes. This power which only tears men's bodies to pieces has never been so horribly abused as the intellectual power, the imaginative power, the poetic, religious power than can enslave men's souls. As a teacher of Greek I gave the intellectual man weapons against the common man. I now want to give the common man weapons against the intellectual man. I love the common people. I want to arm them against the lawyer, the doctor, the priest, the literary man, the professor, the artist, and the politician, who, once in authority, are the most dangerous, disastrous, and tyrannical of all the fools, rascals, and impostors. I want a democratic power strong enough to force the intellectual oligarchy to use its genius for the general good or else perish.

BARBARA. Is there no higher power than that (*pointing to the shell*)?

CUSINS. Yes: but that power can destroy the higher powers just as a tiger can destroy a man: therefore man must master that power first. I admitted this when the Turks and Greeks were last at war. My best pupil went out to fight for Hellas. My parting gift to him was not a copy of Plato's Republic, but a revolver and a hundred Undershaft cartridges. The blood of every Turk he shot—if he shot any—is on my head as well as on Undershaft's. That act committed me to this place for ever. Your father's challenge has beaten me. Dare I make war on war? I dare. I must. I will. And now, is it all over between us?

BARBARA (*touched by his evident dread of her answer*). Silly baby Dolly! How could it be?

CUSINS (*overjoyed*). Then you—you—you— Oh for my drum! (*He flourishes imaginary drumsticks.*)

BARBARA (*angered by his levity*). Take care, Dolly, take care. Oh, if only I could get away from you and from father and from it all! if I could have the wings of a dove and fly away to heaven!

CUSINS. And leave m e!

BARBARA. Yes, you, and all the other naughty mischievous children of men. But I cant. I was happy in the Salvation Army for a moment. I escaped from the world into a paradise of enthusiasms and prayer and soul saving; but the moment our money ran short, it all came back to Bodger: it was he who saved our people: he, and the Prince of Darkness, my papa. Undershaft and Bodger: their hands stretch everywhere: when we feed a starving fellow creature, it is with their bread, because there is no other bread; when we tend the sick, it is in the hospitals they endow; if we turn from the churches they build, we must kneel on the stones of the streets they pave. As long as that lasts, there is no getting away from them. Turning our backs on Bodger and Undershaft is turning our backs on life.

CUSINS. I thought you were determined to turn your back on the wicked side of life.

BARBARA. There is no wicked side: life is all one. And I never wanted to shirk my share in whatever evil must be endured, whether it be sin or suffering. I wish I could cure you of middle-class ideas, Dolly.

CUSINS (*gasping*). Middle cl—! A snub! A social snub to me! from the daughter of a foundling!

BARBARA. That is why I have no class, Dolly: I come straight out of the heart of the whole people. If I were middle-class I should turn my back on my father's business; and we should both live in an artistic drawingroom, with you reading the reviews in one corner, and I in the other at the piano, playing Schumann: both very superior persons, and neither of us a bit of use. Sooner than that, I would sweep out the guncotton shed, or be one of Bodger's barmaids. Do you know what would have happened if you had refused papa's offer?

CUSINS. I wonder!

BARBARA. I should have given you up and married the man who accepted it. After all, my dear old mother has more sense than any of you. I felt like her when I saw this place—felt that I must have it—that never, never, never could I let it go; only she thought it was the houses and the kitchen ranges and the linen and china, when it was really all the human souls to be saved: not weak souls in starved bodies, crying with gratitude for a scrap of bread and treacle, but fullfed, quarrelsome, snobbish, uppish creatures, all standing on their little rights and dignities, and thinking that my father ought to be greatly obliged to them for making so much money for him—and so he ought. That is where salvation is really wanted. My father shall never throw it in my teeth again that my converts were bribed with bread. (*She is transfigured.*) I have got rid of the bribe of bread. I have got rid of the bribe of heaven. Let God's work be done for its own sake: the work he had to create us to do because it cannot be done except by living men and women. When I die, let him be in my debt, not I in his; and let me forgive him as becomes a woman of my rank.

CUSINS. Then the way of life lies through the factory of death?

BARBARA. Yes, through the raising of hell to heaven and of man to God, through the unveiling of an eternal light in the Valley of The Shadow. (*Seizing him with both hands.*) Oh, did you think my courage would never come back? did you believe that I was a deserter? that I, who have stood in the streets, and taken my people to my heart, and talked of the holiest and greatest things with them, could ever turn back and chatter foolishly to fashionable people about nothing in a drawingroom? Never, never, never, never: Major Barbara will die with the colors. Oh! and I have my dear little Dolly boy still; and he has found me my place and my work. Glory Hallelujah! (*She kisses him.*)

CUSINS. My dearest: consider my delicate health. I cannot stand as much happiness as you can.

BARBARA. Yes: it is not easy work being in love with me, is it? But it's good for you. (*She runs to the shed, and calls, childlike*) Mamma! Mamma! (*Bilton comes out of the shed, followed by Undershaft.*) I want Mamma.

UNDERSHAFT. She is taking off her list slippers, dear. (*He passes on to Cusins.*) Well? What does she say?

CUSINS. She has gone right up into the skies.

LADY BRITOMART (*coming from the shed and stopping on the steps, obstructing Sarah, who follows with Lomax. Barbara clutches like a baby at her mother's skirt.*) Barbara: when will you learn to be independent and to act and think for yourself? I know as well as possible what that cry of "Mamma, Mamma," means. Always running to me!

SARAH (*touching Lady Britomart's ribs with her finger tips and imitating a bicycle horn*). Pip! pip!

LADY BRITOMART (*highly indignant*). How dare you say Pip! pip! to me, Sarah? You are both very naughty children. What do you want, Barbara?

BARBARA. I want a house in the village to live in with Dolly. (*Dragging at the skirt.*) Come and tell me which one to take.

UNDERSHAFT (*to Cusins*). Six o'clock tomorrow morning, my young friend.

THE END

CÆSAR AND CLEOPATRA

PROLOGUE

In the doorway of the temple of Ra in Memphis. Deep gloom. An august personage with a hawk's head is mysteriously visible by his own light in the darkness within the temple. He surveys the modern audience with great contempt; and finally speaks the following words to them.

Peace! Be silent and hearken unto me, ye quaint little islanders. Give ear, ye men with white paper on your breasts and nothing written thereon (to signify the innocency of your minds). Hear me, ye women who adorn yourselves alluringly and conceal your thoughts from your men, leading them to believe that ye deem them wondrous strong and masterful whilst in truth ye hold them in your hearts as children without judgment. Look upon my hawk's head; and know that I am Ra, who was once in Egypt a mighty god. Ye cannot kneel nor prostrate yourselves; for ye are packed in rows without freedom to move, obstructing one another's vision; neither do any of ye regard it as seemly to do aught until ye see all the rest do so too; wherefore it commonly happens that in great emergencies ye do nothing, though each telleth his fellow that something must be done. I ask you not for worship, but for silence. Let not your men speak nor your women cough; for I am come to draw you back two thousand years over the graves of sixty generations. Ye poor posterity, think not that ye are the first. Other fools before ye have seen the sun rise and set, and the moon change her shape and her hour. As they were so ye are; and yet not so great, for the pyramids my people built stand to this day; whilst the dustheaps on which ye slave, and which ye call empires, scatter in the wind even as ye pile your dead sons' bodies on them to make yet more dust.

Hearken to me then, oh ye compulsorily educated ones. Know that even as there is an old England and a new, and ye stand perplexed between the twain; so in the days when I was worshipped was there an old Rome and a new, and men standing perplexed between them. And the old Rome was poor and little, and greedy and fierce, and evil in many ways; but because its mind was little and its work was simple, it knew its own mind and did its own work; and the gods pitied it and helped it and strengthened it and shielded it; for the gods are patient with littleness. Then the old Rome, like the beggar on horseback, presumed on the favor of the gods, and said, "Lo! there is neither riches nor greatness in our littleness: the road to riches and greatness is through robbery of the poor and slaughter of the weak." So they robbed their own poor until they became great masters of that art, and knew by what laws it could be made to appear seemly and honest. And when they had squeezed their own poor dry, they robbed the poor of other lands, and added those lands to Rome until there came a new Rome, rich and huge. And I, Ra, laughed; for the minds of the Romans remained the same size whilst their dominion spread over the earth.

Now mark me, that ye may understand what ye are presently to see. Whilst the Romans still stood between the old Rome and the new, there arose among them a mighty soldier: Pompey the Great. And the way of the soldier is the way of death; but the way of the gods is the way of life; and so it comes that a god at the end of his way is wise and a soldier at the end of his way is a fool. So Pompey held by the old Rome, in which only soldiers could become great; but the gods turned to the new Rome, in which any man with wit enough could become what he would. And Pompey's friend Julius Cæsar was on the side of the gods; for he saw that Rome had passed beyond the control of the little old Romans. This Cæsar was a great talker and a politician: he bought men with words and with gold, even as ye are bought. And when they would not be satisfied with words and gold, and demanded also the glories of war, Cæsar in his middle age turned his hand to that trade; and they that were against him when he sought their welfare, bowed down before him when he became a slayer and a conqueror; for such is the nature of you mortals. And as for Pompey, the gods grew tired of his triumphs and his airs of being himself a god; for he talked of law and duty and other matters that concerned not a mere human worm. And the gods smiled on Cæsar; for he lived the life they had given him boldly, and was not forever rebuking us for our indecent ways of creation, and hiding our handiwork as a shameful thing. Ye know well what I mean; for this is one of your own sins.

And thus it fell out between the old Rome and the new, that Cæsar said, "Unless I break the law of Rome, I cannot take my share in ruling her; and the gift of ruling that the gods gave me will perish without fruit." But Pompey said, "The law is above all; and if thou break it thou shalt die." Then said Cæsar, "I will break it: kill me who can." And he broke it. And Pompey went for him, as ye say, with a great army to slay him and uphold the old Rome. So Cæsar fled across the Adriatic sea; for the high gods had a lesson to teach him, which lesson they shall also teach you in due time if ye continue to forget them and to worship that cad among gods, Mammon. Therefore before they raised Cæsar to be master of the world, they were minded to throw him down in the dust, even beneath the feet of Pompey, and blacken his face before the nations. And Pompey they raised higher than ever, he and his laws and his high mind that aped the gods, so that his fall might be the more terrible. And Pompey followed Cæsar, and overcame him with all the majesty of old Rome, and stood over him and over the whole world even as ye stand over it with your fleet that covers thirty miles of the sea. And when Cæsar was brought down to utter nothingness, he made a last stand to die honorably, and did not despair; for he said, "Against me there is Pompey, and the old Rome, and the law and the legions: all all against me; but high above these are the gods; and Pompey is a fool." And the gods laughed and approved; and on the field of Pharsalia the impossible came to pass; the blood and iron ye pin your faith on fell before the spirit of man; for the spirit of man is the will of the gods; and Pompey's power crumbled in his hand, even as the power of imperial Spain crumbled when it was set against your fathers in the days when England was little, and knew her own mind, and had a mind to know instead of a circulation of newspapers. Wherefore look to it, lest some little people whom ye would enslave rise up and become in the hand of God the scourge of your boastings and your injustices and your lusts and stupidities.

And now, would ye know the end of Pompey, or will ye sleep while a god speaks? Heed my words well; for Pompey went where ye are gone, even to Egypt, where there was a Roman occupation even as there was but now a British one. And Cæsar pursued Pompey to Egypt: a Roman fleeing, and a Roman pursuing: dog eating dog. And the Egyptians said, "Lo: these Romans which have lent money to our kings and levied a distraint upon us with their arms, call for ever upon us to be loyal to them by betraying our own country to them. But now behold two Romes! Pompey's Rome and Cæsar's Rome! To which of the twain shall we pretend to be loyal?" So they turned in their perplexity to a soldier that had once served Pompey, and that knew the way of Rome and was full of her lusts. And they said to him, "Lo: in thy country dog eats dog; and both dogs are coming to eat us: what counsel hast thou to give us?" And this soldier, whose name was Lucius Septimius, and whom ye shall presently see before ye, replied, "Ye shall diligently consider which is the bigger dog of the two; and ye shall kill the other dog for his sake and thereby earn his favor." And the Egyptians said, "Thy counsel is expedient; but if we kill a man outside the law we set ourselves in the place of the gods; and this we dare not do. But thou, being a Roman, art accustomed to this kind of killing; for thou hast imperial instincts. Wilt thou therefore kill the lesser dog for us?" And he said, "I will; for I have made my home in Egypt; and I desire consideration and influence among you." And they said, "We knew well thou wouldst not do it for nothing: thou shalt have thy reward."

Now when Pompey came, he came alone in a little galley, putting his trust in the law and the constitution. And it was plain to the people of Egypt that Pompey was now but a very small dog. So when he set his foot on the shore he was greeted by his old comrade Lucius Septimius, who welcomed him with one hand and with the other smote off his head, and kept it as it were a pickled cabbage to make a present to Cæsar. And mankind shuddered; but the gods laughed; for Septimius was but a knife that Pompey had sharpened; and when it turned against his own throat they said that Pompey had better have made Septimius a ploughman than so brave and readyhanded a slayer. Therefore again I bid you beware, ye who would all be Pompeys if ye dared; for war is a wolf that may come to your own door.

Are ye impatient with me? Do ye crave for a story of an unchaste woman? Hath the name of Cleopatra tempted ye hither? Ye foolish ones; Cleopatra is as yet but a child that is whipped by her nurse. And what I am about to shew you for the good of your souls is how Cæsar, seeking Pompey in Egypt, found Cleopatra; and how he received that present of a pickled cabbage that was once the head of Pompey; and what things happened between the old Cæsar and the child queen before he left Egypt and battled his way back to Rome to be slain there as Pompey was slain, by men in whom the spirit of Pompey still lived. All this ye shall see; and ye shall marvel, after your ignorant manner, that men twenty centuries ago were already just such as you, and spoke and lived as ye speak and live, no worse and no better, no wiser and no sillier. And the two thousand years that have past are to me, the god Ra, but a moment; nor is this day any other than the day in which Cæsar set foot in the land of my people. And now I leave you; for ye are a dull folk, and instruction is wasted on you; and I had not spoken so much but that it is in the nature of a god to struggle for ever with the dust and the darkness, and to drag from them, by the force of his longing for the divine, more life and more light. Settle ye therefore in your seats and keep silent; for ye are about to hear a man speak, and a great man he was, as ye count greatness. And fear not that I shall speak to you again:

the rest of the story must ye learn from them that lived it. Farewell; and do not presume to applaud me. (*The temple vanishes in utter darkness.*)

[1912].

ACT I

An October night on the Syrian border of Egypt towards the end of the XXXIII Dynasty, in the year 706 by Roman computation, afterwards reckoned by Christian computation as 48 B.C. *A great radiance of silver fire, the dawn of a moonlit night, is rising in the east. The stars and the cloudless sky are our own contemporaries, nineteen and a half centuries younger than we know them; but you would not guess that from their appearance. Below them are two notable drawbacks of civilization: a palace, and soldiers. The palace, an old, low, Syrian building of whitened mud, is not so ugly as Buckingham Palace; and the officers in the courtyard are more highly civilized than modern English officers: for example, they do not dig up the corpses of their dead enemies and mutiliate them, as we dug up Cromwell and the Mahdi. They are in two groups: one intent on the gambling of their captain Belzanor, a warrior of fifty, who, with his spear on the ground beside his knee, is stooping to throw dice with a sly-looking young Persian recruit; the other gathered about a guardsman who has just finished telling a naughty story (still current in English barracks) at which they are laughing uproariously. They are about a dozen in number, all highly aristocratic young Egyptian guardsmen, handsomely equipped with weapons and armor, very unEnglish in point of not being ashamed of and uncomfortable in their professional dress; on the contrary, rather ostentatiously and arrogantly warlike, as valuing themselves on their military caste.*

Belzanor is a typical veteran, tough and wilful; prompt, capable and crafty where brute force will serve; helpless and boyish when it will not: an effective sergeant, an incompetent general, a deplorable dictator. Would, if influentially connected, be employed in the two last capacities by a modern European State on the strength of his success in the first. Is rather to be pitied just now in view of the fact that Julius Cæsar is invading his country. Not knowing this, is intent on his game with the Persian, whom, as a foreigner, he considers quite capable of cheating him.

His subalterns are mostly handsome young fellows whose interest in the game and the story symbolizes with tolerable completeness the main interests in life of which they are conscious. Their spears are leaning against the walls, or lying on the ground ready to their hands. The corner of the courtyard forms a triangle of which one side is the front of the palace, with a doorway, the other a wall with a gateway. The storytellers are on the palace side: the gamblers, on the gateway side. Close to the gateway, against the wall, is a stone block high enough to enable a Nubian sentinel, standing on it, to look over the wall. The yard is lighted by a torch stuck in the wall. As the laughter from the group round the storyteller dies away, the kneeling Persian, winning the throw, snatches up the stake from the ground.

BELZANOR. By Apis, Persian, thy gods are good to thee.

THE PERSIAN. Try yet again, O captain. Double or quits!

BELZANOR. No more. I am not in the vein.

THE SENTINEL (*poising his javelin as he peers over the wall*). Stand. Who goes there?

They all start, listening. A strange voice replies from without.

VOICE. The bearer of evil tidings.

BELZANOR (*calling to the sentry*). Pass him.

THE SENTINEL (*grounding his javelin*). Draw near, O bearer of evil tidings.

BELZANOR (*pocketing the dice and picking up his spear*). Let us receive this man with honor. He bears evil tidings.

The guardsmen seize their spears and gather about the gate, leaving a way through for the new comer.

PERSIAN (*rising from his knee*). Are evil tidings, then, so honorable?

BELZANOR. O barbarous Persian, hear my instruction. In Egypt the bearer of good tidings is sacrificed to the gods as a thank offering; but no god will accept the blood of the messenger of evil. When we have good tidings, we are careful to send them in the mouth of the cheapest slave we can find. Evil tidings are borne by young noblemen who desire to bring themselves into notice. (*They join the rest at the gate.*)

THE SENTINEL. Pass, O young captain; and bow the head in the House of the Queen.

VOICE. Go anoint thy javelin with fat of swine, O Blackamoor; for before morning the Romans will make thee eat it to the very butt.

The owner of the voice, a fairhaired dandy, dressed in a different fashion to that affected by the guardsmen, but no less extravagantly, comes through the gateway laughing. He is somewhat battlestained; and his left forearm, bandaged, comes through a torn sleeve. In his right hand he carries a Roman sword in its sheath. He swaggers down the courtyard, the Persian on his right, Belzanor on his left, and the guardsmen crowding down behind him.

BELZANOR. Who art thou that laughest in the House of Cleopatra the Queen, and in the teeth of Belzanor, the captain of her guard?

THE NEW COMER. I am Bel Affris, descended from the gods.

BELZANOR (*ceremoniously*). Hail, cousin!

ALL (*except the Persian*). Hail, cousin!

PERSIAN. All the Queen's guards are descended from the gods, O stranger, save myself. I am Persian, and descended from many kings.

BEL AFFRIS (*to the guardsmen*). Hail, cousins! (*To the Persian, condescendingly*) Hail, mortal!

BELZANOR. You have been in battle, Bel Affris; and you are a soldier among soldiers. You will not let the Queen's women have the first of your tidings.

BEL AFFRIS. I have no tidings, except that we shall have our throats cut presently, women, soldiers, and all.

PERSIAN (*to Belzanor*). I told you so.

THE SENTINEL (*who has been listening*). Woe, alas!

BEL AFFRIS (*calling to him*). Peace, peace, poor Ethiop: destiny is with the gods who painted thee black. (*To Belzanor*) What has this mortal (*indicating the Persian*) told you?

BELZANOR. He says that the Roman Julius Cæsar, who has landed on our shores with a handful of followers, will make himself master of Egypt. He is afraid of the Roman soldiers. (*The guardsmen laugh with boisterous scorn.*) Peasants, brought up to scare crows and follow the plough. Sons of smiths and millers and tanners! And we nobles, consecrated to arms, descended from the gods!

PERSIAN. Belzanor: the gods are not always good to their poor relations.

BELZANOR (*hotly, to the Persian*). Man to man, are we worse than the slaves of Cæsar?

BEL AFFRIS (*stepping between them*). Listen, cousin. Man to man, we Egyptians are as gods above the Romans.

THE GUARDSMEN (*exultingly*). Aha!

BEL AFFRIS. But this Cæsar does not pit man against man: he throws a legion at you where you are weakest as he throws a stone from a catapult; and that legion is as a man with one head, a thousand arms, and no religion. I have fought against them; and I know.

BELZANOR (*derisively*). Were you frightened, cousin?

The guardsmen roar with laughter, their eyes sparkling at the wit of their captain.

BEL AFFRIS. No, cousin; but I was beaten. They were frightened (perhaps); but they scattered us like chaff.

The guardsmen, much damped, utter a growl of contemptuous disgust.

BELZANOR. Could you not die?

BEL AFFRIS. No: that was too easy to be worthy of a descendant of the gods. Besides, there was no time: all was over in a moment. The attack came just where we least expected it.

BELZANOR. That shews that the Romans are cowards.

BEL AFFRIS. They care nothing about cowardice, these Romans: they fight to win. The pride and honor of war are nothing to them.

PERSIAN. Tell us the tale of the battle. What befell?

THE GUARDSMEN (*gathering eagerly round Bell Affris*). Ay: the tale of the battle.

BEL AFFRIS. Know then, that I am a novice in the guard of the temple of Ra in Memphis, serving neither Cleopatra nor her brother Ptolemy, but only the high gods. We went a journey to inquire of Ptolemy why he had driven Cleopatra into Syria, and how we of Egypt should deal with the Roman Pompey, newly come to our shores after his defeat by Cæsar at Pharsalia. What, think ye, did we learn? Even that Cæsar is coming also in hot pursuit of his foe, and that Ptolemy has slain Pompey, whose severed head he holds in readiness to present to the conqueror. (*Sensation among the guardsmen.*) Nay, more: we found that Cæsar is already come; for we had not made half a day's journey on our way back when we came upon a city rabble flying from his legions, whose landing they had gone out to withstand.

BELZANOR. And ye, the temple guard! did ye not withstand these legions?

BEL AFFRIS. What man could, that we did. But there came the sound of a trumpet whose voice was as the cursing of a black mountain. Then saw we a moving wall of shields coming towards us. You know how the heart burns when you charge a fortified wall; but how if the fortified wall were to charge you?

PERSIAN (*exulting in having told them so*). Did I not say it?

BEL AFFRIS. When the wall came nigh, it changed into a line of men—common fellows enough, with helmets, leather tunics, and breastplates. Every man of them flung his javelin: the one that came my way drove through my shield as through a papyrus—lo there! (*he points to the bandage on his left arm*) and would have gone through my neck had I not stooped. They were charging at the double then, and were upon us with short swords almost as soon as their javelins. When a man is close to you with such a sword, you can do nothing with our weapons: they are all too long.

PERSIAN. What did you do?

BEL AFFRIS. Doubled my fist and smote my Roman on the

sharpness of his jaw. He was but mortal after all: he lay down in a stupor; and I took his sword and laid it on. (*Drawing the sword*) Lo! a Roman sword with Roman blood on it!

THE GUARDSMEN (*approvingly*). Good! (*They take the sword and hand it round, examining it curiously.*)

PERSIAN. And your men?

BEL AFFRIS. Fled. Scattered like sheep.

BELZANOR (*furiously*). The cowardly slaves! Leaving the descendants of the gods to be butchered!

BEL AFFRIS (*with acid coolness*). The descendants of the gods did not stay to be butchered, cousin. The battle was not to the strong; but the race was to the swift. The Romans, who have no chariots, sent a cloud of horsemen in pursuit, and slew multitudes. Then our high priest's captain rallied a dozen descendants of the gods and exhorted us to die fighting. I said to myself: surely it is safer to stand than to lose my breath and be stabbed in the back; so I joined our captain and stood. Then the Romans treated us with respect; for no man attacks a lion when the field is full of sheep, except for the pride and honor of war, of which these Romans know nothing. So we escaped with our lives; and I am come to warn you that you must open your gates to Cæsar; for his advance guard is scarce an hour behind me; and not an Egyptian warrior is left standing between you and his legions.

THE SENTINEL. Woe, alas! (*He throws down his javelin and flies into the palace.*)

BELZANOR. Nail him to the door, quick! (*The guardsmen rush for him with their spears; but he is too quick for them.*) Now this news will run through the palace like fire through stubble.

BEL AFFRIS. What shall we do to save the women from the Romans?

BELZANOR. Why not kill them?

PERSIAN. Because we should have to pay blood money for some of them. Better let the Romans kill them: it is cheaper.

BELZANOR (*awestruck at his brain power*). O subtle one! O serpent!

BEL AFFRIS. But your Queen?

BELZANOR. True. we must carry off Cleopatra.

BEL AFFRIS. Will ye not await her command?

BELZANOR. Command! a girl of sixteen! Not we. At Memphis ye deem her a Queen: here we know better. I will take her on the crupper of my horse. When we soldiers have carried her out of Cæsar's reach, then the priests and the nurses and the rest of them can pretend she is queen again, and put their commands into her mouth.

PERSIAN. Listen to me, Belzanor.

BELZANOR. Speak, O subtle beyond thy years.

PERSIAN. Cleopatra's brother Ptolemy is at war with her. Let us sell her to him.

THE GUARDSMEN. O subtle one! O serpent!

BELZANOR. We dare not. We are descended from the gods; but Cleopatra is descended from the river Nile; and the lands of our fathers will grow no grain if the Nile rises not to water them. Without our father's gifts we should live the lives of dogs.

PERSIAN. It is true: the Queen's guard cannot live on its pay. But hear me further, O ye kinsmen of Osiris.

THE GUARDSMEN. Speak, O subtle one. Hear the serpent begotten!

PERSIAN. Have I heretofore spoken truly to you of Cæsar. when you thought I mocked you?

GUARDSMEN. Truly, truly.

BELZANOR (*reluctantly admitting it*). So Bel Affris says.

PERSIAN. Hear more of him, then. This Cæsar is a great lover of women: he makes them his friends and counsellors.

BELZANOR. Faugh! This rule of women will be the ruin of Egypt.

PERSIAN. Let it rather be the ruin of Rome! Cæsar grows old now: he is past fifty and full of labors and battles. He is too old for the young women; and the old women are too wise to worship him.

BEL AFFRIS. Take heed, Persian. Cæsar is by this time almost within earshot.

PERSIAN. Cleopatra is not yet a woman: neither is she wise. But she already troubles men's wisdom.

BELZANOR. Ay: that is because she is descended from the river Nile and a black kitten of the sacred White Cat. What then?

PERSIAN. Why, sell her secretly to Ptolemy, and then offer

ourselves to Cæsar as volunteers to fight for the overthrow of her brother and the rescue of our Queen, the Great Granddaughter of the Nile.

THE GUARDSMEN. O serpent!

PERSIAN. He will listen to us if we come with her picture in our mouths. He will conquer and kill her brother, and reign in Egypt with Cleopatra for his Queen. And we shall be her guard.

GUARDSMEN. O subtlest of all the serpents! O admiration! O wisdom!

BEL AFFRIS. He will also have arrived before you have done talking, O word spinner.

BELZANOR. That is true. (*An affrighted uproar in the palace interrupts him.*) Quick: the flight has begun: guard the door. (*They rush to the door and form a cordon before it with their spears. A mob of women-servants and nurses surges out. Those in front recoil from the spears, screaming to those behind to keep back. Belzanor's voice dominates the disturbance as he shouts*) Back there. In again, unprofitable cattle.

THE GUARDSMEN. Back, unprofitable cattle.

BELZANOR. Send us out Ftatateeta, the Queen's chief nurse.

THE WOMEN (*calling into the palace*). Ftatateeta, Ftatateeta. Come, come. Speak to Belzanor.

A WOMAN. Oh, keep back. You are thrusting me on the spearheads.

A huge grim woman, her face covered with a network of tiny wrinkles, and her eyes old, large, and wise; sinewy handed, very tall, very strong; with the mouth of a bloodhound and the jaws of a bulldog, appears on the threshold. She is dressed like a person of consequence in the palace, and confronts the guardsmen insolently.

FTATATEETA. Make way for the Queen's chief nurse.

BELZANOR (*with solemn arrogance*). Ftatateeta: I am Belzanor, the captain of the Queen's guard, descended from the gods.

FTATATEETA (*retorting his arrogance with interest*). Belzanor: I am Ftatateeta, the Queen's chief nurse; and your divine ancestors were proud to be painted on the wall in the pyramids of the kings whom my fathers served.

The women laugh triumphantly.

BELZANOR (*with grim humor*). Ftatateeta: daughter of a long-tongued, swivel-eyed chameleon, the Romans are at hand. (*A cry of terror from the women: they would fly but for the spears.*) Not even the descendants of the gods can resist them; for they have each man seven arms, each carrying seven spears. The blood in their veins is boiling quicksilver; and their wives become mothers in three hours, and are slain and eaten the next day.

A shudder of horror from the women. Ftatateeta, despising them and scorning the soldiers, pushes her way through the crowd and confronts the spear points undismayed.

FTATATEETA. Then fly and save yourselves, O cowardly sons of the cheap clay gods that are sold to fish porters; and leave us to shift for ourselves.

BELZANOR. Not until you have first done our bidding, O terror of manhood. Bring out Cleopatra the Queen to us and then go whither you will.

FTATATEETA (*with a derisive laugh*). Now I know why the gods have taken her out of our hands. (*The guardsmen start and look at one another.*) Know, thou foolish soldier, that the Queen has been missing since an hour past sun down.

BELZANOR (*furiously*). Hag: you have hidden her to sell to Cæsar or her brother. (*He grasps her by the left wrist, and drags her, helped by a few of the guard, to the middle of the courtyard, where, as they fling her on her knees, he draws a murderous looking knife.*) Where is she? Where is she? or—(*He threatens to cut her throat.*)

FTATATEETA (*savagely*). Touch me, dog; and the Nile will not rise on your fields for seven times seven years of famine.

BELZANOR (*frightened, but desperate*). I will sacrifice: I will pay. Or stay. (*To the Persian*) You, O subtle one: your father's lands lie far from the Nile. Slay her.

PERSIAN (*threatening her with his knife*). Persia has but one god; yet he loves the blood of old women. Where is Cleopatra?

FTATATEETA. Persian: as Osiris lives, I do not know. I chid her for bringing evil days upon us by talking to the sacred cats of the priests, and carrying them in her arms. I told her she would be left alone here when the Romans came as a punishment for her disobedience. And now she is gone—run away—hidden. I speak the truth. I call Osiris to witness—

THE WOMEN (*protesting officiously*). She speaks the truth, Belzanor.

BELZANOR. You have frightened the child: she is hiding. Search—quick—into the palace—search every corner.

The guards, led by Belzanor, shoulder their way into the palace through the flying crowd of women, who escape through the courtyard gate.

FTATATEETA (*screaming*). Sacrilege! Men in the Queen's chambers! Sa—(*Her voice dies away as the Persian puts his knife to her throat.*)

BEL AFFRIS (*laying a hand on Ftatateeta's left shoulder*). Forbear her yet a moment, Persian. (*To Ftatateeta, very significantly*) Mother: your gods are asleep or away hunting; and the sword is at your throat. Bring us to where the Queen is hid, and you shall live.

FTATATEETA (*contemptuously*). Who shall stay the sword in the hand of a fool, if the high gods put it there? Listen to me, ye young men without understanding. Cleopatra fears me; but she fears the Romans more. There is but one power greater in her eyes than the wrath of the Queen's nurse and the cruelty of Cæsar; and that is the power of the Sphinx that sits in the desert watching the way to the sea. What she would have it know, she tells into the ears of the sacred cats; and on her birthday she sacrifices to it and decks it with poppies. Go ye therefore into the desert and seek Cleopatra in the shadow of the Sphinx; and on your heads see to it that no harm comes to her.

BEL AFFRIS (*to the Persian*). May we believe this, O subtle one?

PERSIAN. Which way come the Romans?

BEL AFFRIS. Over the desert, from the sea, by this very Sphinx.

PERSIAN (*to Ftatateeta*). O mother of guile! O aspic's tongue! You have made up this tale so that we two may go into the desert and perish on the spears of the Romans. (*Lifting his knife*) Taste death.

FTATATEETA. Not from thee, baby. (*She snatches his ankle from under him and flies stooping along the palace wall, vanishing in the darkness within its precinct. Bel Affris roars with laughter as the Persian tumbles. The guardsmen rush out of the palace with Belzanor and a mob of fugitives, mostly carrying bundles.*)

PERSIAN. Have you found Cleopatra?

BELZANOR. She is gone. We have searched every corner.

THE NUBIAN SENTINEL (*appearing at the door of the palace*). Woe! Alas! Fly, fly!

BELZANOR. What is the matter now?

THE NUBIAN SENTINEL. The sacred white cat has been stolen.

ALL. Woe! Woe! (*General panic. They all fly with cries of consternation. The torch is thrown down and extinguished in the rush. Darkness. The noise of the fugitives dies away. Dead silence. Suspense. Then the blackness and stillness break softly into silver mist and strange airs as the wind-swept harp of Memnon plays at the dawning of the moon. It rises full over the desert; and a vast horizon comes into relief, broken by a huge shape which soon reveals itself in the spreading radiance as a Sphinx pedestalled on the sands. The light still clears, until the upraised eyes of the image are distinguished looking straight forward and upward in infinite fearless vigil, and a mass of color between its great paws defines itself as a heap of red poppies on which a girl lies motionless, her silken vest heaving gently and regularly with the breathing of a dreamless sleeper, and her braided hair glittering in a shaft of moonlight like a bird's wing.*

Suddenly there comes from afar a vaguely fearful sound [it might be the bellow of a Minotaur softened by great distance] and Memnon's music stops. Silence: then a few faint high-ringing trumpet notes. Then silence again. Then a man comes from the south with stealing steps, ravished by the mystery of the night, all wonder, and halts, lost in contemplation, opposite the left flank of the Sphinx, whose bosom, with its burden, is hidden from him by its massive shoulder.)

THE MAN. Hail, Sphinx: salutation from Julius Cæsar! I have wandered in many lands, seeking the lost regions from which my birth into this world exiled me, and the company of creatures such as I myself. I have found flocks and pastures, men and cities, but no other Cæsar, no air native to me, no man kindred to me, none who can do my day's deed, and think my night's thought. In the little world yonder, Sphinx, my place is as high as yours in this great desert; only I wander, and you sit still; I conquer, and you endure; I work and wonder, you watch and wait; I look up and am dazzled, look down and am darkened, look round and am puzzled, whilst your eyes never turn from looking out—out of the world—to the lost region—the home from which we have strayed. Sphinx, you and I, strangers to the race of men, are no strangers to one another: have I not been conscious of you and of this place since I was born? Rome is a madman's dream: this is my Reality. These starry lamps of yours I have seen from afar in Gaul, in Britain, in Spain, in Thessaly, signalling great secrets to some eternal sentinel below, whose post I never could find. And here at last is their sentinel—an image of the constant and immortal part of my life, silent, full of thoughts, alone in the silver desert. Sphinx, Sphinx: I have climbed mountains at night to hear in the distance the stealthy footfall of the winds that chase your sands in forbidden play—our invisible children, O Sphinx, laughing in whispers. My way hither was the way of destiny; for I am he of whose genius you are the symbol: part brute, part woman, and part God—nothing of man in me at all. Have I read your riddle, Sphinx?

THE GIRL (*who has wakened, and peeped cautiously from her nest to see who is speaking*). Old gentleman.

CÆSAR (*starting violently, and clutching his sword*). Immortal gods!

THE GIRL. Old gentleman: don't run away.

CÆSAR (*stupefied*). "Old gentleman: don't run away!!!" This! to Julius Cæsar!

THE GIRL (*urgently*). Old gentleman.

CÆSAR. Sphinx: you presume on your centuries. I am younger than you, though your voice is but a girl's voice as yet.

THE GIRL. Climb up here, quickly; or the Romans will come and eat you.

CÆSAR (*running forward past the Sphinx's shoulder, and seeing her*). A child at its breast! A divine child!

THE GIRL. Come up quickly. You must get up at its side and creep round.

CÆSAR (*amazed*). Who are you?

THE GIRL. Cleopatra, Queen of Egypt.

CÆSAR. Queen of the Gypsies, you mean.

CLEOPATRA. You must not be disrespectful to me, or the Sphinx will let the Romans eat you. Come up. It is quite cosy here.

CÆSAR (*to himself*). What a dream! What a magnificent dream! Only let me not wake, and I will conquer ten continents to pay for dreaming it out to the end. (*He climbs to the Sphinx's flank, and presently reappears to her on the pedestal, stepping round its right shoulder.*)

CLEOPATRA. Take care. That's right. Now sit down: you may have its other paw. (*She seats herself comfortably on its left paw.*) It is very powerful and will protect us; but (*shivering, and with plaintive loneliness*) it would not take any notice of me or keep me company. I am glad you have come: I was very lonely. Did you happen to see a white cat anywhere?

CÆSAR (*sitting slowly down on the right paw in extreme wonderment*). Have you lost one?

CLEOPATRA. Yes: the sacred white cat: is it not dreadful? I brought him here to sacrifice him to the Sphinx; but when we got a little way from the city a black cat called him, and he jumped out of my arms and ran away to it. Do you think that the black cat can have been my great-great-great-grand-mother?

CÆSAR (*staring at her*). Your great-great-great-grand-mother! Well, why not? Nothing would surprise me on this night of nights.

CLEOPATRA. I think it must have been. My great-grand-mother's great-grandmother was a black kitten of the sacred white cat; and the river Nile made her his seventh wife. That is why my hair is so wavy. And I always want to be let do as I like, no matter whether it is the will of the gods or not: that is because my blood is made with Nile water.

CÆSAR. What are you doing here at this time of night? Do you live here?

CLEOPATRA. Of course not: I am the Queen; and I shall live in the palace at Alexandria when I have killed my brother, who drove me out of it. When I am old enough I shall do just what I like. I shall be able to poison the slaves and see them wriggle, and pretend to Ftatateeta that she is going to be put into the fiery furnace.

CÆSAR. Hm! Meanwhile why are you not at home and in bed?

CLEOPATRA. Because the Romans are coming to eat us all. You are not at home and in bed either.

CÆSAR (*with conviction*). Yes I am. I live in a tent; and I am now in that tent, fast asleep and dreaming. Do you suppose that I believe you are real, you impossible little dream witch?

CLEOPATRA. (*giggling and leaning trustfully towards him*). You are a funny old gentleman. I like you.

CÆSAR. Ah, that spoils the dream. Why don't you dream that I am young?

CLEOPATRA. I wish you were; only I think I should be more afraid of you. I like men, especially young men with round strong arms; but I am afraid of them. You are old and rather thin and stringy; but you have a nice voice; and I like to have somebody to talk to, though I think you are a little mad. It is the moon that makes you talk to yourself in that silly way.

CÆSAR. What! you heard that, did you? I was saying my prayers to the great Sphinx.

CLEOPATRA. But this isn't the great Sphinx.

CÆSAR (*much disappointed, looking up at the statue*). What!

CLEOPATRA. This is only a dear little kitten of the Sphinx. Why, the great Sphinx is so big that it has a temple between its paws. This is my pet Sphinx. Tell me: do you think the Romans have any sorcerers who could take us away from the Sphinx by magic?

CÆSAR. Why? Are you afraid of the Romans?

CLEOPATRA (*very seriously*). Oh, they would eat us if they caught us. They are barbarians. Their chief is called Julius Cæsar. His father was a tiger and his mother a burning mountain; and his nose is like an elephant's trunk. (*Cæsar involuntarily rubs his nose.*) They all have long noses, and ivory tusks, and little tails, and seven arms with a hundred arrows in each; and they live on human flesh.

CÆSAR. Would you like me to show you a real Roman?

CLEOPATRA (*terrified*). No. You are frightening me.

CÆSAR. No matter: this is only a dream—

CLEOPATRA (*excitedly*). It is not a dream: it is not a dream.

See, see. (*She plucks a pin from her hair and jabs it repeatedly into his arm.*)

CÆSAR. Ffff—Stop. (*Wrathfully*) How dare you?

CLEOPATRA (*abashed*). You said you were dreaming. (*Whimpering*) I only wanted to shew you—

CÆSAR (*gently*). Come, come: don't cry. A queen mustn't cry. (*He rubs his arm, wondering at the reality of the smart.*) Am I awake? (*He strikes his hand against the Sphinx to test its solidity. It feels so real that he begins to be alarmed, and says perplexedly*) Yes, I— (*quite panic-stricken*) no: impossible: madness, madness! (*Desperately*) Back to camp—to camp. (*He rises to spring down from the pedestal.*)

CLEOPATRA (*flinging her arms in terror round him*). No: you shan't leave me. No, no, no: don't go. I'm afraid—afraid of the Romans.

CÆSAR (*as the conviction that he is really awake forces itself on him*). Cleopatra: can you see my face well?

CLEOPATRA. Yes. It is so white in the moonlight.

CÆSAR. Are you sure it is the moonlight that makes me look whiter than an Egyptian? (*Grimly*) Do you notice that I have a rather long nose?

CLEOPATRA (*recoiling, paralyzed by a terrified suspicion*). Oh!

CÆSAR. It is a Roman nose, Cleopatra.

CLEOPATRA. Ah! (*With a piercing scream she springs up; darts round the left shoulder of the Sphinx; scrambles down to the sand; and falls on her knees in frantic supplication, shrieking.*) Bite him in two, Sphinx: bite him in two. I meant to sacrifice the white cat—I did indeed—I (*Cæsar, who has slipped down from the pedestal, touches her on the shoulder.*) Ah! (*She buries her head in her arms.*)

CÆSAR. Cleopatra: shall I teach you a way to prevent Cæsar from eating you?

CLEOPATRA (*clinging to him piteously*). Oh do, do, do. I will steal Ftatateeta's jewels and give them to you. I will make the river Nile water your lands twice a year.

CÆSAR. Peace, peace, my child. Your gods are afraid of the Romans: you see the Sphinx dare not bite me, nor prevent me carrying you off to Julius Cæsar.

CLEOPATRA (*in pleading murmurings*). You won't, you won't. You said you wouldn't.

CÆSAR. Cæsar never eats women.

CLEOPATRA (*springing up full of hope*). What!

CÆSAR (*impressively*). But he eats girls (*she relapses*) and cats. Now you are a silly little girl; and you are descended from the black kitten. You are both a girl and a cat.

CLEOPATRA (*trembling*). And will he eat me?

CÆSAR. Yes; unless you make him believe that you are a woman.

CLEOPATRA. Oh, you must get a sorcerer to make a woman of me. Are you a sorcerer?

CÆSAR. Perhaps. But it will take a long time; and this very night you must stand face to face with Cæsar in the palace of your fathers.

CLEOPATRA. No, no. I daren't.

CÆSAR. Whatever dread may be in your soul—however terrible Cæsar may be to you—you must confront him as a brave woman and a great queen; and you must feel no fear. If your hand shakes: if your voice quavers; then—night and death! (*She moans.*) But if he thinks you worthy to rule, he will set you on the throne by his side and make you the real ruler of Egypt.

CLEOPATRA (*despairingly*). No: he will find me out: he will find me out.

CÆSAR (*rather mournfully*). He is easily deceived by women. Their eyes dazzle him: and he sees them not as they are, but as he wishes them to appear to him.

CLEOPATRA (*hopefully*). Then we will cheat him. I will put on Ftatateeta's head-dress; and he will think me quite an old woman.

CÆSAR. If you do that he will eat you at one mouthful.

CLEOPATRA. But I will give him a cake with my magic opal and seven hairs of the white cat baked in it; and—

CÆSAR (*abruptly*). Pah! you are a little fool. He will eat your cake and you too. (*He turns contemptuously from her.*)

CLEOPATRA (*running after him and clinging to him*). Oh, please, p l e a s e! I will do whatever you tell me. I will be good! I will be your slave. (*Again the terrible bellowing note sounds across the desert, now closer at hand. It is the bucina, the Roman war trumpet.*)

CÆSAR. Hark!

CLEOPATRA (*trembling*). What was that?

CÆSAR. Cæsar's voice.

CLEOPATRA (*pulling at his hand*). Let us run away. Come. Oh, come.

CÆSAR. You are safe with me until you stand on your throne to receive Cæsar. Now lead me thither.

CLEOPATRA (*only too glad to get away*). I will, I will. (*Again the bucina*) Oh, come, come, come: the gods are angry. Do you feel the earth shaking?

CÆSAR. It is the tread of Cæsar's legions.

CLEOPATRA (*drawing him away*). This way, quickly. And let us look for the white cat as we go. It is he that has turned you into a Roman.

CÆSAR. Incorrigible, oh, incorrigible! Away! (*He follows her, the bucina sounding louder as they steal across the desert. The moonlight wanes: the horizon again shows black against the sky, broken only by the fantastic silhouette of the Sphinx. The sky itself vanishes in darkness, from which there is no relief until the gleam of a distant torch falls on great Egyptian pillars supporting the roof of a majestic corridor. At the further end of this corridor a Nubian slave appears carrying the torch. Cæsar, still led by Cleopatra, follows him. They come down the corridor, Cæsar peering keenly about at the strange architecture, and at the pillar shadows between which, as the passing torch makes them hurry noiselessly backwards, figures of men with wings and hawks' heads, and vast black marble cats, seem to flit in and out of ambush. Further along, the wall turns a corner and makes a spacious transept in which Cæsar sees, on his right, a throne, and behind the throne a door. On each side of the throne is a slender pillar with a lamp on it.*)

CÆSAR. What place is this?

CLEOPATRA. This is where I sit on the throne when I am allowed to wear my crown and robes. (*The slave holds his torch to shew the throne.*)

CÆSAR. Order the slave to light the lamps.

CLEOPATRA (*shyly*). Do you think I may?

CÆSAR. Of course. You are the Queen. (*She hesitates.*) Go on.

CLEOPATRA (*timidly, to the slave*). Light all the lamps.

FTATATEETA (*suddenly coming from behind the throne*). Stop. (*The slave stops. She turns sternly to Cleopatra, who quails like a naughty child.*) Who is this you have with you; and how dare you order the lamps to be lighted without my permission? (*Cleopatra is dumb with apprehension.*)

CÆSAR. Who is she?

CLEOPATRA. Ftatateeta.

FTATATEETA (*arrogantly*). Chief nurse to—

CÆSAR (*cutting her short*). I speak to the Queen. Be silent. (*To Cleopatra*) Is this how your servants know their places? Send her away; and do you (*to the slave*) do as the Queen has bidden. (*The slave lights the lamps. Meanwhile Cleopatra stands hesitating, afraid of Ftatateeta.*) You are the Queen: send her away.

CLEOPATRA (*cajoling*). Ftatateeta, dear: you must go away—just for a little.

CÆSAR. You are not commanding her to go away; you are begging her. You are no Queen. You will be eaten. Farewell. (*He turns to go.*)

CLEOPATRA (*clutching him*). No, no, no. Don't leave me.

CÆSAR. A Roman does not stay with queens who are afraid of their slaves.

CLEOPATRA. I am not afraid. Indeed I am not afraid.

FTATATEETA. We shall see who is afraid here. (*Menacingly*) Cleopatra—

CÆSAR. On your knees, woman: am I also a child that you dare trifle with me? (*He points to the floor at Cleopatra's feet. Ftatateeta, half cowed, half savage, hesitates. Cæsar calls to the Nubian.*) Slave. (*The Nubian comes to him.*) Can you cut off a head? (*The Nubian nods and grins ecstatically, showing all his teeth. Cæsar takes his sword by the scabbard, ready to offer the hilt to the Nubian, and turns again to Ftatateeta, repeating his gesture.*) Have you remembered yourself, mistress?

Ftatateeta, crushed, kneels before Cleopatra, who can hardly believe her eyes.

FTATATEETA (*hoarsely*). O Queen, forget not thy servant in the days of thy greatness.

CLEOPATRA (*blazing with excitement*). Go. Begone. Go away. (*Ftatateeta rises with stooped head, and moves backwards towards the door. Cleopatra watches her submission eagerly, almost clapping her hands, which are trembling. Suddenly she cries*) Give me something to beat her with. (*She snatches a snake-skin from the throne and dashes after Ftatateeta, whirling it like a scourge in the air. Cæsar makes a bound and manages to catch her and hold her while Ftatateeta escapes.*)

CÆSAR. You scratch, kitten, do you?

CLEOPATRA (*breaking from him*). I will beat somebody. I will beat him. (*She attacks the slave.*) There, there, there! (*The slave flies for his life up the corridor and vanishes. She throws the snake-skin away and jumps on the step of the throne with her arms waving, crying*) I am a real Queen at last—a real, real Queen! Cleopatra the Queen! (*Cæsar shakes his head dubiously, the advantage of the change seeming open to question from the point of view of the general welfare of Egypt. She turns and looks at him exultantly. Then she jumps down from the step, runs to him, and flings her arms round him rapturously, crying*) Oh, I love you for making me a Queen.

CÆSAR. But queens love only kings.

CLEOPATRA. I will make all the men I love kings. I will make you a king. I will have many young kings, with round, strong arms; and when I am tired of them I will whip them to death; but you shall always be my king: my nice, kind, wise, good old king.

CÆSAR. Oh, my wrinkles, my wrinkles! And my child's heart! You will be the most dangerous of all Cæsar's conquests.

CLEOPATRA (*appalled*). Cæsar! I forgot Cæsar. (*Anxiously*) You will tell him that I am a Queen, will you not?—a real Queen. Listen! (*stealthily coaxing him*) let us run away and hide until Cæsar is gone.

CÆSAR. If you fear Cæsar, you are no true Queen; and though you were to hide beneath a pyramid, he would go straight to it and lift it with one hand. And then—! (*He chops his teeth together.*)

CLEOPATRA (*trembling*). Oh!

CÆSAR. Be afraid if you dare. (*The note of the bucina resounds again in the distance. She moans with fear. Cæsar exults in it, exclaiming*) Aha! Cæsar approaches the throne of Cleopatra. Come: take your place. (*He takes her hand and leads her to the throne. She is too downcast to speak.*) Ho, there, Teetatota. How do you call your slaves?

CLEOPATRA (*spiritlessly, as she sinks on the throne and cowers there, shaking*). Clap your hands.

He claps his hands. Ftatateeta returns.

CÆSAR. Bring the Queen's robes, and her crown, and her women; and prepare her.

CLEOPATRA (*eagerly—recovering herself a little*). Yes, the crown, Ftatateeta: I shall wear the crown.

FTATATEETA. For whom must the Queen put on her state?

CÆSAR. For a citizen of Rome. A king of kings, Totateeta.

CLEOPATRA (*stamping at her*). How dare you ask questions? Go and do as you are told. (*Ftatateeta goes out with a grim smile. Cleopatra goes on eagerly, to Cæsar*) Cæsar will know that I am a Queen when he sees my crown and robes, will he not?

CÆSAR. No. How shall he know that you are not a slave dressed up in the Queen's ornaments?

CLEOPATRA. You must tell him.

CÆSAR. He will not ask me. He will know Cleopatra by her pride, her courage, her majesty, and her beauty. (*She looks very doubtful.*) Are you trembling?

CLEOPATRA (*shivering with dread*). No, I—I—(*in a very sickly voice*) No.

Ftatateeta and three women come in with the regalia.

FTATATEETA. Of all the Queen's women, these three alone are left. The rest are fled. (*They begin to deck Cleopatra, who submits, pale and motionless.*)

CÆSAR. Good, good. Three are enough. Poor Cæsar generally has to dress himself.

FTATATEETA (*contemptuously*). The Queen of Egypt is not a Roman barbarian. (*To Cleopatra*) Be brave, my nursling. Hold up your head before this stranger.

CÆSAR (*admiring Cleopatra, and placing the crown on her head*). Is it sweet or bitter to be a Queen, Cleopatra?

CLEOPATRA. Bitter.

CÆSAR. Cast out fear; and you will conquer Cæsar. Tota: are the Romans at hand?

FTATATEETA. They are at hand; and the guard has fled.

THE WOMEN (*wailing subduedly*). Woe to us!

The Nubian comes running down the hall.

NUBIAN. The Romans are in the courtyard. (*He bolts through the door. With a shriek, the women fly after him. Ftatateeta's jaw expresses savage resolution: she does not budge. Cleopatra can hardly restrain herself from following them. Cæsar grips her wrist, and looks steadfastly at her. She stands like a martyr.*)

CÆSAR. The Queen must face Cæsar alone. Answer, "So be it."

CLEOPATRA (*white*). So be it.

CÆSAR (*releasing her*). Good.

A tramp and tumult of armed men is heard. Cleopatra's terror increases. The bucina sounds close at hand, followed by a formidable clangor of trumpets. This is too much for Cleopatra: she utters a cry and darts towards the door. Ftatateeta stops her ruthlessly.

FTATATEETA. You are my nursling. You have said "So be it"; and if you die for it, you must make the Queen's word good. (*She hands Cleopatra to Cæsar, who takes her back, almost beside herself with apprehension, to the throne.*)

CÆSAR. Now, if you quail—! (*He seats himself on the throne.*)

She stands on the step, all but unconscious, waiting for death. The Roman soldiers troop in tumultuously through the corridor, headed by their ensign with his eagle, and their bucinator, a burly fellow with his instrument coiled round his body, its brazen bell shaped like the head of a howling wolf. When they reach the transept, they stare in amazement at the throne; dress into ordered rank opposite it; draw their swords and lift them in the air with a shout of Hail, C æ s a r. Cleopatra turns and stares wildly at Cæsar; grasps the situation; and, with a great sob of relief, falls into his arms.

END OF ACT I.

ACT II

Alexandria. A hall on the first floor of the Palace, ending in a loggia approached by two steps. Through the arches of the loggia the Mediterranean can be seen, bright in the morning sun. The clean lofty walls, painted with a procession of the Egyptian theocracy, presented in profile as flat ornament, and the absence of mirrors, sham perspectives, stuffy upholstery and textiles, make the place handsome, wholesome, simple and cool, or, as a rich English manufacturer would express it, poor, bare, ridiculous and unhomely. For Tottenham Court Road civilization is to this Egyptian civilization as glass bead and tattoo civilization is to Tottenham Court Road.

The young king Ptolemy Dionysus (aged ten) is at the top of the steps, on his way in through the loggia, led by his guardian Pothinus, who has him by the hand. The court is assembled to receive him. It is made up of men and women (some of the women being officials) of various complexions and races, mostly Egyptian; some of them, comparatively fair, from lower Egypt; some, much darker, from upper Egypt; with a few Greeks and Jews. Prominent in a group on Ptolemy's right hand is Theodotus, Ptolemy's tutor. Another group, on Ptolemy's left, is headed by Achillas, the general of Ptolemy's troops. Theodotus is a little old man, whose features are as cramped and wizened as his limbs, except his tall straight forehead, which occupies more space than all the rest of his face. He maintains an air of magpie keenness and profundity, listening to what the others say with the sarcastic vigilance of a philosopher listening to the exercises of his disciples. Achillas is a tall handsome man of thirty-five, with a fine black beard curled like the coat of a poodle. Apparently not a clever man, but distinguished and dignified. Pothinus is a vigorous man of fifty, a eunuch, passionate, energetic and quick witted, but of common mind and character; impatient and unable to control his temper. He has fine tawny hair, like fur. Ptolemy, the King, looks much older than an English boy of ten; but he has the childish air, the habit of being in leading strings, the mixture of impotence and petulance, the appearance of being excessively washed, combed and dressed by other hands, which is exhibited by court-bred princes of all ages.

All receive the King with reverences. He comes down the steps to a chair of state which stands a little to his right, the only seat in the hall. Taking his place before it, he looks nervously for instructions to Pothinus, who places himself at his left hand.

POTHINUS. The King of Egypt has a word to speak.

THEODOTUS (*in a squeak which he makes impressive by sheer self-opinionativeness*). Peace for the King's word!

PTOLEMY (*without any vocal inflexions: he is evidently repeating a lesson*). Take notice of this all of you. I am the firstborn son of Auletes the Flute Blower who was your King. My sister Berenice drove him from his throne and reigned in his stead—but—but (*he hesitates*)—

POTHINUS (*stealthily prompting*)—but the gods would not suffer—

PTOLEMY. Yes—the gods would not suffer—not suffer—(*he stops; then, crestfallen*) I forget what the gods would not suffer.

THEODOTUS. Let Pothinus, the King's guardian, speak for the King.

POTHINUS (*suppressing his impatience with difficulty*). The King wished to say that the gods would not suffer the impiety of his sister to go unpunished.

PTOLEMY (*hastily*). Yes: I remember the rest of it. (*He

resumes his monotone.) Therefore the gods sent a stranger, one Mark Antony, a Roman captain of horsemen, across the sands of the desert and he set my father again upon the throne. And my father took Berenice my sister and struck her head off. And now that my father is dead yet another of his daughters, my sister Cleopatra, would snatch the kingdom from me and reign in my place. But the gods would not suffer (*Pothinus coughs admonitorily*)—the gods—the gods would not suffer—

POTHINUS (*prompting*)—will not maintain—

PTOLEMY. Oh yes—will not maintain such iniquity, they will give her head to the axe even as her sister's. But with the help of the witch Ftatateeta, she hath cast a spell on the Roman Julius Cæsar to make him uphold her false pretence to rule in Egypt. Take notice then that I will not suffer—that I will not suffer—(*pettishly, to Pothinus*) What is it that I will not suffer?

POTHINUS (*suddenly exploding with all the force and emphasis of political passion*). The King will not suffer a foreigner to take from him the throne of our Egypt. (*A shout of applause.*) Tell the King, Achillas, how many soldiers and horsemen follow the Roman?

THEODOTUS. Let the King's general speak!

ACHILLAS. But two Roman legions, O King. Three thousand soldiers and scarce a thousand horsemen.

The court breaks into derisive laughter; and a great chattering begins, amid which Rufio, a Roman officer, appears in the loggia. He is a burly, black-bearded man of middle age, very blunt, prompt and rough, with small clear eyes, and plump nose and cheeks, which, however, like the rest of his flesh, are in ironhard condition.

RUFIO (*from the steps*). Peace, ho! (*The laughter and chatter cease abruptly.*) Cæsar approaches.

THEODOTUS (*with much presence of mind*). The King permits the Roman commander to enter!

Cæsar, plainly dressed, but wearing an oak wreath to conceal his baldness, enters from the loggia, attended by Britannus, his secretary, a Briton, about forty, tall, solemn, and already slightly bald, with a heavy, drooping, hazel-colored moustache trained so as to lose its ends in a pair of trim whiskers. He is carefully dressed in blue, with portfolio, inkhorn, and reed pen at his girdle. His serious air and sense of the importance of the business in hand is in marked contrast to the kindly interest of Cæsar, who looks at the scene, which is new to him, with the frank curiosity of a child, and then turns to the King's chair: Britannus and Rufio posting themselves near the steps at the other side.

CÆSAR (*looking at Pothinus and Ptolemy*). Which is the King? the man or the boy?

POTHINUS. I am Pothinus, the guardian of my lord the King.

CÆSAR (*patting Ptolemy kindly on the shoulder*). So you are the King. Dull work at your age, eh? (*To Pothinus*) Your servant, Pothinus. (*He turns away unconcernedly and comes slowly along the middle of the hall, looking from side to side at the courtiers until he reaches Achillas.*) And this gentleman?

THEODOTUS. Achillas, the King's general.

CÆSAR (*to Achillas, very friendly*). A general, eh? I am a general myself. But I began too old, too old. Health and many victories, Achillas!

ACHILLAS. As the gods will, Cæsar.

CÆSAR (*turning to Theodotus*). And you, sir, are—?

THEODOTUS. Theodotus, the King's tutor.

CÆSAR. You teach men how to be kings, Theodotus. That is very clever of you. (*Looking at the gods on the walls as he turns away from Theodotus and goes up again to Pothinus.*) And this place?

POTHINUS. The council chamber of the chancellors of the King's treasury, Cæsar.

CÆSAR. Ah! that reminds me. I want some money.

POTHINUS. The King's treasury is poor, Cæsar.

CÆSAR. Yes: I notice that there is but one chair in it.

RUFIO (*shouting gruffly*). Bring a chair there, some of you, for Cæsar.

PTOLEMY (*rising shyly to offer his chair*). Cæsar—

CÆSAR (*kindly*). No, no, my boy: that is your chair of state. Sit down.

He makes Ptolemy sit down again. Meanwhile Rufio, looking about him, sees in the nearest corner an image of the god Ra, represented as a seated man with the head of a hawk.

Before the image is a bronze tripod, about as large as a three-legged stool, with a stick of incense burning on it. Rufio, with Roman resourcefulness and indifference to foreign superstitions, promptly seizes the tripod; shakes off the incense; blows away the ash; and dumps it down behind Cæsar, nearly in the middle of the hall.

RUFIO. Sit on that, Cæsar.

A shiver runs through the court, followed by a hissing whisper of Sacrilege!

CÆSAR (*seating himself*). Now, Pothinus, to business. I am badly in want of money.

BRITANNUS (*disapproving of these informal expressions*). My master would say that there is a lawful debt due to Rome by Egypt, contracted by the King's deceased father to the Triumvirate; and that it is Cæsar's duty to his country to require immediate payment.

CÆSAR (*blandly*). Ah, I forgot. I have not made my companions known here. Pothinus: this is Britannus, my secretary. He is an islander from the western end of the world, a day's voyage from Gaul. (*Britannus bows stiffly.*) This gentleman is Rufio, my comrade in arms. (*Rufio nods.*) Pothinus: I want sixteen hundred talents.

The courtiers, appalled, murmur loudly, and Theodotus and Achillas appeal mutely to one another against so monstrous a demand.

POTHINUS (*aghast*). Forty million sesterces! Impossible. There is not so much money in the King's treasury.

CÆSAR (*encouragingly*). O n l y sixteen hundred talents, Pothinus. Why count it in sesterces? A sestertius is only worth a loaf of bread.

POTHINUS. And a talent is worth a racehorse. I say it is impossible. We have been at strife here, because the King's sister Cleopatra falsely claims his throne. The King's taxes have not been collected for a whole year.

CÆSAR. Yes they have, Pothinus. My officers have been collecting them all the morning. (*Renewed whisper and sensation, not without some stifled laughter, among the courtiers.*)

RUFIO (*bluntly*). You must pay, Pothinus. Why waste words? You are getting off cheaply enough.

POTHINUS (*bitterly*). Is it possible that Cæsar, the conqueror of the world, has time to occupy himself with such a trifle as our taxes?

CÆSAR. My friend: taxes are the chief business of a conqueror of the world.

POTHINUS. Then take warning, Cæsar. This day, the treasures of the temples and the gold of the King's treasury shall be sent to the mint to be melted down for our ransom in the sight of the people. They shall see us sitting under bare walls and drinking from wooden cups. And their wrath be on your head, Cæsar, if you force us to this sacrilege!

CÆSAR. Do not fear, Pothinus: the people know how well wine tastes in wooden cups. In return for your bounty, I will settle this dispute about the throne for you, if you will. What say you?

POTHINUS. If I say no, will that hinder you?

RUFIO (*defiantly*). No.

CÆSAR. You say the matter has been at issue for a year, Pothinus. May I have ten minutes at it?

POTHINUS. You will do your pleasure, doubtless.

CÆSAR. Good! But first, let us have Cleopatra here.

THEODOTUS. She is not in Alexandria: she is fled into Syria.

CÆSAR. I think not. (*To Rufio*) Call Totateeta.

RUFIO (*calling*). Ho there, Teetatota.

Ftatateeta enters the loggia, and stands arrogantly at the top of the steps.

FTATATEETA. Who pronounces the name of Ftatateeta, the Queen's chief nurse?

CÆSAR. Nobody can pronounce it, Tota, except yourself. Where is your mistress?

Cleopatra, who is hiding behind Ftatateeta, peeps out at them, laughing. Cæsar rises.

CÆSAR. Will the Queen favor us with her presence for a moment?

CLEOPATRA (*pushing Ftatateeta aside and standing haughtily on the brink of the steps*). Am I to behave like a Queen?

CÆSAR. Yes.

Cleopatra immediately comes down to the chair of state; seizes Ptolemy and drags him out of his seat; then takes his place in the chair. Ftatateeta seats herself on the step of the loggia, and sits there, watching the scene with sybilline intensity.

PTOLEMY (*mortified, and struggling with his tears*). Cæsar: this is how she treats me always. If I am a king why is she allowed to take everything from me?

CLEOPATRA. You are not to be King, you little cry-baby. You are to be eaten by the Romans.

CÆSAR (*touched by Ptolemy's distress*). Come here, my boy, and stand by me.

Ptolemy goes over to Cæsar, who, resuming his seat on the tripod, takes the boy's hand to encourage him. Cleopatra, furiously jealous, rises and glares at them.

CLEOPATRA (*with flaming cheeks*). Take your throne: I don't want it. (*She flings away from the chair, and approaches Ptolemy, who shrinks from her.*) Go this instant and sit down in your place.

CÆSAR. Go, Ptolemy. Always take a throne when it is offered to you.

RUFIO. I hope you will have the good sense to follow your own advice when we return to Rome, Cæsar.

Ptolemy slowly goes back to the throne, giving Cleopatra a wide berth, in evident fear of her hands. She takes his place beside Cæsar.

CÆSAR. Pothinus—

CLEOPATRA (*interrupting him*). Are you not going to speak to me?

CÆSAR. Be quiet. Open your mouth again before I give you leave; and you shall be eaten.

CLEOPATRA. I am not afraid. A queen must not be afraid. Eat my husband there, if you like: he is afraid.

CÆSAR (*starting*). Your husband! What do you mean?

CLEOPATRA (*pointing to Ptolemy*). That little thing.

The two Romans and the Briton stare at one another in amazement.

THEODOTUS. Cæsar: you are a stranger here, and not conversant with our laws. The kings and queens of Egypt may not marry except with their own royal blood. Ptolemy and Cleopatra are born king and consort just as they are born brother and sister.

BRITANNUS (*shocked*). Cæsar: this is not proper.

THEODOTUS (*outraged*). How!

CÆSAR (*recovering his self-possession*). Pardon him, Theodotus: he is a barbarian, and thinks that the customs of his tribe and island are the laws of nature.

BRITANNUS. On the contrary, Cæsar, it is these Egyptians who are barbarians; and you do wrong to encourage them. I say it is a scandal.

CÆSAR. Scandal or not, my friend, it opens the gate of peace. (*He rises and addresses Pothinus seriously.*) Pothinus: hear what I propose.

RUFIO. Hear Cæsar there.

CÆSAR. Ptolemy and Cleopatra shall reign jointly in Egypt.

ACHILLAS. What of the King's younger brother and Cleopatra's younger sister?

RUFIO (*explaining*). There is another little Ptolemy, Cæsar: so they tell me.

CÆSAR. Well, the little Ptolemy can marry the other sister; and we will make them both a present of Cyprus.

POTHINUS (*impatiently*). Cyprus is of no use to anybody.

CÆSAR. No matter; you shall have it for the sake of peace.

BRITANNUS (*unconsciously anticipating a later statesman*). Peace with honor, Pothinus.

POTHINUS (*mutinously*). Cæsar: be honest. The money you demand is the price of our freedom. Take it; and leave us to settle our own affairs.

THE BOLDER COURTIERS (*encouraged by Pothinus's tone and Cæsar's quietness*). Yes, yes. Egypt for the Egyptians!

The conference now becomes an altercation, the Egyptians becoming more and more heated. Cæsar remains unruffled; but Rufio grows fiercer and doggeder, and Britannus haughtily indignant.

RUFIO (*contemptuously*). Egypt for the Egyptians! Do you forget that there is a Roman army of occupation here, left by Aulus Gabinius when he set up your toy king for you?

ACHILLAS (*suddenly asserting himself*). And now under my command. *I* am the Roman general here, Cæsar.

CÆSAR (*tickled by the humor of the situation*). And also the Egyptian general, eh?

POTHINUS (*triumphantly*). That is so, Cæsar.

CÆSAR (*to Achillas*). So you can make war on the Egyptians in the name of Rome, and on the Romans—on me, if necessary—in the name of Egypt?

ACHILLAS. That is so, Cæsar.

CÆSAR. And which side are you on at present, if I may presume to ask, general?

ACHILLAS. On the side of the right and of the gods.

CÆSAR. Hm! How many men have you?

ACHILLAS. That will appear when I take the field.

RUFIO (*truculently*). Are your men Romans? If not, it matters not how many there are, provided you are no stronger than 500 to ten.

POTHINUS. It is useless to try to bluff us, Rufio. Cæsar has been defeated before and may be defeated again. A few weeks ago Cæsar was flying for his life before Pompey: a few months hence he may be flying for his life before Cato and Juba of Numidia, the African King.

ACHILLAS (*following up Pothinus's speech menacingly*). What can you do with 4,000 men?

THEODOTUS (*following up Achillas's speech with a raucous squeak*). And without money? Away with you.

ALL THE COURTIERS (*shouting fiercely and crowding towards Cæsar*). Away with you. Egypt for the Egyptians! Begone.

Rufio bites his beard, too angry to speak. Cæsar sits as comfortably as if he were at breakfast, and the cat were clamoring for a piece of Finnan-haddie.

CLEOPATRA. Why do you let them talk to you like that, Cæsar? Are you afraid?

CÆSAR. Why, my dear, what they say is quite true.

CLEOPATRA. But if you go away, I shall not be Queen.

CÆSAR. I shall not go away until you are Queen.

POTHINUS. Achillas: if you are not a fool, you will take that girl whilst she is under your hand.

RUFIO (*daring them*). Why not take Cæsar as well, Achillas?

POTHINUS (*retorting the defiance with interest*). Well said, Rufio. Why not?

RUFIO. Try, Achillas. (*Calling*) Guard there.

The loggia immediately fills with Cæsar's soldiers, who stand, sword in hand, at the top of the steps, waiting the word to charge from their centurion, who carries a cudgel.

For a moment the Egyptians face them proudly: then they retire sullenly to their former places.

BRITANNUS. You are Cæsar's prisoners, all of you.

CÆSAR (*benevolently*). Oh, no, no, no. By no means. Cæsar's guests, gentlemen.

CLEOPATRA. Won't you cut their heads off?

CÆSAR. What! Cut off your brother's head?

CLEOPATRA. Why not? He would cut off mine, if he got the chance. Wouldn't you, Ptolemy?

PTOLEMY (*pale and obstinate*). I would. I will, too, when I grow up.

Cleopatra is rent by a struggle between her newly-acquired dignity as a queen, and a strong impulse to put out her tongue at him. She takes no part in the scene which follows, but watches it with curiosity and wonder, fidgeting with the restlessness of a child, and sitting down on Cæsar's tripod when he rises.

POTHINUS. Cæsar: if you attempt to detain us—

RUFIO. He will succeed, Egyptian: make up your mind to that. We hold the palace, the beach, and the eastern harbor. The road to Rome is open; and you shall travel it if Cæsar chooses.

CÆSAR (*courteously*). I could do no less, Pothinus, to secure the retreat of my own soldiers. I am accountable for every life among them. But you are free to go. So are all here, and in the palace.

RUFIO (*aghast at this clemency*). What! Renegades and all?

CÆSAR (*softening the expression*). Roman army of occupation and all, Rufio.

POTHINUS (*desperately*). Then I make a last appeal to Cæsar's justice. I shall call a witness to prove that but for us, the Roman army of occupation, led by the greatest soldier in the world, would now have Cæsar at its mercy. (*Calling through the loggia*) Ho, there, Lucius Septimius (*Cæsar starts, deeply moved*): if my voice can reach you, come forth and testify before Cæsar.

CÆSAR (*shrinking*). No, no.

THEODOTUS. Yes, I say. Let the military tribune bear witness.

Lucius Septimius, a clean shaven, trim athlete of about 40, with symmetrical features, resolute mouth, and handsome, thin Roman nose, in the dress of a Roman officer, comes in through the loggia and confronts Cæsar, who hides his face with his robe for a moment; then, mastering himself, drops it, and confronts the tribune with dignity.

POTHINUS. Bear witness, Lucius Septimius. Cæsar came hither in pursuit of his foe. Did we shelter his foe?

LUCIUS. As Pompey's foot touched the Egyptian shore, his head fell by the stroke of my sword.

THEODOTUS (*with viperish relish*). Under the eyes of his wife and child! Remember that, Cæsar! They saw it from the ship he had just left. We have given you a full and sweet measure of vengeance.

CÆSAR (*with horror*). Vengeance!

POTHINUS. Our first gift to you, as your galley came into the roadstead, was the head of your rival for the empire of the world. Bear witness, Lucius Septimius: is it not so?

LUCIUS. It is so. With this hand, that slew Pompey, I placed his head at the feet of Cæsar.

CÆSAR. Murderer! So would you have slain Cæsar, had Pompey been victorious at Pharsalia.

LUCIUS. Woe to the vanquished, Cæsar! When I served Pompey, I slew as good men as he, only because he conquered them. His turn came at last.

THEODOTUS (*flatteringly*). The deed was not yours, Cæsar, but ours—nay, mine; for it was done by my counsel. Thanks to us, you keep your reputation for clemency, and have your vengeance too.

CÆSAR. Vengeance! Vengeance! Oh, if I could stoop to vengeance, what would I not exact from you as the price of this murdered man's blood. (*They shrink back, appalled and disconcerted.*) Was he not my son-in-law, my ancient friend, for 20 years the master of great Rome, for 30 years the compeller of victory? Did not I, as a Roman, share his glory? Was the Fate that forced us to fight for the mastery of the world, of our making? Am I Julius Cæsar, or am I a wolf, that you fling to me the grey head of the old soldier, the laurelled conqueror, the mighty Roman, treacherously struck down by this callous ruffian, and then claim my gratitude for it! (*To Lucius Septimius*) Begone: you fill me with horror.

LUCIUS (*cold and undaunted*). Pshaw! you have seen severed heads before, Cæsar, and severed right hands too, I think; some thousands of them, in Gaul, after you vanquished Vercingetorix. Did you spare him, with all your clemency? Was that vengeance?

CÆSAR. No, by the gods! would that it had been! Vengeance at least is human. No, I say: those severed right hands, and the brave Vercingetorix basely strangled in a vault beneath the Capitol, were (*with shuddering satire*) a wise severity, a necessary protection to the commonwealth, a duty of statesmanship—follies and fictions ten times bloodier than honest vengeance! What a fool was I then! To think that men's lives should be at the mercy of such fools! (*Humbly*) Lucius Septimius, pardon me: why should the slayer of Vercingetorix rebuke the slayer of Pompey? You are free to go with the rest. Or stay if you will: I will find a place for you in my service.

LUCIUS. The odds are against you, Cæsar. I go. (*He turns to go out through the loggia.*)

RUFIO (*full of wrath at seeing his prey escaping*). That means that he is a Republican.

LUCIUS (*turning defiantly on the loggia steps*). And what are you?

RUFIO. A Cæsarian, like all Cæsar's soldiers.

CÆSAR (*courteously*). Lucius: believe me, Cæsar is no Cæsarian. Were Rome a true republic, then were Cæsar the first of Republicans. But you have made your choice. Farewell.

LUCIUS. Farewell. Come, Achillas, whilst there is yet time.

Cæsar, seeing that Rufio's temper threatens to get the worse of him, puts his hand on his shoulder and brings him down the hall out of harm's way, Britannus accompanying them and posting himself on Cæsar's right hand. This movement brings the three in a little group to the place occupied by Achillas, who moves haughtily away and joins Theodotus on the other side. Lucius Septimius goes out through the soldiers in the loggia. Pothinus, Theodotus and Achillas follow him with the courtiers, very mistrustful of the soldiers, who close up in their rear and go out after them, keeping them moving without much ceremony. The King is left in his chair, piteous, obstinate, with twitching face and fingers.

During these movements Rufio maintains an energetic grumbling, as follows:—

RUFIO (*as Lucius departs*). Do you suppose he would let us go if he had our heads in his hands?

CÆSAR. I have no right to suppose that his ways are any baser than mine.

RUFIO. Psha!

CÆSAR. Rufio: if I take Lucius Septimius for my model, and become exactly like him, ceasing to be Cæsar, will you serve me still?

BRITANNUS. Cæsar: this is not good sense. Your duty to Rome demands that her enemies should be prevented from doing further mischief. (*Cæsar, whose delight in the moral eye-to-business of his British secretary is inexhaustible, smiles indulgently.*)

RUFIO. It is no use talking to him, Britannus: you may save your breath to cool your porridge. But mark this, Cæsar. Clemency is very well for you; but what is it for your soldiers, who have to fight to-morrow the men you spared yesterday? You may give what orders you please; but I tell you that your next victory will be a massacre, thanks to your clemency. *I*, for one, will take no prisoners. I will kill my enemies in the field; and then you can preach as much clemency as you please: I shall never have to fight them again. And now, with your leave, I will see these gentry off the premises. (*He turns to go.*)

CÆSAR (*turning also and seeing Ptolemy*). What! have they left the boy alone! Oh shame, shame!

RUFIO (*taking Ptolemy's hand and making him rise*). Come, your majesty!

PTOLEMY (*to Cæsar, drawing away his hand from Rufio*). Is he turning me out of my palace?

RUFIO (*grimly*). You are welcome to stay if you wish.

CÆSAR (*kindly*). Go, my boy. I will not harm you; but you will be safer away, among your friends. Here you are in the lion's mouth.

PTOLEMY (*turning to go*). It is not the lion I fear, but (*looking at Rufio*) the jackal. (*He goes out through the loggia.*)

CÆSAR (*laughing approvingly*). Brave boy!

CLEOPATRA (*jealous of Cæsar's approbation, calling after Ptolemy*). Little silly. You think that very clever.

CÆSAR. Britannus: attend the King. Give him in charge to that Pothinus fellow. (*Britannus goes out after Ptolemy.*)

RUFIO (*pointing to Cleopatra*). And this piece of goods? What is to be done with h e r? However, I suppose I may leave that to you. (*He goes out through the loggia.*)

CLEOPATRA (*flushing suddenly and turning on Cæsar*). Did you mean me to go with the rest?

CÆSAR (*a little preoccupied, goes with a sigh to Ptolemy's chair, whilst she waits for his answer with red cheeks and clenched fists*). You are free to do just as you please, Cleopatra.

CLEOPATRA. Then you do not care whether I stay or not?

CÆSAR (*smiling*). Of course I had rather you stayed.

CLEOPATRA. Much, m u c h rather?

CÆSAR (*nodding*). Much, much rather.

CLEOPATRA. Then I consent to stay, because I am asked. But I do not want to, mind.

CÆSAR. That is quite understood. (*Calling*) Totateeta.

Ftatateeta, still seated, turns her eyes on him with a sinister expression, but does not move.

CLEOPATRA (*with a splutter of laughter*). Her name is not Totateeta: it is Ftatateeta. (*Calling*) Ftatateeta. (*Ftatateeta instantly rises and comes to Cleopatra.*)

CÆSAR (*stumbling over the name*). Tfatafeeta will forgive the erring tongue of a Roman. Tota: the Queen will hold her state here in Alexandria. Engage women to attend upon her; and do all that is needful.

FTATATEETA. Am I then the mistress of the Queen's household?

CLEOPATRA (*sharply*). No: *I* am the mistress of the Queen's household. Go and do as you are told, or I will have you thrown into the Nile this very afternoon, to poison the poor crocodiles.

CÆSAR (*shocked*). Oh no, no.

CLEOPATRA. Oh yes, yes. You are very sentimental, Cæsar; but you are clever; and if you do as I tell you, you will soon learn to govern.

Cæsar, quite dumbfounded by this impertinence, turns in his chair and stares at her.

Ftatateeta, smiling grimly, and showing a splendid set of teeth, goes, leaving them alone together.

CÆSAR. Cleopatra: I really think I must eat you, after all.

CLEOPATRA (*kneeling beside him and looking at him with eager interest, half real, half affected to shew how intelligent she is*). You must not talk to me now as if I were a child.

CÆSAR. You have been growing up since the Sphinx introduced us the other night; and you think you know more than I do already.

CLEOPATRA (*taken down, and anxious to justify herself*). No: that would be very silly of me: of course I know that. But—(*suddenly*) are you angry with me?

CÆSAR. No.

CLEOPATRA (*only half believing him*). Then why are you so thoughtful?

CÆSAR (*rising*). I have work to do, Cleopatra.

CLEOPATRA (*drawing back*). *Work!* (Offended) You are tired of talking to me; and that is your excuse to get away from me.

CÆSAR (*sitting down again to appease her*). Well, well: another minute. But then—work!

CLEOPATRA. Work! what nonsense! You must remember that you are a king now: I have made you one. Kings don't work.

CÆSAR. Oh! Who told you that, little kitten? Eh?

CLEOPATRA. My father was King of Egypt; and he never worked. But he was a great king, and cut off my sister's head because she rebelled against him and took the throne from him.

CÆSAR. Well; and how did he get his throne back again?

CLEOPATRA (*eagerly, her eyes lighting up*). I will tell you. A beautiful young man, with strong round arms, came over the desert with many horsemen, and slew my sister's husband and gave my father back his throne. (*Wistfully*) I was only twelve then. Oh, I wish he would come again, now that I am a queen. I would make him my husband.

CÆSAR. It might be managed, perhaps; for it was I who sent that beautiful young man to help your father.

CLEOPATRA (*enraptured*). You know him!

CÆSAR (*nodding*). I do.

CLEOPATRA. Has he come with you? (*Cæsar shakes his head: she is cruelly disappointed.*) Oh, I wish he had, I wish he had. If only I were a little older; so that he might not think me a mere kitten, as you do! But perhaps that is because y o u are old. He is many, m a n y years younger than you, is he not?

CÆSAR (*as if swallowing a pill*). He is somewhat younger.

CLEOPATRA. Would he be my husband, do you think, if I asked him?

CÆSAR. Very likely.

CLEOPATRA. But I should not like to ask him. Could you not persuade him to ask me—without knowing that I wanted him to?

CÆSAR (*touched by her innocence of the beautiful young man's character*). My poor child!

CLEOPATRA. Why do you say that as if you were sorry for me? Does he love anyone else?

CÆSAR. I am afraid so.

CLEOPATRA (*tearfully*). Then I shall not be his first love.

CÆSAR. Not quite the first. He is greatly admired by women.

CLEOPATRA. I wish I could be the first. But if he loves me, I will make him kill all the rest. Tell me: is he still beautiful? Do his strong round arms shine in the sun like marble?

CÆSAR. He is in excellent condition—considering how much he eats and drinks.

CLEOPATRA. Oh, you must not say common, earthly things about him; for I love him. He is a god.

CÆSAR. He is a great captain of horsemen, and swifter of foot than any other Roman.

CLEOPATRA. What is his real name?

CÆSAR (*puzzled*). His r e a l name?

CLEOPATRA. Yes. I always call him Horus, because Horus is the most beautiful of our gods. But I want to know his real name.

CÆSAR. His name is Mark Antony.

CLEOPATRA (*musically*). Mark Antony, Mark Antony, Mark Antony! What a beautiful name! (*She throws her arms around Cæsar's neck.*) Oh, how I love you for sending him to help my father! Did you love my father very much?

CÆSAR. No, my child, but your father, as you say, never worked. I always work. So when he lost his crown he had to promise me 16,000 talents to get it back for him.

CLEOPATRA. Did he ever pay you?

CÆSAR. Not in full.

CLEOPATRA. He was quite right: it was too dear. The whole world is not worth 16,000 talents.

CÆSAR. That is perhaps true, Cleopatra. Those Egyptians who work paid as much of it as he could drag from them. The rest is still due. But as I most likely shall not get it, I must go back to my work. So you must run away for a little and send my secretary to me.

CLEOPATRA (*coaxing*). No: I want to stay and hear you talk about Mark Antony.

CÆSAR. But if I do not get to work, Pothinus and the rest of them will cut us off from the harbor; and then the way from Rome will be blocked.

CLEOPATRA. No matter: I don't want you to go back to Rome.

CÆSAR. But you want Mark Antony to come from it.

CLEOPATRA (*springing up*). Oh yes, yes, yes: I forgot. Go quickly and work, Cæsar; and keep the way over the sea open for my Mark Antony. (*She runs out through the loggia, kissing her hand to Mark Antony across the sea.*)

CÆSAR (*going briskly up the middle of the hall to the loggia steps*). Ho, Britannus. (*He is startled by the entry of a wounded Roman soldier, who confronts him from the upper step.*) What now?

SOLDIER (*pointing to his bandaged head*). This, Cæsar; and two of my comrades killed in the market place.

CÆSAR (*quiet, but attending*). Ay. Why?

SOLDIER. There is an army come to Alexandria, calling itself the Roman army.

CÆSAR. The Roman army of occupation. Ay?

SOLDIER. Commanded by one Achillas.

CÆSAR. Well?

SOLDIER. The citizens rose against us when the army entered the gates. I was with two others in the market place when the news came. They set upon us. I cut my way out; and here I am.

CÆSAR. Good. I am glad to see you alive. (*Rufio enters the loggia hastily, passing behind the soldier to look out through one of the arches at the quay beneath.*) Rufio, we are besieged.

RUFIO. What! Already?

CÆSAR. Now or to-morrow: what does it matter? We s h a l l be besieged.

Britannus runs in.

BRITANNUS. Cæsar—

CÆSAR (*anticipating him*). Yes: I know. (*Rufio and Britannus come down the hall from the loggia at opposite sides, past Cæsar, who waits for a moment near the step to say to the soldier*) Comrade: give the word to turn out on the beach and stand by the boats. Get your wound attended to. Go. (*The soldier hurries out. Cæsar comes down the hall between Rufio and Britannus.*) Rufio: we have some ships in the west harbor. Burn them.

RUFIO (*staring*). Burn them!!

CÆSAR. Take every boat we have in the east harbor, and seize the Pharos—that island with the lighthouse. Leave half our men behind to hold the beach and the quay outside this palace: that is the way home.

RUFIO (*disapproving strongly*). Are we to give up the city?

CÆSAR. We have not got it, Rufio. This palace we have; and—what is that building next door?

RUFIO. The theatre.

CÆSAR. We will have that too: it commands the strand. For the rest, Egypt for the Egyptians!

RUFIO. Well, you know best, I suppose. Is that all?

CÆSAR. That is all. Are those ships burnt yet?

RUFIO. Be easy: I shall waste no more time (*He runs out.*)

BRITANNUS. Cæsar: Pothinus demands speech of you. In my opinion he needs a lesson. His manner is most insolent.

CÆSAR. Where is he?

BRITANNUS. He waits without.

CÆSAR. Ho there! admit Pothinus.

Pothinus appears in the loggia, and comes down the hall very haughtily to Cæsar's left hand.

CÆSAR. Well, Pothinus?

POTHINUS. I have brought you our ultimatum, Cæsar.

CÆSAR. Ultimatum! The door was open: you should have gone out through it before you declared war. You are my prisoner now. (*He goes to the chair and loosens his toga.*)

POTHINUS (*scornfully*). I y o u r prisoner! Do you know that you are in Alexandria, and that King Ptolemy, with an army outnumbering your little troop a hundred to one, is in possession of Alexandria?

CÆSAR (*unconcernedly taking off his toga and throwing it on the chair*). Well, my friend, get out if you can. And tell your friends not to kill any more Romans in the market place. Otherwise my soldiers, who do not share my celebrated clemency, will probably kill you. Britannus: pass the word to the guard: and fetch my armor. (*Britannus runs out. Rufio returns.*) Well?

RUFIO (*pointing from the loggia to a cloud of smoke drifting over the harbor*). See there! (*Pothinus runs eagerly up the steps to look out.*)

CÆSAR. What, ablaze already! Impossible!

RUFIO. Yes, five good ships, and a barge laden with oil grappled to each. But it is not my doing: the Egyptians have saved me the trouble. They have captured the west harbor.

CÆSAR (*anxiously*). And the east harbor? The lighthouse, Rufio?

RUFIO (*with a sudden splutter of raging ill usage, coming down to Cæsar and scolding him*). Can I embark a legion in five minutes? The first cohort is already on the beach. We can do no more. If you want faster work, come and do it yourself.

CÆSAR (*soothing him*). Good, good. Patience, Rufio, patience.

RUFIO. Patience! Who is impatient here, you or I? Would I be here, if I could not oversee them from that balcony?

CÆSAR. Forgive me, Rufio; and (*anxiously*) hurry them as much as—

He is interrupted by an outcry as of an old man in the extremity of misfortune. It draws near rapidly; and Theodotus rushes in, tearing his hair, and squeaking the most lamentable exclamations. Rufio steps back to stare at him, amazed at his frantic condition. Pothinus turns to listen.

THEODOTUS (*on the steps, with uplifted arms*). Horror unspeakable! Woe, alas! Help!

RUFIO. What now?

CÆSAR (*frowning*). Who is slain?

THEODOTUS. Slain! Oh, worse than the death of ten thousand men! Loss irreparable to mankind!

RUFIO. What has happened, man?

THEODOTUS (*rushing down the hall between them*). The fire has spread from your ships. The first of the seven wonders of the world perishes. The library of Alexandria is in flames.

RUFIO. Psha! (*Quite relieved, he goes up to the loggia and watches the preparations of the troops on the beach.*)

CÆSAR. Is that all?

THEODOTUS (*unable to believe his senses*). All! Cæsar: will you go down to posterity as a barbarous soldier too ignorant to know the value of books?

CÆSAR. Theodotus: I am an author myself; and I tell you it is better that the Egyptians should live their lives than dream them away with the help of books.

THEODOTUS (*kneeling, with genuine literary emotion: the passion of the pedant*). Cæsar: once in ten generations of men, the world gains an immortal book.

CÆSAR (*inflexible*). If it did not flatter mankind, the common executioner would burn it.

THEODOTUS. Without history, death would lay you beside your meanest soldier.

CÆSAR. Death will do that in any case. I ask no better grave.

THEODOTUS. What is burning there is the memory of mankind.

CÆSAR. A shameful memory. Let it burn.

THEODOTUS (*wildly*). Will you destroy the past?

CÆSAR. Ay, and build the future with its ruins. (*Theodotus, in despair, strikes himself on the temples with his fists.*) But harken, Theodotus, teacher of kings: you who valued Pompey's head no more than a shepherd values an onion, and who now kneel to me, with tears in your old eyes, to plead for a few sheepskins scrawled with errors. I cannot spare you a man or a bucket of water just now; but you shall pass freely out of the palace. Now, away with you to Achillas; and borrow his legions to put out the fire. (*He hurries him to the steps.*)

POTHINUS (*significantly*). You understand, Theodotus: I remain a prisoner.

THEODOTUS. A prisoner!

CÆSAR. Will you stay to talk whilst the memory of mankind is burning? (*Calling through the loggia*) Ho there! Pass Theodotus out. (*To Theodotus*) Away with you.

THEODOTUS (*to Pothinus*). I must go to save the library. (*He hurries out.*)

CÆSAR. Follow him to the gate, Pothinus. Bid him urge your people to kill no more of my soldiers, for your sake.

POTHINUS. My life will cost you dear if you take it, Cæsar. (*He goes out after Theodotus.*)

Rufio, absorbed in watching the embarkation, does not notice the departure of the two Egyptians.

RUFIO (*shouting from the loggia to the beach*). All ready, there?

A CENTURION (*from below*). All ready. We wait for Cæsar.

CÆSAR. Tell them Cæsar is coming—the rogues! (*Calling*) Britannicus. (*This magniloquent version of his secretary's name is one of Cæsar's jokes. In later years it would have meant, quite seriously and officially, Conqueror of Britain.*)

RUFIO (*calling down*). Push off, all except the longboat. Stand by it to embark, Cæsar's guard there. (*He leaves the balcony and comes down into the hall.*) Where are those Egyptians? Is this more clemency? Have you let them go?

CÆSAR (*chuckling*). I have let Theodotus go to save the library. We must respect literature, Rufio.

RUFIO (*raging*). Folly on folly's head! I believe if you could bring back all the dead of Spain, Gaul and Thessaly to life, you would do it that we might have the trouble of fighting them over again.

CÆSAR. Might not the gods destroy the world if their only thought were to be at peace next year? (*Rufio, out of all patience, turns away in anger. Cæsar suddenly grips his sleeve, and adds slyly in his ear*) Besides, my friend: every Egyptian we imprison means imprisoning two Roman soldiers to guard him. Eh?

RUFIO. Agh! I might have known there was some fox's trick behind your fine talking. (*He gets away from Cæsar*

SALES SLIP EDC SET

MERCHANT NAME

TERMINAL NO.

MERCHANT NO.

CARD TYPE/NUMBER

TX.

EXPIRY

BATCH NO.

TRACE NO.

DATE/TIME

REF. NO.

APP. CODE

The issuer of the card identified on this item is authorized to pay the amount shown as total upon proper presentation. I promise to pay such total (together with any other charges due thereon) subject to and in accordance with the agreement governing the use of such card.

I acknowledge satisfactory receipt of relative goods/services.

X

Cardholder's signature

NO REFUND

CUSTOMER COPY

P.1488 (VAT) (2-12/41)

Bangkok Bank SALES SLIP EDC SET

CREDIT CARD VISA

MERCHANT NAME

TERMINAL NO

MERCHANT NO

CARD TYPE/NUMBER

TX | EXPIRY

BATCH NO. | TRACE NO.

DATE/TIME

REF. NO. | APPR CODE

The issuer of the card identified on this item is authorized to pay the amount shown as total upon proper presentation. I promise to pay such total together with any other charges due thereon subject to and in accordance with the agreement governing the use of such card.

I acknowledge satisfactory receipt of relative goods/services.

X

CUSTOMER COPY

Cardholder's signature

with an ill-humored shrug, and goes to the balcony for another look at the preparations; finally goes out.)

CÆSAR. Is Britannus asleep? I sent him for my armor an hour ago. (*Calling*) Britannicus, thou British islander. Britannicus!

Cleopatra runs in through the loggia with Cæsar's helmet and sword, snatched from Britannus, who follows her with a cuirass and greaves. They come down to Cæsar, she to his left hand, Britannus to his right.

CLEOPATRA. I am going to dress you, Cæsar. Sit down. (*He obeys.*) These Roman helmets are so becoming! (*She takes off his wreath.*) Oh! (*She bursts out laughing at him.*)

CÆSAR. What are you laughing at?

CLEOPATRA. You're bald (*beginning with a big B, and ending with a splutter*).

CÆSAR (*almost annoyed*). Cleopatra! (*He rises, for the convenience of Britannus, who puts the cuirass on him.*)

CLEOPATRA. So that is why you wear the wreath—to hide it.

BRITANNUS. Peace, Egyptian: they are the bays of the conqueror. (*He buckles the cuirass.*)

CLEOPATRA. Peace, thou: islander! (*To Cæsar*) You should rub your head with strong spirits of sugar, Cæsar. That will make it grow.

CÆSAR (*with a wry face*). Cleopatra: do you like to be reminded that you are very young?

CLEOPATRA (*pouting*). No.

CÆSAR (*sitting down again, and setting out his leg for Britannus, who kneels to put on his greaves*). Neither do I like to be reminded that I am—middle aged. Let me give you ten of my superfluous years. That will make you 26, and leave me only—no matter. Is it a bargain?

CLEOPATRA. Agreed. 26, mind. (*She puts the helmet on him.*) Oh! How nice! You look only about 50 in it!

BRITANNUS (*looking up severely at Cleopatra*). You must not speak in this manner to Cæsar.

CLEOPATRA. Is it true that when Cæsar caught you on that island, you were painted all over blue?

BRITANNUS. Blue is the color worn by all Britons of good standing. In war we stain our bodies blue; so that though our enemies may strip us of our clothes and our lives, they cannot strip us of our respectability. (*He rises.*)

CLEOPATRA (*with Cæsar's sword*). Let me hang this on. Now you look splendid. Have they made any statues of you in Rome?

CÆSAR. Yes, many statues.

CLEOPATRA. You must send for one and give it to me.

RUFIO (*coming back into the loggia, more impatient than ever*). Now Cæsar: have you done talking? The moment your foot is aboard there will be no holding our men back: the boats will race one another for the lighthouse.

CÆSAR (*drawing his sword and trying the edge*). Is this well set to-day, Britannicus? At Pharsalia it was as blunt as a barrel-hoop.

BRITANNUS. It will split one of the Egyptian's hairs to-day, Cæsar. I have set it myself.

CLEOPATRA (*suddenly throwing her arms in terror round Cæsar*). Oh, you are not really going into battle to be killed?

CÆSAR. No, Cleopatra. No man goes to battle to be killed.

CLEOPATRA. But they do get killed. My sister's husband was killed in battle. You must not go. Let him go (*pointing to Rufio. They all laugh at her*). Oh please, p l e a s e don't go. What will happen to me if you never come back?

CÆSAR (*gravely*). Are you afraid?

CLEOPATRA (*shrinking*). No.

CÆSAR (with quiet authority). Go to the balcony; and you shall see us take the Pharos. You must learn to look on battles. Go. (*She goes, downcast, and looks out from the balcony.*) That is well. Now, Rufio. March.

CLEOPATRA (*suddenly clapping her hands*). Oh, you will not be able to go!

CÆSAR. Why? What now?

CLEOPATRA. They are drying up the harbor with buckets—a multitude of soldiers—over there (*pointing out across the sea to her left*)—they are dipping up the water.

RUFIO (*hastening to look*). It is true. The Egyptian army! Crawling over the edge of the west harbor like locusts. (*With sudden anger he strides down to Cæsar.*) This is your accursed clemency, Cæsar. Theodotus has brought them.

CÆSAR (*delighted at his own cleverness*). I meant him to,

Rufio. They have come to put out the fire. The library will keep them busy whilst we seize the lighthouse. Eh? (*He rushes out buoyantly through the loggia, followed by Britannus.*)

RUFIO (*disgustedly*). More foxing! Agh! (*He rushes off. A shout from the soldiers announces the appearance of Cæsar below.*)

CENTURION (*below*). All aboard. Give way there. (*Another shout.*)

CLEOPATRA (*waving her scarf through the loggia arch*). Goodbye, goodbye, dear Cæsar. Come back safe. Goodbye!

END OF ACT II.

ACT III

The edge of the quay in front of the palace, looking out west over the east harbor of Alexandria to Pharos island, just off the end of which, and connected with it by a narrow mole, is the famous lighthouse, a gigantic square tower of white marble diminishing in size storey by storey to the top, on which stands a cresset beacon. The island is joined to the main land by the Heptastadium, a great mole or causeway five miles long bounding the harbor on the south.

In the middle of the quay a Roman sentinel stands on guard, pilum in hand, looking out to the lighthouse with strained attention, his left hand shading his eyes. The pilum is a stout wooden shaft 4½ feet long, with an iron spit about three feet long fixed in it. The sentinel is so absorbed that he does not notice the approach from the north end of the quay of four Egyptian market porters carrying rolls of carpet, preceded by Ftatateeta and Apollodorus the Sicilian. Apollodorus is a dashing young man of about 24, handsome and debonair, dressed with deliberate æstheticism in the most delicate purples and dove greys, with ornaments of bronze, oxydized silver, and stones of jade and agate. His sword, designed as carefully as a medieval cross, has a blued blade showing through an openwork scabbard of purple leather and filigree. The porters, conducted by Ftatateeta, pass along the quay behind the sentinel to the steps of the palace, where they put down their bales and squat on the ground. Apollodorus does not pass along with them: he halts, amused by the preoccupation of the sentinel.

APOLLODORUS (*calling to the sentinel*). Who goes there, eh?

SENTINEL (*starting violently and turning with his pilum at the charge, revealing himself as a small, wiry, sandy-haired, conscientious young man with an elderly face*). What's this? Stand. Who are you?

APOLLODORUS. I am Apollodorus the Sicilian. Why, man, what are you dreaming of? Since I came through the lines beyond the theatre there, I have brought my caravan past three sentinels, all so busy staring at the lighthouse that not one of them challenged me. Is this Roman discipline?

SENTINEL. We are not here to watch the land but the sea. Cæsar has just landed on the Pharos. (*Looking at Ftatateeta*) What have you here? Who is this piece of Egyptian crockery?

FTATATEETA. Apollodorus: rebuke this Roman dog; and bid him bridle his tongue in the presence of Ftatateeta, the mistress of the Queen's household.

APOLLODORUS. My friend: this is a great lady, who stands high with Cæsar.

SENTINEL (*not at all impressed, pointing to the carpets*). And what is all this truck?

APOLLODORUS. Carpets for the furnishing of the Queen's apartments in the palace. I have picked them from the best carpets in the world; and the Queen shall choose the best of my choosing.

SENTINEL. So you are the carpet merchant?

APOLLODORUS (*hurt*). My friend: I am a patrician.

SENTINEL. A patrician! A patrician keeping a shop instead of following arms!

APOLLODORUS. I do not keep a shop. Mine is a temple of the arts. I am a worshipper of beauty. My calling is to choose beautiful things for beautiful Queens. My motto is Art for Art's sake.

SENTINEL. That is not the password.

APOLLODORUS. It is a universal password.

SENTINEL. I know nothing about universal passwords. Either give me the password for the day or get back to your shop.

Ftatateeta, roused by his hostile tone, steals towards the edge of the quay with the step of a panther, and gets behind him.

APOLLODORUS. How if I do neither?

SENTINEL. Then I will drive this pilum through you.

APOLLODORUS. At your service, my friend. (*He draws his sword, and springs to his guard with unruffled grace.*)

FTATATEETA (*suddenly seizing the sentinel's arms from behind*). Thrust your knife into the dog's throat, Apollodorus. (*The chivalrous Apollodorus laughingly shakes his head; breaks ground away from the sentinel towards the palace; and lowers his point.*)

SENTINEL (*struggling vainly*). Curse on you! Let me go. Help ho!

FTATATEETA (*lifting him from the ground*). Stab the little Roman reptile. Spit him on your sword.

A couple of Roman soldiers, with a centurion, come running along the edge of the quay from the north end. They rescue their comrade, and throw off Ftatateeta, who is sent reeling away on the left hand of the sentinel.

CENTURION (*an unattractive man of fifty, short in his speech and manners, with a vine wood cudgel in his hand*). How now? What is all this?

FTATATEETA (*to Apollodorus*). Why did you not stab him? There was time!

APOLLODORUS. Centurion: I am here by order of the Queen to—

CENTURION (*interrupting him*). The Queen! Yes, yes: (*to the sentinel*) pass him in. Pass all these bazaar people into the Queen, with their goods. But mind you pass no one out that you have not passed in—not even the Queen herself.

SENTINEL. This old woman is dangerous: she is as strong as three men. She wanted the merchant to stab me.

APOLLODORUS. Centurion: I am not a merchant. I am a patrician and a votary of art.

CENTURION. Is the woman your wife?

APOLLODORUS (*horrified*). No, no! (*Correcting himself politely*) Not that the lady is not a striking figure in her own way. But (*emphatically*) she is n o t my wife.

FTATATEETA (*to the Centurion*). Roman: I am Ftatateeta, the mistress of the Queen's household.

CENTURION. Keep your hands off our men, mistress; or I will have you pitched into the harbor, though you were as strong as ten men. (*To his men*) To your posts: march! (*He returns with his men the way they came.*)

FTATATEETA (*looking malignantly after him*). We shall see whom Isis loves best: her servant Ftatateeta or a dog of a Roman.

SENTINEL (*to Apollodorus, with a wave of his pilum towards the palace*). Pass in there; and keep your distance. (*Turning to Ftatateeta*) Come within a yard of me, you old crocodile; and I will give you this (*the pilum*) in your jaws.

CLEOPATRA (*calling from the palace*). Ftatateeta, Ftatateeta.

FTATATEETA (*looking up, scandalized*). Go from the window, go from the window. There are men here.

CLEOPATRA. I am coming down.

FTATATEETA (*distracted*). No, no. What are you dreaming of? O ye gods, ye gods! Apollodorus: bid your men pick up your bales; and in with me quickly.

APOLLODORUS. Obey the mistress of the Queen's household.

FTATATEETA (*impatiently, as the porters stoop to lift the bales*). Quick, quick: she will be out upon us. (*Cleopatra comes from the palace and runs across the quay to Ftatateeta.*) Oh that ever I was born!

CLEOPATRA (*eagerly*). Ftatateeta: I have thought of something. I want a boat—at once.

FTATATEETA. A boat! No, no: you cannot. Apollodorus: speak to the Queen.

APOLLODORUS (*gallantly*). Beautiful queen: I am Apollodorus the Sicilian, your servant, from the bazaar. I have brought you the three most beautiful Persian carpets in the world to choose from.

CLEOPATRA. I have no time for carpets to-day. Get me a boat.

FTATATEETA. What whim is this? You cannot go on the water except in the royal barge.

APOLLODORUS. Royalty, Ftatateeta, lies not in the barge but in the Queen. (*To Cleopatra*) The touch of your majesty's foot on the gunwale of the meanest boat in the harbor will make it royal. (*He turns to the harbor and calls seaward*) Ho there, boatman! Pull in to the steps.

CLEOPATRA. Apollodorus: you are my perfect knight; and I will always buy my carpets through you. (*Apollodorus bows joyously. An oar appears above the quay; and the boatman, a bullet-headed, vivacious, grinning fellow, burnt almost black by the sun, comes up a flight of steps from the water on the sentinel's right, oar in hand, and waits at the top.*) Can you row, Apollodorus?

APOLLODORUS. My oars shall be your majesty's wings. Whither shall I row my Queen?

CLEOPATRA. To the lighthouse. Come. (*She makes for the steps.*)

SENTINEL (*opposing her with his pilum at the charge*). Stand. You cannot pass.

CLEOPATRA (*flushing angrily*). How dare you? Do you know that I am the Queen?

SENTINEL. I have my orders. You cannot pass.

CLEOPATRA. I will make Cæsar have you killed if you do not obey me.

SENTINEL. He will do worse to me if I disobey my officer. Stand back.

CLEOPATRA. Ftatateeta: strangle him.

SENTINEL (*alarmed—looking apprehensively at Ftatateeta, and brandishing his pilum*). Keep off, there.

CLEOPATRA (*running to Apollodorus*). Apollodorus: make your slaves help us.

APOLLODORUS. I shall not need their help, lady. (*He draws his sword.*) Now, soldier: choose which weapon you will defend yourself with. Shall it be sword against pilum, or sword against sword?

SENTINEL. Roman against Sicilian, curse you. Take that. (*He hurls his pilum at Apollodorus, who drops expertly on one knee. The pilum passes whizzing over his head and falls harmless. Apollodorus, with a cry of triumph, springs up and attacks the sentinel, who draws his sword and defends himself, crying*) Ho there, guard. Help!

Cleopatra, half frightened, half delighted, takes refuge near the palace, where the porters are squatting among the bales. The boatman, alarmed, hurries down the steps out of harm's way, but stops, with his head just visible above the edge of the quay, to watch the fight. The sentinel is handicapped by his fear of an attack in the rear from Ftatateeta. His swordsmanship, which is of a rough and ready sort, is heavily taxed, as he has occasionally to strike at her to keep her off between a blow and a guard with Apollodorus. The Centurion returns with several soldiers. Apollodorus springs back towards Cleopatra as this reinforcement confronts him.

CENTURION (*coming to the sentinel's right hand*). What is this? What now?

SENTINEL (*panting*). I could do well enough by myself if it weren't for the old woman. Keep her off me: that is all the help I need.

CENTURION. Make your report, soldier. What has happened?

FTATATEETA. Centurion: he would have slain the Queen.

SENTINEL (*bluntly*). I would, sooner than let her pass. She wanted to take boat, and go—so she said—to the lighthouse. I stopped her, as I was ordered to; and she set this fellow on me. (*He goes to pick up his pilum and returns to his place with it.*)

CENTURION (*turning to Cleopatra*). Cleopatra: I am loth to offend you; but without Cæsar's express order we dare not let you pass beyond the Roman lines.

APOLLODORUS. Well, Centurion; and has not the lighthouse been within the Roman lines since Cæsar landed there?

CLEOPATRA. Yes, yes. Answer that, if you can.

CENTURION (*to Apollodorus*). As for you, Apollodorus, you may thank the gods that you are not nailed to the palace door with a pilum for your meddling.

APOLLODORUS (*urbanely*). My military friend, I was not born to be slain by so ugly a weapon. When I fall, it will be (*holding up his sword*) by this white queen of arms, the only weapon fit for an artist. And now that you are convinced that we do not want to go beyond the lines, let me finish killing your sentinel and depart with the Queen.

CENTURION (*as the sentinel makes an angry demonstration*). Peace there. Cleopatra. I must abide by my orders, and not by the subtleties of this Sicilian. You must withdraw into the palace and examine your carpets there.

CLEOPATRA (*pouting*). I will not: I am the Queen. Cæsar does not speak to me as you do. Have Cæsar's centurions changed manners with his scullions?

CENTURION (*sulkily*). I do my duty. That is enough for me.

APOLLODORUS. Majesty: when a stupid man is doing something he is ashamed of, he always declares that it is his duty.

CENTURION (*angry*). Apollodorus—

APOLLODORUS (*interrupting him with defiant elegance*). I will make amends for that insult with my sword at fitting time and place. Who says artist, says duellist. (*To Cleopatra*) Hear my counsel, star of the east. Until word comes to these soldiers from Cæsar himself, you are a prisoner. Let me go to him with a message from you, and a present; and before the sun has stooped half way to the arms of the sea, I will bring you back Cæsar's order of release.

CENTURION (*sneering at him*). And you will sell the Queen the present, no doubt.

APOLLODORUS. Centurion: the Queen shall have from me, without payment, as the unforced tribute of Sicilian taste to Egyptian beauty, the richest of these carpets for her present to Cæsar.

CLEOPATRA (*exultantly, to the Centurion*). Now you see what an ignorant common creature you are!

CENTURION (*curtly*). Well, a fool and his wares are soon parted. (*He turns to his men.*) Two more men to this post here; and see that no one leaves the palace but this man and his merchandize. If he draws his sword again inside the lines, kill him. To your posts. March.

He goes out, leaving two auxiliary sentinels with the other.

APOLLODORUS (*with polite goodfellowship*). My friends: will you not enter the palace and bury our quarrel in a bowl of wine? (*He takes out his purse, jingling the coins in it.*) The Queen has presents for you all.

SENTINEL (*very sulky*). You heard our orders. Get about your business.

FIRST AUXILIARY. Yes: you ought to know better. Off with you.

SECOND AUXILIARY (*looking longingly at the purse—this sentinel is a hooknosed man, unlike his comrade, who is squab faced*). Do not tantalize a poor man.

APOLLODORUS (*to Cleopatra*). Pearl of Queens: the Centurion is at hand; and the Roman soldier is incorruptible when his officer is looking. I must carry your word to Cæsar.

CLEOPATRA (*who has been meditating among the carpets*). Are these carpets very heavy?

APOLLODORUS. It matters not how heavy. There are plenty of porters.

CLEOPATRA. How do they put the carpets into boats? Do they throw them down?

APOLLODORUS. Not into small boats, majesty. It would sink them.

CLEOPATRA. Not into that man's boat, for instance? (*Pointing to the boatman.*)

APOLLODORUS. No. Too small.

CLEOPATRA. But you can take a carpet to Cæsar in it if I send one?

APOLLODORUS. Assuredly.

CLEOPATRA. And you will have it carried gently down the steps and take great care of it?

APOLLODORUS. Depend on me.

CLEOPATRA. Great, g r e a t care?

APOLLODORUS. More than of my own body.

CLEOPATRA. You will promise me not to let the porters drop it or throw it about?

APOLLODORUS. Place the most delicate glass goblet in the palace in the heart of the roll, Queen; and if it be broken, my head shall pay for it.

CLEOPATRA. Good. Come, Ftatateeta. (*Ftatateeta comes to her. Apollodorus offers to squire them into the palace.*) No, Apollodorus, you must not come. I will choose a carpet for myself. You must wait here. (*She runs into the palace.*)

APOLLODORUS (*to the porters*). Follow this lady (*indicating Ftatateeta*); and obey her.

The porters rise and take up their bales.

FTATATEETA (*addressing the porters as if they were vermin*). This way. And take your shoes off before you put your feet on those stairs.

She goes in, followed by the porters with the carpets. Meanwhile Apollodorus goes to the edge of the quay and looks out over the harbor. The sentinels keep their eyes on him malignantly.

APOLLODORUS (*addressing the sentinel*). My friend—

SENTINEL (*rudely*). Silence there.

FIRST AUXILIARY. Shut your muzzle, you.

SECOND AUXILIARY (*in a half whisper, glancing apprehensively towards the north end of the quay*). Can't you wait a bit?

APOLLODORUS. Patience, worthy three-headed donkey. (*They mutter ferociously; but he is not at all intimidated.*) Listen: were you set here to watch me, or to watch the Egyptians?

SENTINEL. We know our duty.

APOLLODORUS. Then why don't you do it? There is something going on over there. (*Pointing southwestward to the mole.*)

SENTINEL (*sulkily*). I do not need to be told what to do by the like of you.

APOLLODORUS. Blockhead. (*He begins shouting*) Ho there, Centurion, Hoiho!

SENTINEL. Curse your meddling. (*Shouting*) Hoiho! Alarm! Alarm!

FIRST AND SECOND AUXILIARIES. Alarm! alarm! Hoiho!

The Centurion comes running in with his guard.

CENTURION. What now? Has the old woman attacked you again? (*Seeing Apollodorus*) Are y o u here still?

APOLLODORUS (*pointing as before*). See there. The Egyptians are moving. They are going to recapture the Pharos. They will attack by sea and land: by land along the great mole; by sea from the west harbor. Stir yourselves, my military friends: the hunt is up. (*A clangor of trumpets from several points along the quay.*) Aha! I told you so.

CENTURION (*quickly*). The two extra men pass the alarm to the south posts. One man keep guard here. The rest with me—quick.

The two auxiliary sentinels run off to the south. The Centurion and his guard run off northward; and immediately afterwards the bucina sounds. The four porters come from the palace carrying a carpet, followed by Ftatateeta.

SENTINEL (*handling his pilum apprehensively*). You again! (*The porters stop.*)

FTATATEETA. Peace, Roman fellow: you are now single-handed. Apollodorus: this carpet is Cleopatra's present to Cæsar. It has rolled up in it ten precious goblets of the thinnest Iberian crystal, and a hundred eggs of the sacred blue pigeon. On your honor, let not one of them be broken.

APOLLODORUS. On my head be it. (*To the porters*) Into the boat with them carefully.

The porters carry the carpet to the steps.

FIRST PORTER (*looking down at the boat*). Beware what you do, sir. Those eggs of which the lady speaks must weigh more than a pound apiece. This boat is too small for such a load.

BOATMAN (*excitedly rushing up the steps*). Oh thou injurious porter! Oh thou unnatural son of a she-camel! (*To Apollodorus*) My boat, sir, hath often carried five men. Shall it not carry your lordship and a bale of pigeons' eggs? (*To the porter*) Thou mangey dromedary, the gods shall punish thee for this envious wickedness.

FIRST PORTER (*stolidly*). I cannot quit this bale now to beat thee; but another day I will lie in wait for thee.

APOLLODORUS (*going between them*). Peace there. If the boat were but a single plank, I would get to Cæsar on it.

FTATATEETA (*anxiously*). In the name of the gods, Apollodorus, run no risks with that bale.

APOLLODORUS. Fear not, thou venerable grotesque: I guess its great worth. (*To the porters*) Down with it, I say; and gently; or ye shall eat nothing but stick for ten days.

The boatman goes down the steps, followed by the porters with the bale: Ftatateeta and Apollodorus watching from the edge.

APOLLODORUS. Gently, my sons, my children—(*with sudden alarm*) gently, ye dogs. Lay it level in the stern—so—'tis well.

FTATATEETA (*screaming down at one of the porters*). Do not step on it, do not step on it. Oh thou brute beast!

FIRST PORTER (*ascending*). Be not excited, mistress: all is well.

FTATATEETA (*panting*). All well! Oh, thou hast given my heart a turn! (*She clutches her side, gasping.*)

The four porters have now come up and are waiting at the stairhead to be paid.

APOLLODORUS. Here, ye hungry ones. (*He gives money to the first porter, who holds it in his hand to shew to the others. They crowd greedily to see how much it is, quite prepared, after the Eastern fashion, to protest to heaven against their patron's stinginess. But his liberality overpowers them.*)

FIRST PORTER. O bounteous prince!

SECOND PORTER. O lord of the bazaar!

THIRD PORTER. O favored of the gods!

FOURTH PORTER. O father to all the porters of the market!

SENTINEL (*enviously, threatening them fiercely with his pilum*). Hence, dogs: off. Out of this. (*They fly before him northward along the quay.*)

APOLLODORUS. Farewell, Ftatateeta. I shall be at the lighthouse before the Egyptians. (*He descends the steps.*)

FTATATEETA. The gods speed thee and protect my nursling!

The sentry returns from chasing the porters and looks down at the boat, standing near the stairhead lest Ftatateeta should attempt to escape.

APOLLODORUS (*from beneath, as the boat moves off*). Farewell, valiant pilum pitcher.

SENTINEL. Farewell, shopkeeper.

APOLLODORUS. Ha, ha! Pull, thou brave boatman, pull. Soho-o-o-o-o! (*He begins to sing in barcarolle measure to the rhythm of the oars.*)

My heart, my heart, spread out thy wings:
Shake off thy heavy load of love—

Give me the oars, O son of a snail.

SENTINEL (*threatening Ftatateeta*). Now mistress: back to your henhouse. In with you.

FTATATEETA (*falling on her knees and stretching her hands over the waters*). Gods of the seas, bear her safely to the shore!

SENTINEL. Bear who safely? What do you mean?

FTATATEETA (*looking darkly at him*). Gods of Egypt and of Vengeance, let this Roman fool be beaten like a dog by his captain for suffering her to be taken over the waters.

SENTINEL. Accursed one: is she then in the boat? (*He calls over the sea*) Hoiho, there, boatman! Hoiho!

APOLLODORUS (*singing in the distance*).

My heart, my heart, be whole and free:
Love is thine only enemy.

Meanwhile, Rufio, the morning's fighting done, sits munching dates on a faggot of brushwood outside the door of the lighthouse, which towers gigantic to the clouds on his left. His helmet, full of dates, is between his knees; and a leathern bottle of wine is by his side. Behind him the great stone pedestal of the lighthouse is shut in from the open sea by a low stone parapet, with a couple of steps in the middle to the broad coping. A huge chain with a hook hangs down from the lighthouse crane above his head. Faggots like the one he sits on lie beneath it ready to be drawn up to feed the beacon.

Cæsar is standing on the step at the parapet looking out anxiously, evidently ill at ease. Britannus comes out of the lighthouse door.

RUFIO. Well, my British islander. Have you been up to the top?

BRITANNUS. I have. I reckon it at 200 feet high.

RUFIO. Anybody up there?

BRITANNUS. One elderly Tyrian to work the crane; and his son, a well conducted youth of 14.

RUFIO (*looking at the chain*). What! An old man and a boy work that! Twenty men, you mean.

BRITANNUS. Two only, I assure you. They have counterweights, and a machine with boiling water in it which I do not understand: it is not of British design. They use it to haul up barrels of oil and faggots to burn in the brazier on the roof.

RUFIO. But—

BRITANNUS. Excuse me: I came down because there are messengers coming along the mole to us from the island. I must see what their business is. (*He hurries out past the lighthouse.*)

CÆSAR (*coming away from the parapet, shivering and out of sorts*). Rufio: this has been a mad expedition. We shall be beaten. I wish I knew how our men are getting on with that barricade across the great mole.

RUFIO (*angrily*). Must I leave my food and go starving to bring you a report?

CÆSAR (*soothing him nervously*). No, Rufio, no. Eat, my son, eat. (*He takes another turn, Rufio chewing dates meanwhile.*) The Egyptians cannot be such fools as not to storm the barricade and swoop down on us here before it is finished. It is the first time I have ever run an avoidable risk. I should not have come to Egypt.

RUFIO. An hour ago you were all for victory.

CÆSAR (*apologetically*). Yes: I was a fool—rash, Rufio—boyish.

RUFIO. Boyish! Not a bit of it. Here. (*Offering him a handful of dates*)

CÆSAR. What are these for?

RUFIO. To eat. That's what's the matter with you. When a man comes to your age, he runs down before his midday meal. Eat and drink; and then have another look at our chances.

CÆSAR (*taking the dates*). My age! (*He shakes his head and bites a date.*) Yes, Rufio: I am an old man—worn out now—true, quite true. (*He gives way to melancholy contemplation, and eats another date.*) Achillas is still in his prime: Ptolemy is a boy. (*He eats another date, and plucks up a little.*) Well, every dog has his day; and I have had mine: I cannot complain. (*With sudden cheerfulness*) These dates are not bad, Rufio. (*Britannus returns, greatly excited, with a leathern bag. Cæsar is himself again in a moment.*) What now?

BRITANNUS (*triumphantly*). Our brave Rhodian mariners have captured a treasure. There! (*He throws the bag down at Cæsar's feet.*) Our enemies are delivered into our hands.

CÆSAR. In that bag?

BRITANNUS. Wait till you hear, Cæsar. This bag contains all the letters which have passed between Pompey's party and the army of occupation here.

CÆSAR. Well?

BRITANNUS (*impatient of Cæsar's slowness to grasp the situation*). Well, we shall now know who your foes are. The name of every man who has plotted against you since you crossed the Rubicon may be in these papers, for all we know.

CÆSAR. Put them in the fire.

BRITANNUS. Put them—!!!! (*He gasps.*)

CÆSAR. In the fire. Would you have me waste the next three years of my life in proscribing and condemning men who will be my friends when I have proved that my friendship is worth more than Pompey's was—than Cato's is. O incorrigible British islander: am I a bull dog, to seek quarrels merely to shew how stubborn my jaws are?

BRITANNUS. But your honor—the honor of Rome—

CÆSAR. I do not make human sacrifices to my honor, as your Druids do. Since you will not burn these, at least I can drown them. (*He picks up the bag and throws it over the parapet into the sea.*)

BRITANNUS. Cæsar: this is mere eccentricity. Are traitors to be allowed to go free for the sake of a paradox?

RUFIO (*rising*). Cæsar: when the islander has finished preaching, call me again. I am going to have a look at the boiling water machine. (*He goes into the lighthouse.*)

BRITANNUS (*with genuine feeling*). O Cæsar, my great master, if I could but persuade you to regard life seriously, as men do in my country!

CÆSAR. Do they truly do so, Britannus?

BRITANNUS. Have you not been there? Have you not seen them? What Briton speaks as you do in your moments of levity? What Briton neglects to attend the services at the sacred grove? What Briton wears clothes of many colors as you do, instead of plain blue, as all solid, well esteemed men should? These are moral questions with us.

CÆSAR. Well, well, my friend: some day I shall settle down and have a blue toga, perhaps. Meanwhile, I must get on as best I can in my flippant Roman way. (*Apollodorus comes past the lighthouse.*) What now?

BRITANNUS (*turning quickly, and challenging the stranger with official haughtiness*). What is this? Who are you? How did you come here?

APOLLODORUS. Calm yourself, my friend: I am not going to eat you. I have come by boat, from Alexandria, with precious gifts for Cæsar.

CÆSAR. From Alexandria!

BRITANNUS (*severely*). That is Cæsar, sir.

RUFIO (*appearing at the lighthouse door*). What's the matter now?

APOLLODORUS. Hail, great Cæsar! I am Apollodorus the Sicilian, an artist.

BRITANNUS. An artist! Why have they admitted this vagabond?

CÆSAR. Peace, man. Apollodorus is a famous patrician amateur.

BRITANNUS (*disconcerted*). I crave the gentleman's pardon. (*To Cæsar*) I understood him to say that he was a professional. (*Somewhat out of countenance, he allows Apollodorus to approach Cæsar, changing places with him. Rufio, after looking Apollodorus up and down with marked disparagement, goes to the other side of the platform.*)

CÆSAR. You are welcome, Apollodorus. What is your business?

APOLLODORUS. First, to deliver to you a present from the Queen of Queens.

CÆSAR. Who is that?

APOLLODORUS. Cleopatra of Egypt.

CÆSAR (*taking him into his confidence in his most winning manner*). Apollodorus: this is no time for playing with presents. Pray you, go back to the Queen, and tell her that if all goes well I shall return to the palace this evening.

APPOLODORUS. Cæsar: I cannot return. As I approached the lighthouse, some fool threw a great leathern bag into the sea. It broke the nose of my boat; and I had hardly time to get myself and my charge to the shore before the poor little cockleshell sank.

CÆSAR. I am sorry, Apollodorus. The fool shall be rebuked. Well, well: what have you brought me? The Queen will be hurt if I do not look at it.

RUFIO. Have we time to waste on this trumpery? The Queen is only a child.

CÆSAR. Just so: that is why we must not disappoint her. What is the present, Apollodorus?

APOLLODORUS. Cæsar: it is a Persian carpet—a beauty! And in it are—so I am told—pigeons' eggs and crystal goblets and fragile precious things. I dare not for my head have it carried up that narrow ladder from the causeway.

RUFIO. Swing it up by the crane, then. We will send the

eggs to the cook; drink our wine from the goblets; and the carpet will make a bed for Cæsar.

APOLLODORUS. The crane! Cæsar: I have sworn to tender this bale of carpet as I tender my own life.

CÆSAR (*cheerfully*). Then let them swing you up at the same time; and if the chain breaks, you and the pigeons' eggs will perish together. (*He goes to the chain and looks up along it, examining it curiously*).

APOLLODORUS (*to Britannus*). Is Cæsar serious?

BRITANNUS. His manner is frivolous because he is an Italian; but he means what he says.

APOLLODORUS. Serious or not, he spake well. Give me a squad of soldiers to work the crane.

BRITANNUS. Leave the crane to me. Go and await the descent of the chain.

APOLLODORUS. Good. You will presently see me there (*turning to them all and pointing with an eloquent gesture to the sky above the parapet*) rising like the sun with my treasure.

He goes back the way he came. Britannus goes into the lighthouse.

RUFIO (*ill-humoredly*). Are you really going to wait here for this foolery, Cæsar?

CÆSAR (*backing away from the crane as it gives signs of working*). Why not?

RUFIO. The Egyptians will let you know why not if they have the sense to make a rush from the shore end of the mole before our barricade is finished. And here we are waiting like children to see a carpet full of pigeons' eggs.

The chain rattles, and is drawn up high enough to clear the parapet. It then swings round out of sight behind the lighthouse.

CÆSAR. Fear not, my son Rufio. When the first Egyptian takes his first step along the mole, the alarm will sound; and we two will reach the barricade from our end before the Egyptians reach it from their end—we two, Rufio: I, the old man, and you, his biggest boy. And the old man will be there first. So peace; and give me some more dates.

APOLLODORUS (*from the causeway below*). Soho, haul away. So-ho-o-o-o! (*The chain is drawn up and comes round again from behind the lighthouse. Apollodorus is swinging in the air with his bale of carpet at the end of it. He breaks into song as he soars above the parapet.*)

Aloft, aloft, behold the blue
That never shone in woman's eyes—

Easy there: stop her. (*He ceases to rise.*) Further round! (*The chain comes forward above the platform.*)

RUFIO (*calling up*). Lower away there. (*The chain and its load begin to descend.*)

APOLLODORUS (*calling up*). Gently—slowly—mind the eggs.

RUFIO (*calling up*). Easy there—slowly—slowly.

Apollodorus and the bale are deposited safely on the flags in the middle of the platform. Rufio and Cæsar help Apollodorus to cast off the chain from the bale.

RUFIO. Haul up.

The chain rises clear of their heads with a rattle. Britannus comes from the lighthouse and helps them to uncord the carpet.

APOLLODORUS (*when the cords are loose*). Stand off, my friends: let Cæsar see. (*He throws the carpet open.*)

RUFIO. Nothing but a heap of shawls. Where are the pigeons' eggs?

APOLLODORUS. Approach, Cæsar; and search for them among the shawls.

RUFIO (*drawing his sword*). Ha, treachery! Keep back, Cæsar: I saw the shawl move: there is something alive there.

BRITANNUS (*drawing his sword*). It is a serpent.

APOLLODORUS. Dares Cæsar thrust his hand into the sack where the serpent moves?

RUFIO (*turning on him*). Treacherous dog—

CÆSAR. Peace. Put up your swords. Apollodorus: your serpent seems to breathe very regularly. (*He thrusts his hand under the shawls and draws out a bare arm.*) This is a pretty little snake.

RUFIO (*drawing out the other arm*). Let us have the rest of you.

They pull Cleopatra up by the wrists into a sitting position. Britannus, scandalized, sheathes his sword with a drive of protest.

CLEOPATRA (*gasping*). Oh, I'm smothered. Oh, Cæsar; a

man stood on me in the boat; and a great sack of something fell upon me out of the sky; and then the boat sank, and then I was swung up into the air and bumped down.

CÆSAR (*petting her as she rises and takes refuge on his breast*). Well, never mind: here you are safe and sound at last.

RUFIO. Ay; and now that she is here, what are we to do with her?

BRITANNUS. She cannot stay here, Cæsar, without the companionship of some matron.

CLEOPATRA (*jealously, to Cæsar, who is obviously perplexed*). Aren't you glad to see me?

CÆSAR. Yes, yes; *I* am very glad. But Rufio is very angry; and Britannus is shocked.

CLEOPATRA (*contemptuously*). You can have their heads cut off, can you not?

CÆSAR. They would not be so useful with their heads cut off as they are now, my sea bird.

RUFIO (*to Cleopatra*). We shall have to go away presently and cut some of your Egyptians' heads off. How will you like being left here with the chance of being captured by that little brother of yours if we are beaten?

CLEOPATRA. But you mustn't leave me alone. Cæsar, you will not leave me alone, will you?

RUFIO. What! not when the trumpet sounds and all our lives depends on Cæsar's being at the barricade before the Egyptians reach it? Eh?

CLEOPATRA. Let them lose their lives: they are only soldiers.

CÆSAR (*gravely*). Cleopatra: when that trumpet sounds, we must take every man his life in his hand, and throw it in the face of Death. And of my soldiers who have trusted me there is not one whose hand I shall not hold more sacred than your head. (*Cleopatra is overwhelmed. Her eyes fill with tears.*) Apollodorus: you must take her back to the palace.

APOLLODORUS. Am I a dolphin, Cæsar, to cross the seas with young ladies on my back? My boat is sunk: all yours are either at the barricade or have returned to the city. I will hail one if I can: that is all I can do. (*He goes back to the causeway.*)

CLEOPATRA (*struggling with her tears*). It does not matter. I will not go back. Nobody cares for me.

CÆSAR. Cleopatra—

CLEOPATRA. You want me to be killed.

CÆSAR (*still more gravely*). My poor child: your life matters little here to anyone but yourself. (*She gives way altogether at this, casting herself down on the faggots weeping. Suddenly a great tumult is heard in the distance, bucinas and trumpets sounding through a storm of shouting. Britannus rushes to the parapet and looks along the mole. Cæsar and Rufio turn to one another with quick intelligence.*)

CÆSAR. Come, Rufio.

CLEOPATRA (*scrambling to her knees and clinging to him*). No, no. Do not leave me, Cæsar. (*He snatches his skirt from her clutch.*) Oh!

BRITANNUS (*from the parapet*). Cæsar: we are cut off. The Egyptians have landed from the west harbor between us and the barricade!!!

RUFIO (*running to see*). Curses! It is true. We are caught like rats in a trap.

CÆSAR (*ruthfully*). Rufio, Rufio: my men at the barricade are between the sea party and the shore party. I have murdered them.

RUFIO (*coming back from the parapet to Cæsar's right hand*). Ay: that comes of fooling with this girl here.

APOLLODORUS (*coming up quickly from the causeway*). Look over the parapet, Cæsar.

CÆSAR. We have looked, my friend. We must defend ourselves here.

APOLLODORUS. I have thrown the ladder into the sea. They cannot get in without it.

RUFIO. Ay; and we cannot get out. Have you thought of that?

APOLLODORUS. Not get out! Why not? You have ships in the east harbor.

BRITANNUS (*hopefully, at the parapet*). The Rhodian galleys are standing in towards us already. (*Cæsar quickly joins Britannus at the parapet.*)

RUFIO (*to Apollodorus, impatiently*). And by what road are we to walk to the galleys, pray?

APOLLODORUS (*with gay, defiant rhetoric*). By the road that leads everywhere—the diamond path of the sun and moon. Have you never seen the child's shadow play of The Broken Bridge? "Ducks and geese with ease get over"—eh? (*He throws away his cloak and cap, and binds his sword on his back.*)

RUFIO. What are you talking about?

APOLLODORUS. I will shew you. (*Calling to Britannus*) How far off is the nearest galley?

BRITANNUS. Fifty fathom.

CÆSAR. No, no: they are further off than they seem in this clear air to your British eyes. Nearly quarter of a mile, Apollodorus.

APOLLODORUS. Good. Defend yourselves here until I send you a boat from that galley.

RUFIO. Have you wings, perhaps?

APOLLODORUS. Water wings, soldier. Behold!

He runs up the steps between Cæsar and Britannus to the coping of the parapet; springs into the air; and plunges head foremost into the sea.

CÆSAR (*like a schoolboy—wildly excited*). Bravo, bravo! (*Throwing off his cloak*) By Jupiter, I will do that too.

RUFIO (*seizing him*). You are mad. You shall not.

CÆSAR. Why not? Can I not swim as well as he?

RUFIO (*frantic*). Can an old fool dive and swim like a young one? He is twenty-five and you are fifty.

CÆSAR (*breaking loose from Rufio*). Old!!!

BRITANNUS (*shocked*). Rufio: you forget yourself.

CÆSAR. I will race you to the galley for a week's pay, father Rufio.

CLEOPATRA. But me! me!! me!!! what is to become of me?

CÆSAR. I will carry you on my back to the galley like a dolphin. Rufio: when you see me rise to the surface, throw her in: I will answer for her. And then in with you after her, both of you.

CLEOPATRA. No, no, NO. I shall be drowned.

BRITANNUS. Cæsar: I am a man and a Briton, not a fish. I must have a boat. I cannot swim.

CLEOPATRA. Neither can I.

CÆSAR (*to Britannus*). Stay here, then, alone, until I recapture the lighthouse: I will not forget you. Now, Rufio.

RUFIO. You have made up your mind to this folly?

CÆSAR. The Egyptians have made it up for me. What else is there to do? And mind where you jump: I do not want to get your fourteen stone in the small of my back as I come up. (*He runs up the steps and stands on the coping.*)

BRITANNUS (*anxiously*). One last word, Cæsar. Do not let yourself be seen in the fashionable part of Alexandria until you have changed your clothes.

CAESAR (*calling over the sea*). Ho, Apollodorus: (*he points skyward and quotes the barcarolle.*)

The white upon the blue above—

APOLLODORUS (*swimming in the distance.*)

Is purple on the green below—

CÆSAR (*exultantly*). Aha! (*He plunges into the sea.*)

CLEOPATRA (*running excitedly to the steps*). Oh, let me see. He will be drowned. (*Rufio seizes her.*) Ah—ah—ah—ah! (*He pitches her screaming into the sea. Rufio and Britannus roar with laughter.*)

RUFIO (*looking down after her*). He has got her. (*To Britannus*) Hold the fort, Briton. Cæsar will not forget you. (*He springs off.*)

BRITANNUS (*running to the steps to watch them as they swim*). All safe, Rufio?

RUFIO (*swimming*). All safe.

CÆSAR (*swimming further off*). Take refuge up there by the beacon; and pile the fuel on the trap door, Britannus.

BRITANNUS (*calling in reply*). I will first do so, and then commend myself to my country's gods. (*A sound of cheering from the sea. Britannus gives full vent to his excitement.*) The boat has reached him: Hip, hip, hip, hurrah!

END OF ACT III.

ACT IV

Cleopatra's sousing in the east harbor of Alexandria was in October 48 B.C. In March 47 she is passing the afternoon in her boudoir in the palace, among a bevy of her ladies, listening to a slave girl who is playing the harp in the middle of the room. The harpist's master, an old musician, with a lined face, prominent brows, white beard, moustache and eyebrows twisted and horned at the ends, and a consciously keen and pretentious expression, is squatting on the floor close to her on her right, watching her performance. Ftatateeta is in attendance near the door, in front of a group of female slaves. Except the harp player all are seated: Cleopatra in a chair opposite the door on the other side of the room; the rest on the ground. Cleopatra's ladies are all young, the most conspicuous being Charmian and Iras, her favorites. Charmian is a hatchet faced, terra cotta colored little goblin, swift in her movements, and neatly finished at the hands and feet. Iras is a plump, goodnatured creature, rather fatuous, with a profusion of red hair, and a tendency to giggle on the slightest provocation.

CLEOPATRA. Can I—

FTATATEETA (*insolently, to the player*). Peace, thou! The Queen speaks. (*The player stops.*)

CLEOPATRA (*to the old musician*). I want to learn to play

the harp with my own hands. Cæsar loves music. Can you teach me?

MUSICIAN. Assuredly I and no one else can teach the Queen. Have I not discovered the lost method of the ancient Egyptians, who could make a pyramid tremble by touching a bass string? All the other teachers are quacks: I have exposed them repeatedly.

CLEOPATRA. Good: you shall teach me. How long will it take?

MUSICIAN. Not very long: only four years. Your Majesty must first become proficient in the philosophy of Pythagoras.

CLEOPATRA. Has she (*indicating the slave*) become proficient in the philosophy of Pythagoras?

MUSICIAN. Oh, she is but a slave. She learns as a dog learns.

CLEOPATRA. Well, then, I will learn as a dog learns; for she plays better than you. You shall give me a lesson every day for a fortnight. (*The musician hastily scrambles to his feet and bows profoundly.*) After that, whenever I strike a false note you shall be flogged; and if I strike so many that there is not time to flog you, you shall be thrown into the Nile to feed the crocodiles. Give the girl a piece of gold; and send them away.

MUSICIAN (*much taken aback*). But true art will not be thus forced.

FTATATEETA (*pushing him out*). What is this? Answering the Queen, forsooth. Out with you.

He is pushed out by Ftatateeta, the girl following with her harp, amid the laughter of the ladies and slaves.

CLEOPATRA. Now, can any of you amuse me? Have you any stories or any news?

IRAS. Ftatateeta—

CLEOPATRA. Oh, Ftatateeta, Ftatateeta, always Ftatateeta. Some new tale to set me against her.

IRAS. No: this time Ftatateeta has been virtuous. (*All the ladies laugh—not the slaves.*) Pothinus has been trying to bribe her to let him speak with you.

CLEOPATRA (*wrathfully*). Ha! you all sell audiences with me, as if I saw whom you please, and not whom I please. I should like to know how much of her gold piece that harp girl will have to give up before she leaves the palace.

IRAS. We can easily find out that for you.

The ladies laugh.

CLEOPATRA (*frowning*). You laugh; but take care, take care. I will find out some day how to make myself served as Cæsar is served.

CHARMIAN. Old hooknose! (*They laugh again.*)

CLEOPATRA (*revolted*). Silence. Charmian: do not you be a silly little Egyptian fool. Do you know why I allow you all to chatter impertinently just as you please, instead of treating you as Ftatateeta would treat you if she were Queen?

CHARMIAN. Because you try to imitate Cæsar in everything; and he lets everybody say what they please to him.

CLEOPATRA. No; but because I asked him one day why he did so; and he said, "Let your women talk; and you will learn something from them." "What have I to learn from them?" I said. "What they are," said he; and oh! you should have seen his eyes as he said it. You would have curled up, you shallow things. (*They laugh. She turns fiercely on Iras.*) At whom are you laughing—at me or at Cæsar?

IRAS. At Cæsar.

CLEOPATRA. If you were not a fool, you would laugh at me; and if you were not a coward you would not be afraid to tell me so. (*Ftatateeta returns.*) Ftatateeta: they tell me that Pothinus has offered you a bribe to admit him to my presence.

FTATATEETA (*protesting*). Now by my father's gods—

CLEOPATRA (*cutting her short despotically*). Have I not told you not to deny things? You would spend the day calling your father's gods to witness to your virtues if I let you. Go take the bribe; and bring in Pothinus. (*Ftatateeta is about to reply.*) Don't answer me. Go.

Ftatateeta goes out; and Cleopatra rises and begins to prowl to and fro between her chair and the door, meditating. All rise and stand.

IRAS (*as she reluctantly rises*). Heigho! I wish Cæsar were back in Rome.

CLEOPATRA (*threateningly*). It will be a bad day for you all when he goes. Oh, if I were not ashamed to let him see that I am as cruel at heart as my father, I would make you repent that speech! Why do you wish him away?

CHARMIAN. He makes you so terribly prosy and serious and learned and philosophical. It is worse than being religious, at our ages. (*The ladies laugh.*)

CLEOPATRA. Cease that endless cackling, will you. Hold your tongues.

CHARMIAN (*with mock resignation*). Well, well: we must try to live up to Cæsar.

They laugh again. Cleopatra rages silently as she continues to prowl to and fro. Ftatateeta comes back with Pothinus, who halts on the threshold.

FTATATEETA (*at the door*). Pothinus craves the ear of the—

CLEOPATRA. There, there: that will do: let him come in. (*She resumes her seat. All sit down except Pothinus, who advances to the middle of the room. Ftatateeta takes her former place.*) Well, Pothinus: what is the latest news from your rebel friends?

POTHINUS (*haughtily*). I am no friend of rebellion. And a prisoner does not receive news.

CLEOPATRA. You are no more a prisoner than I am—than Cæsar is. These six months we have been besieged in this palace by my subjects. You are allowed to walk on the beach among the soldiers. Can I go further myself, or can Cæsar?

POTHINUS. You are but a child, Cleopatra, and do not understand these matters.

The ladies laugh, Cleopatra looks inscrutably at him.

CHARMIAN. I see you do not know the latest news, Pothinus.

POTHINUS. What is that?

CHARMIAN. That Cleopatra is no longer a child. Shall I tell you how to grow much older, and much, m u c h wiser in one day?

POTHINUS. I should prefer to grow wiser without growing older.

CHARMIAN. Well, go up to the top of the lighthouse; and get somebody to take you by the hair and throw you into the sea. (*The ladies laugh.*)

CLEOPATRA. She is right, Pothinus: you will come to the shore with much conceit washed out of you. (*The ladies laugh. Cleopatra rises impatiently.*) Begone, all of you. I will speak with Pothinus alone. Drive them out, Ftatateeta. (*They run out laughing. Ftatateeta shuts the door on them.*) What are y o u waiting for?

FTATATEETA. It is not meet that the Queen remain alone with—

CLEOPATRA (*interrupting her*). Ftatateeta: must I sacrifice you to your father's gods to teach you that *I* am Queen of Egypt, and not you?

FTATATEETA (*indignantly*). You are like the rest of them. You want to be what these Romans call a New Woman. (*She goes out, banging the door.*)

CLEOPATRA (*sitting down again*). Now, Pothinus: why did you bribe Ftatateeta to bring you hither?

POTHINUS (*studying her gravely*). Cleopatra: what they tell me is true. You are changed.

CLEOPATRA. Do you speak with Cæsar every day for six months: and y o u will be changed.

POTHINUS. It is the common talk that you are infatuated with this old man.

CLEOPATRA. Infatuated? What does that mean? Made foolish, is it not? Oh no: I wish I were.

POTHINUS. You wish you were made foolish! How so?

CLEOPATRA. When I was foolish, I did what I liked, except when Ftatateeta beat me; and even then I cheated her and did it by stealth. Now that Cæsar has made me wise, it is no use my liking or disliking; I do what must be done, and have no time to attend to myself. That is not happiness; but it is greatness. If Cæsar were gone, I think I could govern the Egyptians; for what Cæsar is to me, I am to the fools around me.

POTHINUS (*looking hard at her*). Cleopatra: this may be the vanity of youth.

CLEOPATRA. No, no: it is not that I am so clever, but that the others are so stupid.

POTHINUS (*musingly*). Truly, that is the great secret.

CLEOPATRA. Well, now tell me what you came to say?

POTHINUS (*embarrassed*). I! Nothing.

CLEOPATRA. Nothing!

POTHINUS. At least—to beg for my liberty: that is all.

CLEOPATRA. For that you would have knelt to Cæsar. No,

Pothinus: you came with some plan that depended on Cleopatra being a little nursery kitten. Now that Cleopatra is a Queen, the plan is upset.

POTHINUS (*bowing his head submissively*). It is so.

CLEOPATRA (*exultant*). Aha!

POTHINUS (*raising his eyes keenly to her*). Is Cleopatra then indeed a Queen, and no longer Cæsar's prisoner and slave?

CLEOPATRA. Pothinus: we are all Cæsar's slaves—all we in this land of Egypt—whether we will or no. And she who is wise enough to know this will reign when Cæsar departs.

POTHINUS. You harp on Cæsar's departure.

CLEOPATRA. What if I do?

POTHINUS. Does he not love you?

CLEOPATRA. Love me! Pothinus: Cæsar loves no one. Who are those we love? Only those whom we do not hate: all people are strangers and enemies to us except those we love. But it is not so with Cæsar. He has no hatred in him: he makes friends with everyone as he does with dogs and children. His kindness to me is a wonder: neither mother, father, nor nurse have ever taken so much care for me, or thrown open their thoughts to me so freely.

POTHINUS. Well: is not this love?

CLEOPATRA. What! When he will do as much for the first girl he meets on his way back to Rome? Ask his slave, Britannus: he has been just as good to him. Nay, ask his very horse! His kindness is not for anything in me: it is in his own nature.

POTHINUS. But how can you be sure that he does not love you as men love women?

CLEOPATRA. Because I cannot make him jealous. I have tried.

POTHINUS. Hm! Perhaps I should have asked, then, do you love him?

CLEOPATRA. Can one love a god? Besides, I love another Roman: one whom I saw long before Cæsar—no god, but a man—one who can love and hate—one whom I can hurt and who would hurt me.

POTHINUS. Does Cæsar know this?

CLEOPATRA. Yes.

POTHINUS. And he is not angry?

CLEOPATRA. He promises to send him to Egypt to please me!

POTHINUS. I do not understand this man.

CLEOPATRA (*with superb contempt*). You understand Cæsar! How could you? (*Proudly*) I do—by instinct.

POTHINUS (*deferentially, after a moment's thought*). Your Majesty caused me to be admitted to-day. What message has the Queen for me?

CLEOPATRA. This. You think that by making my brother king, you will rule in Egypt, because you are his guardian and he is a little silly.

POTHINUS. The Queen is pleased to say so.

CLEOPATRA. The Queen is pleased to say this also. That Cæsar will eat up you, and Achillas, and my brother, as a cat eats up mice; and that he will put on this land of Egypt as a shepherd puts on his garment. And when he has done that, he will return to Rome, and leave Cleopatra here as his viceroy.

POTHINUS (*breaking out wrathfully*). That he will never do. We have a thousand men to his ten; and we will drive him and his beggarly legions into the sea.

CLEOPATRA (*with scorn, getting up to go*). You rant like any common fellow. Go, then, and marshal your thousands; and make haste; for Mithridates of Pergamos is at hand with reinforcements for Cæsar. Cæsar has held you at bay with two legions: we shall see what he will do with twenty.

POTHINUS. Cleopatra—

CLEOPATRA. Enough, enough: Cæsar has spoiled me for talking to weak things like you. (*She goes out. Pothinus, with a gesture of rage, is following, when Ftatateeta enters and stops him.*)

POTHINUS. Let me go forth from this hateful place.

FTATATEETA. What angers you?

POTHINUS. The curse of all the gods of Egypt be upon her! She has sold her country to the Roman, that she may buy it back from him with her kisses.

FTATATEETA. Fool: did she not tell you that she would have Cæsar gone?

POTHINUS. You listened?

FTATATEETA. I took care that some honest woman should be at hand whilst you were with her.

POTHINUS. Now by the gods—

FTATATEETA. Enough of your gods! Cæsar's gods are all powerful here. It is no use you coming to Cleopatra: you are only an Egyptian. She will not listen to any of her own race: she treats us all as children.

POTHINUS. May she perish for it!

FTATATEETA (*balefully*). May your tongue wither for that wish! Go! send for Lucius Septimius, the slayer of Pompey. He is a Roman: may be she will listen to him. Begone!

POTHINUS (*darkly*). I know to whom I must go now.

FTATATEETA (*suspiciously*). To whom, then?

POTHINUS. To a greater Roman than Lucius. And mark this, mistress. You thought, before Cæsar came, that Egypt should presently be ruled by you and your crew in the name of Cleopatra. I set myself against it—

FTATATEETA (*interrupting him—wrangling*). Ay; that it might be ruled by you and y o u r crew in the name of Ptolemy.

POTHINUS. Better me, or even you, than a woman with a Roman heart; and that is what Cleopatra is now become. Whilst I live, she shall never rule. So guide yourself accordingly. (*He goes out.*)

It is by this time drawing on to dinner time. The table is laid on the roof of the palace; and thither Rufio is now climbing, ushered by a majestic palace official, wand of office in hand, and followed by a slave carrying an inlaid stool. After many stairs they emerge at last into a massive colonnade on the roof. Light curtains are drawn between the columns on the north and east to soften the westering sun. The official leads Rufio to one of these shaded sections. A cord for pulling the curtains apart hangs down between the pillars.

THE OFFICIAL (*bowing*). The Roman commander will await Cæsar here.

The slave sets down the stool near the southernmost column, and slips out through the curtains.

RUFIO (*sitting down, a little blown*). Pouf! That was a climb. How high have we come?

THE OFFICIAL. We are on the palace roof, O Beloved of Victory!

RUFIO. Good! The Beloved of Victory has no more stairs to get up.

A second official enters from the opposite end, walking backwards.

THE SECOND OFFICIAL. Cæsar approaches.

Cæsar, fresh from the bath, clad in a new tunic of purple silk, comes in beaming and festive, followed by two slaves carrying a light couch, which is hardly more than an elaborately designed bench. They place it near the northmost of the two curtained columns. When this is done they slip out through the curtains; and the two officials, formally bowing, follow them. Rufio rises to receive Cæsar.

CÆSAR (*coming over to him*). Why, Rufio! (*Surveying his dress with an air of admiring astonishment*) A new baldrick! A new golden pommel to your sword! And you have had your hair cut! But not your beard—? impossible! (*He sniffs at Rufio's beard.*) Yes, perfumed, by Jupiter Olympus!

RUFIO (*growling*). Well: is it to please myself?

CÆSAR (*affectionately*). No, my son Rufio, but to please me—to celebrate my birthday.

RUFIO (*contemptuously*). Your birthday! You always have a birthday when there is a pretty girl to be flattered or an ambassador to be conciliated. We had seven of them in ten months last year.

CÆSAR (*contritely*). It is true, Rufio! I shall never break myself of these petty deceits.

RUFIO. Who is to dine with us—besides Cleopatra?

CÆSAR. Apollodorus the Sicilian.

RUFIO. That popinjay!

CÆSAR. Come! the popinjay is an amusing dog—tells a story; sings a song; and saves us the trouble of flattering the Queen. What does she care for old politicians and camp-fed bears like us? No: Apollodorus is good company, Rufio, good company.

RUFIO. Well, he can swim a bit and fence a bit: he might be worse, if he only knew how to hold his tongue.

CÆSAR. The gods forbid he should ever learn! Oh, this military life! this tedious, brutal life of action! That is the worst of us Romans: we are mere doers and drudgers: a swarm of bees turned into men. Give me a good talker—one with wit and imagination enough to live without continually doing something!

RUFIO. Ay! a nice time he would have of it with you when dinner was over! Have you noticed that I am before my time?

CÆSAR. Aha! I thought that meant something. What is it?

RUFIO. Can we be overheard here?

CÆSAR. Our privacy invites eavesdropping. I can remedy that. (*He claps his hands twice. The curtains are drawn, revealing the roof garden with a banqueting table set across in the middle for four persons, one at each end, and two side by side. The side next to Cæsar and Rufio is blocked with golden wine vessels and basins. A gorgeous major-domo is superintending the laying of the table by a staff of slaves. The colonnade goes round the garden at both sides to the further end, where a gap in it, like a great gateway, leaves the view open to the sky beyond the western edge of the roof, except in the middle, where a life size image of Ra, seated on a huge plinth, towers up, with hawk head and crown of asp and disk. His altar, which stands at his feet, is a single white stone.*) Now everybody can see us, nobody will think of listening to us. (*He sits down on the bench left by the two slaves.*)

RUFIO (*sitting down on his stool*). Pothinus wants to speak to you. I advise you to see him: there is some plotting going on here among the women.

CÆSAR. Who is Pothinus?

RUFIO. The fellow with hair like squirrel's fur—the little King's bear leader, whom you kept prisoner.

CÆSAR (*annoyed*). And has he not escaped?

RUFIO. No.

CÆSAR (*rising imperiously*). Why not? You have been guarding this man instead of watching the enemy. Have I not told you always to let prisoners escape unless there are special orders to the contrary? Are there not enough mouths to be fed without him?

RUFIO. Yes; and if you would have a little sense and let me cut his throat, you would save his rations. Anyhow, he won't escape. Three sentries have told him they would put a pilum through him if they saw him again. What more can they do? He prefers to stay and spy on us. So would I if I had to do with generals subject to fits of clemency.

CÆSAR (*resuming his seat, argued down*). Hm! And so he wants to see me.

RUFIO. Ay, I have brought him with me. He is waiting there (*jerking his thumb over his shoulder*) under guard.

CÆSAR. And you want me to see him?

RUFIO (*obstinately*). I don't want anything. I daresay you will do what you like. Don't put it on to me.

CÆSAR (*with an air of doing it expressly to indulge Rufio*). Well, well: let us have him.

RUFIO (*calling*). Ho there, guard! Release your man and send him up. (*Beckoning*) Come along!

Pothinus enters and stops mistrustfully between the two, looking from one to the other.

CÆSAR (*graciously*). Ah, Pothinus! You are welcome. And what is the news this afternoon?

POTHINUS. Cæsar: I come to warn you of a danger, and to make you an offer.

CÆSAR. Never mind the danger. Make the offer.

RUFIO. Never mind the offer. What's the danger?

POTHINUS. Cæsar: you think that Cleopatra is devoted to you.

CÆSAR (*gravely*). My friend: I already know what I think. Come to your offer.

POTHINUS. I will deal plainly. I know not by what strange gods you have been enabled to defend a palace and a few yards of beach against a city and an army. Since we cut you off from Lake Mareotis, and you dug wells in the salt sea sand and brought up buckets of fresh water from them, we have known that your gods are irresistible, and that you are a worker of miracles. I no longer threaten you—

RUFIO (*sarcastically*). Very handsome of you, indeed.

POTHINUS. So be it: you are the master. Our gods sent the north west winds to keep you in our hands; but you have been too strong for them.

CÆSAR (*gently urging him to come to the point*). Yes, yes, my friend. But what then?

RUFIO. Spit it out, man. What have you to say?

POTHINUS. I have to say that you have a traitress in your camp, Cleopatra—

THE MAJOR-DOMO (*at the table, announcing*). The Queen! (*Cæsar and Rufio rise.*)

RUFIO (*aside to Pothinus*). You should have spat it out sooner, you fool. Now it is too late.

Cleopatra, in gorgeous raiment, enters in state through the gap in the colonnade, and comes down past the image of Ra and past the table to Cæsar. Her retinue, headed by Ftatateeta, joins the staff at the table. Cæsar gives Cleopatra his seat, which she takes.

CLEOPATRA (*quickly, seeing Pothinus*). What is h e doing here?

CÆSAR (*seating himself beside her, in the most amiable of tempers*). Just going to tell me something about you. You shall hear it. Proceed, Pothinus.

POTHINUS (*disconcerted*). Cæsar— (*He stammers.*)

CÆSAR. Well, out with it.

POTHINUS. What I have to say is for your ear, not for the Queen's.

CLEOPATRA (*with subdued ferocity*). There are means of making you speak. Take care.

POTHINUS (*defiantly*). Cæsar does not employ those means.

CÆSAR. My friend: when a man has anything to tell in this world, the difficulty is not to make him tell it, but to prevent him from telling it too often. Let me celebrate my birthday by setting you free. Farewell: we shall not meet again.

CLEOPATRA (*angrily*). Cæsar: this mercy is foolish.

POTHINUS (*to Cæsar*). Will you not give me a private audience? Your life may depend on it. (*Cæsar rises loftily.*)

RUFIO (*aside to Pothinus*). Ass! Now we shall have some heroics.

CÆSAR (*oratorically*). Pothinus—

RUFIO (*interrupting him*). Cæsar: the dinner will spoil if you begin preaching your favourite sermon about life and death.

CLEOPATRA (*priggishly*). Peace, Rufio. I desire to hear Cæsar.

RUFIO (*bluntly*). Your Majesty has heard it before. You repeated it to Apollodorus last week; and he thought it was all your own. (*Cæsar's dignity collapses. Much tickled, he sits down again and looks roguishly at Cleopatra, who is furious. Rufio calls as before.*) Ho there, guard! Pass the prisoner out.

He is released. (*To Pothinus*) Now off with you. You have lost your chance.

POTHINUS (*his temper overcoming his prudence*). I w i l l speak.

CÆSAR (*to Cleopatra*). You see. Torture would not have wrung a word from him.

POTHINUS. Cæsar: you have taught Cleopatra the arts by which the Romans govern the world.

CÆSAR. Alas! they cannot even govern themselves. What then?

POTHINUS. What then? Are you so besotted with her beauty that you do not see that she is impatient to reign in Egypt alone, and that her heart is set on your departure?

CLEOPATRA (*rising*). Liar!

CÆSAR (*shocked*). What! Protestations! Contradictions!

CLEOPATRA (*ashamed, but trembling with suppressed rage*). No, I do not deign to contradict. Let him talk. (*She sits down again.*)

POTHINUS. From her own lips I have heard it. You are to be her catspaw: you are to tear the crown from her brother's head and set it on her own, delivering us all into her hand—delivering yourself also. And then Cæsar can return to Rome, or depart through the gate of death, which is nearer and surer.

CÆSAR (*calmly*). Well, my friend; and is not this very natural?

POTHINUS (*astonished*). Natural! Then you do not resent treachery?

CÆSAR. Resent! O thou foolish Egyptian, what have I to do with resentment? Do I resent the wind when it chills me, or the night when it makes me stumble in the darkness? Shall I resent youth when it turns from age, and ambition when it turns from servitude? To tell me such a story as this is but to tell me that the sun will rise to-morrow.

CLEOPATRA (*unable to contain herself*). But it is false—false. I swear it.

CÆSAR. It is true, though you swore it a thousand times, and believed all you swore. (*She is convulsed with emotion. To screen her, he rises and takes Pothinus to Rufio, saying*) Come, Rufio: let us see Pothinus past the guard. I have a word to say to him. (*Aside to them*) We must give the Queen a moment to recover herself. (*Aloud*) Come. (*He takes Pothinus and Rufio out with him, conversing with them meanwhile.*) Tell your friends, Pothinus, that they must not think I am opposed to a reasonable settlement of the country's affairs— (*They pass out of hearing.*)

CLEOPATRA (*in a stifled whisper*). Ftatateeta, Ftatateeta.

FTATATEETA (*hurrying to her from the table and petting her*). Peace, child: be comforted—

CLEOPATRA (*interrupting her*). Can they hear us?

FTATATEETA. No, dear heart, no.

CLEOPATRA. Listen to me. If he leaves the palace alive, never see my face again.

FTATATEETA. He? Poth—

CLEOPATRA (*striking her on the mouth*). Strike his life out as I strike his name from your lips. Dash him down from the wall. Break him on the stones. Kill, kill, k i l l him.

FTATATEETA (*shewing all her teeth*). The dog shall perish.

CLEOPATRA. Fail in this, and you go out from before me for ever.

FTATATEETA (*resolutely*). So be it. You shall not see my face until his eyes are darkened.

Cæsar comes back, with Apollodorus, exquisitely dressed, and Rufio.

CLEOPATRA (*to Ftatateeta*). Come soon—soon. (*Ftatateeta turns her meaning eyes for a moment on her mistress; then goes grimly away past Ra and out. Cleopatra runs like a gazelle to Cæsar*) So you have come back to me, Cæsar. (*Caressingly*) I thought you were angry. Welcome, Apollodorus. (*She gives him her hand to kiss, with her other arm about Cæsar.*)

APOLLODORUS. Cleopatra grows more womanly beautiful from week to week.

CLEOPATRA. Truth, Apollodorus?

APOLLODORUS. Far, far short of the truth! Friend Rufio threw a pearl into the sea: Cæsar fished up a diamond.

CÆSAR. Cæsar fished up a touch of rheumatism, my friend. Come: to dinner! to dinner! (*They move towards the table.*)

CLEOPATRA (*skipping like a young fawn*). Yes, to dinner. I have ordered s u c h a dinner for you, Cæsar!

CÆSAR. Ay? What are we to have?

CLEOPATRA. Peacocks' brains.

CÆSAR (*as if his mouth watered*). Peacocks' brains, Apollodorus!

APOLLODORUS. Not for me. I prefer nightingales' tongues. (*He goes to one of the two covers set side by side.*)

CLEOPATRA. Roast boar, Rufio!

RUFIO (*gluttonously*). Good! (*He goes to the seat next Apollodorus, on his left.*)

CÆSAR (*looking at his seat, which is at the end of the table, to Ra's left hand*). What has become of my leathern cushion?

CLEOPATRA (*at the opposite end*). I have got new ones for you.

THE MAJOR-DOMO. These cushions, Cæsar, are of Maltese gauze, stuffed with rose leaves.

CÆSAR. Rose leaves! Am I a caterpillar? (*He throws the cushions away and seats himself on the leather mattress underneath.*)

CLEOPATRA. What a shame! My new cushions!

THE MAJOR-DOMO (*at Cæsar's elbow*). What shall we serve to whet Cæsar's appetite?

CÆSAR. What have you got?

THE MAJOR-DOMO. Sea hedgehogs, black and white sea acorns, sea nettles, beccaficoes, purple shellfish—

CÆSAR. Any oysters?

THE MAJOR-DOMO. Assuredly.

CÆSAR. B r i t i s h oysters?

THE MAJOR-DOMO (*assenting*). British oysters, Cæsar.

CÆSAR. Oysters, then. (*The Major-Domo signs to a slave at each order; and the slave goes out to execute it.*) I have been in Britain—that western land of romance—the last piece of earth on the edge of the ocean that surrounds the world. I went there in search of its famous pearls. The British pearl was a fable; but in searching for it I found the British oyster.

APOLLODORUS. All posterity will bless you for it. (*To the Major-Domo*) Sea hedgehogs for me.

RUFIO. Is there nothing solid to begin with?

THE MAJOR-DOMO. Fieldfares with asparagus—

CLEOPATRA (*interrupting*). Fattened fowls! have some fattened fowls, Rufio.

RUFIO. Ay, that will do.

CLEOPATRA (*greedily*). Fieldfares for me.

THE MAJOR-DOMO. Cæsar will deign to choose his wine? Sicilian, Lesbian, Chian—

RUFIO (*contemptuously*). All Greek.

APOLLODORUS. Who would drink Roman wine when he could get Greek? Try the Lesbian, Cæsar.

CÆSAR. Bring me my barley water.

RUFIO (*with intense disgust*). Ugh! Bring me my Falernian. (*The Falernian is presently brought to him.*)

CLEOPATRA (*pouting*). It is waste of time giving you dinners, Cæsar. My scullions would not condescend to your diet.

CÆSAR (*relenting*). Well, well: let us try the Lesbian. (*The Major-Domo fills Cæsar's goblet; then Cleopatra's and Apollodorus's.*) But when I return to Rome, I will make laws against these extravagances. I will even get the laws carried out.

CLEOPATRA (*coaxingly*). Never mind. To-day you are to be like other people: idle, luxurious, and kind. (*She stretches her hand to him along the table.*)

CÆSAR. Well, for once I will sacrifice my comfort—(*kissing her hand*) there! (*He takes a draught of wine*) Now are you satisfied?

CLEOPATRA. And you no longer believe that I long for your departure for Rome?

CÆSAR. I no longer believe anything. My brains are asleep. Besides, who knows whether I shall return to Rome?

RUFIO (*alarmed*). How? Eh? What?

CÆSAR. What has Rome to shew me that I have not seen already? One year of Rome is like another, except that I grow older, whilst the crowd in the Appian Way is always the same age.

APOLLODORUS. It is no better here in Egypt. The old men, when they are tired of life, say, "We have seen everything except the source of the Nile."

CÆSAR (*his imagination catching fire*). And why not see that? Cleopatra: will you come with me and track the flood to its cradle in the heart of the regions of mystery? Shall we leave Rome behind us—Rome, that has achieved greatness only to learn how greatness destroys nations of men who are not great! Shall I make you a new kingdom, and build you a holy city there in the great unknown?

CLEOPATRA (*rapturously*). Yes, yes. You shall.

RUFIO. Ay: now he will conquer Africa with two legions before we come to the roast boar.

APOLLODORUS. Come: no scoffing. This is a noble scheme: in it Cæsar is no longer merely the conquering soldier, but the creative poet-artist. Let us name the holy city, and consecrate it with Lesbian wine.

CÆSAR. Cleopatra shall name it herself.

CLEOPATRA. It shall be called Cæsar's Gift to his Beloved.

APOLLODORUS. No, no. Something vaster than that—something universal, like the starry firmament.

CÆSAR (*prosaically*). Why not simply The Cradle of the Nile?

CLEOPATRA. No: the Nile is my ancestor; and he is a god. Oh! I have thought of something. The Nile shall name it himself. Let us call upon him. (*To the Major-Domo*) Send for him. (*The three men stare at one another; but the Major-Domo goes out as if he had received the most matter-of-fact order.*) And (*to the retinue*) away with you all.

The retinue withdraws, making obeisance.

A priest enters, carrying a miniature sphinx with a tiny tripod before it. A morsel of incense is smoking in the tripod. The priest comes to the table and places the image in the middle of it. The light begins to change to the magenta purple of the Egyptian sunset, as if the god had brought a strange colored shadow with him. The three men are determined not to be impressed; but they feel curious in spite of themselves.

CÆSAR. What hocus-pocus is this?

CLEOPATRA. You shall see. And it is not hocus-pocus. To do it properly, we should kill something to please him; but perhaps he will answer Cæsar without that if we spill some wine to him.

APOLLODORUS (*turning his head to look up over his shoulder at Ra*). Why not appeal to our hawkheaded friend here?

CLEOPATRA. (*nervously*). Sh! He will hear you and be angry.

RUFIO (*phlegmatically*). The source of the Nile is out of his district, I expect.

CLEOPATRA. No: I will have my city named by nobody but my dear little sphinx, because it was in its arms that Cæsar found me asleep. (*She languishes at Cæsar; then turns curtly to the priest*) Go. I am a priestess, and have power to take your charge from you. (*The priest makes a reverence and goes out.*) Now let us call on the Nile all together. Perhaps he will rap on the table.

CÆSAR. What! table rapping! Are such superstitions still believed in this year 707 of the Republic?

CLEOPATRA. It is no superstition: our priests learn lots of things from the tables. Is it not so, Apollodorus?

APOLLODORUS. Yes: I profess myself a converted man. When Cleopatra is priestess, Apollodorus is devotee. Propose the conjuration.

CLEOPATRA. You must say with me, "Send us thy voice, Father Nile."

ALL FOUR (*holding their glasses together before the idol*). Send us thy voice, Father Nile.

The death cry of a man in mortal terror and agony answers them. Appalled, the men set down their glasses, and listen. Silence. The purple deepens in the sky. Cæsar, glancing at Cleopatra, catches her pouring out her wine before the god with gleaming eyes, and mute assurances of gratitude and worship. Apollodorus springs up and runs to the edge of the roof to peer down and listen.

CÆSAR (*looking piercingly at Cleopatra*). What was that?

CLEOPATRA (*petulantly*). Nothing. They are beating some slave.

CÆSAR. Nothing!

RUFIO. A man with a knife in him, I'll swear.

CÆSAR (*rising*). A murder!

APOLLODORUS (*at the back, waving his hand for silence*). S-sh! Silence. Did you hear that?

CÆSAR. Another cry?

APOLLODORUS (*returning to the table*). No, a thud. Something fell on the beach, I think.

RUFIO (*grimly, as he rises*). Something with bones in it, eh?

CÆSAR (*shuddering*). Hush, hush, Rufio. (*He leaves the

table and returns to the colonnade: Rufio following at his left elbow, and Apollodorus at the other side.)

CLEOPATRA (*still in her place at the table*). Will you leave me, Cæsar? Apollodorus: are you going?

APOLLODORUS. Faith, dearest Queen, my appetite is gone.

CÆSAR. Go down to the courtyard, Apollodorus; and find out what has happened.

Apollodorus nods and goes out, making for the staircase by which Rufio ascended.

CLEOPATRA. Your soldiers have killed somebody, perhaps. What does it matter?

The murmur of a crowd rises from the beach below. Cæsar and Rufio look at one another.

CÆSAR. This must be seen to. (*He is about to follow Apollodorus when Rufio stops him with a hand on his arm. Ftatateeta comes back by the far end of the roof, with dragging steps, a drowsy satiety in her eyes and in the corners of the bloodhound lips. For a moment Cæsar suspects that she is drunk with wine. Not so Rufio: he knows well the red vintage that has inebriated her.*)

RUFIO (*in a low tone*). There is some mischief between those two.

FTATATEETA. The Queen looks again on the face of her servant.

Cleopatra looks at her for a moment with an exultant reflection of her murderous expression. Then she flings her arms round her; kisses her repeatedly and savagely; and tears off her jewels and heaps them on her. The two men turn from the spectacle to look at one another. Ftatateeta drags herself sleepily to the altar; kneels before Ra; and remains there in prayer. Cæsar goes to Cleopatra, leaving Rufio in the colonnade.

CÆSAR (*with searching earnestness*). Cleopatra: what has happened?

CLEOPATRA (*in mortal dread of him, but with her utmost cajolery*). Nothing, dearest Cæsar. (*With sickly sweetness, her voice almost failing*) Nothing. I am innocent. (*She approaches him affectionately*) Dear Cæsar: are you angry with me? Why do you look at me so? I have been here with you all the time. How can I know what has happened?

CÆSAR (*reflectively*). That is true.

CLEOPATRA (*greatly relieved, trying to caress him*). Of course it is true. (*He does not respond to the caress.*) You know it is true, Rufio.

The murmur without suddenly swells to a roar and subsides.

RUFIO. I shall know presently. (*He makes for the altar in the burly trot that serves him for a stride, and touches Ftatateeta on the shoulder.*) Now, mistress: I shall want you. (*He orders her, with a gesture, to go before him.*)

FTATATEETA (*rising and glowering at him*). My place is with the Queen.

CLEOPATRA. She has done no harm, Rufio.

CÆSAR (*to Rufio*). Let her stay.

RUFIO (*sitting down on the altar*). Very well. Then my place is here too; and you can see what is the matter for yourself. The city is in a pretty uproar, it seems.

CÆSAR (*with grave displeasure*). Rufio: there is a time for obedience.

RUFIO. And there is a time for obstinacy. (*He folds his arms doggedly.*)

CÆSAR (*to Cleopatra*). Send her away.

CLEOPATRA (*whining in her eagerness to propitiate him*). Yes, I will. I will do whatever you ask me, Cæsar, always because I love you. Ftatateeta: go away.

FTATATEETA. The Queen's word is my will. I shall be at hand for the Queen's call. (*She goes out past Ra, as she came.*)

RUFIO (*following her*). Remember, Cæsar, y o u r body guard also is within call. (*He follows her out.*)

Cleopatra, presuming upon Cæsar's submission to Rufio, leaves the table and sits down on the bench in the colonnade.

CLEOPATRA. Why do you allow Rufio to treat you so? You should teach him his place.

CÆSAR. Teach him to be my enemy, and to hide his thoughts from me as you are now hiding yours.

CLEOPATRA (*her fears returning*). Why do you say that, Cæsar? Indeed, indeed, I am not hiding anything. You are wrong to treat me like this. (*She stifles a sob.*) I am only a child; and you turn into stone because you think some one has been killed. I cannot bear it. (*She purposely breaks down and *weeps. He looks at her with profound sadness and complete coldness. She looks up to see what effect she is producing. Seeing that he is unmoved, she sits up, pretending to struggle with her emotion and to put it bravely away.*) But there: I know you hate tears: you shall not be troubled with them. I know you are not angry, but only sad; only I am so silly, I cannot help being hurt when you speak coldly. Of course you are quite right: it is dreadful to think of anyone being killed or even hurt; and I hope nothing really serious has—(*Her voice dies away under his contemptuous penetration.*)

CÆSAR. What has frightened you into this? What have you done? (*A trumpet sounds on the beach below.*) Aha! that sounds like the answer.

CLEOPATRA (*sinking back trembling on the bench and covering her face with her hands*). I have not betrayed you, Cæsar: I swear it.

CÆSAR. I know that. I have not trusted you. (*He turns from her, and is about to go out when Apollodorus and Britannus drag in Lucius Septimius to him. Rufio follows. Cæsar shudders.*) Again, Pompey's murderer!

RUFIO. The town has gone mad, I think. They are for tearing the palace down and driving us into the sea straight away. We laid hold of this renegade in clearing them out of the courtyard.

CÆSAR. Release him. (*They let go his arms.*) What has offended the citizens, Lucius Septimius?

LUCIUS. What did you expect, Cæsar? Pothinus was a favorite of theirs.

CÆSAR. What has happened to Pothinus? I set him free, here, not half an hour ago. Did they not pass him out?

LUCIUS. Ay, through the gallery arch sixty feet above ground, with three inches of steel in his ribs. He is as dead as Pompey. We are quits now, as to killing—you and I.

CÆSAR (*shocked*). Assassinated!—our prisoner, our guest! (*He turns reproachfully on Rufio*) Rufio—

RUFIO (*emphatically—anticipating the question*). Whoever did it was a wise man and a friend of yours (*Cleopatra is greatly emboldened*); but none of us had a hand in it. So it is no use to frown at me. (*Cæsar turns and looks at Cleopatra.*)

CLEOPATRA (*violently—rising*). He was slain by order of the

Queen of Egypt. I am not Julius Cæsar the dreamer, who allows every slave to insult him. Rufio has said I did well: now the others shall judge me too. (*She turns to the others.*) This Pothinus sought to make me conspire with him to betray Cæsar to Achillas and Ptolemy. I refused; and he cursed me and came privily to Cæsar to accuse me of his own treachery. I caught him in the act; and he insulted me—me, the Queen! to my face. Cæsar would not avenge me; he spoke him fair and set him free. Was I right to avenge myself? Speak, Lucius.

LUCIUS. I do not gainsay it. But you will get little thanks from Cæsar for it.

CLEOPATRA. Speak, Apollodorus. Was I wrong?

APOLLODORUS. I have only one word of blame, most beautiful. You should have called upon me, your knight; and in fair duel I should have slain the slanderer.

CLEOPATRA (*passionately*). I will be judged by your very slave, Cæsar. Britannus: speak. Was I wrong?

BRITANNUS. Were treachery, falsehood, and disloyalty left unpunished, society must become like an arena full of wild beasts, tearing one another to pieces. Cæsar is in the wrong.

CÆSAR (*with quiet bitterness*). And so the verdict is against me, it seems.

CLEOPATRA (*vehemently*). Listen to me, Cæsar. If one man in all Alexandria can be found to say that I did wrong, I swear to have myself crucified on the door of the palace by my own slaves.

CÆSAR. If one man in all the world can be found, now or forever, to k n o w that you did wrong, that man will have either to conquer the world as I have, or be crucified by it. (*The uproar in the streets again reaches them.*) Do you hear? These knockers at your gate are also believers in vengeance and in stabbing. You have slain their leader: it is right that they shall slay you. If you doubt it, ask your four counsellors here. And then in the name of that right (*he emphasizes the word with great scorn*) shall I not slay them for murdering their Queen, and be slain in my turn by their countrymen as the invader of their fatherland? Can Rome do less then than slay these slayers too, to shew the world how Rome avenges her sons and her honor? And so to the end of history, murder shall breed murder, always in the name of right and honor and peace, until the gods are tired of blood and create a race that can understand. (*Fierce uproar. Cleopatra becomes white with terror.*) Hearken, you who must not be insulted. Go near enough to catch their words: you will find them bitterer than the tongue of Pothinus. (*Loftily wrapping himself up in an impenetrable dignity.*) Let the Queen of Egypt now give her orders for vengeance, and take her measures for defence; for she has renounced Cæsar. (*He turns to go.*)

CLEOPATRA (*terrified, running to him and falling on her knees*). You will not desert me, Cæsar. You will defend the palace.

CÆSAR. You have taken the powers of life and death upon you. I am only a dreamer.

CLEOPATRA. But they will kill me.

CÆSAR. And why not?

CLEOPATRA. In pity—

CÆSAR. Pity! What! has it come to this so suddenly, that nothing can save you now but pity? Did it save Pothinus?

She rises, wringing her hands, and goes back to the bench in despair. Apollodorus shews his sympathy with her by quietly posting himself behind the bench. The sky has by this time become the most vivid purple, and soon begins to change to a glowing pale orange, against which the colonnade and the great image show darklier and darklier.

RUFIO. Cæsar: enough of preaching. The enemy is at the gate.

CÆSAR (*turning on him and giving way to his wrath*). Ay; and what has held him baffled at the gate all these months? Was it my folly, as you deem it, or your wisdom? In this Egyptian Red Sea of blood, whose hand has held all your heads above the waves? (*Turning on Cleopatra*) And yet, when Cæsar says to such an one, "Friend, go free," you, clinging for your little life to my sword, dare steal out and stab him in the back? And you, soldiers and gentlemen, and honest servants as you forget that you are, applaud this assassination, and say, "Cæsar is in the wrong." By the gods, I am tempted to open my hand and let you all sink into the flood.

CLEOPATRA (*with a ray of cunning hope*). But, Cæsar, if you do, you will perish yourself.

Cæsar's eyes blaze.

RUFIO (*greatly alarmed*). Now, by great Jove, you filthy little Egyptian rat, that is the very word to make him walk out alone into the city and leave us here to be cut to pieces. (*Desperately, to Cæsar*) Will you desert us because we are a parcel of fools? I mean no harm by killing: I do it as a dog kills a cat, by instinct. We are all dogs at your heels; but we have served you faithfully.

CÆSAR (*relenting*). Alas, Rufio, my son, my son: as dogs we are like to perish now in the streets.

APOLLODORUS (*at his post behind Cleopatra's seat*). Cæsar, what you say has an Olympian ring in it: it must be right; for it is fine art. But I am still on the side of Cleopatra. If we must die, she shall not want the devotion of a man's heart nor the strength of a man's arm.

CLEOPATRA (*sobbing*). But I don't want to die.

CÆSAR (*sadly*). Oh, ignoble, ignoble!

LUCIUS (*coming forward between Cæsar and Cleopatra*). Hearken to me, Cæsar. It may be ignoble; but I also mean to live as long as I can.

CÆSAR. Well, my friend, you are likely to outlive Cæsar. Is it any magic of mine, think you, that has kept your army and this whole city at bay for long? Yesterday, what quarrel had they with me that they should risk their lives against me? But to-day we have flung them down their hero murdered; and now every man of them is set upon clearing out this nest of assassins—for such we are and no more. Take courage then; and sharpen your sword. Pompey's head has fallen; and Cæsar's head is ripe.

APOLLODORUS. Does Cæsar despair?

CÆSAR (*with infinite pride*). He who has never hoped can never despair. Cæsar, in good or bad fortune, looks his fate in the face.

LUCIUS. Look it in the face, then; and it will smile as it always has on Cæsar.

CÆSAR (*with involuntary haughtiness*). Do you presume to encourage me?

LUCIUS. I offer you my services. I will change sides if you will have me.

CÆSAR (*suddenly coming down to earth again, and looking sharply at him, divining that there is something behind the offer*). What! At this point?

LUCIUS (*firmly*). At this point.

RUFIO. Do you suppose Cæsar is mad, to trust you?

LUCIUS. I do not ask him to trust me until he is victorious. I ask for my life, and for a command in Cæsar's army. And since Cæsar is a fair dealer, I will pay in advance.

CÆSAR. Pay! How?

LUCIUS. With a piece of good news for you.

Cæsar divines the news in a flash.

RUFIO. What news?

CÆSAR (*with an elate and buoyant energy which makes Cleopatra sit up and stare*). What news! What news, did you say, my son Rufio? The relief has arrived: what other news remains for us? Is it not so, Lucius Septimius? Mithridates of Pergamos is on the march.

LUCIUS. He has taken Pelusium.

CÆSAR (*delighted*). Lucius Septimius: you are henceforth my officer. Rufio: the Egyptians must have sent every soldier from the city to prevent Mithridates crossing the Nile. There is nothing in the streets now but mob—mob!

LUCIUS. It is so. Mithridates is marching by the great road to Memphis to cross above the Delta. Achillas will fight him there.

CÆSAR (*all audacity*). Achillas shall fight Cæsar there. See, Rufio. (*He runs to the table; snatches a napkin; and draws a plan on it with his finger dipped in wine, whilst Rufio and Lucius Septimius crowd about him to watch, all looking closely, for the light is now almost gone.*) Here is the palace (*pointing to his plan*): here is the theatre. You (*to Rufio*) take twenty men and pretend to go by that street (*pointing it out*); and whilst they are stoning you, out go the cohorts by this and this. My streets are right, are they, Lucius?

LUCIUS. Ay, that is the fig market—

CÆSAR (*too much excited to listen to him*). I saw them the day we arrived. Good! (*He throws the napkin on the table and comes down again into the colonnade.*) Away, Britannus:

tell Petronius that within an hour half our forces must take ship for the western lake. See to my horse and armor. (*Britannus runs out.*) With the rest, *I* shall march round the lake and up the Nile to meet Mithridates. Away, Lucius; and give the word.

Lucius hurries out after Britannus.

RUFIO. Come: this is something like business.

CÆSAR (*buoyantly*). Is it not, my only son? (*He claps his hands. The slaves hurry in to the table.*) No more of this mawkish revelling: away with all this stuff: shut it out of my sight and be off with you. (*The slaves begin to remove the table; and the curtains are drawn, shutting in the colonnade.*) You understand about the streets, Rufio?

RUFIO. Ay, I think I do. I will get through them, at all events.

The bucina sounds busily in the courtyard beneath.

CÆSAR. Come, then: we must talk to the troops and hearten them. You down to the beach: I to the courtyard. (*He makes for the staircase.*)

CLEOPATRA (*rising from her seat, where she has been quite neglected all this time, and stretching out her hands timidly to him*). Cæsar.

CÆSAR (*turning*). Eh?

CLEOPATRA. Have you forgotten me?

CÆSAR (*indulgently*). I am busy now, my child, busy. When I return your affairs shall be settled. Farewell; and be good and patient.

He goes, preoccupied and quite indifferent. She stands with clenched fists, in speechless rage and humiliation.

RUFIO. That game is played and lost, Cleopatra. The woman always gets the worst of it.

CLEOPATRA (*haughtily*). Go. Follow your master.

RUFIO (*in her ear, with rough familiarity*). A word first. Tell your executioner that if Pothinus had been properly killed—i n t h e t h r o a t—he would not have called out. Your man bungled his work.

CLEOPATRA (*enigmatically*). How do you know it was a man?

RUFIO (*startled, and puzzled*). It was not you: you were with us when it happened. (*She turns her back scornfully on him. He shakes his head, and draws the curtains to go out. It is now a magnificent moonlit night. The table has been removed. Ftatateeta is seen in the light of the moon and stars, again in prayer before the white altar-stone of Ra. Rufio starts; closes the curtains again softly; and says in a low voice to Cleopatra*) Was it she? with her own hand?

CLEOPATRA (*threateningly*). Whoever it was, let my enemies beware of her. Look to it, Rufio, you who dare make the Queen of Egypt a fool before Cæsar.

RUFIO (*looking grimly at her*). I will look to it, Cleopatra. (*He nods in confirmation of the promise, and slips out through the curtains, loosening his sword in its sheath as he goes.*)

ROMAN SOLDIERS (*in the courtyard below*). Hail, Cæsar! Hail, hail!

Cleopatra listens. The bucina sounds again, followed by several trumpets.

CLEOPATRA (*wringing her hands and calling*). Ftatateeta. Ftatateeta. It is dark; and I am alone. Come to me. (*Silence.*) Ftatateeta. (*Louder.*) Ftatateeta. (*Silence*). *In a panic she snatches the cord and pulls the curtains apart.*

Ftatateeta is lying dead on the altar of Ra, with her throat cut. Her blood deluges the white stone.

END OF ACT IV.

ACT V

High noon. Festival and military pageant on the esplanade before the palace. In the east harbor Cæsar's galley, so gorgeously decorated that it seems to be rigged with flowers, is alongside the quay, close to the steps Apollodorus descended when he embarked with the carpet. A Roman guard is posted there in charge of a gangway, whence a red floorcloth is laid down the middle of the esplanade, turning off to the north opposite the central gate in the palace front, which shuts in the esplanade on the south side. The broad steps of the gate, crowded with Cleopatra's ladies, all in their gayest attire, are like a flower garden. The façade is lined by her guard, officered by the same gallants to whom Bel Affris announced the coming of Cæsar six months before in the old palace on the Syrian border. The north side is lined by Roman soldiers, with the townsfolk on tiptoe behind them, peering over their heads at the cleared esplanade, in which the officers stroll about, chatting. Among these are Belzanor and the Persian; also the Centurion, vinewood cudgel in hand, battle worn, thick-booted, and much outshone, both socially and decoratively, by the Egyptian officers.

Apollodorus makes his way through the townsfolk and calls to the officers from behind the Roman line.

APOLLODORUS. Hullo! May I pass?

CENTURION. Pass Apollodorus the Sicilian there! (*The soldiers let him through.*)

BELZANOR. Is Cæsar at hand?

APOLLODORUS. Not yet. He is still in the market place. I could not stand any more of the roaring of the soldiers! After half an hour of the enthusiasm of an army, one feels the need of a little sea air.

PERSIAN. Tell us the news. Hath he slain the priests?

APOLLODORUS. Not he. They met him in the market place with ashes on their heads and their gods in their hands. They placed the gods at his feet. The only one that was worth looking at was Apis: a miracle of gold and ivory work. By my advice he offered the chief priest two talents for it.

BELZANOR (*appalled*). Apis the all-knowing for two talents! What said the chief priest?

APOLLODORUS. He invoked the mercy of Apis, and asked for five.

BELZANOR. There will be famine and tempest in the land for this.

PERSIAN. Pooh! Why did not Apis cause Cæsar to be vanquished by Achillas? Any fresh news from the war, Apollodorus?

APOLLODORUS. The little King Ptolemy was drowned.

BELZANOR. Drowned! How?

APOLLODORUS. With the rest of them. Cæsar attacked them from three sides at once and swept them into the Nile. Ptolemy's barge sank.

BELZANOR. A marvelous man, this Cæsar! Will he come soon, think you?

APOLLODORUS. He was settling the Jewish question when I left.

A flourish of trumpets from the north, and commotion among the townsfolk, announces the approach of Cæsar.

PERSIAN. He has made short work of them. Here he comes. (*He hurries to his post in front of the Egyptian lines.*)

BELZANOR (*following him*). Ho there! Cæsar comes.

The soldiers stand at attention, and dress their lines. Apollodorus goes to the Egyptian line.

CENTURION (*hurrying to the gangway guard*). Attention there! Cæsar comes.

Cæsar arrives in state with Rufio: Britannus following. The soldiers receive him with enthusiastic shouting.

CÆSAR. I see my ship awaits me. The hour of Cæsar's farewell to Egypt has arrived. And now, Rufio, what remains to be done before I go?

RUFIO (*at his left hand*). You have not yet appointed a Roman governor for this province.

CÆSAR (*looking whimsically at him, but speaking with perfect gravity*). What say you to Mithridates of Pergamos, my reliever and rescuer, the great son of Eupator?

RUFIO. Why, that you will want him elsewhere. Do you forget that you have some three or four armies to conquer on your way home?

CÆSAR. Indeed! Well, what say you to yourself?

RUFIO (*incredulously*). I! I a governor! What are you dreaming of? Do you not know that I am only the son of a freedman?

CÆSAR (*affectionately*). Has not Cæsar called you his son? (*Calling to the whole assembly*) Peace awhile there; and hear me.

THE ROMAN SOLDIERS. Hear Cæsar.

CÆSAR. Hear the service, quality, rank and name of the Roman governor. By service, Cæsar's shield; by quality, Cæsar's friend; by rank, a Roman soldier. (*The Roman soldiers give a triumphant shout.*) By name, Rufio. (*They shout again.*)

RUFIO (*kissing Cæsar's hand*). Ay: I am Cæsar's shield; but of what use shall I be when I am no longer on Cæsar's arm? Well, no matter— (*He becomes husky, and turns away to recover himself.*)

CÆSAR. Where is that British Islander of mine?

BRITANNUS (*coming forward on Cæsar's right hand*). Here, Cæsar.

CÆSAR. Who bade you, pray, thrust yourself into the battle of the Delta, uttering the barbarous cries of your native land, and affirming yourself a match for any four of the Egyptians, to whom you applied unseemly epithets?

BRITANNUS. Cæsar: I ask you to excuse the language that escaped me in the heat of the moment.

CÆSAR. And how did you, who cannot swim, cross the canal with us when we stormed the camp?

BRITANNUS. Cæsar: I clung to the tail of your horse.

CÆSAR. These are not the deeds of a slave, Britannicus, but of a free man.

BRITANNUS. Cæsar: I was born free.

CÆSAR. But they call you Cæsar's slave.

BRITANNUS. Only as Cæsar's slave have I found real freedom.

CÆSAR (*moved*). Well said. Ungrateful that I am, I was about to set you free; but now I will not part from you for a million talents. (*He claps him friendlily on the shoulder. Britannus, gratified, but a trifle shamefaced, takes his hand and kisses it sheepishly.*)

BELZANOR (*to the Persian*). This Roman knows how to make men serve him.

PERSIAN. Ay: men too humble to become dangerous rivals to him.

BELZANOR. O subtle one! O cynic!

CÆSAR (*seeing Apollodorus in the Egyptian corner and calling to him*). Apollodorus: I leave the art of Egypt in your charge. Remember: Rome loves art and will encourage it ungrudgingly.

APOLLODORUS. I understand, Cæsar. Rome will produce no art itself; but it will buy up and take away whatever the other nations produce.

CÆSAR. What! Rome produce no art! Is peace not an art? is war not an art? is government not an art? is civilization not an art? All these we give you in exchange for a few ornaments. You will have the best of the bargain. (*Turning to Rufio*) And now, what else have I to do before I embark? (*Trying to recollect*) There is something I cannot remember: what c a n it be? Well, well: it must remain undone: we must not waste this favorable wind. Farewell, Rufio.

RUFIO. Cæsar: I am loth to let you go to Rome without your shield. There are too many daggers there.

CÆSAR. It matters not: I shall finish my life's work on my way back; and then I shall have lived long enough. Besides: I have always disliked the idea of dying: I had rather be killed. Farewell.

RUFIO (*with a sigh, raising his hands and giving Cæsar up as incorrigible*). Farewell. (*They shake hands.*)

CÆSAR (*waving his hand to Apollodorus*). Farewell, Apollodorus, and my friends, all of you. Aboard!

The gangway is run out from the quay to the ship. As Cæsar moves towards it, Cleopatra, cold and tragic, cunningly dressed in black, without ornaments or decoration of any kind, and thus making a striking figure among the brilliantly dressed bevy of ladies as she passes through it, comes from the palace and stands on the steps. Cæsar does not see her until she speaks.

CLEOPATRA. Has Cleopatra no part in this leave taking?

CÆSAR (*enlightened*). Ah, I k n e w there was something. (*To Rufio*) How could you let me forget her, Rufio? (*Hastening to her*) Had I gone without seeing you, I should never have forgiven myself. (*He takes her hands, and brings her into the middle of the esplanade. She submits stonily.*) Is this mourning for me?

CLEOPATRA. No.

CÆSAR (*remorsefully*). Ah, that was thoughtless of me! It is for your brother.

CLEOPATRA. No.

CÆSAR. For whom, then?

CLEOPATRA. Ask the Roman governor whom you have left us.

CÆSAR. Rufio?

CLEOPATRA. Yes: Rufio. (*She points at him with deadly scorn.*) He who is to rule here in Cæsar's name, in Cæsar's way, according to Cæsar's boasted laws of life.

CÆSAR (*dubiously*). He is to rule as he can, Cleopatra. He has taken the work upon him, and will do it in his own way.

CLEOPATRA. Not in your way, then?

CÆSAR (*puzzled*). What do you mean by my way?

CLEOPATRA. Without punishment. Without revenge. Without judgment.

CÆSAR (*approvingly*). Ay: that is the right way, the great way, the only possible way in the end. (*To Rufio*) Believe it, Rufio, if you can.

RUFIO. Why, I believe it, Cæsar. You have convinced me of it long ago. But look you. You are sailing for Numidia to-day. Now tell me: if you meet a hungry lion there, you will not punish it for wanting to eat you?

CÆSAR (*wondering what he is driving at*). No.

RUFIO. Nor revenge upon it the blood of those it has already eaten.

CÆSAR. No.

RUFIO. Nor judge it for its guiltiness.

CÆSAR. No.

RUFIO. What, then, will you do to save your life from it?

CÆSAR (*promptly*). Kill it, man, without malice, just as it would kill me. What does this parable of the lion mean?

RUFIO. Why, Cleopatra had a tigress that killed men at her bidding. I thought she might bid it kill you some day. Well, had I not been Cæsar's pupil, what pious things might I not have done to that tigress? I might have punished it. I might have revenged Pothinus on it.

CÆSAR (*interjects*). Pothinus!

RUFIO (*continuing*). I might have judged it. But I put all these follies behind me; and, without malice, only cut its throat. And that is why Cleopatra comes to you in mourning.

CLEOPATRA (*vehemently*). He has shed the blood of my servant Ftatateeta. On your head be it as upon his, Cæsar, if you hold him free of it.

CÆSAR (*energetically*). On my head be it, then; for it was well done. Rufio: had you set yourself in the seat of the judge, and with hateful ceremonies and appeals to the gods handed that woman over to some hired executioner to be slain before the people in the name of justice, never again would I have touched your hand without a shudder. But this was natural slaying: I feel no horror at it.

Rufio, satisfied, nods at Cleopatra, mutely inviting her to mark that.

CLEOPATRA (*pettish and childish in her impotence*). No: not when a Roman slays an Egyptian. All the world will now see how unjust and corrupt Cæsar is.

CÆSAR (*taking her hands coaxingly*). Come: do not be angry with me. I am sorry for that poor Totateeta. (*She laughs in spite of herself.*) Aha! you are laughing. Does that mean reconciliation?

CLEOPATRA (*angry with herself for laughing*). No, n o, NO!! But it is so ridiculous to hear you call her Totateeta.

CÆSAR. What! As much a child as ever, Cleopatra! Have I not made a woman of you after all?

CLEOPATRA. Oh, it is you who are a great baby: you make me seem silly because you will not behave seriously. But you have treated me badly; and I do not forgive you.

CÆSAR. Bid me farewell.

CLEOPATRA. I will not.

CÆSAR (*coaxing*). I will send you a beautiful present from Rome.

CLEOPATRA (*proudly*). Beauty from Rome to Egypt indeed! What can Rome give me that Egypt cannot give me?

APOLLODORUS. That is true, Cæsar. If the present is to be really beautiful, I shall have to buy it for you in Alexandria.

CÆSAR. You are forgetting the treasures for which Rome is most famous, my friend. You cannot buy them in Alexandria.

APOLLODORUS. What are they, Cæsar?

CÆSAR. Her sons. Come, Cleopatra: forgive me and bid me farewell; and I will send you a man, Roman from head to heel and Roman of the noblest; not old and ripe for the knife; not lean in the arms and cold in the heart; not hiding a bald head under his conqueror's laurels; not stooped with the weight of the world on his shoulders; but brisk and fresh, strong and young, hoping in the morning, fighting in the day, and revelling in the evening. Will you take such an one in exchange for Cæsar?

CLEOPATRA (*palpitating*). His name, his name?

CÆSAR. Shall it be Mark Antony? (*She throws herself into his arms.*)

RUFIO. You are a bad hand at a bargain, mistress, if you will swap Cæsar for Antony.

CÆSAR. So now you are satisfied.

CLEOPATRA. You will not forget.

CÆSAR. I will not forget. Farewell: I do not think we shall meet again. Farewell. (*He kisses her on the forehead. She is much affected and begins to sniff. He embarks.*)

THE ROMAN SOLDIERS (*as he sets his foot on the gangway*). Hail, Cæsar; and farewell!

He reaches the ship and returns Rufio's wave of the hand.

APOLLODORUS (*to Cleopatra*). No tears, dearest Queen: they stab your servant to the heart. He will return some day.

CLEOPATRA. I hope not. But I can't help crying all the

same. (*She waves her handkerchief to Cæsar; and the ship begins to move.*)

THE ROMAN SOLDIERS (*drawing their swords and raising them in the air*). Hail, Cæsar!

THE END

NOTES TO CÆSAR AND CLEOPATRA

CLEOPATRA'S CURE FOR BALDNESS

For the sake of conciseness in a hurried situation I have made Cleopatra recommend rum. This, I am afraid, is an anachronism: the only real one in the play. To balance it, I give a couple of the remedies she actually believed in. They are quoted by Galen from Cleopatra's book on Cosmetic.

"For bald patches, powder red sulphuret of arsenic and take it up with oak gum, as much as it will bear. Put on a rag and apply, having soaped the place well first. I have mixed the above with a foam of nitre, and it worked well."

Several other receipts follow, ending with: "The following is the best of all, acting for fallen hairs, when applied with oil or pomatum; acts also for falling off of eyelashes or for people getting bald all over. It is wonderful. Of domestic mice burnt, one part; of vine rag burnt, one part; of horse's teeth burnt, one part; of bear's grease one; of deer's marrow one; of reed bark one. To be pounded when dry, and mixed with plenty of honey till it gets the consistency of honey; then the bear's grease and marrow to be mixed (when melted), the medicine to be put in a brass flask, and the bald part rubbed til it sprouts."

Concerning these ingredients, my fellow-dramatist, Gilbert Murray, who, as a Professor of Greek, has applied to classical antiquity the methods of high scholarship (my own method is pure divination), writes to me as follows: "Some of this I don't understand, and possibly Galen did not, as he quotes your heroine's own language. Foam of nitre is, I think, something like soapsuds. Reed bark is an odd expression. It might mean the outside membrane of a reed: I do not know what it ought to be called. In the burnt mice receipt I take it that you first mixed the solid powders with honey, and then added the grease. I expect Cleopatra preferred it because in most of the others you have to lacerate the skin, prick it, or rub it till it bleeds. I do not know what vine rag is. I translate literally."

Apparent Anachronisms

The only way to write a play which shall convey to the general public an impression of antiquity is to make the characters speak blank verse and abstain from reference to steam, telegraphy, or any of the material conditions of their existence. The more ignorant men are, the more convinced are they that their little parish and their little chapel is an apex to which civilization and philosophy have painfully struggled up the pyramid of time from a desert of savagery. Savagery, they think, became barbarism; barbarism became ancient civilization; ancient civilization became Pauline Christianity; Pauline Christianity became Roman Catholicism; Roman Catholicism became the Dark Ages; and the Dark Ages were finally enlightened by the Protestant instincts of the English race. The whole process is summed up as Progress with a capital P. And any elderly gentleman of Progressive temperament will testify that the improvement since he was a boy is enormous.

Now if we count the generations of Progressive elderly gentlemen since, say, Plato, and add together the successive enormous improvements to which each of them has testified, it will strike us at once as an unaccountable fact that the world, instead of having been improved in 67 generations out of all recognition, presents, on the whole, a rather less dignified appearance in Ibsen's Enemy of the People than in Plato's Republic. And in truth, the period of time covered by history is far too short to allow of any perceptible progress in the popular sense of Evolution of the Human Species. The notion that there has been any such Progress since Cæsar's time (less than 20 centuries) is too absurd for discussion. All the savagery, barbarism, dark ages and the rest of it of which we have any record as existing in the past, exists at the present moment. A British carpenter or stone-mason may point out that he gets twice as much money for his labor as his father did in the same trade, and that his suburban house, with its bath, its cottage piano, its drawingroom suite, and its album of photographs, would have shamed the plainness of his grandmother's. But the descendants of feudal barons, living in squalid lodgings on a salary of fifteen shillings a week instead of in castles on princely revenues, do not congratulate the world on the change. Such changes, in fact, are not to the point. It has been known, as far back as our records go, that man running wild in the woods is different to man kennelled in a city slum; that a dog seems to understand a shepherd better than a hewer of wood and drawer of water can understand an astronomer; and that breeding, gentle nurture and luxurious food and shelter will produce a kind of man with whom the common laborer is socially incompatible. The same thing is true of horses and dogs. Now there is clearly room for great changes in the world by increasing the percentage of individuals who are carefully bred and gently nurtured, even to finally making the most of every man and woman born. But that possibility existed in the days of the Hittites as much as it does to-day. It does not give the slightest real support to the common assumption that the civilized contemporaries of the Hittites were unlike their civilized descendants to-day.

This would appear the tritest commonplace if it were not that the ordinary citizen's ignorance of the past combines with his idealization of the present to mislead and flatter him. Our latest book on the new railway across Asia describes the dulness of the Siberian farmer and the vulgar pursepride of the Siberian man of business without the least consciousness that the sting of contemptuous instances given might have been saved by writing simply, "Farmers and provincial plutocrats in Siberia are exactly what they are in England." The latest professor descanting on the civilization of the Western Empire in the fifth century feels bound to assume, in the teeth of his own researches, that the Christian was one sort of animal and the Pagan another. It might as well be assumed, as indeed it generally is assumed by implication, that a murder committed with a poisoned arrow is different to a murder committed with a Mauser rifle. All such notions are illusions. Go back to the first syllable of recorded time, and there you will find your Christian and your Pagan, your yokel and your poet, helot and hero, Don Quixote and Sancho, Tamino and Papageno, Newton and bushman unable to count eleven, all alive and contemporaneous, and all convinced that they are the heirs of all the ages and the privileged recipients of THE truth (all others damnable heresies), just as you have them to-day, flourishing in countries each of which is the bravest and best that ever sprang at Heaven's command from out the azure main.

Again, there is the illusion of "increased command over Nature," meaning that cotton is cheap and that ten miles of country road on a bicycle have replaced four on foot. But even if man's increased command over Nature included any increased command over himself (the only sort of command relevant to his evolution into a higher being), the fact remains that it is only by running away from the increased command over Nature to country places where Nature is still in primitive command over Man that he can recover from the effects of the smoke, the stench, the foul air, the overcrowding, the racket, the ugliness, the dirt which the cheap cotton costs us. If manufacturing activity means Progress, the town must be more advanced than the country; and the field laborers and village artizans of to-day must be much less changed from the servants of Job than the proletariat of modern London from the proletariat of Cæsar's Rome. Yet the cockney proletarian is so inferior to the village laborer that it is only by steady recruiting from the country that London is kept alive. This does not seem as if the change since Job's time were Progress in the popular sense: quite the reverse. The common stock of discoveries in physics has accumulated a little: that is all.

One more illustration. Is the Englishman prepared to admit that the American is his superior as a human being? I ask this question because the scarcity of labor in America relatively to the demand for it has led to a development of machinery there, and a consequent "increase of command over Nature" which makes many of our English methods appear almost medieval to the up-to-date Chicagoan. This means that the American has an advantage over the Englishman of exactly the same nature that the Englishman has over the contemporaries of Cicero. Is the Englishman prepared to draw the same conclusion in both cases? I think not. The American, of course, will draw it cheerfully; but I must then ask him whether, since a modern negro has a greater "command over Nature" than Washington had, we are also to accept the conclusion, involved in his former one, that humanity has progressed from Washington to the *fin de siècle* negro.

Finally, I would point out that if life is crowned by its success and devotion in industrial organization and ingenuity, we had better worship the ant and the bee (as moralists urge us to do in our childhood), and humble ourselves before the arrogance of the birds of Aristophanes.

My reason then for ignoring the popular conception of Progress in Cæsar and Cleopatra is that there is no reason to suppose that any Progress has taken place since their time. But even if I shared the popular delusion, I do not see that I could have made any essential difference in the play. I can only imitate humanity as I know it. Nobody knows whether Shakespear thought that ancient Athenian joiners, weavers, or bellows menders were any different from Elizabethan ones; but it is quite certain that he could not have made them so, unless, indeed, he had played the literary man and made Quince say, not, "Is all our company here?" but, "Bottom: was not that Socrates that passed us at the Piræus with Glaucon and Polemarchus on his way to the house of Kephalus." And so on.

CLEOPATRA

Cleopatra was only sixteen when Cæsar went to Egypt; but in Egypt sixteen is a riper age than it is in England. The childishness I have ascribed to her, as far as it is childishness of character and not lack of experience, is not a matter of years. It may be observed in our own climate at the present day in many women of fifty. It is a mistake to suppose that the difference between wisdom and folly has anything to do with the difference between physical age and physical youth.

Some women are younger at seventy than most women at seventeen.

It must be borne in mind, too, that Cleopatra was a queen, and was therefore not the typical Greek-cultured, educated Egyptian lady of her time. To represent her by any such type would be as absurd as to represent George IV by a type founded on the attainments of Sir Isaac Newton. It is true that an ordinarily well educated Alexandrian girl of her time would no more have believed bogey stories about the Romans than the daughter of a modern Oxford professor would believe them about the Germans (though, by the way, it is possible to talk great nonsense at Oxford about foreigners when we are at war with them). But I do not feel bound to believe that Cleopatra was well educated. Her father, the illustrious Flute Blower, was not at all a parent of the Oxford professor type. And Cleopatra was a chip of the old block.

Britannus

I find among those who have read this play in manuscript a strong conviction that an ancient Briton could not possibly have been like a modern one. I see no reason to adopt this curious view. It is true that the Roman and Norman conquests must have for a time disturbed the normal British type produced by the climate. But Britannus, born before these events, represents the unadulterated Briton who fought Cæsar and impressed Roman observers much as we should expect the ancestors of Mr. Podsnap to impress the cultivated Italians of their time.

I am told that it is not scientific to treat national character as a product of climate. This only shews the wide difference between common knowledge and the intellectual game called science. We have men of exactly the same stock, and speaking the same language, growing in Great Britain, in Ireland, and in America. The result is three of the most distinctly marked nationalities under the sun. Racial characteristics are quite another matter. The difference between a Jew and a Gentile has nothing to do with the difference between an Englishman and a German. The characteristics of Britannus are local characteristics, not race characteristics. In an ancient Briton they would, I take it, be exaggerated, since modern Britain, disforested, drained, urbanified and consequently cosmopolized, is presumably less characteristically British than Cæsar's Britain.

And again I ask does anyone who, in the light of a competent knowledge of his own age, has studied history from contemporary documents, believe that 67 generations of promiscuous marriage have made any appreciable difference in the human fauna of these isles? Certainly I do not.

JULIUS CÆSAR

As to Cæsar himself, I have purposely avoided the usual anachronism of going to Cæsar's books, and concluding that the style is the man. That is only true of authors who have the specific literary genius, and have practised long enough to attain complete self-expression in letters. It is not true even on these conditions in an age when literature is conceived as a game of style, and not as a vehicle of self-expression by the author. Now Cæsar was an amateur stylist writing books of travel and campaign histories in a style so impersonal that the authenticity of the later volumes is disputed. They reveal some of his qualities just as the Voyage of a Naturalist Round the World reveals some of Darwin's, without expressing his private personality. An Englishman reading them would say that Cæsar was a man of great common sense and good taste, meaning thereby a man without originality or moral courage.

In exhibiting Cæsar as a much more various person than the historian of the Gallic wars, I hope I have not succumbed unconsciously to the dramatic illusion to which all great men owe part of their reputation and some the whole of it. I admit that reputations gained in war are specially questionable. Able civilians taking up the profession of arms, like Cæsar and Cromwell, in middle age, have snatched all its laurels from opponent commanders bred to it, apparently because capable persons engaged in military pursuits are so scarce that the existence of two of them at the same time in the same hemisphere is extremely rare. The capacity of any conqueror is therefore more likely than not to be an illusion produced by the incapacity of his adversary. At all events, Cæsar might have won his battles without being wiser than Charles XII or Nelson or Joan of Arc, who were, like most modern "self-made" millionaires, half-witted geniuses, enjoying the worship accorded by all races to certain forms of insanity. But Cæsar's victories were only advertisements for an eminence that would never have become popular without them. Cæsar is greater off the battle field than on it. Nelson off his quarterdeck was so quaintly out of the question that when his head was injured at the battle of the Nile, and his conduct became for some years openly scandalous, the difference was not important enough to be noticed. It may, however, be said that peace hath her illusory reputations no less than war. And it is certainly true that in civil life mere capacity for work—the power of killing a dozen secretaries under you, so to speak, as a life-or-death courier kills horses—enables men with common ideas and superstitions to distance all competitors in the strife of political ambition. It was this power of work that astonished Cicero as the most prodigious of Cæsar's gifts, as it astonished later observers in Napoleon before it wore him out. How if Cæsar were nothing but a Nelson and a Gladstone combined! a prodigy of vitality without any special quality of mind! nay, with ideas that were worn out before he was born, as Nelson's and Gladstone's were! I have considered that possibility too, and rejected it. I cannot cite all the stories about Cæsar which seem to me to shew that he was genuinely original; but let me at least point out that I have been careful to attribute nothing but originality to him. Originality gives a man an air of frankness, generosity, and magnanimity by enabling him to estimate the value of truth, money, or success in any particular instance quite independently of convention and moral generalization. He therefore will not, in the ordinary Treasury bench fashion, tell a lie which everybody knows to be a lie (and consequently expects him as a matter of good taste to tell). His lies are not found out: they pass for candors. He understands the paradox of money, and gives it away when he can get most for it: in other words, when its value is least, which is just when a common man tries hardest to get it. He knows that the real moment of success is not the moment apparent to the crowd. Hence, in order to produce an impression of complete disinterestedness and magnanimity, he has only to act with entire selfishness; and this is perhaps the only sense in which a man can be said to be *naturally* great. It is in this sense that I have represented Cæsar as great. Having virtue, he has no need of goodness. He is neither forgiving, frank, nor generous, because a man who is too great to resent has nothing to forgive; a man who says things that other people are afraid to say need be no more frank than Bismarck was; and there is no generosity in giving things you do not want to people of whom you intend to make use. This distinction between virtue and goodness is not understood in England: hence the poverty of our drama in heroes. Our stage attempts at them are mere goody-goodies. Goodness, in its popular British sense of self-denial, implies that man is vicious by nature, and that supreme goodness is supreme martyrdom. Not sharing that pious opinion, I have not given countenance to it in any of my plays. In this follow I the precedent of the ancient myths, which represent the hero as vanquishing his enemies, not in fair fight, but with enchanted sword, superequine horse and magical invulnerability, the possession of which, from the vulgar moralistic point of view, robs his exploits of any merit whatever.

As to Cæsar's sense of humor, there is no more reason to assume he lacked it than to assume that he was deaf or blind. It is said that on the occasion of his assassination by a conspiracy of moralists (its always your moralist who makes assassination a duty, on the scaffold or off it), he defended himself until the good Brutus struck him, when he exclaimed, "What! you too, Brutus!" and disdained further fight. If this be true, he must have been an incorrigible comedian. But even if we waive this story, or accept the traditional sentimental interpretaton of it, there is still abundant evidence of his lightheartedness and adventurousness. Indeed it is clear from his whole history that what has been called his ambition was an instinct for exploration. He had much more of Columbus and Franklin in him than of Henry V.

However, nobody need deny Cæsar a share, at least, of the qualities I have attributed to him. All men, much more Julius Cæsars, possess all qualities in some degree. The really interesting question is whether I am right in assuming that the way to produce an impression of greatness is by exhibiting a man, not as mortifying his nature by doing his duty, in the manner which our system of putting little men into great positions (not having enough great men in our influential families to go around) forces us to inculcate, but as simply doing what he naturally wants to do. For this raises the question whether our world has not been wrong in its moral theory for the last 2,500 years or so. It must be a constant puzzle to many of us that the Christian era, so excellent in its intentions, should have been practically such a very discreditable episode in the history of the race. I doubt if this is altogether due to the vulgar and sanguinary sensationalism of our religious legends, with their substitution of gross physical torments and public executions for the passion of humanity. Islam, substituting voluptuousness for torment (a merely superficial difference, it is true) has done no better. It may have been the failure of Christianity to emancipate itself from expiatory theories of moral responsibility, guilt, innocence, reward, punishment, and the rest of it, that baffled its intention of changing the world. But these are bound up in all philosophies of creation as opposed to cosmism. They may therefore be regarded as the price we pay for popular religion.

THE DOCTOR'S DILEMMA

PREFACE ON DOCTORS

It is not the fault of our doctors that the medical service of the community, as at present provided for, is a murderous absurdity. That any sane nation, having observed that you could provide for the supply of bread by giving bakers a pecuniary interest in baking for you, should go on to give a surgeon a pecuniary interest in cutting off your leg, is enough to make one despair of political humanity. But that is precisely what we have done. And the more appalling the mutilation, the more the mutilator is paid. He who corrects the ingrowing toe-nail receives a few shillings: he who cuts your inside out receives hundreds of guineas, except when he does it to a poor person for practice.

Scandalized voices murmur that these operations are necessary. They may be. It may also be necessary to hang a man or pull down a house. But we take good care not to make the hangman and the housebreaker the judges of that. If we did, no man's neck would be safe and no man's house stable. But we do make the doctor the judge, and fine him anything from sixpence to several hundred guineas if he decides in our favor. I cannot knock my shins severely without forcing on some surgeon the difficult question, "Could I not make a better use of a pocketful of guineas than this man is making of his leg? Could he not write as well—or even better—on one leg than on two? And the guineas would make all the difference in the world to me just now. My wife—my pretty ones—the leg may mortify—it is always safer to operate—he will be well in a fortnight—artificial legs are now so well made that they are really better than natural ones—evolution is towards motors and leglessness, &c., &c., &c.''

Now there is no calculation that an engineer can make as to the behavior of a girder under a strain, or an astronomer as to the recurrence of a comet, more certain than the calculation that under such circumstances we shall be dismembered unnecessarily in all directions by surgeons who believe the operations to be necessary solely because they want to perform them. The process metaphorically called bleeding the rich man is performed not only metaphorically but literally every day by surgeons who are quite as honest as most of us. After all, what harm is there in it? The surgeon need not take off the rich man's (or woman's) leg or arm: he can remove the appendix or the uvula, and leave the patient none the worse after a fortnight or so in bed, whilst the nurse, the general practitioner, the apothecary, and the surgeon will be the better.

Doubtful Character Borne by the Medical Profession

Again I hear the voices indignantly muttering old phrases about the high character of a noble profession and the honor and conscience of its members. I must reply that the medical profession has not a high character: it has an infamous character. I do not know a single thoughtful and well-informed person who does not feel that the tragedy of illness at present is that it delivers you helplessly into the hands of a profession which you deeply mistrust, because it not only advocates and practises the most revolting cruelties in the pursuit of knowledge, and justifies them on grounds which would equally justify practising the same cruelties on yourself or your children, or burning down London to test a patent fire extinguisher, but, when it has shocked the public, tries to reassure it with lies of breath-bereaving brazenness. That is the character the medical profession has got just now. It may be deserved or it may not: there it is at all events, and the doctors who have not realized this are living in a fool's paradise. As to the honor and conscience of doctors, they have as much as any other class of men, no more and no less. And what other men dare pretend to be impartial where they have a strong pecuniary interest on one side? Nobody supposes that doctors are less virtuous than judges; but a judge whose salary and reputation depended on whether the verdict was for plaintiff or defendant, prosecutor or prisoner, would be as little trusted as a general in the pay of the enemy. To offer me a doctor as my judge, and then weight his decision with a bribe of a large sum of money and a virtual guarantee that if he makes a mistake it can never be proved against him, is to go wildly beyond the ascertained strain which human nature will bear. It is simply unscientific to allege or believe that doctors do not under existing circumstances perform unnecessary operations and manufacture and prolong lucrative illnesses. The only ones who can claim to be above suspicion are those who are so much sought after that their cured patients are immediately replaced by fresh ones. And there is this curious psychological fact to be remembered: a serious illness or a death advertizes the doctor exactly as a hanging advertizes the barrister who defended the person hanged. Suppose, for example, a royal personage gets something wrong with his throat, or has a pain in his inside. If a doctor effects some trumpery cure with a wet compress or a peppermint lozenge nobody takes the least notice of him. But if he operates on the throat and kills the patient, or extirpates an internal organ and keeps the whole nation palpitating for days whilst the patient hovers in pain and fever between life and death, his fortune is made: every rich man who omits to call him in when the same symptoms appear in his household is held not to have done his utmost duty to the patient. The wonder is that there is a king or queen left alive in Europe.

Doctors' Consciences

There is another difficulty in trusting to the honor and conscience of a doctor. Doctors are just like other Englishmen: most of them have no honor and no conscience: what they commonly mistake for these is sentimentality and an intense dread of doing anything that everybody else does not do, or omitting to do anything that everybody else does. This of course does amount to a sort of working or rule-of-thumb conscience; but it means that you will do anything, good or bad, provided you get enough people to keep you in countenance by doing it also. It is the sort of conscience that makes it possible to keep order on a pirate ship, or in a troop of brigands. It may be said that in the last analysis there is no other sort of honor or conscience in existence—that the assent of the majority is the only sanction known to ethics. No doubt this holds good in political practice. If mankind knew the facts, and agreed with the doctors, then the doctors would be in the right; and any person who thought otherwise would be a lunatic. But mankind does not agree, and does not know the facts. All that can be said for medical popularity is that until there is a practicable alternative to blind trust in the doctor, the truth about the doctor is so terrible that we dare not face it. Molière saw through the doctors; but he had to call them in just the same. Napoleon had no illusions about them; but he had to die under their treatment just as much as the most credulous ignoramus that ever paid sixpence for a bottle of strong medicine. In this predicament most people, to save themselves from unbearable mistrust and misery, or from being driven by their conscience into actual conflict with the law, fall back on the old rule that if you cannot have what you believe in you must believe in what you have. When your child is ill or your wife dying, and you happen to be very fond of them, or even when, if you are not fond of them, you are human enough to forget every personal grudge before the spectacle of a fellow creature in pain or peril, what you want is comfort, reassurance, something to clutch at, were it but a straw. This the doctor brings you. You have a wildly urgent feeling that something must be done; and the doctor does something. Sometimes what he does kills the patient; but you do not know that; and the doctor assures you that all that human skill could do has been done. And nobody has the brutality to say to the newly bereft father, mother, husband, wife, brother, or sister, "You have killed your lost darling by your credulity."

THE PECULIAR PEOPLE

Besides, the calling in of the doctor is now compulsory except in cases where the patient is an adult and not too ill to decide the steps to be taken. We are subject to prosecution for manslaughter or for criminal neglect if the patient dies without the consolations of the medical profession. This menace is kept before the public by the Peculiar People. The Peculiars, as they are called, have gained their name by believing that the Bible is infallible, and taking their belief quite seriously. The Bible is very clear as to the treatment of illness. The Epistle of James, chapter v., contains the following explicit directions:

> 14. Is any sick among you? let him call for the elders of the Church; and let them pray over him, anointing him with oil in the name of the Lord:
>
> 15. And the prayer of faith shall save the sick, and the Lord shall raise him up; and if he have committed sins, they shall be forgiven him.

The Peculiars obey these instructions and dispense with doctors. They are therefore prosecuted for manslaughter when their children die.

When I was a young man, the Peculiars were usually acquitted. The prosecution broke down when the doctor in the witness box was asked whether, if the child had had medical attendance, it would have lived. It was, of course, impossible for any man of sense and honor to assume divine omniscience by answering this in the affirmative, or indeed pretending to be able to answer it at all. And on this the judge had to instruct the jury that they must acquit the prisoner. Thus a judge with a keen sense of law (a very rare phenomenon on the Bench, by the way) was spared the possibility of having to sentence one prisoner (under the Blasphemy Laws) for questioning the authority of Scripture, and another for ignorantly and superstitiously accepting it as a guide for conduct. To-day all this is changed. The doctor never hesitates to claim divine omniscience, nor to clamor for laws to punish any scepticism on the part of laymen. A modern doctor thinks nothing of signing the death certificate of one of his own diphtheria patients, and then going into the witness box and swearing a Peculiar into prison for six months by assuring the jury, on oath, that if the prisoner's child, dead of diphtheria, had been placed under his treatment instead of that of St. James, it would not have died. And he does so not only with impunity, but with public applause, though the logical course would be to prosecute him either for the murder of his own patient or for perjury in the case of St. James. Yet no barrister, apparently, dreams of asking for the statistics of the relative case-mortality in diphtheria among the Peculiars or among the believers in doctors, on which alone any valid opinion could be founded. The barrister is as superstitious as the doctor is infatuated; and the Peculiar goes unpitied to his cell, though nothing whatever has been proved except that his child does without the interference of a doctor as effectually as any of the hundreds of children who die every day of the same diseases in the doctor's care.

Recoil of the Dogma of Medical Infallibility on the Doctor

On the other hand, when the doctor is in the dock, or is the defendant in an action for malpractice, he has to struggle against the inevitable result of his former pretences to infinite knowledge and unerring skill. He has taught the jury and the judge, and even his own counsel, to believe that every doctor can, with a glance at the tongue, a touch on the pulse, and a reading of the clinical thermometer, diagnose with absolute certainty a patient's complaint, also that on dissecting a dead body he can infallibly put his finger on the cause of death, and, in cases where poisoning is suspected, the nature of the poison used. Now all this supposed exactness and infallibility is imaginary; and to treat a doctor as if his mistakes were necessarily malicious or corrupt malpractices (an inevitable deduction from the postulate that the doctor, being omniscient, cannot make mistakes) is as unjust as to blame the nearest apothecary for not being prepared to supply you with sixpennyworth of the elixir of life, or the nearest motor garage for not having perpetual motion on sale in gallon tins. But if apothecaries and motor car makers habitually advertized elixir of life and perpetual motion, and succeeded in creating a strong general belief that they could supply it, they would find themselves in an awkward position if they were indicted for allowing a customer to die, or for burning a chauffeur by putting petrol into his car. That is the predicament the doctor finds himself in when he has to defend himself against a charge of malpractice by a plea of ignorance and fallibility. His plea is received with flat incredulity; and he gets little sympathy, even from laymen who know, because he has brought the incredulity on himself. If he escapes, he can only do so by opening the eyes of the jury to the facts that medical science is as yet very imperfectly differentiated from common curemongering witchcraft; that diagnosis, though it means in many instances (including even the identification of pathogenic bacilli under the microscope) only a choice among terms so loose that they would not be accepted as definitions in any difficult matter on which doctors often differ; and that the very best medical opinion and treatment varies widely from doctor to doctor, one practitioner prescribing six or seven scheduled poisons for so familiar a disease as enteric fever where another will not tolerate drugs at all; one starving a patient whom another would stuff; one urging an operation which another would regard as unnecessary and dangerous; one giving alcohol and meat which another would sternly forbid, &c., &c., &c.: all these discrepancies arising not between the opinion of good doctors and bad ones (the medical contention is, of course, that a bad doctor is an impossibility), but between practitioners of equal eminence and authority. Usually it is impossible to persuade the jury that these facts are facts. Juries seldom notice facts; and they have been taught to regard any doubts of the omniscience and omnipotence of doctors as blasphemy. Even the fact that doctors themselves die of the very diseases they profess to cure passes unnoticed. We do not shoot out our lips and shake our heads, saying, "They save others: themselves they cannot save": their reputation stands, like an African king's palace, on a foundation of dead bodies; and the result is that the verdict goes against the defendant when the defendant is a doctor accused of malpractice.

Fortunately for the doctors, they very seldom find themselves in this position, because it is so difficult to prove anything against them. The only evidence that can decide a case of malpractice is expert evidence: that is, the evidence of other doctors; and every doctor will allow a colleague to decimate a whole countryside sooner than violate the bond of professional etiquet by giving him away. It is the nurse who gives the doctor away in private, because every nurse has some particular doctor whom she likes; and she usually assures her patients that all the others are disastrous noodles, and soothes the tedium of the sick-bed by gossip about their blunders. She will even give a doctor away for the sake of making the patient believe that she knows more than the doctor. But she dare not, for her livelihood, give the doctor away in public. And the doctors stand by one another at all costs. Now and then some doctor in an unassailable position, like the late Sir William Gull, will go into the witness box and say what he really thinks about the way a patient has been treated; but such behavior is considered little short of infamous by his colleagues.

WHY DOCTORS DO NOT DIFFER

The truth is, there would never be any public agreement among doctors if they did not agree to agree on the main point of the doctor being always in the right. Yet the two guinea man never thinks that the five shilling man is right: if he did, he would be understood as confessing to an overcharge of £1:17s.; and on the same ground the five shilling man cannot encourage the notion that the owner of the sixpenny surgery round the corner is quite up to his mark. Thus even the layman has to be taught that infallibility is not quite infallible, because there are two qualities of it to be had at two prices.

But there is no agreement even in the same rank at the same price. During the first great epidemic of influenza towards the end of the nineteenth century a London evening paper sent round a journalist-patient to all the great consultants of that day, and published their advice and prescriptions; a proceeding passionately denounced by the medical papers as a breach of confidence of these eminent physicians. The case was the same; but the prescriptions were different, and so was the advice. Now a doctor cannot think his own treatment right and at the same time think his colleague right in prescribing a different treatment when the patient is the same. Anyone who has ever known doctors well enough to hear medical shop talked without reserve knows that they are full of stories about each other's blunders and errors, and that the theory of their omniscience and omnipotence no more holds good among themselves than it did with Molière and Napoleon. But for this very reason no doctor dare accuse another of malpractice. He is not sure enough of his own opinion to ruin another man by it. He knows that if such conduct were tolerated in his profession no doctor's livelihood or reputation would be worth a year's purchase. I do not blame him: I should do the same myself. But the effect of this state of things is to make the medical profession a conspiracy to hide its own shortcomings. No doubt the same may be said of all professions. They are all conspiracies against the laity; and I do not suggest that the medical conspiracy is either better or worse than the military conspiracy, the legal conspiracy, the sacerdotal conspiracy, the pedagogic conspiracy, the royal and aristocratic conspiracy, the literary and artistic conspiracy, and the innumerable industrial, commercial, and financial conspiracies, from the trade unions to the great exchanges, which make up the huge conflict which we call society. But it is less suspected. The Radicals who used to advocate, as an indispensable preliminary to social reform, the strangling of the last king with the entrails of the last priest, substituted compulsory vaccination for compulsory baptism without a murmur.

The Craze for Operations

Thus everything is on the side of the doctor. When men die of disease they are said to die from natural causes. When they recover (and they mostly do) the doctor gets the credit of curing them. In surgery all operations are recorded as successful if the patient can be got out of the hospital or nursing home alive, though the subsequent history of the case may be such as would make an honest surgeon vow never to recommend or perform the operation again. The large range of operations which consist of amputating limbs and extirpating organs admits of no direct verification of their necessity. There is a fashion in operations as there is in sleeves and skirts: the triumph of some surgeon who has at last found out how to make a once desperate operation fairly safe is usually followed by a rage for that operation not only among the doctors, but actually among their patients. There are men and women whom the operating table seems to fascinate: half-alive people who through vanity, or hypochondria, or a craving to be the constant objects of anxious attention or what not, lose such feeble sense as they ever had of the value of their own organs and limbs. They seem to care as little for mutilation as lobsters or lizards, which at least have the excuse that they grow new claws and new tails if they lose the old ones. Whilst this book was being prepared for the press a case was tried in the Courts, of a man who sued a railway company for damages because a train had run over him and amputated both his legs. He lost his case because it was proved that he had deliberately contrived the occurrence himself for the sake of getting an idler's pension at the expense of the railway company, being too dull to realize how much more he had to lose than to gain by the bargain even if he had won his case and received damages above his utmost hopes.

This amazing case makes it possible to say, with some prospect of being believed, that there is in the classes who can afford to pay for fashionable operations a sprinkling of persons so incapable of appreciating the relative importance of preserving their bodily integrity (including the capacity for parentage) and the pleasure of talking about themselves and hearing themselves talked about as the heroes and heroines of sensational operations, that they tempt surgeons to operate on them not only with huge fees, but with personal solicitation. Now it cannot be too often repeated that when an operation is once performed, nobody can ever prove that it was unnecessary. If I refuse to allow my leg to be amputated, its mortification and my death may prove that I was wrong; but if I let the leg go, nobody can ever prove that it would not have mortified had I been obstinate. Operation is therefore the safe side for the surgeon as well as the lucrative side. The result is that we hear of "conservative surgeons" as a distinct class of practitioners who make it a rule not to operate if they can possibly help it, and who are sought after by the people who have vitality enough to regard an operation as a last resort. But no surgeon is bound to take the conservative view. If he believes that an organ is at best a useless survival, and that if he extirpates it the patient will be well and none the worse in a fortnight, whereas to await the natural cure would mean a month's illness, then he is clearly justified in recommending the operation even if the cure without operation is as certain as anything of the kind ever can be. Thus the conservative surgeon and the radical or extirpatory surgeon may both be right as far as the ultimate cure is concerned; so that their consciences do not help them out of their differences.

Credulity and Chloroform

There is no harder scientific fact in the world than the fact that belief can be produced in practically unlimited quantity and intensity, without observation or reasoning, and even in defiance of both, by the simple desire to believe founded on a strong interest in believing. Everybody recognizes this in the case of the amatory infatuations of the adolescents who see angels and heroes in obviously (to others) commonplace and even objectionable maidens and youths. But it holds good over the entire field of human activity. The hardest-headed materialist will become a consulter of table-rappers and slate-writers if he loses a child or a wife so beloved that the desire to revive and communicate with them becomes irresistible. The cobbler believes that there is nothing like leather. The Imperalist who regards the conquest of England by a foreign power as the worst of political misfortunes believes that the conquest of a foreign power by England would be a boon to the conquered. Doctors are no more proof against such illusions than other men. Can anyone then doubt that under existing conditions a great deal of unnecessary and mischievous operating is bound to go on, and that patients are encouraged to imagine that modern surgery and anesthesia have made operations much less serious matters than they really are? When doctors write or speak to the public about operations, they imply, and often say in so many words, that chloroform has made surgery painless. People who have been operated on know better. The patient does not feel the knife, and the operation is therefore enormously facilitated for the surgeon; but the patient pays for the anesthesia with hours of wretched sickness; and when that is over there is the pain of the wound made by the surgeon, which has to heal like any other wound. This is why operating surgeons, who are usually out of the house with their fee in their pockets before the patient has recovered consciousness, and who therefore see nothing of the suffering witnessed by the general practitioner and the nurse, occasionally talk of operations very much as the hangman in Barnaby Rudge talked of executions, as if being operated on were a luxury in sensation as well as in price.

Medical Poverty

To make matters worse, doctors are hideously poor. The Irish gentleman doctor of my boyhood, who took nothing less than a guinea, though he might pay you four visits for it, seems to have no equivalent nowadays in English society. Better be a railway porter than an ordinary English general practitioner. A railway porter has from eighteen to twenty-three shillings a week from the Company merely as a retainer; and his additional fees from the public, if we leave the third-class two-penny tip out of account (and I am by no means sure that even this reservation need be made), are equivalent to doctor's fees in the case of second-class passengers, and double doctor's fees in the case of first. Any class of educated men thus treated tends to become a brigand class, and doctors are no exception to the rule. They are offered disgraceful prices for advice and medicine. Their patients are for the most part so poor and so ignorant that good advice would be resented as impracticable and wounding. When you are so poor that you cannot afford to refuse eighteenpence from a man who is too poor to pay you any more, it is useless to tell him that what he or his sick child needs is not medicine, but more leisure, better clothes, better food, and a better drained and ventilated house. It is kinder to give him a bottle of something almost as cheap as water, and tell him to come again with another eighteenpence if it does not cure him. When you have done that over and over again every day for a week, how much scientific conscience have you left? If you are weak-minded enough to cling desperately to your eighteenpence as denoting a certain social superiority to the sixpenny doctor, you will be miserably poor all your life; whilst the sixpenny doctor, with his low prices and quick turnover of patients, visibly makes much more than you do and kills no more people.

A doctor's character can no more stand out against such conditions than the lungs of his patients can stand out against bad ventilation. The only way in which he can preserve his self-respect is by forgetting all he ever learnt of science, and clinging to such help as he can give without cost merely by being less ignorant and more accustomed to sick-beds than his patients. Finally, he acquires a certain skill at nursing cases under poverty-stricken domestic conditions, just as women who have been trained as domestic servants in some huge institution with lifts, vacuum cleaners, electric lighting, steam heating, and machinery that turns the kitchen into a laboratory and engine house combined, manage, when they are sent out into the world to drudge as general servants, to pick up their business in a new way, learning the slatternly habits and wretched makeshifts of homes where even bundles of kindling wood are luxuries to be anxiously economized.

THE SUCCESSFUL DOCTOR

The doctor whose success blinds public opinion to medical poverty is almost as completely demoralized. His promotion means that his practice becomes more and more confined to the idle rich. The proper advice for most of their ailments is typified in Abernethy's "Live on sixpence a day and earn it." But here, as at the other end of the scale, the right advice is neither agreeable nor practicable. And every hypochondriacal rich lady or gentleman who can be persuaded that he or she is a lifelong invalid means anything from fifty to five hundred pounds a year for the doctor. Operations enable a surgeon to earn similar sums in a couple of hours; and if the surgeon also keeps a nursing home, he may make considerable profits at the same time by running what is the most expensive kind of hotel. These gains are so great that they undo much of the moral advantage which the absence of grinding pecuniary anxiety gives the rich doctor over the poor one. It is true that the temptation to prescribe a sham treatment because the real treatment is too dear for either patient or doctor does not exist for the rich doctor. He always has plenty of genuine cases which can afford genuine treatment; and these provide him with enough sincere scientific professional work to save him from the ignorance, obsolescence, and atrophy of scientific conscience into which his poorer colleagues sink. But on the other hand his expenses are enormous. Even as a bachelor, he must, at London west end rates, make over a thousand a year before he can afford even to insure his life. His house, his servants, and his equipage (or autopage) must be on the scale to which his patients are accustomed, though a couple of rooms with a camp bed in one of them might satisfy his own requirements. Above all, the income which provides for these outgoings stops the moment he himself stops working. Unlike the man of business, whose managers, clerks, warehousemen and laborers keep his business going whilst he is in bed or in his club, the doctor cannot earn a farthing by deputy. Though he is exceptionally exposed to infection, and has to face all weathers at all hours of the night and day, often not enjoying a complete night's rest for a week, the money stops coming in the moment he stops going out; and therefore illness has special terrors for him, and success no certain permanence. He dare not stop making hay while the sun shines; for it may set at any time. Men do not resist pressure of this intensity. When they come under it as doctors they pay unnecessary visits; they write prescriptions that are as absurd as the rub of chalk with which an Irish tailor once charmed away a wart from my father's finger; they conspire with surgeons to promote operations; they nurse the delusions of the *malade imaginaire* (who is always really ill because, as there is no such thing as perfect health, nobody is ever really well); they exploit human folly, vanity, and fear of death as ruthlessly as their own health, strength, and patience are exploited by selfish hypochondriacs. They must do all these things or else run pecuniary risks that no man can fairly be asked to run. And the healthier the world becomes, the more they are compelled to live by imposture and the less by that really helpful activity of which all doctors get enough to preserve them from utter corruption. For even the most hardened humbug who ever prescribed ether tonics to ladies whose need for tonics is of precisely the same character as the need of poorer women for a glass of gin, has to help a mother through child-bearing often enough to feel that he is not living wholly in vain.

THE PSYCHOLOGY OF SELF-RESPECT IN SURGEONS

The surgeon, though often more unscrupulous than the general practitioner, retains his self-respect more easily. The human conscience can subsist on very questionable food. No man who is occupied in doing a very difficult thing, and doing it very well, ever loses his self-respect. The shirk, the duffer, the malingerer, the coward, the weakling, may be put out of countenance by his own failures and frauds; but the man who does evil skilfully, energetically, masterfully, grows prouder and bolder at every crime. The common man may have to found his self-respect on sobriety, honesty and industry; but a Napoleon needs no such props for his sense of dignity. If Nelson's conscience whispered to him at all in the silent watches of the night, you may depend on it it whispered about the Baltic and the Nile and Cape St. Vincent, and not about his unfaithfulness to his wife. A man who robs little children when no one is looking can hardly have much self-respect or even self-esteem; but an accomplished burglar must be proud of himself. In the play to which I am at present preluding I have represented an artist who is so entirely satisfied with his artistic conscience, even to the point of dying like a saint with its support, that he is utterly selfish and unscrupulous in every other relation without feeling at the smallest disadvantage. The same thing may be observed in women who have a genius for personal attractiveness: they expend more thought, labor, skill, inventiveness, taste and endurance on making themselves lovely than would suffice to keep a dozen ugly women honest; and this enables them to maintain a high opinion of themselves, and an angry contempt for unattractive and personally careless women, whilst they lie and cheat and slander and sell themselves without a blush. The truth is, hardly any of us have ethical energy enough for more than one really inflexible point of honor. Andrea del Sarto, like Louis Dubedat in my play, must have expended on the attainment of his great mastery of design and his originality in fresco painting more conscientiousness and industry than go to the making of the reputations of a dozen ordinary mayors and churchwardens; but (if Vasari is to be believed) when the King of France entrusted him with money to buy pictures for him, he stole it to spend on his wife. Such cases are not confined to eminent artists. Unsuccessful, unskilful men are often much more scrupulous than successful ones. In the ranks of ordinary skilled labor many men are to be found who earn good wages and are never out of a job because they are strong, indefatigable, and skilful, and who therefore are bold in a high opinion of themselves; but they are selfish and tyrannical, gluttonous and drunken, as their wives and children know to their cost.

Not only do these talented energetic people retain their self-respect through shameful misconduct: they do not even lose the respect of others, because their talents benefit and interest everybody, whilst their vices affect only a few. An actor, a painter, a composer, an author, may be as selfish as he likes without reproach from the public if only his art is superb; and he cannot fulfil this condition without sufficient effort and sacrifice to make him feel noble and martyred in spite of his selfishness. It may even happen that the selfishness of an artist may be a benefit to the public by enabling him to concentrate himself on their gratification with a recklessness of every other consideration that makes him highly dangerous to those about him. In sacrificing others to himself he is sacrificing them to the public he gratifies; and the public is quite content with that arrangement. The public actually has an interest in the artist's vices.

It has no such interest in the surgeon's vices. The surgeon's art is exercised at its expense, not for its gratification.

We do not go to the operating table as we go to the theatre, to the picture gallery, to the concert room, to be entertained and delighted: we go to be tormented and maimed, lest a worse thing should befall us. It is of the most extreme importance to us that the experts on whose assurance we face this horror and suffer this mutilation should have no interests but our own to think of; should judge our cases scientifically; and should feel about them kindly. Let us see what guarantees we have: first for the science, and then for the kindness.

Are Doctors Men of Science?

I presume nobody will question the existence of a widely spread popular delusion that every doctor is a man of science. It is escaped only in the very small class which understands by science something more than conjuring with retorts and spirit lamps, magnets and microscopes, and discovering magical cures for disease. To a sufficiently ignorant man every captain of a trading schooner is a Galileo, every organ-grinder a Beethoven, every piano-tuner a Helmholtz, every Old Bailey barrister a Solon, every Seven Dials pigeon dealer a Darwin, every scrivener a Shakespear, every locomotive engine a miracle, and its driver no less wonderful than George Stephenson. As a matter of fact, the rank and file of doctors are no more scientific than their tailors; or, if you prefer to put it in the reverse way, their tailors are no less scientific than they. Doctoring is an art, not a science: any layman who is interested in science sufficiently to take in one of the scientific journals and follow the literature of the scientific movement, knows more about it than those doctors (probably a large majority) who are not interested in it, and practise only to earn their bread. Doctoring is not even the art of keeping people in health (no doctor seems able to advise you what to eat any better than his grandmother or the nearest quack): it is the art of curing illnesses. It does happen exceptionally that a practising doctor makes a contribution to science (my play describes a very notable one); but it happens much oftener that he draws disastrous conclusions from his clinical experience because he has no conception of scientific method, and believes, like any rustic, that the handling of evidence and statistics needs no expertness. The distinction between a quack doctor and a qualified one is mainly that only the qualified one is authorized to sign death certificates, for which both sorts seem to have about equal occasion. Unqualified practitioners now make large incomes as hygienists, and are resorted to as frequently by cultivated amateur scientists who understand quite well what they are doing as by ignorant people who are simply dupes. Bone-setters make fortunes under the very noses of our greatest surgeons from educated and wealthy patients; and some of the most successful doctors on the register use quite heretical methods of treating disease, and have qualified themselves solely for convenience. Leaving out of account the village witches who prescribe spells and sell charms, the humblest professional healers in this country are the herbalists. These men wander through the fields on Sunday seeking for herbs with magic properties of curing disease, preventing childbirth, and the like. Each of them believes that he is on the verge of a great discovery, in which Virginia Snake Root will be an ingredient, heaven knows why! Virginia Snake Root fascinates the imagination of the herbalist as mercury used to fascinate the alchemists. On week days he keeps a shop in which he sells packets of pennyroyal, dandelion, &c., labelled with little lists of the diseases they are supposed to cure, and apparently do cure to the satisfaction of the people who keep on buying them. I have never been able to perceive any distinction between the science of the herbalist and that of the duly registered doctor. A relative of mine recently consulted a doctor about some of the ordinary symptoms which indicate the need for a holiday and a change. The doctor satisfied himself that the patient's heart was a little depressed. Digitalis being a drug labelled as a heart specific by the profession, he promptly administered a stiff dose. Fortunately the patient was a hardy old lady who was not easily killed. She recovered with no worse result than her conversion to Christian Science, which owes its vogue quite as much to public despair of doctors as to superstition. I am not, observe, here concerned with the question as to whether the dose of digitalis was judicious or not; the point is, that a farm laborer consulting a herbalist would have been treated in exactly the same way.

BACTERIOLOGY AS A SUPERSTITION

The smattering of science that all—even doctors—pick up from the ordinary newspapers nowadays only makes the doctor more dangerous than he used to be. Wise men used to take care to consult doctors qualified before 1860, who were usually contemptuous of or indifferent to the germ theory and bacteriological therapeutics; but now that these veterans have mostly retired or died, we are left in the hands of the generations which, having heard of microbes much as St. Thomas Aquinas heard of angels, suddenly concluded that the whole art of healing could be summed up in the formula: Find the microbe and kill it. And even that they did not know how to do. The simplest way to kill most microbes is to throw them into an open street or river and let the sun shine on them, which explains the fact that when great cities have recklessly thrown all their sewage into the open river the water has sometimes been cleaner twenty miles below the city than thirty miles above it. But doctors instinctively avoid all facts that are reassuring, and eagerly swallow those that make it a marvel that anyone could possibly survive three days in an atmosphere consisting mainly of countless pathogenic germs. They conceive microbes as immortal until slain by a germicide administered by a duly qualified medical man. All through Europe people are adjured, by public notices and even under legal penalties, not to throw their microbes into the sunshine, but to collect them carefully in a handkerchief; shield the handkerchief from the sun in the darkness and warmth of the pocket; and send it to a laundry to be mixed up with everybody else's handkerchiefs, with results only too familiar to local health authorities.

In the first frenzy of microbe killing, surgical instruments were dipped in carbolic oil, which was a great improvement on not dipping them in anything at all and simply using them dirty; but as microbes are so fond of carbolic oil that they swarm in it, it was not a success from the anti-microbe point of view. Formalin was squirted into the circulation of consumptives until it was discovered that formalin nourishes the tubercle bacillus handsomely and kills men. The popular theory of disease is the common medical theory: namely, that every disease had its microbe duly created in the garden of Eden, and has been steadily propagating itself and producing widening circles of malignant disease ever since. It was plain from the first that if this had been even approximately true, the whole human race would have been wiped out by the plague long ago, and that every epidemic, instead of fading out as mysteriously as it rushed in, would spread over the whole world. It was also evident that the characteristic microbe of a disease might be a symptom instead of a cause. An unpunctual man is always in a hurry; but it does not follow that hurry is the cause of unpunctuality: on the contrary, what is the matter with the patient is sloth. When Florence Nightingale said bluntly that if you overcrowded your soldiers in dirty quarters there would be an outbreak of smallpox among them, she was snubbed as an ignorant female who did not know that smallpox can be produced only by the importation of its specific microbe.

If this was the line taken about smallpox, the microbe of which has never yet been run down and exposed under the microscope by the bacteriologist, what must have been the ardor of conviction as to tuberculosis, tetanus, enteric fever, Maltese fever, diphtheria, and the rest of the diseases in which the characteristic bacillus had been identified! When there was no bacillus it was assumed that, since no disease could exist without a bacillus, it was simply eluding observation. When the bacillus was found, as it frequently was, in persons who were not suffering from the disease, the theory was saved by simply calling the bacillus an impostor, or pseudobacillus. The same boundless credulity which the public exhibit as to a doctor's power of diagnosis was shown by the doctors themselves as to the analytic microbe hunters. These witch finders would give you a certificate of the ultimate constitution of anything from a sample of the water from your well to a scrap of your lungs, for seven-and-sixpence. I do not suggest that the analysts were dishonest. No doubt they carried the analysis as far as they could afford to carry it for the money. No doubt also they could afford to carry it far enough to be of some use. But the fact remains that just as doctors perform for half-a-crown, without the least misgiving, operations which could not be thoroughly and safely performed with due scientific rigor and the requisite apparatus by an unaided private practitioner for less than some thousands of pounds, so did they proceed on the assumption that they could get the last word of science as to the constituents of their pathological samples for a two hours cab fare.

Economic Difficulties of Immunization

I have heard doctors affirm and deny almost every possible proposition as to disease and treatment. I can remember the time when doctors no more dreamt of consumption and pneumonia being infectious than they now dream of sea-sickness being infectious, or than so great a clinical observer as Sydenham dreamt of smallpox being infectious. I have heard doctors deny that there is such a thing as infection. I have heard them deny the existence of hydrophobia as a specific disease differing from tetanus. I have heard them defend prophylactic measures and prophylactic legislation as the sole and certain salvation of mankind from zymotic disease; and I have heard them denounce both as malignant spreaders of cancer and lunacy. But the one objection I have never heard from a doctor is the objection that prophylaxis by the inoculatory methods most in vogue is an economic impossibility under our private practice system. They buy some stuff from somebody for a shilling, and inject a pennyworth of it under their patient's skin for half-a-crown, concluding that, since this primitive rite pays the somebody and pays them, the problem of prophylaxis has been satisfactorily solved. The results are sometimes no worse than the ordinary results of dirt getting into cuts; but neither the doctor nor the patient is quite satisfied unless the inoculation "takes"; that is, unless it produces perceptible illness and disablement. Sometimes both doctor and patient get more value in this direction than they bargain for. The results of ordinary private-practice-inoculation at their worst are bad enough to be indistinguishable from those of the most discreditable and dreaded disease known; and doctors, to save the credit of the inoculation, have been driven to accuse their patient or their patient's parents of having contracted this disease independently of the inoculation, an excuse which naturally does not make the family any more resigned, and leads to public recriminations in which the doctors, forgetting everything but the immediate quarrel, naively excuse themselves by admitting, and even claiming as a point in their favor, that it is often impossible to distinguish the disease produced by their inoculation and the disease they have accused the patient of contracting. And both parties assume that what is at issue is the scientific soundness of the prophylaxis. It never occurs to them that the particular pathogenic germ which they intended to introduce into the patient's system may be quite innocent of the catastrophe, and that the casual dirt introduced with it may be at fault. When, as in the case of smallpox or cowpox, the germ has not yet been detected, what you inoculate is simply undefined matter that has been scraped off an anything but chemically clean calf suffering from the disease in question. You take your chance of the germ being in the scrapings, and, lest you should kill it, you take no precautions against other germs being in it as well. Anything may happen as the result of such an inoculation. Yet this is the only stuff of the kind which is prepared and supplied even in State establishments: that is, in the only establishments free from the commercial temptation to adulterate materials and scamp precautionary processes.

Even if the germ were identified, complete precautions would hardly pay. It is true that microbe farming is not expensive. The cost of breeding and housing two head of cattle would provide for the breeding and housing of enough microbes to inoculate the entire population of the globe since human life first appeared on it. But the precautions necessary to insure that the inoculation shall consist of nothing else but the required germ in the proper state of attenuation are a very different matter from the precautions necessary in the distribution and consumption of beefsteaks. Yet people expect to find vaccines and antitoxins and the like retailed at "popular prices" in private enterprise shops just as they expect to find ounces of tobacco and papers of pins.

The Perils of Inoculation

The trouble does not end with the matter to be inoculated. There is the question of the condition of the patient. The discoveries of Sir Almroth Wright have shewn that the appalling results which led to the hasty dropping in 1894 of Koch's tuberculin were not accidents, but perfectly orderly and inevitable phenomena following the injection of dangerously strong "vaccines" at the wrong moment, and reinforcing the disease instead of stimulating the resistance to it. To ascertain the right moment a laboratory and a staff of experts are needed. The general practitioner, having no such laboratory and no such experience, has always chanced it, and insisted, when he was unlucky, that the results were not due to the inoculation, but to some other cause: a favorite and not very tactful one being the drunkenness or licentiousness of the patient. But though a few doctors have now learnt the danger of inoculating without any reference to the patient's "opsonic index" at the moment of inoculation, and though those other doctors who are denouncing the danger as imaginary and opsonin as a craze or a fad, obviously do so because it involves an operation which they have neither the means nor the knowledge to perform, there is still no grasp of the economic change in the situation. They have never been warned that the practicability of any method of extirpating disease depends not only on its efficacy, but on its cost. For example, just at present the world has run raving mad on the subject of radium, which has excited our credulity precisely as the apparitions at Lourdes excited the credulity of Roman Catholics. Suppose it were ascertained that every child in the world could be rendered absolutely immune from all disease during its entire life by taking half an ounce of radium to every pint of its milk. The world would be none the healthier, because not even a Crown Prince—no, not even the son of a Chicago Meat King, could afford the treatment. Yet it is doubtful whether doctors would refrain from prescribing it on that ground. The recklessness with which they now recommend wintering in Egypt or at Davos to people who cannot afford to go to Cornwall, and the orders given for champagne jelly and old port in households where such luxuries must obviously be acquired at the cost of stinting necessaries, often make one wonder whether it is possible for a man to go through a medical training and retain a spark of common sense.

This sort of inconsiderateness gets cured only in the classes where poverty, pretentious as it is even at its worst, cannot pitch its pretences high enough to make it possible for the doctor (himself often no better off than the patient) to assume that the average income of an English family is about £2,000 a year, and that it is quite easy to break up a home, sell an old family seat at a sacrifice, and retire into a foreign sanatorium devoted to some "treatment" that did not exist two years ago and probably will not exist (except as a pretext for keeping an ordinary hotel) two years hence. In a poor practice the doctor must find cheap treatments for cheap people, or humiliate and lose his patients either by prescribing beyond their means or sending them to the public hospitals. When it comes to prophylactic inoculation, the alternative lies between the complete scientific process, which can only be brought down to a reasonable cost by being very highly organized as a public service in a public institution, and such cheap, nasty, dangerous and scientifically spurious imitations as ordinary vaccination, which seems not unlikely to be ended, like its equally vaunted forerunner, XVIII. century inoculation, by a purely reactionary law making all sorts of vaccination, scientific or not, criminal offences. Naturally, the poor doctor (that is, the average doctor) defends ordinary vaccination frantically, as it means to him the bread of his children. To secure the vehement and practically unanimous support of the rank and file of the medical profession for any sort of treatment or operation, all that is necessary is that it can be easily practised by a rather shabbily dressed man in a surgically dirty room in a surgically dirty house without any assistance, and that the materials for it shall cost, say, a penny, and the charge for it to a patient with £100 a year be half-a-crown. And, on the other hand, a hygienic measure has only to be one of such refinement, difficulty, precision and costliness as to be quite beyond the resources of private practice, to be ignored or angrily denounced as a fad.

Trade Unionism and Science

Here we have the explanation of the savage rancor that so amazes people who imagine that the controversy concerning vaccination is a scientific one. It has really nothing to do with science. The medical profession, consisting for the most part of very poor men struggling to keep up appearances beyond their means, find themselves threatened with the extinction of a considerable part of their incomes: a part, too, that is easily and regularly earned, since it is independent of disease, and brings every person born into the nation, healthy or not, to the doctors. To boot, there is the occasional windfall of an epidemic, with its panic and rush for revaccination. Under such circumstances, vaccination would be defended desperately were it twice as dirty, dangerous, and unscientific in method as it actually is. The note of fury in the defence, the feeling that the anti-vaccinator is doing a cruel, ruinous, inconsiderate thing in a mood of malignant folly: all this, so puzzling to the observer who knows nothing of the economic side of the question, and only sees that the anti-vaccinator, having nothing whatever to gain and a good deal to lose by placing himself in opposition to the law and to the outcry that adds private persecution to legal penalties, can have no interest in the matter except the interest of a reformer in abolishing a corrupt and mischievous superstition, becomes intelligible the moment the tragedy of medical poverty and the lucrativeness of cheap vaccination is taken into account.

In the face of such economic pressure as this, it is silly to expect that medical teaching, any more than medical practice, can possibly be scientific. The test to which all methods of treatment are finally brought is whether they are lucrative to doctors or not. It would be difficult to cite any proposition less obnoxious to science than that advanced by Hahnemann: to wit, that drugs which in large doses produce certain symptoms, counteract them in very small doses, just as in more modern practice it is found that a sufficiently small inoculation with typhoid rallies our powers to resist the disease instead of prostrating us with it. But Hahnemann and his followers were frantically persecuted for a century by generations of apothecary-doctors whose incomes depended on the quantity of drugs they could induce their patients to swallow. These two cases of ordinary vaccination and homeopathy are typical of all the rest. Just as the object of a trade union under existing conditions must finally be, not to improve the technical quality of the work done by its members, but to secure a living wage for them, so the object of the medical profession today is to secure an income for the private doctor; and to this consideration all concern for science and public health must give way when the two come into conflict. Fortunately they are not always in conflict. Up to a certain point doctors, like carpenters and masons, must earn their living by doing the work that the public wants from them; and as it is not in the nature of things possible that such public want should be based on unmixed disutility, it may be admitted that doctors have their uses, real as well as imaginary. But just as the best carpenter or mason will resist the introduction of a machine that is likely to throw him out of work, or the public technical education of unskilled laborers' sons to compete with him, so the doctor will resist with all his powers of persecution every advance of science that threatens his income. And as the advance of scientific hygiene tends to make the private doctor's visits rarer, and the public inspector's frequenter, whilst the advance of scientific therapeutics is in the direction of treatments that involve highly organized laboratories, hospitals, and public institutions generally, it unluckily happens that the organization of private practitioners which we call the medical profession is coming more and more to represent, not science, but desperate and embittered antiscience: a statement of things which is likely to get worse until the average doctor either depends upon or hopes for an appointment in the public health service for his livelihood.

So much for our guarantees as to medical science. Let us now deal with the more painful subject of medical kindness.

Doctors and Vivisection

The importance to our doctors of a reputation for the tenderest humanity is so obvious, and the quantity of benevolent work actually done by them for nothing (a great deal of it from sheer good nature) so large, that at first sight it seems unaccountable that they should not only throw all their credit away, but deliberately choose to band themselves publicly with outlaws and scoundrels by claiming that in the pursuit of their professional knowledge they should be free from the restraints of law, of honor, of pity, of remorse, of everything that distinguishes an orderly citizen from a South Sea buccaneer, or a philosopher from an inquisitor. For here we look in vain for either an economic or a sentimental motive. In every generation fools and blackguards have made this claim; and honest and reasonable men, led by the strongest contemporary minds, have repudiated it and exposed its crude rascality. From Shakespear and Dr. Johnson to Ruskin and Mark Twain, the natural abhorrence of sane mankind for the vivisector's cruelty, and the contempt of able thinkers for his imbecile casuistry, have been expressed by the most popular spokesmen of humanity. If the medical profession were to outdo the Anti-Vivisection Societies in a general professional protest against the practice and principles of the vivisectors, every doctor in the kingdom would gain substantially by the immense relief and reconciliation which would follow such a reassurance of the humanity of the doctor. Not one doctor in a thousand is a vivisector, or has any interest in vivisection, either pecuniary or intellectual, or would treat his dog cruelly or allow anyone else to do it. It is true that the doctor complies with the professional fashion of defending vivisection, and assuring you that people like Shakespear and Dr. Johnson and Ruskin and Mark Twain are ignorant sentimentalists, just as he complies with any other silly fashion: the mystery is, how it became the fashion in spite of its being so injurious to those who follow it. Making all possible allowance for the effect of the brazen lying of the few men who bring a rush of despairing patients to their doors by professing in letters to the newspapers to have learnt from vivisection how to cure certain diseases, and the assurances of the sayers of smooth things that the practice is quite painless under the law, it is still difficult to find any civilized motive for an attitude by which the medical profession has everything to lose and nothing to gain.

The Primitive Savage Motive

I say civilized motive advisedly; for primitive tribal motives are easy enough to find. Every savage chief who is not a Mahomet learns that if he wishes to strike the imagination of his tribe—and without doing that he cannot rule them—he must terrify or revolt them from time to time by acts of hideous cruelty or disgusting unnaturalness. We are far from being as superior to such tribes as we imagine. It is very doubtful indeed whether Peter the Great could have effected the changes he made in Russia if he had not fascinated and intimidated his people by his monstrous cruelties and grotesque escapades. Had he been a nineteenth-century king of England, he would have had to wait for some huge accidental calamity: a cholera epidemic, a war, or an insurrection, before waking us up sufficiently to get anything done. Vivisection helps the doctor to rule us as Peter ruled the Russians. The notion that the man who does dreadful things is superhuman, and that therefore he can also do wonderful things either as ruler, avenger, healer, or what not, is by no means confined to barbarians. Just as the manifold wickednesses and stupidities of our criminal code are supported, not by any general comprehension of law or study of jurisprudence, not even by simple vindictiveness, but by the superstition that a calamity of any sort must be expiated by a human sacrifice; so the wickednesses and stupidities of our medicine men are rooted in superstitions that have no more to do with science than the traditional ceremony of christening an ironclad has to do with the effectiveness of its armament. We have only to turn to Macaulay's description of the treatment of Charles II. in his last illness to see how strongly his physicians felt that their only chance of cheating death was by outraging nature in tormenting and disgusting their unfortunate patient. True, this was more than two centuries ago; but I have heard my own nineteenth-century grandfather describe the cupping and firing and nauseous medicines of his time with perfect credulity as to their beneficial effects; and some more modern treatments appear to me quite as barbarous. It is in this way that vivisection pays the doctor. It appeals to the fear and credulity of the savage in us; and without fear and credulity half the private doctor's occupation and seven-eighths of his influence would be gone.

The Higher Motive. The Tree of Knowledge

But the greatest force of all on the side of vivisection is the mighty and indeed divine force of curiosity. Here we have no decaying tribal instinct which men strive to root out of themselves as they strive to root out the tiger's lust for blood. On the contrary, the curiosity of the ape, or of the child who pulls out the legs and wings of a fly to see what it will do without them, or who, on being told that a cat dropped out of the window will always fall on its legs, immediately tries the experiment on the nearest cat from the highest window in the house (I protest I did it myself from the first floor only), is as nothing compared to the thirst for knowledge of the philosopher, the poet, the biologist, and the naturalist. I have always despised Adam because he had to be tempted by the woman, as she was by the serpent, before he could be induced to pluck the apple from the tree of knowledge. I should have swallowed every apple on the tree the moment the owner's back was turned. When Gray said "Where ignorance is bliss, 'tis folly to be wise," he forgot that it is godlike to be wise; and since nobody wants bliss particularly, or could stand more than a very brief taste of it if it were attainable, and since everybody, by the deepest law of the Life Force, desires to be godlike, it is stupid, and indeed blasphemous and despairing, to hope that the thirst for knowledge will either diminish or consent to be subordinated to any other end whatsoever. We shall see later on that the claim that has arisen in this way for the unconditioned pursuit of knowledge is as idle as all dreams of unconditioned activity; but none the less the right to knowledge must be regarded as a fundamental human right. The fact that men of science have had to fight so hard to secure its recognition, and are still so vigorously persecuted when they discover anything that is not quite palatable to vulgar people, makes them sorely jealous for that right; and when they hear a popular outcry for the suppression of a method of research which has an air of being scientific, their first instinct is to rally to the defence of that method without further consideration, with the result that they sometimes, as in the case of vivisection, presently find themselves fighting on a false issue.

The Flaw in the Argument

I may as well pause here to explain their error. The right to know is like the right to live. It is fundamental and unconditional in its assumption that knowledge, like life, is a desirable thing, though any fool can prove that ignorance is bliss, and that "a little knowledge is a dangerous thing" (a little being the most that any of us can attain), as easily as that the pains of life are more numerous and constant than its pleasures, and that therefore we should all be better dead. The logic is unimpeachable; but its only effect is to make us say that if these are the conclusions logic leads to, so much the worse for logic, after which curt dismissal of Folly, we continue living and learning by instinct: that is, as of right. We legislate on the assumption that no man may be killed on the strength of a demonstration that he would be happier in his grave, not even if he is dying slowly of cancer and begs the doctor to despatch him quickly and mercifully. To get killed lawfully he must violate somebody else's right to live by committing murder. But he is by no means free to live unconditionally. In society he can exercise his right to live only under very stiff conditions. In countries where there is compulsory military service he may even have to throw away his individual life to save the life of the community.

It is just so in the case of the right to knowledge. It is a right that is as yet very imperfectly recognized in practice. But in theory it is admitted that an adult person in pursuit of knowledge must not be refused it on the ground that he would be better or happier without it. Parents and priests may forbid knowledge to those who accept their authority; and social taboo may be made effective by acts of legal persecution under cover of repressing blasphemy, obscenity, and sedition; but no government now openly forbids its subjects to pursue knowledge on the ground that knowledge is in itself a bad thing, or that it is possible for any of us to have too much of it.

LIMITATIONS OF THE RIGHT TO KNOWLEDGE

But neither does any government exempt the pursuit of knowledge, any more than the pursuit of life, liberty, and happiness (as the American Constitution puts it), from all social conditions. No man is allowed to put his mother into the stove because he desires to know how long an adult woman will survive at a temperature of 500° Fahrenheit, no matter how important or interesting that particular addition to the store of human knowledge may be. A man who did so would have short work made not only of his right to knowledge, but of his right to live and all his other rights at the same time. The right to knowledge is not the only right; and its exercise must be limited by respect for other rights, and for its own exercise by others. When a man says to Society, "May I torture my mother in pursuit of knowledge?" Society replies, "No." If he pleads, "What! Not even if I have a chance of finding out how to cure cancer by doing it?" Society still says, "Not even then." If the scientist, making the best of his disappointment, goes on to ask may he torture a dog, the stupid and callous people who do not realize that a dog is a fellow-creature and sometimes a good friend, may say Yes, though Shakespear, Dr. Johnson and their like may say No. But even those who say "You may torture *a* dog" never say "You may torture *my* dog." And nobody says, "Yes, because in the pursuit of knowledge you may do as you please." Just as even the stupidest people say, in effect, "If you cannot attain to knowledge without burning your mother you must do without knowledge," so the wisest people say, "If you cannot attain to knowledge without torturing a dog, you must do without knowledge."

A FALSE ALTERNATIVE

But in practice you cannot persuade any wise man that this alternative can ever be forced on anyone but a fool, or that a fool can be trusted to learn anything from any experiment, cruel or humane. The Chinaman who burnt down his house to roast his pig was no doubt honestly unable to conceive any less disastrous way of cooking his dinner; and the roast must have been spoiled after all (a perfect type of the average vivisectionist experiment); but this did not prove that the Chinaman was right: it only proved that the Chinaman was an incapable cook and, fundamentally, a fool.

Take another celebrated experiment: one in sanitary reform. In the days of Nero Rome was in the same predicament as London to-day. If some one would burn down London, and it were rebuilt, as it would now have to be, subject to the sanitary by-laws and Building Act provisions enforced by the London County Council, it would be enormously improved; and the average lifetime of Londoners would be considerably prolonged. Nero argued in the same way about Rome. He employed incendiaries to set it on fire; and he played the harp in scientific raptures whilst it was burning. I am so far of Nero's way of thinking that I have often said, when consulted by despairing sanitary reformers, that what London needs to make her healthy is an earthquake. Why, then, it may be asked, do not I, as a public-spirited man, employ incendiaries to set it on fire, with a heroic disregard of the consequences to myself and others? Any vivisector would, if he had the courage of his opinions. The reasonable answer is that London can be made healthy without burning her down; and that as we have not enough civic virtue to make her healthy in a humane and economical way, we should not have enough to rebuild her in that way. In the old Hebrew legend, God lost patience with the world as Nero did with Rome, and drowned everybody except a single family. But the result was that the progeny of that family reproduced all the vices of their predecessors so exactly that the misery caused by the flood might just as well have been spared: things went on just as they did before. In the same way, the lists of diseases which vivisection claims to have cured is long; but the returns of the Registrar-General shew that people still persist in dying of them as if vivisection had never been heard of. Any fool can burn down a city or cut an animal open; and an exceptionally foolish fool is quite likely to promise enormous benefits to the race as the result of such activities. But when the constructive, benevolent part of the business comes to be done, the same want of imagination, the same stupidity and cruelty, the same laziness and want of perseverance that prevented Nero or the vivisector from devising or pushing through humane methods, prevents him from bringing order out of the chaos and happiness out of the misery he has made. At one time it seemed reasonable enough to declare that it was impossible to find whether or not there was a stone inside a man's body except by exploring it with a knife, or to find out what the sun is made of without visiting it in a balloon. Both these impossibilities have been achieved, but not by vivisectors. The Röntgen rays need not hurt the patient; and spectrum analysis involves no destruction. After such triumphs of humane experiment and reasoning, it is useless to assure us that there is no other key to knowledge except cruelty. When the vivisector offers us that assurance, we reply simply and contemptuously, "You mean that you are not clever or humane or energetic enough to find one."

Cruelty for its own Sake

It will now, I hope, be clear why the attack on vivisection is not an attack on the right to knowledge: why, indeed, those who have the deepest conviction of the sacredness of that right are the leaders of the attack. No knowledge is finally impossible of human attainment; for even though it may be beyond our present capacity, the needed capacity is not unattainable. Consequently no method of investigation is the only method; and no law forbidding any particular method can cut us off from the knowledge we hope to gain by it. The only knowledge we lose by forbidding cruelty is knowledge at first hand of cruelty itself, which is precisely the knowledge humane people wish to be spared.

But the question remains: Do we all really wish to be spared that knowledge? Are humane methods really to be preferred to cruel ones? Even if the experiments come to nothing, may not their cruelty be enjoyed for its own sake, as a sensational luxury? Let us face these questions boldly, not shrinking from the fact that cruelty is one of the primitive pleasures of mankind, and that the detection of its Protean disguises as law, education, medicine, discipline, sport and so forth, is one of the most difficult of the unending tasks of the legislator.

Our Own Cruelties

At first blush it may seem not only unnecessary, but even indecent, to discuss such a proposition as the elevation of cruelty to the rank of a human right. Unnecessary, because no vivisector confesses to a love of cruelty for its own sake or claims any general fundamental right to be cruel. Indecent, because there is an accepted convention to repudiate cruelty; and vivisection is only tolerated by the law on condition that, like judicial torture, it shall be done as mercifully as the nature of the practice allows. But the moment the controversy becomes embittered, the recriminations bandied between the opposed parties bring us face-to-face with some very ugly truths. On one occasion I was invited to speak at a large Anti-Vivisection meeting in the Queen's Hall in London. I found myself on the platform with fox hunters, tame stag hunters, men and women whose calendar was divided, not by pay days and quarter days, but by seasons for killing animals for sport: the fox, the hare, the otter, the partridge and the rest having each its appointed date for slaughter. The ladies among us wore hats and cloaks and head-dresses obtained by wholesale massacres, ruthless trappings, callous extermination of our fellow creatures. We insisted on our butchers supplying us with white veal, and were large and constant consumers of *pâté de foie gras;* both comestibles being obtained by revolting methods. We sent our sons to public schools where indecent flogging is a recognized method of taming the young human animal. Yet we were all in hysterics of indignation at the cruelties of the vivisectors. These, if any were present, must have smiled sardonically at such inhuman humanitarians, whose daily habits and fashionable amusements cause more suffering in England in a week than all the vivisectors of Europe do in a year. I made a very effective speech, not exclusively against vivisection, but against cruelty; and I have never been asked to speak since by that Society, nor do I expect to be, as I should probably give such offence to its most affluent subscribers that its attempts to suppress vivisection would be seriously hindered. But that does not prevent the vivisectors from freely using the ''youre another'' retort, and using it with justice.

We must therefore give ourselves no airs of superiority when denouncing the cruelties of vivisection. We all do just as horrible things, with even less excuse. But in making that admission we are also making short work of the virtuous airs with which we are sometimes referred to the humanity of the medical profession as a guarantee that vivisection is not abused—much as if our burglars should assure us that they are too honest to abuse the practice of burgling. We are, as a matter of fact, a cruel nation; and our habit of disguising our vices by giving polite names to the offences we are determined to commit does not, unfortunately for my own comfort, impose on me. Vivisectors can hardly pretend to be better than the classes from which they are drawn, or those above them; and if these classes are capable of sacrificing animals in various cruel ways under cover of sport, fashion, education, discipline, and even, when the cruel sacrifices are human sacrifices, of political economy, it is idle for the vivisector to pretend that he is incapable of practising cruelty for pleasure or profit or both under the cloak of science. We are all tarred with the same brush; and the vivisectors are not slow to remind us of it, and to protest vehemently against being branded as exceptionally cruel and as devisers of horrible instruments of torture by people whose main notion of enjoyment is cruel sport, and whose requirements in the way of villainously cruel traps occupy pages of the catalogue of the Army and Navy Stores.

The Scientific Investigation of Cruelty

There is in man a specific lust for cruelty which infects even his passion of pity and makes it savage. Simple disgust at cruelty is very rare. The people who turn sick and faint and those who gloat are often alike in the pains they take to witness executions, floggings, operations or any other exhibitions of suffering, especially those involving bloodshed, blows, and laceration. A craze for cruelty can be developed just as a craze for drink can; and nobody who attempts to ignore cruelty as a possible factor in the attraction of vivisection and even of antivivisection, or in the credulity with which we accept its excuses, can be regarded as a scientific investigator of it. Those who accuse vivisectors of indulging the well-known passion of cruelty under the cloak of research are therefore putting forward a strictly scientific psychological hypothesis, which is also simple, human, obvious, and probable. It may be as wounding to the personal vanity of the vivisector as Darwin's Origin of Species was to the people who could not bear to think that they were cousins to the monkeys (remember Goldsmith's anger when he was told that he could not move his upper jaw); but science has to consider only the truth of the hypothesis, and not whether conceited people will like it or not. In vain do the sentimental champions of vivisection declare themselves the most humane of men, inflicting suffering only to relieve it, scrupulous in the use of anesthetics, and void of all passion except the passion of pity for a disease-ridden world. The really scientific investigator answers that the question cannot be settled by hysterical protestations, and that if the vivisectionist rejects deductive reasoning, he had better clear his character by his own favorite method of experiment.

Suggested Laboratory Tests of the Vivisector's Emotions

Take the hackneyed case of the Italian who tortured mice, ostensibly to find out about the effects of pain rather less than the nearest dentist could have told him, and who boasted of the ecstatic sensations (he actually used the word love) with which he carried out his experiments. Or the gentleman who starved sixty dogs to death to establish the fact that a dog deprived of food gets progressively lighter and weaker, becoming remarkably emaciated, and finally dying: an undoubted truth, but ascertainable without laboratory experiments by a simple enquiry addressed to the nearest policeman, or, failing him, to any sane person in Europe. The Italian is diagnosed as a cruel voluptuary: the dog-starver is passed over as such a hopeless fool that it is impossible to take any interest in him. Why not test the diagnosis scientifically? Why not perform a careful series of experiments on persons under the influence of voluptuous ecstasy, so as to ascertain its physiological symptoms? Then perform a second series on persons engaged in mathematical work or machine designing, so as to ascertain the symptoms of cold scientific activity? Then note the symptoms of a vivisector performing a cruel experiment; and compare them with the voluptuary symptoms and the mathematical symptoms? Such experiments would be quite as interesting and important as any yet undertaken by the vivisectors. They might open a line of investigation which would finally make, for instance, the ascertainment of the guilt or innocence of an accused person a much exacter process than the very fallible methods of our criminal courts. But instead of proposing such an investigation, our vivisectors offer us all the pious protestations and all the huffy recriminations that any common unscientific mortal offers when he is accused of unworthy conduct.

Routine

Yet most vivisectors would probably come triumphant out of such a series of experiments, because vivisection is now a routine, like butchering or hanging or flogging; and many of the men who practise it do so only because it has been established as part of the profession they have adopted. Far from enjoying it, they have simply overcome their natural repugnance and become indifferent to it, as men inevitably become indifferent to anything they do often enough. It is this dangerous power of custom that makes it so difficult to convince the common sense of mankind that any established commercial or professional practice has its root in passion. Let a routine once spring from passion, and you will presently find thousands of routineers following it passionlessly for a livelihood. Thus it always seems strained to speak of the religious convictions of a clergyman, because nine out of ten clergymen have no religious convictions: they are ordinary officials carrying on a routine of baptizing, marrying, and churching; praying, reciting, and preaching; and, like solicitors or doctors, getting away from their duties with relief to hunt, to garden, to keep bees, to go into society, and the like. In the same way many people do cruel and vile things without being in the least cruel or vile, because the routine to which they have been brought up is superstitiously cruel and vile.

To say that every man who beats his children and every schoolmaster who flogs a pupil is a conscious debauchee is absurd: thousands of dull, conscientious people beat their children conscientiously, because they were beaten themselves and think children ought to be beaten. The ill-tempered vulgarity that instinctively strikes at and hurts a thing that annoys it (and all children are annoying), and the simple stupidity that requires from a child perfection beyond the reach of the wisest and best adults (perfect truthfulness coupled with perfect obedience is quite a common condition of leaving a child unwhipped), produce a good deal of flagellation among people who not only do not lust after it, but who hit the harder because they are angry at having to perform an uncomfortable duty. These people will beat merely to assert their authority, or to carry out what they conceive to be a divine order on the strength of the precept of Solomon recorded in the Bible, which carefully adds that Solomon completely spoilt his own son and turned away from the god of his fathers to the sensuous idolatry in which he ended his days.

In the same way we find men and women practising vivisection as senselessly as a humane butcher, who adores his fox terrier, will cut a calf's throat and hang it up by its heels to bleed slowly to death because it is the custom to eat veal and insist on its being white; or as a German purveyor nails a goose to a board and stuffs it with food because fashionable people eat *pâté de foie gras*; or as the crew of a whaler breaks in on a colony of seals and clubs them to death in wholesale massacre because ladies want sealskin jackets; or as fanciers blind singing birds with hot needles, and mutilate the ears and tails of dogs and horses. Let cruelty or kindness or anything else once become customary and it will be practised by people to whom it is not at all natural, but whose rule of life is simply to do only what everybody else does, and who would lose their employment and starve if they indulged in any peculiarity. A respectable man will lie daily, in speech and in print, about the qualities of the article he lives by selling, because it is customary to do so. He will flog his boy for telling a lie, because it is customary to do so. He will also flog him for not telling a lie if the boy tells inconvenient or disrespectful truths, because it is customary to do so. He will give the same boy a present on his birthday, and buy him a spade and bucket at the seaside, because it is customary to do so, being all the time neither particularly mendacious, nor particularly cruel, nor particularly generous, but simply incapable of ethical judgment or independent action.

Just so do we find a crowd of petty vivisectionists daily committing atrocities and stupidities, because it is the custom to do so. Vivisection is customary as part of the routine of preparing lectures in medical schools. For instance, there are two ways of making the action of the heart visible to students. One, a barbarous, ignorant, and thoughtless way, is to stick little flags into a rabbit's heart and let the students see the flags jump. The other, an elegant, ingenious, well-informed, and instructive way, is to put a sphygmograph on the student's wrist and let him see a record of his heart's action traced by a needle on a slip of smoked paper. But it has become the custom for lecturers to teach from the rabbit; and the lecturers are not original enough to get out of their groove. Then there are the demonstrations which are made by cutting up frogs with scissors. The most humane man, however repugnant the operation may be to him at first, cannot do it at lecture after lecture for months without finally—and that very soon—feeling no more for the frog than if he were cutting up pieces of paper. Such clumsy and lazy ways of teaching are based on the cheapness of frogs and rabbits. If machines were as cheap as frogs, engineers would not only be taught the anatomy of machines and the functions of their parts: they would also have machines misused and wrecked before them so that they might learn as much as possible by using their eyes, and as little as possible by using their brains and imaginations. Thus we have, as part of the routine of teaching, a routine of vivisection which soon produces complete indifference to it on the part even of those who are naturally humane. If they pass on from the routine of lecture preparation, not into general practice, but into research work, they carry this acquired indifference with them into the laboratory, where any atrocity is possible, because all atrocities satisfy curiosity. The routine man is in the majority in his profession always: consequently the moment his practice is tracked down to its source in human passion there is a great and quite sincere poohpoohing from himself, from the mass of the profession, and from the mass of the public, which sees that the average doctor is much too commonplace and decent a person to be capable of passionate wickedness of any kind.

Here then, we have in vivisection, as in all the other tolerated and instituted cruelties, this anti-climax: that only a negligible percentage of those who practise and consequently defend it get any satisfaction out of it. As in Mr. Galsworthy's play Justice the useless and detestable torture of solitary imprisonment is shewn at its worst without the introduction of a single cruel person into the drama, so it would be possible to represent all the torments of vivisection dramatically without introducing a single vivisector who had not felt sick at his first experience in the laboratory. Not that this can exonerate any vivisector from suspicion of enjoying his work (or *her* work: a good deal of the vivisection in medical schools is done by women). In every autobiography which records a real experience of school or prison life, we find that here and there among the routineers there is to be found the genuine amateur, the orgiastic flogging schoolmaster or the nagging warder, who has sought out a cruel profession for the sake of its cruelty. But it is the genuine routineer who is the bulwark of the practice, because, though you can excite public fury against a Sade, a Bluebeard, or a Nero, you cannot rouse any feeling against dull Mr. Smith doing his duty: that is, doing the usual thing. He is so obviously no better and no worse than anyone else that it is difficult to conceive that the things he does are abominable. If you would see public dislike surging up in a moment against an individual, you must watch one who does something unusual, no matter how sensible it may be. The name of Jonas Hanway lives as that of a brave man because he was the first who dared to appear in the streets of this rainy island with an umbrella.

The Old Line between Man and Beast

But there is still a distinction to be clung to by those who dare not tell themselves the truth about the medical profession because they are so helplessly dependent on it when death threatens the household. That distinction is the line that separates the brute from the man in the old classification. Granted, they will plead, that we are all cruel; yet the tame-stag-hunter does not hunt men; and the sportsman who lets a leash of greyhounds loose on a hare would be horrified at the thought of letting them loose on a human child. The lady who gets her cloak by flaying a sable does not flay a negro; nor does it ever occur to her that her veal cutlet might be improved on by a slice of tender baby.

Now there was a time when some trust could be placed in this distinction. The Roman Catholic Church still maintains, with what it must permit me to call a stupid obstinacy, and in spite of St. Francis and St. Anthony, that animals have no souls and no rights; so that you cannot sin against an animal, or against God by anything you may choose to do to an animal. Resisting the temptation to enter on an argument as to whether you may not sin against your own soul if you are unjust or cruel to the least of those whom St. Francis called his little brothers, I have only to point out here that nothing could be more despicably superstitious in the opinion of a vivisector than the notion that science recognizes any such step in evolution as the step from a physical organism to an immortal soul. That conceit has been taken out of all our men of science, and out of all our doctors, by the evolutionists; and when it is considered how completely obsessed biological science has become in our days, not by the full scope of evolution, but by that particular method of it which has neither sense nor purpose nor life nor anything human, much less godlike, in it: by the method, that is, of so-called Natural Selection (meaning no selection at all, but mere dead accident and luck), the folly of trusting the vivisectors to hold the human animal any more sacred than the other animals becomes so clear that it would be waste of time to insist further on it. As a matter of fact the man who once concedes to the vivisector the right to put a dog outside the laws of honor and fellowship, concedes to him also the right to put himself outside them; for he is nothing to the vivisector but a more highly developed, and consequently more interesting-to-experiment-on vertebrate than the dog.

VIVISECTING THE HUMAN SUBJECT

I have in my hand a printed and published account by a doctor of how he tested his remedy for pulmonary tuberculosis, which was, to inject a powerful germicide directly into the circulation by stabbing a vein with a syringe. He was one of those doctors who are able to command public sympathy by saying, quite truly, that when they discovered that the proposed treatment was dangerous, they experimented thenceforth on themselves. In this case the doctor was devoted enough to carry his experiments to the point of running serious risks, and actually making himself very uncomfortable. But he did not begin with himself. His first experiment was on two hospital patients. On receiving a message from the hospital to the effect that these two martyrs to therapeutic science had all but expired in convulsions, he experimented on a rabbit, which instantly dropped dead. It was then, and not until then, that he began to experiment on himself, with the germicide modified in the direction indicated by the experiments made on the two patients and the rabbit. As a good many people countenance vivisection because they fear that if the experiments are not made on rabbits they will be made on themselves, it is worth noting that in this case, where both rabbits and men were equally available, the men, being, of course, enormously more instructive, and costing nothing, were experimented on first. Once grant the ethics of the vivisectionists and you not only sanction the experiment on the human subject, but make it the first duty of the vivisector. If a guinea pig may be sacrificed for the sake of the very little that can be learnt from it, shall not a man be sacrificed for the sake of the great deal that can be learnt from him? At all events, he *is* sacrificed, as this typical case shows. I may add (not that it touches the argument) that the doctor, the patients, and the rabbit all suffered in vain, as far as the hoped-for rescue of the race from pulmonary consumption is concerned.

"THE LIE IS A EUROPEAN POWER"

Now at the very time when the lectures describing these experiments were being circulated in print and discussed eagerly by the medical profession, the customary denials that patients are experimented on were as loud, as indignant, as high-minded as ever, in spite of the few intelligent doctors who point out rightly that all treatments are experiments on the patient. And this brings us to an obvious but mostly overlooked weakness in the vivisector's position: that is, his inevitable forfeiture of all claim to have his word believed. It is hardly to be expected that a man who does not hesitate to vivisect for the sake of science will hesitate to lie about it afterwards to protect it from what he deems the ignorant sentimentality of the laity. When the public conscience stirs uneasily and threatens suppression, there is never wanting some doctor of eminent position and high character who will sacrifice himself devotedly to the cause of science by coming forward to assure the public on his honor that all experiments on animals are completely painless; although he must know that the very experiments which first provoked the anti-vivisection movement by their atrocity were experiments to ascertain the physiological effects of the sensation of extreme pain (the much more interesting physiology of pleasure remains uninvestigated) and that all experiments in which sensation is a factor are voided by its suppression. Besides, vivisection may be painless in cases where the experiments are very cruel. If a person scratches me with a poisoned dagger so gently that I do not feel the scratch, he has achieved a painless vivisection; but if I presently die in torment I am not likely to consider that his humanity is amply vindicated by his gentleness. A cobra's bite hurts so little that the creature is almost, legally speaking, a vivisector who inflicts no pain. By giving his victims chloroform before biting them he could comply with the law completely.

Here, then, is a pretty deadlock. Public support of vivisection is founded almost wholly on the assurances of the vivisectors that great public benefits may be expected from the practice. Not for a moment do I suggest that such a defence would be valid even if proved. But when the witnesses begin by alleging that in the cause of science all the customary ethical obligations (which include the obligation to tell the truth) are suspended, what weight can any reasonable person give to their testimony? I would rather swear fifty lies than take an animal which had licked my hand in good fellowship and torture it. If I did torture the dog, I should certainly not have the face to turn round and ask how any person dare suspect an honorable man like myself of telling lies. Most sensible and humane people would, I hope, reply flatly that honorable men do not behave dishonorably even to dogs. The murderer who, when asked by the chaplain whether he had any other crimes to confess, replied indignantly, "What do you take me for?" reminds us very strongly of the vivisectors who are so deeply hurt when their evidence is set aside as worthless.

An Argument which would Defend any Crime

The Achilles heel of vivisection, however, is not to be found in the pain it causes, but in the line of argument by which it is justified. The medical code regarding it, is simply criminal anarchism at its very worst. Indeed no criminal has yet had the impudence to argue as every vivisector argues. No burglar contends that as it is admittedly important to have money to spend, and as the object of burglary is to provide the burglar with money to spend, and as in many instances it has achieved this object, therefore the burglar is a public benefactor and the police are ignorant sentimentalists. No highway robber has yet harrowed us with denunciations of the puling moralist who allows his child to suffer all the evils of poverty because certain faddists think it dishonest to garotte an alderman. Thieves and assassins understand quite well that there are paths of acquisition, even of the best things, that are barred to all men of honor. Again, has the silliest burglar ever pretended that to put a stop to burglary is to put a stop to industry? All the vivisections that have been performed since the world began have produced nothing so important as the innocent and honorable discovery of radiography; and one of the reasons why radiography was not discovered sooner was that the men whose business it was to discover new clinical methods were coarsening and stupefying themselves with the sensual villainies and cutthroat's casuistries of vivisection. The law of the conservation of energy holds good in physiology as in other things: every vivisector is a deserter from the army of honorable investigators. But the vivisector does not see this. He not only calls his methods scientific: he contends that there are no other scientific methods. When you express your natural loathing for his cruelty and your natural contempt for his stupidity, he imagines that you are attacking science. Yet he has no inkling of the method and temper of science. The point at issue being plainly whether he is a rascal or not, he not only insists that the real point is whether some hotheaded anti-vivisectionist is a liar (which he proves by ridiculously unscientific assumptions as to the degree of accuracy attainable in human statement), but never dreams of offering any scientific evidence by his own methods.

There are many paths to knowledge already discovered; and no enlightened man doubts that there are many more waiting to be discovered. Indeed, all paths lead to knowledge; because even the vilest and stupidest action teaches us something about vileness and stupidity, and may accidentally teach us a good deal more: for instance, a cutthroat learns (and perhaps teaches) the anatomy of the carotid artery and jugular vein; and there can be no question that the burning of St. Joan of Arc must have been a most instructive and interesting experiment to a good observer, and could have been made more so if it had been carried out by skilled physiologists under laboratory conditions. The earthquake in San Francisco proved invaluable as an experiment in the stability of giant steel buildings; and the ramming of the Victoria by the Camperdown settled doubtful points of the greatest importance in naval warfare. According to vivisectionist logic our builders would be justified in producing artificial earthquakes with dynamite, and our admirals in contriving catastrophes at naval manœuvres, in order to follow up the line of research thus accidentally discovered.

The truth is, if the acquisition of knowledge justifies every sort of conduct, it justifies any sort of conduct, from the illumination of Nero's feasts by burning human beings alive (another interesting experiment) to the simplest act of kindness. And in the light of that truth it is clear that the exemption of the pursuit of knowledge from the laws of honor is the most hideous conceivable enlargement of anarchy; worse, by far, than an exemption of the pursuit of money or political power, since these can hardly be attained without some regard for at least the appearances of human welfare, whereas a curious devil might destroy the whole race in torment, acquiring knowledge all the time from his highly interesting experiment. There is more danger in one respectable scientist countenancing such a monstrous claim than in fifty assassins or dynamitards. The man who makes it is ethically imbecile; and whoever imagines that it is a scientific claim has not the faintest conception of what science means. The paths to knowledge are countless. One of these paths is a path through darkness, secrecy, and cruelty. When a man deliberately turns from all other paths and goes down that one, it is scientific to infer that what attracts him is not knowledge, since there are other paths to that, but cruelty. With so strong and scientific a case against him, it is childish for him to stand on his honor and reputation and high character and the credit of a noble profession and so forth: he must clear himself either by reason or by experiment, unless he boldly contends that evolution has retained a passion of cruelty in man just because it is indispensable to the fulness of his knowledge.

Thou Art the Man

I shall not be at all surprised if what I have written above has induced in sympathetic readers a transport of virtuous indignation at the expense of the medical profession. I shall not damp so creditable and salutary a sentiment; but I must point out that the guilt is shared by all of us. It is not in his capacity of healer and man of science that the doctor vivisects or defends vivisection, but in his entirely vulgar lay capacity. He is made of the same clay as the ignorant, shallow, credulous, half-miseducated, pecuniarily anxious people who call him in when they have tried in vain every bottle and every pill the advertizing druggist can persuade them to buy. The real remedy for vivisection is the remedy for all the mischief that the medical profession and all the other professions are doing: namely, more knowledge. The juries which send the poor Peculiars to prison, and give vivisectionists heavy damages against humane persons who accuse them of cruelty; the editors and councillors and student-led mobs who are striving to make Vivisection one of the watchwords of our civilization, are not doctors: they are the British public, all so afraid to die that they will cling frantically to any idol which promises to cure all their diseases, and crucify anyone who tells them that they must not only die when their time comes, but die like gentlemen. In their paroxysms of cowardice and selfishness they force the doctors to humor their folly and ignorance. How complete and inconsiderate their ignorance is can only be realized by those who have some knowledge of vital statistics, and of the illusions which beset Public Health legislation.

What the Public Wants and Will Not Get

The demands of this poor public are not reasonable, but they are quite simple. It dreads disease and desires to be protected against it. But it is poor and wants to be protected cheaply. Scientific measures are too hard to understand, too costly, too clearly tending towards a rise in the rates and more public interference with the insanitary, because insufficiently financed, private house. What the public wants, therefore, is a cheap magic charm to prevent, and a cheap pill or potion to cure, all disease. It forces all such charms on the doctors.

The Vaccination Craze

Thus it was really the public and not the medical profession that took up vaccination with irresistible faith, sweeping the invention out of Jenner's hand and establishing it in a form which he himself repudiated. Jenner was not a man of science; but he was not a fool; and when he found that people who had suffered from cowpox either by contagion in the milking shed or by vaccination, were not, as he had supposed, immune from smallpox, he ascribed the cases of immunity which had formerly misled him to a disease of the horse, which, perhaps because we do not drink its milk and eat its flesh, is kept at a greater distance in our imagination than our foster mother the cow. At all events, the public, which had been boundlessly credulous about the cow, would not have the horse on any terms; and to this day the law which prescribes Jennerian vaccination is carried out with an anti-Jennerian inoculation because the public would have it so in spite of Jenner. All the grossest lies and superstitions which have disgraced the vaccination craze were taught to the doctors by the public. It was not the doctors who first began to declare that all our old men remember the time when almost every face they saw in the street was horribly pitted with smallpox, and that all this disfigurement has vanished since the introduction of vaccination. Jenner himself alluded to this imaginary phenomenon before the introduction of vaccination, and attributed it to the older practice of smallpox inoculation, by which Voltaire, Catherine II. and Lady Mary Wortley Montagu so confidently expected to see the disease made harmless. It was not Jenner who set people declaring that smallpox, if not abolished by vaccination, had at least been made much milder: on the contrary, he recorded a pre-vaccination epidemic in which none of the persons attacked went to bed or considered themselves as seriously ill. Neither Jenner, nor any other doctor ever, so far as I know, inculcated the popular notion that everybody got smallpox as a matter of course before vaccination was invented. That doctors get infected with these delusions, and are in their unprofessional capacity as members of the public subject to them like other men, is true; but if we had to decide whether vaccination was first forced on the public by the doctors or on the doctors by the public, we should have to decide against the public.

Statistical Illusions

Public ignorance of the laws of evidence and of statistics can hardly be exaggerated. There may be a doctor here and there who in dealing with the statistics of disease has taken at least the first step towards sanity by grasping the fact that as an attack of even the commonest disease is an exceptional event, apparently overwhelming statistical evidence in favor of any prophylactic can be produced by persuading the public that everybody caught the disease formerly. Thus if a disease is one which normally attacks fifteen per cent of the population, and if the effect of a prophylactic is actually to increase the proportion to twenty per cent, the publication of this figure of twenty per cent will convince the public that the prophylactic has reduced the percentage by eighty per cent instead of increasing it by five, because the public, left to itself and to the old gentlemen who are always ready to remember, on every possible subject, that things used to be much worse than they are now (such old gentlemen greatly outnumber the laudatores tempori acti), will assume that the former percentage was about 100. The vogue of the Pasteur treatment of hydrophobia, for instance, was due to the assumption by the public that every person bitten by a rabid dog necessarily got hydrophobia. I myself heard hydrophobia discussed in my youth by doctors in Dublin before a Pasteur Institute existed, the subject having been brought forward there by the scepticism of an eminent surgeon as to whether hydrophobia is really a specific disease or only ordinary tetanus induced (as tetanus was then supposed to be induced) by a lacerated wound. There were no statistics available as to the proportion of dog bites that ended in hydrophobia; but nobody ever guessed that the cases could be more than two or three per cent of the bites. On me, therefore, the results published by the Pasteur Institute produced no such effect as they did on the ordinary man who thinks that the bite of a mad dog means certain hydrophobia. It seemed to me that the proportion of deaths among the cases treated at the Institute was rather higher, if anything, than might have been expected had there been no Institute in existence. But to the public every Pasteur patient who did not die was miraculously saved from an agonizing death by the beneficent white magic of that most trusty of all wizards, the man of science.

Even trained statisticians often fail to appreciate the extent to which statistics are vitiated by the unrecorded assumptions of their interpreters. Their attention is too much occupied with the cruder tricks of those who make a corrupt use of statistics for advertizing purposes. There is, for example, the percentage dodge. In some hamlet, barely large enough to have a name, two people are attacked during a smallpox epidemic. One dies: the other recovers. One has vaccination marks: the other has none. Immediately either the vaccinists or the anti-vaccinists publish the triumphant news that at such and such a place not a single vaccinated person died of smallpox whilst 100 per cent of the unvaccinated perished miserably; or, as the case may be, that 100 per cent of the unvaccinated recovered whilst the vaccinated succumbed to the last man. Or, to take another common instance, comparisons which are really comparisons between two social classes with different standards of nutrition and education are palmed off as comparisons between the results of a certain medical treatment and its neglect. Thus it is easy to prove that the wearing of tall hats and the carrying of umbrellas enlarges the chest, prolongs life, and confers comparative immunity from disease; for the statistics shew that the classes which use these articles are bigger, healthier, and live longer than the class which never dreams of possessing such things. It does not take much perspicacity to see that what really makes this difference is not the tall hat and the umbrella, but the wealth and nourishment of which they are evidence, and that a gold watch or membership of a club in Pall Mall might be proved in the same way to have the like sovereign virtues. A university degree, a daily bath, the owning of thirty pairs of trousers, a knowledge of Wagner's music, a pew in church, anything, in short, that implies more means and better nurture than the mass of laborers enjoy, can be statistically palmed off as a magic-spell conferring all sorts of privileges.

In the case of a prophylactic enforced by law, this illusion is intensified grotesquely, because only vagrants can evade it. Now vagrants have little power of resisting any disease: their death rate and their case-mortality rate is always high relatively to that of respectable folk. Nothing is easier, therefore, than to prove that compliance with any public regulation produces the most gratifying results. It would be equally easy even if the regulation actually raised the death-rate, provided it did not raise it sufficiently to make the average householder, who cannot evade regulations, die as early as the average vagrant who can.

The Surprises of Attention and Neglect

There is another statistical illusion which is independent of class differences. A common complaint of houseowners is that the Public Health Authorities frequently compel them to instal costly sanitary appliances which are condemned a few years later as dangerous to health, and forbidden under penalties. Yet these discarded mistakes are always made in the first instance on the strength of a demonstration that their introduction has reduced the death-rate. The explanation is simple. Suppose a law were made that every child in the nation should be compelled to drink a pint of brandy per month, but that the brandy must be administered only when the child was in good health, with its digestion and so forth working normally, and its teeth either naturally or artificially sound. Probably the result would be an immediate and startling reduction in child mortality, leading to further legislation increasing the quantity of brandy to a gallon. Not until the brandy craze had been carried to a point at which the direct harm done by it would outweigh the incidental good, would an anti-brandy party be listened to. That incidental good would be the substitution of attention to the general health of children for the neglect which is now the rule so long as the child is not actually too sick to run about and play as usual. Even if this attention were confined to the children's teeth, there would be an improvement which it would take a good deal of brandy to cancel.

This imaginary case explains the actual case of the sanitary appliances which our local sanitary authorities prescribe today and condemn tomorrow. No sanitary contrivance which the mind of even the very worst plumber can devize could be as disastrous as that total neglect for long periods which gets avenged by pestilences that sweep through whole continents, like the black death and the cholera. If it were proposed at this time of day to discharge all the sewage of London crude and untreated into the Thames, instead of carrying it, after elaborate treatment, far out into the North Sea, there would be a shriek of horror from all our experts. Yet if Cromwell had done that instead of doing nothing, there would probably have been no Great Plague of London. When the Local Health Authority forces every householder to have his sanitary arrangements thought about and attended to by somebody whose special business it is to attend to such things, then it matters not how erroneous or even directly mischievous may be the specific measures taken: the net result at first is sure to be an improvement. Not until attention has been effectually substituted for neglect as the general rule, will the statistics begin to shew the merits of the particular methods of attention adopted. And as we are far from having arrived at this stage, being as to health legislation only at the beginning of things, we have practically no evidence yet as to the value of methods. Simple and obvious as this is, nobody seems as yet to discount the effect of substituting attention for neglect in drawing conclusions from health statistics. Everything is put to the credit of the particular method employed, although it may quite possibly be raising the death rate by five per thousand whilst the attention incidental to it is reducing the death rate fifteen per thousand. The net gain of ten per thousand is credited to the method, and made the excuse for enforcing more of it.

Stealing Credit from Civilization

There is yet another way in which specifics which have no merits at all, either direct or incidental, may be brought into high repute by statistics. For a century past civilization has been cleaning away the conditions which favor bacterial fevers. Typhus, once rife, has vanished: plague and cholera have been stopped at our frontiers by a sanitary blockade. We still have epidemics of smallpox and typhoid; and diphtheria and scarlet fever are endemic in the slums. Measles, which in my childhood was not regarded as a dangerous disease, has now become so mortal that notices are posted publicly urging parents to take it seriously. But even in these cases the contrast between the death and recovery rates in the rich districts and in the poor ones has led to the general conviction among experts that bacterial diseases are preventible; and they already are to a large extent prevented. The dangers of infection and the way to avoid it are better understood than they used to be. It is barely twenty years since people exposed themselves recklessly to the infection of consumption and pneumonia in the belief that these diseases were not "catching." Nowadays the troubles of consumptive patients are greatly increased by the growing disposition to treat them as lepers. No doubt there is a good deal of ignorant exaggeration and cowardly refusal to face a human and necessary share of the risk. That has always been the case. We now know that the medieval horror of leprosy was out of all proportion to the danger of infection, and was accompanied by apparent blindness to the infectiousness of smallpox, which has since been worked up by our disease terrorists into the position formerly held by leprosy. But the scare of infection, though it sets even doctors talking as if the only really scientific thing to do with a fever patient is to throw him into the nearest ditch and pump carbolic acid on him from a safe distance until he is ready to be cremated on the spot, has led to much greater care and cleanliness. And the net result has been a series of victories over disease.

Now let us suppose that in the early nineteenth century somebody had come forward with a theory that typhus fever always begins in the top joint of the little finger; and that if this joint be amputated immediately after birth, typhus fever will disappear. Had such a suggestion been adopted, the theory would have been triumphantly confirmed; for as a matter of fact, typhus fever *has* disappeared. On the other hand cancer and madness have increased (statistically) to an appalling extent. The opponents of the little finger theory would therefore be pretty sure to allege that the amputations were spreading cancer and lunacy. The vaccination controversy is full of such contentions. So is the controversy as to the docking of horses' tails and the cropping of dogs' ears. So is the less widely known controversy as to circumcision and the declaring certain kinds of flesh unclean by the Jews. To advertize any remedy or operation, you have only to pick out all the most reassuring advances made by civilization, and boldly present the two in the relation of cause and effect: the public will swallow the fallacy without a wry face. It has no idea of the need for what is called a control experiment. In Shakespear's time and for long after it, mummy was a favorite medicament. You took a pinch of the dust of a dead Egyptian in a pint of the hottest water you could bear to drink; and it did you a great deal of good. This, you thought, proved what a sovereign healer mummy was. But if you had tried the control experiment of taking the hot water without the mummy, you might have found the effect exactly the same, and that any hot drink would have done as well.

BIOMETRIKA

Another difficulty about statistics is the technical difficulty of calculation. Before you can even make a mistake in drawing your conclusion from the correlations established by your statistics you must ascertain the correlations. When I turn over the pages of Biometrika, a quarterly journal in which is recorded the work done in the field of biological statistics by Professor Karl Pearson and his colleagues, I am out of my depth at the first line, because mathematics are to me only a concept: I never used a logarithm in my life, and could not undertake to extract the square root of four without misgiving. I am therefore unable to deny that the statistical ascertainment of the correlations between one thing and another must be a very complicated and difficult technical business, not to be tackled successfully except by high mathematicians; and I cannot resist Professor Karl Pearson's immense contempt for, and indignant sense of grave social danger in, the unskilled guesses of the ordinary sociologist.

Now the man in the street knows nothing of Biometrika: all he knows is that "you can prove anything by figures," though he forgets this the moment figures are used to prove anything he wants to believe. If he did take in Biometrika he would probably become abjectly credulous as to all the conclusions drawn in it from the correlations so learnedly worked out; though the mathematician whose correlations would fill a Newton with admiration may, in collecting and accepting data and drawing conclusions from them, fall into quite crude errors by just such popular oversights as I have been describing.

PATIENT-MADE THERAPEUTICS

To all these blunders and ignorances doctors are no less subject than the rest of us. They are not trained in the use of evidence, nor in biometrics, nor in the psychology of human credulity, nor in the incidence of economic pressure. Further, they must believe, on the whole, what their patients believe, just as they must wear the sort of hat their patients wear. The doctor may lay down the law despotically enough to the patient at points where the patient's mind is simply blank; but when the patient has a prejudice the doctor must either keep it in countenance or lose his patient. If people are persuaded that night air is dangerous to health and that fresh air makes them catch cold, it will not be possible for a doctor to make his living in private practice if he prescribes ventilation. We have to go back no further than the days of The Pickwick Papers to find ourselves in a world where people slept in four-post beds with curtains drawn closely round to exclude as much air as possible. Had Mr. Pickwick's doctor told him that he would be much healthier if he slept on a camp bed by an open window, Mr. Pickwick would have regarded him as a crank and called in another doctor. Had he gone on to forbid Mr. Pickwick to drink brandy and water whenever he felt chilly, and assured him that if he were deprived of meat or salt for a whole year, he would not only not die, but would be none the worse, Mr. Pickwick would have fled from his presence as from that of a dangerous madman. And in these matters the doctor cannot cheat his patient. If he has no faith in drugs or vaccination, and the patient has, he can cheat him with colored water and pass his lancet through the flame of a spirit lamp before scratching his arm. But he cannot make him change his daily habits without knowing it.

The Reforms also come from the Laity

In the main, then, the doctor learns that if he gets ahead of the superstitions of his patients he is a ruined man; and the result is that he instinctively takes care not to get ahead of them. That is why all the changes come from the laity. It was not until an agitation had been conducted for many years by laymen, including quacks and faddists of all kinds, that the public was sufficiently impressed to make it possible for the doctors to open their minds and their mouths on the subject of fresh air, cold water, temperance, and the rest of the new fashions in hygiene. At present the tables have been turned on many old prejudices. Plenty of our most popular elderly doctors believe that cold tubs in the morning are unnatural, exhausting, and rheumatic; that fresh air is a fad and that everybody is the better for a glass or two of port wine every day; but they no longer dare say as much until they know exactly where they are; for many very desirable patients in country houses have lately been persuaded that their first duty is to get up at six in the morning and begin the day by taking a walk barefoot through the dewy grass. He who shews the least scepticism as to this practice is at once suspected of being "an old-fashioned doctor," and dismissed to make room for a younger man.

In short, private medical practice is governed not by science but by supply and demand; and however scientific a treatment may be, it cannot hold its place in the market if there is no demand for it; nor can the grossest quackery be kept off the market if there is a demand for it.

Fashions and Epidemics

A demand, however, can be inculcated. This is thoroughly understood by fashionable tradesmen, who find no difficulty in persuading their customers to renew articles that are not worn out and to buy things they do not want. By making doctors tradesmen, we compel them to learn the tricks of trade; consequently we find that the fashions of the year include treatments, operations, and particular drugs, as well as hats, sleeves, ballads, and games. Tonsils, vermiform appendices, uvulas, even ovaries are sacrificed because it is the fashion to get them cut out, and because the operations are highly profitable. The psychology of fashion becomes a pathology; for the cases have every air of being genuine: fashions, after all, are only induced epidemics, proving that epidemics can be induced by tradesmen, and therefore by doctors.

The Doctor's Virtues

It will be admitted that this is a pretty bad state of things. And the melodramatic instinct of the public, always demanding that every wrong shall have, not its remedy, but its villain to be hissed, will blame, not its own apathy, superstition, and ignorance, but the depravity of the doctors. Nothing could be more unjust or mischievous. Doctors, if no better than other men, are certainly no worse. I was reproached during the performances of The Doctor's Dilemma at the Court Theatre in 1907 because I made the artist a rascal, the journalist an illiterate incapable, and all the doctors "angels." But I did not go beyond the warrant of my own experience. It has been my luck to have doctors among my friends for nearly forty years (all perfectly aware of my freedom from the usual credulity as to the miraculous powers and knowledge attributed to them); and though I know that there are medical blackguards as well as military, legal, and clerical blackguards (one soon finds that out when one is privileged to hear doctors talking shop among themselves), the fact that I was no more at a loss for private medical advice and attendance when I had not a penny in my pocket than I was later on when I could afford fees on the highest scale, has made it impossible for me to share that hostility to the doctor as a man which exists and is growing as an inevitable result of the present condition of medical practice. Not that the interest in disease and aberrations which turns some men and women to medicine and surgery is not sometimes as morbid as the interest in misery and vice which turns some others to philanthropy and "rescue work." But the true doctor is inspired by a hatred of ill-health, and a divine impatience of any waste of vital forces. Unless a man is led to medicine or surgery through a very exceptional technical aptitude, or because doctoring is a family tradition, or because he regards it unintelligently as a lucrative and gentlemanly profession, his motives in choosing the career of a healer are clearly generous. However actual practice may disillusion and corrupt him, his selection in the first instance is not a selection of a base character.

THE DOCTOR'S HARDSHIPS

A review of the counts in the indictment I have brought against private medical practice will shew that they arise out of the doctor's position as a competitive private tradesman: that is, out of his poverty and dependence. And it should be borne in mind that doctors are expected to treat other people specially well whilst themselves submitting to specially inconsiderate treatment. The butcher and baker are not expected to feed the hungry unless the hungry can pay; but a doctor who allows a fellow-creature to suffer or perish without aid is regarded as a monster. Even if we must dismiss hospital service as really venal, the fact remains that most doctors do a good deal of gratuitous work in private practice all through their careers. And in his paid work the doctor is on a different footing to the tradesman. Although the articles he sells, advice and treatment, are the same for all classes, his fees have to be graduated like the income tax. The successful fashionable doctor may weed his poorer patients out from time to time, and finally use the College of Physicians to place it out of his own power to accept low fees; but the ordinary general practitioner never makes out his bills without considering the taxable capacity of his patients.

Then there is the disregard of his own health and comfort which results from the fact that he is, by the nature of his work, an emergency man. We are polite and considerate to the doctor when there is nothing the matter, and we meet him as a friend or entertain him as a guest; but when the baby is suffering from croup, or its mother has a temperature of 104°, or its grandfather has broken his leg, nobody thinks of the doctor except as a healer and saviour. He may be hungry, weary, sleepy, run down by several successive nights disturbed by that instrument of torture, the night bell; but who ever thinks of this in the face of sudden sickness or accident? We think no more of the condition of a doctor attending a case than of the condition of a fireman at a fire. In other occupations night-work is specially recognized and provided for. The worker sleeps all day; has his breakfast in the evening; his lunch or dinner at midnight; his dinner or supper before going to bed in the morning; and he changes to day-work if he cannot stand night-work. But a doctor is expected to work day and night. In practices which consist largely of workmen's clubs, and in which the patients are therefore taken on wholesale terms and very numerous, the unfortunate assistant, or the principal if he has no assistant, often does not undress, knowing that he will be called up before he has snatched an hour's sleep. To the strain of such inhuman conditions must be added the constant risk of infection. One wonders why the impatient doctors do not become savage and unmanageable, and the patient ones imbecile. Perhaps they do, to some extent. And the pay is wretched, and so uncertain that refusal to attend without payment in advance becomes often a necessary measure of self-defence, whilst the County Court has long ago put an end to the tradition that the doctor's fee is an honorarium. Even the most eminent physicians, as such biographies as those of Paget shew, are sometimes miserably, inhumanly poor until they are past their prime.

In short, the doctor needs our help for the moment much more than we often need his. The ridicule of Molière, the death of a well-informed and clever writer like the late Harold Frederic in the hands of Christian Scientists (a sort of sealing with his blood of the contemptuous disbelief in and dislike of doctors he had bitterly expressed in his books), the scathing and quite justifiable exposure of medical practice in the novel by Mr. Maarten Maartens entitled The New Religion: all these trouble the doctor very little, and are in any case well set off by the popularity of Sir Luke Fildes' famous picture, and by the verdicts in which juries from time to time express their conviction that the doctor can do no wrong. The real woes of the doctor are the shabby coat, the wolf at the door, the tyranny of ignorant patients, the work-day of 24 hours, and the uselessness of honestly prescribing what most of the patients really need: that is, not medicine, but money.

The Public Doctor

What then is to be done?

Fortunately we have not to begin absolutely from the beginning: we already have, in the Medical Officer of Health, a sort of doctor who is free from the worst hardships, and consequently from the worst vices, of the private practitioner. His position depends, not on the number of people who are ill, and whom he can keep ill, but on the number of people who are well. He is judged, as all doctors and treatments should be judged, by the vital statistics of his district. When the death rate goes up his credit goes down. As every increase in his salary depends on the issue of a public debate as to the health of the constituency under his charge, he has every inducement to strive towards the ideal of a clean bill of health. He has a safe, dignified, responsible, independent position based wholly on the public health; whereas the private practitioner has a precarious, shabby-genteel, irresponsible, servile position, based wholly on the prevalence of illness.

It is true, there are grave scandals in the public medical service. The public doctor may be also a private practitioner eking out his earnings by giving a little time to public work for a mean payment. There are cases in which the position is one which no successful practitioner will accept, and where, therefore, incapables or drunkards get automatically selected for the post, *faute de mieux*; but even in these cases the doctor is less disastrous in his public capacity than in his private one: besides, the conditions which produce these bad cases are doomed, as the evil is now recognized and understood. A popular but unstable remedy is to enable local authorities, when they are too small to require the undivided time of such men as the Medical Officers of our great municipalities, to combine for public health purposes so that each may share the services of a highly paid official of the best class; but the right remedy is a larger area as the sanitary unit.

Medical Organization

Another advantage of public medical work is that it admits of organization, and consequently of the distribution of the work in such a manner as to avoid wasting the time of highly qualified experts on trivial jobs. The individualism of private practice leads to an appalling waste of time on trifles. Men whose dexterity as operators or almost divinatory skill in diagnosis are constantly needed for difficult cases, are poulticing whitlows, vaccinating, changing unimportant dressings, prescribing ether drams for ladies with timid leanings towards dipsomania, and generally wasting their time in the pursuit of private fees. In no other profession is the practitioner expected to do all the work involved in it from the first day of his professional career to the last as the doctor is. The judge passes sentence of death; but he is not expected to hang the criminal with his own hands, as he would be if the legal profession were as unorganized as the medical. The bishop is not expected to blow the organ or wash the baby he baptizes. The general is not asked to plan a campaign or conduct a battle at half-past twelve and to play the drum at half-past two. Even if they were, things would still not be as bad as in the medical profession; for in it not only is the first-class man set to do third-class work, but, what is much more terrifying, the third-class man is expected to do first-class work. Every general practitioner is supposed to be capable of the whole range of medical and surgical work at a moment's notice; and the country doctor, who has not a specialist nor a crack consultant at the end of his telephone, often has to tackle without hesitation cases which no sane practitioner in a town would take in hand without assistance. No doubt this develops the resourcefulness of the country doctor, and makes him a more capable man than his suburban colleague; but it cannot develop the second-class man into a first-class one. If the practice of law not only led to a judge having to hang, but the hangman to judge, or if in the army matters were so arranged that it would be possible for the drummer boy to be in command at Waterloo whilst the Duke of Wellington was playing the drum in Brussels, we should not be consoled by the reflection that our hangmen were thereby made a little more judicial-minded, and our drummers more responsible, than in foreign countries where the legal and military professions recognized the advantages of division of labor.

Under such conditions no statistics as to the graduation of professional ability among doctors are available. Assuming that doctors are normal men and not magicians (and it is unfortunately very hard to persuade people to admit so much and thereby destroy the romance of doctoring) we may guess that the medical profession, like the other professions, consists of a small percentage of highly gifted persons at one end, and a small percentage of altogether disastrous duffers at the other. Between these extremes comes the main body of doctors (also, of course, with a weak and a strong end) who can be trusted to work under regulations with more or less aid from above according to the gravity of the case. Or, to put it in terms of the cases, there are cases that present no difficulties, and can be dealt with by a nurse or student at one end of the scale, and cases that require watching and handling by the very highest existing skill at the other; whilst between come the great mass of cases which need visits from the doctor of ordinary ability and from the chiefs of the profession in the proportion of, say, seven to none, seven to one, three to one, one to one, or, for a day or two, none to one. Such a service is organized at present only in hospitals, though in large towns the practice of calling in the consultant acts, to some extent, as a substitute for it. But in the latter case it is quite unregulated except by professional etiquet, which, as we have seen, has for its object, not the health of the patient or of the community at large, but the protection of the doctor's livelihood and the concealment of his errors. And as the consultant is an expensive luxury, he is a last resource rather, as he should be, than a matter of course, in all cases where the general practitioner is not equal to the occasion: a predicament in which a very capable man may find himself at any time through the cropping up of a case of which he has had no clinical experience.

The Social Solution of the Medical Problem

The social solution of the medical problem, then, depends on that large, slowly advancing, pettishly resisted integration of society called generally Socialism. Until the medical profession becomes a body of men trained and paid by the country to keep the country in health it will remain what it is at present: a conspiracy to exploit popular credulity and human suffering. Already our M.O.H.s (Medical Officers of Health) are in the new position: what is lacking is appreciation of the change, not only by the public but by the private doctors. For, as we have seen, when one of the first-rate posts becomes vacant in one of the great cities, and all the leading M.O.H.s compete for it, they must appeal to the good health of the cities of which they have been in charge, and not to the size of the incomes the local private doctors are making out of the ill-health of their patients. If a competitor can prove that he has utterly ruined every sort of medical private practice in a large city except obstetric practice and the surgery of accidents, his claims are irresistible; and this is the ideal at which every M.O.H. should aim. But the profession at large should none the less welcome him and set its house in order for the social change which will finally be its own salvation. For the M.O.H. as we know him is only the beginning of that army of Public Hygiene which will presently take the place in general interest and honor now occupied by our military and naval forces. It is silly that an Englishman should be more afraid of a German soldier than of a British disease germ, and should clamor for more barracks in the same newspapers that protest against more school clinics, and cry out that if the State fights disease for us it makes us paupers, though they never say that if the State fights the Germans for us it makes us cowards. Fortunately, when a habit of thought is silly it only needs steady treatment by ridicule from sensible and witty people to be put out of countenance and perish. Every year sees an increase in the number of persons employed in the Public Health Service, who would formerly have been mere adventurers in the Private Illness Service. To put it another way, a host of men and women who have now a strong incentive to be mischievous and even murderous rogues will have a much stronger, because a much honester, incentive to be not only good citizens but active benefactors to the community. And they will have no anxiety whatever about their incomes.

The Future of Private Practice

It must not be hastily concluded that this involves the extinction of the private practitioner. What it will really mean for him is release from his present degrading and scientifically corrupting slavery to his patients. As I have already shewn, the doctor who has to live by pleasing his patients in competition with everybody who has walked the hospitals, scraped through the examinations, and bought a brass plate, soon finds himself prescribing water to teetotallers and brandy or champagne jelly to drunkards; beefsteaks and stout in one house, and "uric acid free" vegetarian diet over the way; shut windows, big fires, and heavy overcoats to old Colonels, and open air and as much nakedness as is compatible with decency to young faddists, never once daring to say either "I dont know," or "I dont agree." For the strength of the doctor's, as of every other man's position when the evolution of social organization at last reaches his profession, will be that he will always have open to him the alternative of public employment when the private employer becomes too tyrannous. And let no one suppose that the words doctor and patient can disguise from the parties the fact that they are employer and employee. No doubt doctors who are in great demand can be as high-handed and independent as employees are in all classes when a dearth in their labor market makes them indispensable; but the average doctor is not in this position: he is struggling for life in an overcrowded profession, and knows well that "a good bedside manner" will carry him to solvency through a morass of illness, whilst the least attempt at plain dealing with people who are eating too much, or drinking too much, or frowsting too much (to go no further in the list of intemperances that make up so much of family life) would soon land him in the Bankruptcy Court.

Private practice, thus protected, would itself protect individuals, as far as such protection is possible, against the errors and superstitions of State medicine, which are at worst no worse than the errors and superstitions of private practice, being, indeed, all derived from it. Such monstrosities as vaccination are, as we have seen, founded, not on science, but on half-crowns. If the Vaccination Acts, instead of being wholly repealed as they are already half repealed, were strengthened by compelling every parent to have his child vaccinated by a public officer whose salary was completely independent of the number of vaccinations performed by him, and for whom there was plenty of alternative public health work waiting, vaccination would be dead in two years, as the vaccinator would not only not gain by it, but would lose credit through the depressing effects on the vital statistics of his district of the illness and deaths it causes, whilst it would take from him all the credit of that freedom from smallpox which is the result of good sanitary administration and vigilant prevention of infection. Such absurd panic scandals as that of the last London epidemic, where a fee of half-a-crown per re-vaccination produced raids on houses during the absence of parents, and the forcible seizure and re-vaccination of children left to answer the door, can be prevented simply by abolishing the half-crown and all similar follies, paying, not for this or that ceremony of witchcraft, but for immunity from disease, and paying, too, in a rational way. The officer with a fixed salary saves himself trouble by doing his business with the least possible interference with the private citizen. The man paid by the job loses money by not forcing his job on the public as often as possible without reference to its results.

The Technical Problem

As to any technical medical problem specially involved, there is none. If there were, I should not be competent to deal with it, as I am not a technical expert in medicine: I deal with the subject as an economist, a politician, and a citizen exercising my common sense. Everything that I have said applies equally to all the medical techniques, and will hold good whether public hygiene be based on the poetic fancies of Christian Science, the tribal superstitions of the druggist and the vivisector, or the best we can make of our real knowledge. But I may remind those who confusedly imagine that the medical problem is also the scientific problem, that all problems are finally scientific problems. The notion that therapeutics or hygiene or surgery is any more or less scientific than making or cleaning boots is entertained only by people to whom a man of science is still a magician who can cure diseases, transmute metals, and enable us to live for ever. It may still be necessary for some time to come to practise on popular credulity, popular love and dread of the marvellous, and popular idolatry, to induce the poor to comply with the sanitary regulations they are too ignorant to understand. As I have elsewhere confessed, I have myself been responsible for ridiculous incantations with burning sulphur, experimentally proved to be quite useless, because poor people are convinced, by the mystical air of the burning and the horrible smell, that it exorcises the demons of smallpox and scarlet fever and makes it safe for them to return to their houses. To assure them that the real secret is sunshine and soap is only to convince them that you do not care whether they live or die, and wish to save money at their expense. So you perform the incantation; and back they go to their houses, satisfied. A religious ceremony—a poetic blessing of the threshold, for instance—would be much better; but unfortunately our religion is weak on the sanitary side. One of the worst misfortunes of Christendom was that reaction against the voluptuous bathing of the imperial Romans which made dirty habits a part of Christian piety, and in some unlucky places (the Sandwich Islands for example) made the introduction of Christianity also the introduction of disease, because the formulators of the superseded native religion, like Mahomet, had been enlightened enough to introduce as religious duties such sanitary measures as ablution and the most careful and reverent treatment of everything cast off by the human body, even to nail clippings and hairs; and our missionaries thoughtlessly discredited this godly doctrine without supplying its place, which was promptly taken by laziness and neglect. If the priests of Ireland could only be persuaded to teach their flocks that it is a deadly insult to the Blessed Virgin to place her image in a cottage that is not kept up to that high standard of Sunday cleanliness to which all her worshippers must believe she is accustomed, and to represent her as being especially particular about stables because her son was born in one, they might do more in one year than all the Sanitary Inspectors in Ireland could do in twenty; and they could hardly doubt that Our Lady would be delighted. Perhaps they do nowadays; for Ireland is certainly a transfigured country since my youth as far as clean faces and pinafores can transfigure it. In England, where so many of the inhabitants are too gross to believe in poetic faiths, too respectable to tolerate the notion that the stable at Bethany was a common peasant farmer's stable instead of a first-rate racing one, and too savage to believe that anything can really cast out the devil of disease unless it be some terrifying hoodoo of tortures and stinks, the M.O.H. will no doubt for a long time to come have to preach to fools according to their folly, promising miracles, and threatening hideous personal consequences of neglect of by-laws and the like; therefore it will be important that every M.O.H. shall have, with his (or her) other qualifications, a sense of humor, lest (he or she) should come at last to believe all the nonsense that must needs be talked. But he must, in his capacity of an expert advising the authorities, keep the government itself free of superstition. If Italian peasants are so ignorant that the Church can get no hold of them except by miracles, why, miracles there must be. The blood of St. Januarius must liquefy whether the Saint is in the humor or not. To trick a heathen into being a dutiful Christian is no worse than to trick a whitewasher into trusting himself in a room where a smallpox patient has lain, by pretending to exorcise the disease with burning sulphur. But woe to the Church if in deceiving the peasant it also deceives itself; for then the Church is lost, and the peasant too, unless he revolt against it. Unless the Church works the pretended miracle painfully against the grain, and is continually urged by its dislike of the imposture to strive to make the peasant susceptible to the true reasons for behaving well, the Church will become an instrument of his corruption and an exploiter of his ignorance, and will find itself launched upon that persecution of scientific truth of which all priesthoods are accused—and none with more justice than the scientific priesthood.

And here we come to the danger that terrifies so many of us: the danger of having a hygienic orthodoxy imposed on us. But we must face that: in such crowded and poverty ridden civilizations as ours any orthodoxy is better than laisser-faire. If our population ever comes to consist exclusively of well-to-do, highly cultivated, and thoroughly instructed free persons in a position to take care of themselves, no doubt they will make short work of a good deal of official regulation that is now of life-and-death necessity to us; but under existing circumstances, I repeat, almost any sort of attention that democracy will stand is better than neglect. Attention and activity lead to mistakes as well as to successes; but a life spent in making mistakes is not only more honorable but more useful than a life spent doing nothing. The one lesson that comes out of all our theorizing and experimenting is that there is only one really scientific progressive method; and that is the method of trial and error. If you come to that, what is laisser-faire but an orthodoxy? the most tyrannous and disastrous of all the orthodoxies, since it forbids you even to learn.

The Latest Theories

Medical theories are so much a matter of fashion, and the most fertile of them are modified so rapidly by medical practice and biological research, which are international activities, that the play which furnishes the pretext for this preface is already slightly outmoded, though I believe it may be taken as a faithful record for the year (1906) in which it was begun. I must not expose any professional man to ruin by connecting his name with the entire freedom of criticism which I, as a layman, enjoy; but it will be evident to all experts that my play could not have been written but for the work done by Sir Almroth Wright in the theory and practice of securing immunization from bacterial diseases by the inoculation of "vaccines" made of their own bacteria: a practice incorrectly called vaccinetherapy (there is nothing vaccine about it) apparently because it is what vaccination ought to be and is not. Until Sir Almroth Wright, following up on one of Metchnikoff's most suggestive biological romances, discovered that the white corpuscles or phagocytes which attack and devour disease germs for us do their work only when we butter the disease germs appetizingly for them with a natural sauce which Sir Almroth named opsonin, and that our production of this condiment continually rises and falls rhythmically from negligibility to the highest efficiency, nobody had been able even to conjecture why the various serums that were from time to time introduced as having effected marvellous cures, presently made such direful havoc of some unfortunate patient that they had to be dropped hastily. The quantity of sturdy lying that was necessary to save the credit of inoculation in those days was prodigious; and had it not been for the devotion shewn by the military authorities throughout Europe, who would order the entire disappearance of some disease from their armies, and bring it about by the simple plan of changing the name under which the cases were reported, or for our own Metropolitan Asylums Board, which carefully suppressed all the medical reports that revealed the sometimes quite appalling effects of epidemics of revaccination, there is no saying what popular reaction might not have taken place against the whole immunization movement in therapeutics.

The situation was saved when Sir Almroth Wright pointed out that if you inoculated a patient with pathogenic germs at a moment when his powers of cooking them for consumption by the phagocytes was receding to its lowest point, you would certainly make him a good deal worse and perhaps kill him, whereas if you made precisely the same inoculation when the cooking power was rising to one of its periodical climaxes, you would stimulate it to still further exertions and produce just the opposite result. And he invented a technique for ascertaining in which phase the patient happened to be at any given moment. The dramatic possibilities of this discovery and invention will be found in my play. But it is one thing to invent a technique: it is quite another to persuade the medical profession to acquire it. Our general practitioners, I gather, simply declined to acquire it, being mostly unable to afford either the acquisition or the practice of it when acquired. Something simple, cheap, and ready at all times for all comers, is, as I have shewn, the only thing that is economically possible in general practice, whatever may be the case in Sir Almroth's famous laboratory in St. Mary's Hospital. It would have become necessary to denounce opsonin in the trade papers as a fad and Sir Almroth as a dangerous man if his practice in the laboratory had not led him to the conclusion that the customary inoculations were very much too powerful, and that a comparatively infinitesimal dose would not precipitate a negative phase of cooking activity, and might induce a positive one. And thus it happens that the refusal of our general practitioners to acquire the new technique is no longer quite so dangerous in practice as it was when The Doctor's Dilemma was written: nay, that Sir Ralph Bloomfield Bonington's way of administering inoculations as if they were spoonfuls of squills may sometimes work fairly well. For all that, I find Sir Almroth Wright, on the 23rd May, 1910, warning the Royal Society of Medicine that "the clinician has not yet been prevailed upon to reconsider his position," which means that the general practitioner ("the doctor," as he is called in our homes) is going on just as he did before, and could not afford to learn or practice a new technique even if he had ever heard of it. To the patient who does not know about it he will say nothing. To the patient who does, he will ridicule it, and disparage Sir Almroth. What else can he do, except confess his ignorance and starve?

But now please observe how "the whirligig of time brings its revenges." This latest discovery of the remedial virtue of a very, very tiny hair of the dog that bit you reminds us, not only of Arndt's law of protoplasmic reaction to stimuli, according to which weak and strong stimuli provoke opposite reactions, but of Hahnemann's homeopathy, which was founded on the fact alleged by Hahnemann that drugs which produce certain symptoms when taken in ordinary perceptible quantities, will, when taken in infinitesimally small quantities, provoke just the opposite symptoms; so that the drug that gives you a headache will also cure a headache if you take little enough of it. I have already explained that the savage opposition which homeopathy encountered from the medical profession was not a scientific opposition; for nobody seems to deny that some drugs act in the alleged manner. It was opposed simply because doctors and apothecaries lived by selling bottles and boxes of doctor's stuff to be taken in spoonfuls or in pellets as large as peas; and people would not pay as much for drops and globules no bigger than pins' heads. Nowadays, however, the more cultivated folk are beginning to be so suspicious of drugs, and the incorrigibly superstitious people so profusely supplied with patent medicines (the medical advice to take them being wrapped round the bottle and thrown in for nothing) that homeopathy has become a way of rehabilitating the trade of prescription compounding, and is consequently coming into professional credit. At which point the theory of opsonins comes very opportunely to shake hands with it.

Add to the newly triumphant homeopathist and the opsonist that other remarkable innovator, the Swedish masseur, who does not theorize about you, but probes you all over with his powerful thumbs until he finds out your sore spots and rubs them away, besides cheating you into a little wholesome exercise; and you have nearly everything in medical practice to-day that is not flat witchcraft or pure commercial exploitation of human credulity and fear of death. Add to them a good deal of vegetarian and teetotal controversy raging round a clamor for scientific eating and drinking, and resulting in little so far except calling digestion Metabolism and dividing the public between the eminent doctor who tells us that we do not eat enough fish, and his equally eminent colleague who warns us that a fish diet must end in leprosy, and you have all that opposes with any sort of countenance the rise of Christian Science with its cathedrals and congregations and zealots and miracles and cures: all very silly, no doubt, but sane and sensible, poetic and hopeful, compared to the pseudo science of the commercial general practitioner, who foolishly clamors for the prosecution and even the execution of the Christian Scientists when their patients die, forgetting the long death roll of his own patients.

By the time this preface is in print the kaleidoscope may have had another shake; and opsonin may have gone the way of phlogiston at the hands of its own restless discoverer. I will not say that Hahnemann may have gone the way of Diafoirus; for Diafoirus we have always with us. But we shall still pick up all our knowledge in pursuit of some Will o' the Wisp or other. What is called science has always pursued the Elixir of Life and the Philosopher's Stone, and is just as busy after them to-day as ever it was in the days of Paracelsus. We call them by different names: Immunization or Radiology or what not; but the dreams which lure us into the adventures from which we learn are always at bottom the same. Science becomes dangerous only when it imagines that it has reached its goal. What is wrong with priests and popes is that instead of being apostles and saints, they are nothing but empirics who say "I know" instead of "I am learning," and pray for credulity and inertia as wise men pray for scepticism and activity. Such abominations as the Inquisition and the Vaccination Acts are possible only in the famine years of the soul, when the great vital dogmas of honor, liberty, courage, the kinship of all life, faith that the unknown is greater than the known and is only the As Yet Unknown, and resolution to find a manly highway to it, have been forgotten in a paroxysm of littleness and terror in which nothing is active except concupiscence and the fear of death, playing on which any trader can filch a fortune, any blackguard gratify his cruelty, and any tyrant make us his slaves.

Lest this should seem too rhetorical a conclusion for our professional men of science, who are mostly trained not to believe anything unless it is worded in the jargon of those writers who, because they never really understand what they are trying to say, cannot find familiar words for it, and are therefore compelled to invent a new language of nonsense for every book they write, let me sum up my conclusions as dryly as is consistent with accurate thought and live conviction.

1. Nothing is more dangerous than a poor doctor: not even a poor employer or a poor landlord.

2. Of all the anti-social vested interests the worst is the vested interest in ill-health.

3. Remember that an illness is a misdemeanor; and treat the doctor as an accessory unless he notifies every case to the Public Health authority.

4. Treat every death as a possible and under our present system a probable murder, by making it the subject of a reasonably conducted inquest; and execute the doctor, if necessary, *as* a doctor, by striking him off the register.

5. Make up your mind how many doctors the community needs to keep it well. Do not register more or less than this number; and let registration constitute the doctor a civil servant with a dignified living wage paid out of public funds.

6. Municipalize Harley Street.

7. Treat the private operator exactly as you would treat a private executioner.

8. Treat persons who profess to be able to cure disease as you treat fortune tellers.

9. Keep the public carefully informed, by special statistics and announcements of individual cases, of all illnesses of doctors or in their families.

10. Make it compulsory for a doctor using a brass plate to have inscribed on it, in addition to the letters indicating his qualifications, the words "Remember that I too am mortal."

11. In legislation and social organization, proceed on the principle that invalids, meaning persons who cannot keep themselves alive by their own activities, cannot, beyond reason, expect to be kept alive by the activity of others. There is

a point at which the most energetic policeman or doctor, when called upon to deal with an apparently drowned person, gives up artificial respiration, although it is never possible to declare with certainty, at any point short of decomposition, that another five minutes of the exercise would not effect resuscitation. The theory that every individual alive is of infinite value is legislatively impracticable. No doubt the higher the life we secure to the individual by wise social organization, the greater his value is to the community, and the more pains we shall take to pull him through any temporary danger or disablement. But the man who costs more than he is worth is doomed by sound hygiene as inexorably as by sound economics.

12. Do not try to live for ever. You will not succeed.

13. Use your health, even to the point of wearing it out. That is what it is for. Spend all you have before you die; and do not outlive yourself.

14. Take the utmost care to get well born and well brought up. This means that your mother must have a good doctor. Be careful to go to a school where there is what they call a school clinic, where your nutrition and teeth and eyesight and other matters of importance to you will be attended to. Be particularly careful to have all this done at the expense of the nation, as otherwise it will not be done at all, the chances being about forty to one against your being able to pay for it directly yourself, even if you know how to set about it. Otherwise you will be what most people are at present: an unsound citizen of an unsound nation, without sense enough to be ashamed or unhappy about it.

* * *

I am grateful to Hesba Stretton, the authoress of "Jessica's First Prayer," for permission to use the title of one of her stories for this play.

ACT I

On the 15th June 1903, in the early forenoon, a medical student, surname Redpenny, Christian name unknown and of no importance, sits at work in a doctor's consulting-room. He devils for the doctor by answering his letters, acting as his domestic laboratory assistant, and making himself indispensable generally, in return for unspecified advantages involved by intimate intercourse with a leader of his profession, and amounting to an informal apprenticeship and a temporary affiliation. Redpenny is not proud, and will do anything he is asked without reservation of his personal dignity if he is asked in a fellow-creaturely way. He is a wide-open-eyed, ready, credulous, friendly, hasty youth, with his hair and clothes in reluctant transition from the untidy boy to the tidy doctor.

Redpenny is interrupted by the entrance of an old serving-woman who has never known the cares, the preoccupations, the responsibilities, jealousies, and anxieties of personal beauty. She has the complexion of a never-washed gypsy, incurable by any detergent; and she has, not a regular beard and moustaches, which could at least be trimmed and waxed into a masculine presentableness, but a whole crop of small beards and moustaches, mostly springing from moles all over her face. She carries a duster and toddles about meddlesomely, spying out dust so diligently that whilst she is flicking off one speck she is already looking elsewhere for another. In con-

versation she has the same trick, hardly ever looking at the person she is addressing except when she is excited. She has only one manner, and that is the manner of an old family nurse to a child just after it has learnt to walk. She has used her ugliness to secure indulgences unattainable by Cleopatra or Fair Rosamund, and has the further great advantage over them that age increases her qualification instead of impairing it. Being an industrious, agreeable, and popular old soul, she is a walking sermon on the vanity of feminine prettiness. Just as Redpenny has no discovered Christian name, she has no discovered surname, and is known throughout the doctors' quarter between Cavendish Square and the Marylebone Road simply as Emmy.

The consulting-room has two windows looking on Queen Anne Street. Between the two is a marble-topped console, with haunched gilt legs ending in sphinx claws. The huge pier-glass which surmounts it is mostly disabled from reflection by elaborate painting on its surface of palms, ferns, lilies, tulips, and sunflowers. The adjoining wall contains the fireplace, with two arm-chairs before it. As we happen to face the corner we see nothing of the other two walls. On the right of the fireplace, or rather on the right of any person facing the fireplace, is the door. On its left is the writing-table at which Redpenny sits. It is an untidy table with a microscope, several test tubes, and a spirit lamp standing up through its litter of papers. There is a couch in the middle of the room, at right angles to the console, and parallel to the fireplace. A chair stands between the couch and the windowed wall. The windows have green Venetian blinds and rep curtains; and there is a gasalier; but it is a convert to electric lighting. The wall paper and carpets are mostly green, coeval with the gasalier and the Venetian blinds. The house, in fact, was so well furnished in the middle of the century that it stands unaltered to this day and is still quite presentable.

EMMY (*entering and immediately beginning to dust the couch*). Theres a lady bothering me to see the doctor.

REDPENNY (*distracted by the interruption*). Well, she cant see the doctor. Look here: whats the use of telling you that the doctor cant take any new patients, when the moment a knock comes to the door, in you bounce to ask whether he can see somebody?

EMMY. Who asked you whether he could see somebody?

REDPENNY. You did.

EMMY. I said theres a lady bothering me to see the doctor. That isnt asking. It's telling.

REDPENNY. Well, is the lady bothering you any reason for you to come bothering me when I'm busy?

EMMY. Have you seen the papers?

REDPENNY. No.

EMMY. Not seen the birthday honors?

REDPENNY (*beginning to swear*). What the—

EMMY. Now, now, ducky!

REDPENNY. What do you suppose I care about the birthday honors? Get out of this with your chattering. Dr. Ridgeon will be down before I have these letters ready. Get out.

EMMY. Dr. Ridgeon wont never be down any more, young man.

She detects dust on the console and is down on it immediately.

REDPENNY (*jumping up and following her*). What?

EMMY. He's been made a knight. Mind you dont go Dr. Ridgeoning him in them letters. Sir Colenso Ridgeon is to be his name now.

REDPENNY. I'm jolly glad.

EMMY. I never was so taken aback. I always thought his great discoveries was fudge (let alone the mess of them) with his drops of blood and tubes full of Maltese fever and the like. Now he'll have a rare laugh at me.

REDPENNY. Serve you right! It was like your cheek to talk to him about science. (*He returns to his table and resumes his writing.*)

EMMY. Oh, I dont think much of science; and neither will you when youve lived as long with it as I have. Whats on my mind is answering the door. Old Sir Patrick Cullen has been here already and left first congratulations—hadnt time to come up on his way to the hospital, but was determined to be first—coming back, he said. All the rest will be here too: the knocker will be going all day. What I'm afraid of is that the doctor'll want a footman like all the rest, now that he's Sir

Colenso. Mind: dont you go putting him up to it, ducky; for he'll never have any comfort with anybody but me to answer the door. I know who to let in and who to keep out. And that reminds me of the poor lady. I think he ought to see her. She's just the kind that puts him in a good temper. (*She dusts Redpenny's papers.*)

REDPENNY. I tell you he cant see anybody. Do go away, Emmy. How can I work with you dusting all over me like this?

EMMY. I'm not hindering you working—if you call writing letters working. There goes the bell. (*She looks out of the window.*) A doctor's carriage. Thats more congratulations. (*She is going out when Sir Colenso Ridgeon enters.*) Have you finished your two eggs, sonny?

RIDGEON. Yes.

EMMY. Have you put on your clean vest?

RIDGEON. Yes.

EMMY. Thats my ducky diamond! Now keep yourself tidy and dont go messing about and dirtying your hands: the people are coming to congratulate you. (*She goes out.*)

Sir Colenso Ridgeon is a man of fifty who has never shaken off his youth. He has the off-handed manner and the little audacities of address which a shy and sensitive man acquires in breaking himself in to intercourse with all sorts and conditions of men. His face is a good deal lined; his movements are slower than, for instance, Redpenny's; and his flaxen hair has lost its lustre; but in figure and manner he is more the young man than the titled physician. Even the lines in his face are those of overwork and restless scepticism, perhaps partly of curiosity and appetite, rather than of age. Just at present the announcement of his knighthood in the morning papers makes him specially self-conscious, and consequently specially off-hand with Redpenny.

RIDGEON. Have you seen the papers? Youll have to alter the name in the letters if you havnt.

REDPENNY. Emmy has just told me. I'm awfully glad. I—

RIDGEON. Enough, young man, enough. You will soon get accustomed to it.

REDPENNY. They ought to have done it years ago.

RIDGEON. They would have; only they couldnt stand Emmy opening the door, I daresay.

EMMY (*at the door, announcing*). Dr. Shoemaker. (*She withdraws.*)

A middle-aged gentleman, well dressed, comes in with a friendly but propitiatory air, not quite sure of his reception. His combination of soft manners and responsive kindliness, with a certain unseizable reserve and a familiar yet foreign chiselling of feature, reveal the Jew: in this instance the handsome gentlemanly Jew, gone a little pigeon-breasted and stale after thirty, as handsome young Jews often do, but still decidedly good-looking.

THE GENTLEMAN. Do you remember me? Schutzmacher. University College school and Belsize Avenue. Loony Schutzmacher, you know.

RIDGEON. What! Loony! (*He shakes hands cordially.*) Why, man, I thought you were dead long ago. Sit down. (*Schutzmacher sits on the couch: Ridgeon on the chair between it and the window.*) Where have you been these thirty years?

SCHUTZMACHER. In general practice, until a few months ago. I've retired.

RIDGEON. Well done, Loony! I wish *I* could afford to retire. Was your practice in London?

SCHUTZMACHER. No.

RIDGEON. Fashionable coast practice, I suppose.

SCHUTZMACHER. How could I afford to buy a fashionable practice? I hadnt a rap. I set up in a manufacturing town in the midlands in a little surgery at ten shillings a week.

RIDGEON. And made your fortune?

SCHUTZMACHER. Well, I'm pretty comfortable. I have a place in Hertfordshire besides our flat in town. If you ever want a quiet Saturday to Monday, I'll take you down in my motor at an hour's notice.

RIDGEON. Just rolling in money! I wish you rich g.p.'s would teach me how to make some. Whats the secret of it?

SCHUTZMACHER. Oh, in my case the secret was simple enough, though I suppose I should have got into trouble if it had attracted any notice. And I'm afraid you'll think it rather infra dig.

RIDGEON. Oh, I have an open mind. What was the secret?

SCHUTZMACHER. Well, the secret was just two words.

RIDGEON. Not Consultation Free, was it?

SCHUTZMACHER (*shocked*). No, no. Really!

RIDGEON (*apologetic*). Of course not. I was only joking.

SCHUTZMACHER. My two words were simply Cure Guaranteed.

RIDGEON (*admiring*). Cure Guaranteed!

SCHUTZMACHER. Guaranteed. After all, thats what everybody wants from a doctor, isn't it?

RIDGEON. My dear Loony, it was an inspiration. Was it on the brass plate?

SCHUTZMACHER. There was no brass plate. It was a shop window: red, you know, with black lettering. Doctor Leo Schutzmacher, L.R.C.P.M.R.C.S. Advice and medicine sixpence. Cure Guaranteed.

RIDGEON. And the guarantee proved sound nine times out of ten, eh?

SCHUTZMACHER (*rather hurt at so moderate an estimate*). Oh, much oftener than that. You see, most people get well all right if they are careful and you give them a little sensible advice. And the medicine really did them good. Parrish's Chemical Food: phosphates, you know. One tablespoonful to a twelve-ounce bottle of water: nothing better, no matter what the case is.

RIDGEON. Redpenny: make a note of Parrish's Chemical Food.

SCHUTZMACHER. I take it myself, you know, when I feel run down. Good-bye. You dont mind my calling, do you? Just to congratulate you.

RIDGEON. Delighted, my dear Loony. Come to lunch on Saturday next week. Bring your motor and take me down to Hertford.

SCHUTZMACHER. I will. We shall be delighted. Thank you. Good-bye. (*He goes out with Ridgeon, who returns immediately.*)

REDPENNY. Old Paddy Cullen was here before you were up, to be the first to congratulate you.

RIDGEON. Indeed. Who taught you to speak of Sir Patrick Cullen as old Paddy Cullen, you young ruffian?

REDPENNY. You never call him anything else.

RIDGEON. Not now that I am Sir Colenso. Next thing, you fellows will be calling me old Colly Ridgeon.

REDPENNY. We do, at St. Anne's.

RIDGEON. Yach! Thats what makes the medical student the most disgusting figure in modern civilization. No veneration, no manners—no—

EMMY (*at the door, announcing*). Sir Patrick Cullen. (*She retires.*)

Sir Patrick Cullen is more than twenty years older than Ridgeon, not yet quite at the end of his tether, but near it and resigned to it. His name, his plain, downright, sometimes rather arid common sense, his large build and stature, the absence of those odd moments of ceremonial servility by which an old English doctor sometimes shews you what the status of the profession was in England in his youth, and an occasional turn of speech, are Irish; but he has lived all his life in England and is thoroughly acclimatized. His manner to Ridgeon, whom he likes, is whimsical and fatherly: to others he is a little gruff and uninviting, apt to substitute more or less expressive grunts for articulate speech, and generally indisposed, at his age, to make much social effort. He shakes Ridgeon's hand and beams at him cordially and jocularly.

SIR PATRICK. Well, young chap. Is your hat too small for you, eh?

RIDGEON. Much too small. I owe it all to you.

SIR PATRICK. Blarney, my boy. Thank you all the same. (*He sits in one of the arm-chairs near the fireplace. Ridgeon sits on the couch.*) Ive come to talk to you a bit. (*To Redpenny*) Young man: get out.

REDPENNY. Certainly, Sir Patrick. (*He collects his papers and makes for the door.*)

SIR PATRICK. Thank you. Thats a good lad. (*Redpenny vanishes.*) They all put up with me, these young chaps, because I'm an old man, a real old man, not like you. Youre only beginning to give yourself the airs of age. Did you ever see a boy cultivating a moustache? Well, a middle-aged doctor cultivating a grey head is much the same sort of spectacle.

RIDGEON. Good Lord! yes: I suppose so. And I thought that

the days of my vanity were past. Tell me: at what age does a man leave off being a fool?

SIR PATRICK. Remember the Frenchman who asked his grandmother at what age we get free from the temptations of love. The old woman said she didn't know. (*Ridgeon laughs.*) Well, I make you the same answer. But the world's growing very interesting to me now, Colly.

RIDGEON. You keep up your interest in science, do you?

SIR PATRICK. Lord! yes. Modern science is a wonderful thing. Look at your great discovery! Look at all the great discoveries! Where are they leading to? Why, right back to my poor dear old father's ideas and discoveries. He's been dead now over forty years. Oh, it's very interesting.

RIDGEON. Well, theres nothing like progress, is there?

SIR PATRICK. Dont misunderstand me, my boy. I'm not belittling your discovery. Most discoveries are made regularly every fifteen years; and it's fully a hundred and fifty since yours was made last. That's something to be proud of. But your discovery's not new. It's only inoculation. My father practised inoculation until it was made criminal in eighteen-forty. That broke the poor old man's heart, Colly: he died of it. And now it turns out that my father was right after all. Youve brought us back to inoculation.

RIDGEON. I know nothing about smallpox. My line is tuberculosis and typhoid and plague. But of course the principle of all vaccines is the same.

SIR PATRICK. Tuberculosis? M-m-m-m! You've found out how to cure consumption, eh?

RIDGEON. I believe so.

SIR PATRICK. Ah yes. It's very interesting. What is it the old cardinal says in Browning's play? "I have known four and twenty leaders of revolt." Well, I've known over thirty men and found out how to cure consumption. Why do people go on dying of it, Colly? Devilment, I suppose. There was my father's old friend George Boddington of Sutton Coldfield. He discovered the open-air cure in eighteen-forty. He was ruined and driven out of his practice for only opening the windows; and now we wont let a consumptive patient have as much as a roof over his head. Oh, it's very v e r y interesting to an old man.

RIDGEON. You old cynic, you dont believe a bit in my discovery.

SIR PATRICK. No, no: I dont go quite so far as that, Colly. But still, you remember Jane Marsh?

RIDGEON. Jane Marsh? No.

SIR PATRICK. You dont!

RIDGEON. No.

SIR PATRICK. You mean to tell me you dont remember the woman with the tuberculous ulcer on her arm?

RIDGEON (*enlightened*). Oh, your washerwoman's daughter. Was her name Jane Marsh? I forgot.

SIR PATRICK. Perhaps youve forgotten also that you undertook to cure her with Koch's tuberculin.

RIDGEON. And instead of curing her, it rotted her arm right off. Yes: I remember. Poor Jane! However, she makes a good living out of that arm now by shewing it at medical lectures.

SIR PATRICK. Still, that wasnt quite what you intended, was it?

RIDGEON. I took my chance of it.

SIR PATRICK. Jane did, you mean.

RIDGEON. Well, it's always the patient who has to take the chance when an experiment is necessary. And we can find out nothing without experiment.

SIR PATRICK. What did you find out from Jane's case?

RIDGEON. I found out that the inoculation that ought to cure sometimes kills.

SIR PATRICK. I could have told you that. Ive tried these modern inoculations a bit myself. Ive killed people with them; and Ive cured people with them; but I gave them up because I never could tell which I was going to do.

RIDGEON (*taking a pamphlet from a drawer in the writing-table and handing it to him*). Read that the next time you have an hour to spare; and youll find out why.

SIR PATRICK (*grumbling and fumbling for his spectacles*). Oh, bother your pamphlets. Whats the practice of it? (*Looking at the pamphlet*) Opsonin? What the devil is opsonin?

RIDGEON. Opsonin is what you butter the disease germs with to make your white blood corpuscles eat them. (*He sits down again on the couch.*)

SIR PATRICK. Thats not new. Ive heard this notion that the

white corpuscles—what is it that whats his name?—Metchnikoff—calls them?

RIDGEON. Phagocytes.

SIR PATRICK. Aye, phagocytes: yes, yes, yes. Well, I heard this theory that the phagocytes eat up the disease germs years ago: long before you came into fashion. Besides, they dont always eat them.

RIDGEON. They do when you butter them with opsonin.

SIR PATRICK. Gammon.

RIDGEON. No: it's not gammon. What it comes to in practice is this. The phagocytes wont eat the microbes unless the microbes are nicely buttered for them. Well, the patient manufactures the butter for himself all right; but my discovery is that the manufacture of that butter, which I call opsonin, goes on in the system by ups and downs—Nature being always rhythmical, you know—and that what the inoculation does is to stimulate the ups or downs, as the case may be. If we had inoculated Jane Marsh when her butter factory was on the up-grade, we should have cured her arm. But we got in on the down-grade and lost her arm for her. I call the up-grade the positive phase and the down-grade the negative phase. Everything depends on your inoculating at the right moment. Inoculate when the patient is in the negative phase and you kill: inoculate when the patient is in the positive phase and you cure.

SIR PATRICK. And pray how are you to know whether the patient is in the positive or the negative phase?

RIDGEON. Send a drop of the patient's blood to the laboratory at St. Anne's; and in fifteen minutes I'll give you his opsonin index in figures. If the figure is one, inoculate and cure: if it's under point eight, inoculate and kill. Thats my discovery: the most important that has been made since Harvey discovered the circulation of the blood. My tuberculosis patients dont die now.

SIR PATRICK. And mine do when my inoculation catches them in the negative phase, as you call it. Eh?

RIDGEON. Precisely. To inject a vaccine into a patient without first testing his opsonin is as near murder as a respectable practitioner can get. If I wanted to kill a man I should kill him that way.

EMMY (*looking in*). Will you see a lady that wants her husband's lungs cured?

RIDGEON (*impatiently*). No. Havnt I told you I will see nobody? (*To Sir Patrick*) I live in a state of siege ever since it got about that I'm a magician who can cure consumption with a drop of serum. (*To Emmy*) Dont come to me again about people who have no appointments. I tell you I can see nobody.

EMMY. Well, I'll tell her to wait a bit.

RIDGEON (*furious*). Youll tell her I cant see her, and send her away: do you hear?

EMMY (*unmoved*). Well, will you see Mr. Cutler Walpole? He dont want a cure: he only wants to congratulate you.

RIDGEON. Of course. Shew him up. (*She turns to go.*) Stop. (*To Sir Patrick*) I want two minutes more with you between ourselves. (*To Emmy*) Emmy: ask Mr. Walpole to wait just two minutes, while I finish a consultation.

EMMY. Oh, h e' l l wait all right. He's talking to the poor lady. (*She goes out.*)

SIR PATRICK. Well? what is it?

RIDGEON. Dont laugh at me. I want your advice.

SIR PATRICK. Professional advice?

RIDGEON. Yes. Theres something the matter with me. I dont know what it is.

SIR PATRICK. Neither do I. I suppose youve been sounded.

RIDGEON. Yes, of course. Theres nothing wrong with any of the organs: nothing special, anyhow. But I have a curious aching: I dont know where: I cant localize it. Sometimes I think it's my heart: sometimes I suspect my spine. It doesn't exactly hurt me; but it unsettles me completely. I feel that something is going to happen. And there are other symptoms. Scraps of tunes come into my head that seem to me very pretty, though theyre quite commonplace.

SIR PATRICK. Do you hear voices?

RIDGEON. No.

SIR PATRICK. I'm glad of that. When my patients tell me that theyve made a greater discovery than Harvey, and that they hear voices, I lock them up.

RIDGEON. You think I'm mad! Thats just the suspicion that

has come across me once or twice. Tell me the truth: I can bear it.

SIR PATRICK. Youre sure there are no voices?

RIDGEON. Quite sure.

SIR PATRICK. Then it's only foolishness.

RIDGEON. Have you ever met anything like it before in your practice?

SIR PATRICK. Oh, yes: often. It's very common between the ages of seventeen and twenty-two. It sometimes comes on again at forty or thereabouts. Youre a bachelor, you see. It's not serious—if youre careful.

RIDGEON. About my food?

SIR PATRICK. No: about your behavior. Theres nothing wrong with your spine; and theres nothing wrong with your heart; but theres something wrong with your common sense. Youre not going to die; but you may be going to make a fool of yourself. So be careful.

RIDGEON. I see you dont believe in my discovery. Well, sometimes I dont believe in it myself. Thank you all the same. Shall we have Walpole up?

SIR PATRICK. Oh, have him up. (*Ridgeon rings.*) He's a clever operator, is Walpole, though he's only one of your chloroform surgeons. In my early days, you made your man drunk; and the porters and the students held him down; and you had to set your teeth and finish the job fast. Nowadays you work at your ease; and the pain doesn't come until afterwards, when youve taken your cheque and rolled up your bag and left the house. I tell you, Colly, chloroform has done a lot of mischief. It's enabled every fool to be a surgeon.

RIDGEON (*To Emmy, who answers the bell*). Shew Mr. Walpole up.

EMMY. He's talking to the lady.

RIDGEON (*exasperated*). Did I not tell you—

Emmy goes out without heeding him. He gives it up, with a shrug, and plants himself with his back to the console, leaning resignedly against it.

SIR PATRICK. I know your Cutler Walpoles and their like. Theyve found out that a man's body's full of bits and scraps of old organs he has no mortal use for. Thanks to chloroform, you can cut half a dozen of them out without leaving him any the worse, except for the illness and the guineas it costs him. I knew the Walpoles well fifteen years ago. The father used to snip off the ends of people's uvulas for fifty guineas, and paint throats with caustic every day for a year at two guineas a time. His brother-in-law extirpated tonsils for two hundred guineas until he took up women's cases at double the fees. Cutler himself worked hard at anatomy to find something fresh to operate on; and at last he got hold of something he calls the nuciform sac, which he's made quite the fashion. People pay him five hundred guineas to cut it out. They might as well get their hair cut for all the difference it makes; but I suppose they feel important after it. You cant go out to dinner now without your neighbor bragging to you of some useless operation or other.

EMMY (*announcing*). Mr. Cutler Walpole. (*She goes out.*)

Cutler Walpole is an energetic, unhesitating man of forty, with a cleanly modelled face, very decisive and symmetrical about the shortish, salient, rather pretty nose, and the three trimly turned corners made by his chin and jaws. In comparison with Ridgeon's delicate broken lines, and Sir Patrick's softly rugged aged ones, his face looks machine-made and beeswaxed; but his scrutinizing, daring eyes give it life and force. He seems never at a loss, never in doubt: one feels that if he made a mistake he would make it thoroughly and firmly. He has neat, well-nourished hands, short arms, and is built for strength and compactness rather than for height. He is smartly dressed with a fancy waistcoat, a richly colored scarf secured by a handsome ring, ornaments on his watch chain, spats on his shoes, and a general air of the well-to-do sportsman about him. He goes straight across to Ridgeon and shakes hands with him.

WALPOLE. My dear Ridgeon, best wishes! heartiest congratulations! You deserve it.

RIDGEON. Thank you.

WALPOLE. As a man, mind you. You deserve it as a man. The opsonin is simple rot, as any capable surgeon can tell you; but we're all delighted to see your personal qualities officially recognized. Sir Patrick: how are you? I sent you a paper lately about a little thing I invented: a new saw. For shoulder blades.

SIR PATRICK (*meditatively*). Yes: I got it. It's a good saw: a useful, handy instrument.

WALPOLE (*confidently*). I knew youd see its points.

SIR PATRICK. Yes: I remember that saw sixty-five years ago.

WALPOLE. What!

SIR PATRICK. It was called a cabinetmaker's jimmy then.

WALPOLE. Get out! Nonsense! Cabinetmaker be—

RIDGEON. Never mind him, Walpole. He's jealous.

WALPOLE. By the way, I hope I'm not disturbing you two in anything private.

RIDGEON. No no. Sit down. I was only consulting him. I'm rather out of sorts. Overwork, I suppose.

WALPOLE (*swiftly*). I know whats the matter with you. I can see it in your complexion. I can feel it in the grip of your hand.

RIDGEON. What is it?

WALPOLE. Blood-poisoning.

RIDGEON. Blood-poisoning! Impossible.

WALPOLE. I tell you, blood-poisoning. Ninety-five per cent of the human race suffer from chronic blood-poisoning, and die of it. It's as simple as A.B.C. Your nuciform sac is full of decaying matter—undigested food and waste products—rank ptomaines. Now you take my advice, Ridgeon. Let me cut it out for you. You'll be another man afterwards.

SIR PATRICK. Dont you like him as he is?

WALPOLE. No I dont. I dont like any man who hasnt a healthy circulation. I tell you this: in an intelligently governed country people wouldnt be allowed to go about with nuciform sacs, making themselves centres of infection. The operation ought to be compulsory: it's ten times more important than vaccination.

SIR PATRICK. Have you had your own sac removed, may I ask?

WALPOLE (*triumphantly*). I havnt got one. Look at me! Ive no symptoms. I'm as sound as a bell. About five per cent of the population havnt got any; and I'm one of the five per cent. I'll give you an instance. You know Mrs. Jack Foljambe: the smart Mrs. Foljambe? I operated at Easter on her sister-in-law, Lady Gorran, and found she had the biggest sac I ever saw: it held about two ounces. Well, Mrs Foljambe had the right spirit—the genuine hygienic instinct. She couldnt stand her sister-in-law being a clean, sound woman, and she simply a whited sepulchre. So she insisted on my operating on her, too. And by George, sir, she hadnt any sac at all. Not a trace! Not a rudiment! I was so taken aback—so interested, that I forgot to take the sponges out, and was stitching them up inside her when the nurse missed them. Somehow, I'd made sure she'd have an exceptionally large one. (*He sits down on the couch, squaring his shoulders and shooting his hands out of his cuffs as he sets his knuckles akimbo.*)

EMMY (*looking in*). Sir Ralph Bloomfield Bonington.

A long and expectant pause follows this announcement. All look to the door; but there is no Sir Ralph.

RIDGEON (*at last*). Where is he?

EMMY (*looking back*). Drat him, I thought he was following me. He's stayed down to talk to that lady.

RIDGEON (*exploding*). I told you to tell that lady—(EMMY *vanishes.*)

WALPOLE (*jumping up again*). Oh, by the way, Ridgeon, that reminds me. Ive been talking to that poor girl. It's her husband; and she thinks it's a case of consumption: the usual wrong diagnosis: these damned general practitioners ought never to be allowed to touch a patient except under the orders of a consultant. She's been describing his symptoms to me; and the case is as plain as a pikestaff: bad blood-poisoning. Now she's poor. She cant afford to have him operated on. Well, you send him to me: I'll do it for nothing. Theres room for him in my nursing home. I'll put him straight, and feed him up and make her happy. I like making people happy. (*He goes to the chair near the window.*)

EMMY (*looking in*). Here he is.

Sir Ralph Bloomfield Bonington wafts himself into the room. He is a tall man, with a head like a tall and slender egg. He has been in his time a slender man; but now, in his sixth decade, his waistcoat has filled out somewhat. His fair eyebrows arch good-naturedly and uncritically. He has a most musical voice; his speech is a perpetual anthem; and he never tires of the sound of it. He radiates an enormous self-satisfaction, cheering, reassuring, healing by the mere incompatibility of disease or anxiety with his welcome presence.

Even broken bones, it is said, have been known to unite at the sound of his voice: he is a born healer, as independent of mere treatment and skill as any Christian Scientist. When he expands into oratory or scientific exposition, he is as energetic as Walpole; but it is with a bland, voluminous, atmospheric energy, which envelops its subject and its audience, and makes interruption or inattention impossible, and imposes veneration and credulity on all but the strongest minds. He is known in the medical world as B.B.; and the envy aroused by his success in practice is softened by the conviction that he is, scientifically considered, a colossal humbug: the fact being that, though he knows just as much (and just as little) as his contemporaries, the qualifications that pass muster in common men reveal their weakness when hung on his egregious personality.

B.B. Aha! Sir Colenso. S i r Colenso, eh? Welcome to the order of knighthood.

RIDGEON (*shaking hands*). Thank you, B.B.

B.B. What! Sir Patrick! And how are we to-day? a little chilly? a little stiff? but hale and still the cleverest of us all. (*Sir Patrick grunts.*) What! Walpole! the absent-minded beggar: eh?

WALPOLE. What does that mean?

B.B. Have you forgotten the lovely opera singer I sent you to have that growth taken off her vocal cords?

WALPOLE (*springing to his feet*). Great heavens, man, you dont mean to say you sent her for a throat operation!

B.B. (*archly*). Aha! Ha ha! Aha! (*trilling like a lark as he shakes his finger at Walpole*) You removed her nuciform sac. Well, well! force of habit! force of habit! Never mind, ne-e-ever mind. She got back her voice after it, and thinks you the greatest surgeon alive; and so you are, so you are, so you are.

WALPOLE (*in a tragic whisper, intensely serious*). Blood-poisoning. I see. I see. (*He sits down again.*)

SIR PATRICK. And how is a certain distinguished family getting on under your care, Sir Ralph?

B.B. Our friend Ridgeon will be gratified to hear that I have tried his opsonin treatment on little Prince Henry with complete success.

RIDGEON (*startled and anxious*). But how—

B.B. (*continuing*). I suspected typhoid: the head gardener's boy had it; so I just called at St. Anne's one day and got a tube of your very excellent serum. You were out, unfortunately.

RIDGEON. I hope they explained to you carefully—

B.B. (*waving away the absurd suggestion*). Lord bless you, my dear fellow, I didnt need any explanations. I'd left my wife in the carriage at the door; and I'd no time to be taught my business by your young chaps. I know all about it. Ive handled these anti-toxins ever since they first came out.

RIDGEON. But theyre not anti-toxins; and theyre dangerous unless you use them at the right time.

B.B. Of course they are. Everything is dangerous unless you take it at the right time. An apple at breakfast does you good: an apple at bedtime upsets you for a week. There are only two rules for anti-toxins. First, dont be afraid of them: second, inject them a quarter of an hour before meals, three times a day.

RIDGEON (*appalled*). Great heavens, B.B., no, no, no.

B.B. (*sweeping on irresistibly*). Yes, yes, yes, Colly. The proof of the pudding is in the eating, you know. It was an immense success. It acted like magic on the little prince. Up went his temperature; off to bed I packed him; and in a week he was all right again, and absolutely immune from typhoid for the rest of his life. The family were very nice about it: their gratitude was quite touching; but I said they owed it all to you, Ridgeon; and I am glad to think that your knighthood is the result.

RIDGEON. I am deeply obliged to you. (*Overcome, he sits down on the chair near the couch.*)

B.B. Not at all, not at all. Your own merit. Come! come! come! dont give way.

RIDGEON. It's nothing. I was a little giddy just now. Overwork, I suppose.

WALPOLE. Blood-poisoning.

B.B. Overwork! Theres no such thing. I do the work of ten men. Am I giddy? No. NO. If youre not well, you have a disease. It may be a slight one; but it's a disease. And what is a disease? The lodgment in the system of a pathogenic germ, and the multiplication of that germ. What is the remedy? A very simple one. Find the germ and kill it.

SIR PATRICK. Suppose theres no germ?

B.B. Impossible, Sir Patrick: there m u s t be a germ: else how could the patient be ill?

SIR PATRICK. Can you shew me the germ of overwork?

B.B. No; but why? Why? Because, my dear Sir Patrick, though the germ is there, it's invisible. Nature has given it no danger signal for us. These germs—these bacilli—are translucent bodies, like glass, like water. To make them visible you must stain them. Well, my dear Paddy, do what you will, some of them wont stain. They wont take cochineal: they wont take methylene blue; they wont take gentian violet: they wont take any coloring matter. Consequently, though we know, as scientific men, that they exist, we cannot see them. But can you disprove their existence? Can you conceive the disease existing without them? Can you, for instance, shew me a case of diphtheria without the bacillus?

SIR PATRICK. No; but I'll shew you the same bacillus, without the disease, in your own throat.

B.B. No, not the same, Sir Patrick. It is an entirely different bacillus; only the two are, unfortunately, so exactly alike that you cannot see the difference. You must understand, my dear Sir Patrick, that every one of these interesting little creatures has an imitator. Just as men imitate each other, germs imitate each other. There is the genuine diphtheria bacillus discovered by Lœffler; and there is the pseudo-bacillus, exactly like it, which you could find, as you say, in my own throat.

SIR PATRICK. And how do you tell one from the other?

B.B. Well, obviously, if the bacillus is the genuine Lœffler, you have diphtheria; and if it's the pseudo-bacillus, youre quite well. Nothing simpler. Science is always simple and always profound. It is only the half-truths that are dangerous. Ignorant faddists pick up some superficial information about germs; and they write to the papers and try to discredit science. They dupe and mislead many honest and worthy people. But science has a perfect answer to them on every point.

A little learning is a dangerous thing;
Drink deep; or taste not the Pierian spring.

I mean no disrespect to your generation, Sir Patrick: some of you old stagers did marvels through sheer professional intuition and clinical experience; but when I think of the average men of your day, ignorantly bleeding and cupping and purging, and scattering germs over their patients from their clothes and instruments, and contrast all that with the scientific certainty and simplicity of my treatment of the little prince the other day, I cant help being proud of my own generation: the men who were trained on the germ theory, the veterans of the great struggle over Evolution in the seventies. We may have our faults; but at least we are men of science. That is why I am taking up your treatment, Ridgeon, and pushing it. It's scientific. (*He sits down on the chair near the couch.*)

EMMY (*at the door, announcing*). Dr. Blenkinsop.

Dr. Blenkinsop is in very different case from the others. He is clearly not a prosperous man. He is flabby and shabby, cheaply fed and cheaply clothed. He has the lines made by a conscience between his eyes, and the lines made by continual money worries all over his face, cut all the deeper as he has seen better days, and hails his well-to-do colleagues as their contemporary and old hospital friend, though even in this he has to struggle with the difference of poverty and relegation to the poorer middle class.

RIDGEON. How are you, Blenkinsop?

BLENKINSOP. Ive come to offer my humble congratulations. Oh dear! all the great guns are before me.

B.B. (*patronizing, but charming*). How d'ye do, Blenkinsop? How d'ye do?

BLENKINSOP. And Sir Patrick, too! (*Sir Patrick grunts.*)

RIDGEON. Youve met Walpole, of course?

WALPOLE. How d'ye do?

BLENKINSOP. It's the first time Ive had that honor. In my poor little practice there are no chances of meeting you great men. I know nobody but the St. Anne's men of my own day. (*To Ridgeon*) And so youre Sir Colenso. How does it feel?

RIDGEON. Foolish at first. Dont take any notice of it.

BLENKINSOP. I'm ashamed to say I havnt a notion what your great discovery is; but I congratulate you all the same for the sake of old times.

B.B. (*shocked*). But, my dear Blenkinsop, you used to be rather keen on science.

BLENKINSOP. Ah, I used to be a lot of things. I used to have two or three decent suits of clothes, and flannels to go up the river on Sundays. Look at me now: this is my best; and it must last till Christmas. What can I do? Ive never opened a book since I was qualified thirty years ago. I used to read the medical papers at first; but you know how soon a man drops that; besides, I cant afford them; and what are they after all but trade papers, full of advertisements? Ive forgotten all my science: whats the use of my pretending I havnt? But I have great experience: clinical experience; and bedside experience is the main thing, isn't it?

B.B. No doubt; always provided, mind you, that you have a sound scientific theory to correlate your observations at the bedside. Mere experience by itself is nothing. If I take my dog to the bedside with me, he sees what I see. But he learns nothing from it. Why? Because he's not a scientific dog.

WALPOLE. It amuses me to hear you physicians and general practitioners talking about clinical experience. What do you see at the bedside but the outside of the patient? Well: it isnt his outside thats wrong, except perhaps in skin cases. What you want is a daily familiarity with people's insides; and that you can only get at the operating table. I know what I'm talking about: Ive been a surgeon and a consultant for twenty years; and Ive never known a general practitioner right in his diagnosis yet. Bring them a perfectly simple case; and they diagnose cancer, and arthritis, and appendicitis, and every other itis, when any really experienced surgeon can see that it's a plain case of blood-poisoning.

BLENKINSOP. Ah, it's easy for you gentlemen to talk; but what would you say if you had my practice? Except for the workmen's clubs, my patients are all clerks and shopmen. They darent be ill: they cant afford it. And when they break down, what can I do for them? Y o u can send your people to St. Moritz or to Egypt, or recommend horse exercise or motoring or champagne jelly or complete change and rest for six months. *I* might as well order my people a slice of the moon. And the worst of it is, I'm too poor to keep well myself on the cooking I have to put up with. Ive such a wretched digestion; and I look it. How am I to inspire confidence? (*He sits disconsolately on the couch.*)

RIDGEON (*restlessly*). Dont, Blenkinsop: it's too painful. The most tragic thing in the world is a sick doctor.

WALPOLE. Yes, by George; it's like a bald-headed man trying to sell a hair restorer. Thank God I'm a surgeon!

B.B. (*sunnily*). I am never sick. Never had a day's illness in my life. Thats what enables me to sympathize with my patients.

WALPOLE (*interested*). What! youre never ill?

B.B. Never.

WALPOLE. Thats interesting. I believe you have no nuciform sac. If you ever do feel at all queer, I should very much like to have a look.

B.B. Thank you, my dear fellow; but I'm too busy just now.

RIDGEON. I was just telling them when you came in, Blenkinsop, that I have worked myself out of sorts.

BLENKINSOP. Well, it seems presumptuous of me to offer a prescription to a great man like you; but still I have great experience; and if I might recommend a pound of ripe greengages every day half an hour before lunch, I'm sure youd find a benefit. Theyre very cheap.

RIDGEON. What do you say to that, B.B.?

B.B. (*encouragingly*). Very sensible, Blenkinsop: very sensible indeed. I'm delighted to see that you disapprove of drugs.

SIR PATRICK (*grunts*)!

B.B. (*archly*). Aha! Haha! Did I hear from the fireside armchair the bow-wow of the old school defending its drugs? Ah, believe me, Paddy, the world would be healthier if every chemist's shop in England were demolished. Look at the papers! full of scandalous advertisements of patent medicines! a huge commercial system of quackery and poison. Well, whose fault is it? Ours. I say, ours. We set the example. We spread the superstition. We taught the people to believe in bottles of doctor's stuff; and now they buy it at the stores instead of consulting a medical man.

WALPOLE. Quite true. Ive not prescribed a drug for the last fifteen years.

B.B. Drugs can only repress symptoms: they cannot eradicate disease. The true remedy for all diseases is Nature's remedy. Nature and Science are at one, Sir Patrick, believe me; though you were taught differently. Nature has provided, in the white corpuscles as you call them—in the phagocytes as we call them—a natural means of devouring and destroying all disease germs. There is at bottom only one genuinely scientific treatment for all diseases, and that is to stimulate the phagocytes. Stimulate the phagocytes. Drugs are a delusion. Find the germ of the disease; prepare from it a suitable anti-toxin; inject it three times a day quarter of an hour before meals; and what is the result? The phagocytes are stimulated; they devour the disease; and the patient recovers—unless, of course, he's too far gone. That, I take it, is the essence of Ridgeon's discovery.

SIR PATRICK (*dreamily*). As I sit here, I seem to hear my poor old father talking again.

B.B. (*rising in incredulous amazement*). Your father! But, Lord bless my soul, Paddy, your father must have been an older man than you.

SIR PATRICK. Word for word almost, he said what you say. No more drugs. Nothing but inoculation.

B.B. (*almost contemptuously*). Inoculation! Do you mean smallpox inoculation?

SIR PATRICK. Yes. In the privacy of our family circle, sir, my father used to declare his belief that smallpox inoculation was good, not only for smallpox, but for all fevers.

B.B. (*suddenly rising to the new idea with immense interest and excitement*). What! Ridgeon: did you hear that? Sir Patrick: I am more struck by what you have just told me than I can well express. Your father, sir, anticipated a discovery of my own. Listen, Walpole. Blenkinsop: attend one moment. You will all be intensely interested in this. I was put on the track by accident. I had a typhoid case and tetanus case side by side in the hospital: a beadle and a city missionary. Think of what that meant for them, poor fellows! Can a beadle be dignified with typhoid? Can a missionary be eloquent with lockjaw? No. NO. Well, I got some typhoid anti-toxin from Ridgeon and a tube of Muldooley's anti-tetanus serum. But the missionary jerked all my things off the table in one of his paroxysms; and in replacing them I put Ridgeon's tube where Muldooley's ought to have been. The consequence was that I inoculated the typhoid case for tetanus and the tetanus case for typhoid. (*The doctors look greatly concerned. B.B., undamped, smiles triumphantly.*) Well, they recovered. THEY RECOVERED. Except for a touch of St. Vitus's dance the missionary's as well to-day as ever; and the beadle's ten times the man he was.

BLENKINSOP. Ive known things like that happen. They cant be explained.

B.B. (*severely*). Blenkinsop: there is n o t h i n g that cannot be explained by science. What did I do? Did I fold my hands helplessly and say that the case could not be explained? By no means. I sat down and used my brains. I thought the case out on scientific principles. I asked myself why didnt the missionary die of typhoid on top of tetanus, and the beadle of tetanus on top of typhoid? Theres a problem for you, Ridgeon. Think, Sir Patrick. Reflect, Blenkinsop. Look at it without prejudice, Walpole. What is the real work of the anti-toxin? Simply to stimulate the phagocytes. Very well. But so long as you stimulate the phagocytes, what does it matter which particular sort of serum you use for the purpose? Haha! Eh? Do you see? Do you grasp it? Ever since that Ive used all sorts of anti-toxins absolutely indiscriminately, with perfectly satisfactory results. I inoculated the little prince with your stuff, Ridgeon, because I wanted to give you a lift; but two years ago I tried the experiment of treating a scarlet fever case with a sample of hydrophobia serum from the Pasteur Institute, and it answered capitally. It stimulated the phagocytes; and the phagocytes did the rest. That is why Sir Patrick's father found that inoculation cured all fevers. It stimulated the phagocytes. (*He throws himself into his chair, exhausted with the triumph of his demonstration, and beams magnificently on them.*)

EMMY (*looking in*). Mr. Walpole: your motor's come for you; and it's frightening Sir Patrick's horses; so come along quick.

WALPOLE (*rising*). Good-bye, Ridgeon.

RIDGEON. Good-bye; and many thanks.

B.B. You see my point, Walpole?

EMMY. He cant wait, Sir Ralph. The carriage will be into the area if he dont come.

WALPOLE. I'm coming. (*To B.B.*) Theres nothing in your point: phagocytosis is pure rot: the cases are all blood-poisoning; and the knife is the real remedy. Bye-bye, Sir Paddy. Happy to have met you, Mr. Blenkinsop. Now, Emmy. (*He goes out, followed by Emmy.*)

B.B. (*sadly*). Walpole has no intellect. A mere surgeon. Wonderful operator; but, after all, what is operating? Only manual labor. Brain—BRAIN remains master of the situation. The nuciform sac is utter nonsense: theres no such organ. It's a mere accidental kink in the membrane, occurring in perhaps two-and-a-half per cent of the population. Of course I'm glad for Walpole's sake that the operation is fashionable; for he's a dear good fellow; and after all, as I always tell people, the operation will do them no harm: indeed, Ive known the nervous shake-up and the fortnight in bed do people a lot of good after a hard London season; but still it's a shocking fraud. (*Rising*) Well, I must be toddling. Good-bye, Paddy (*Sir Patrick grunts.*) good-bye, good-bye. Good-bye, my dear Blenkinsop, good-bye! Good-bye, Ridgeon. Dont fret about your health: you know what to do: if your liver is sluggish, a little mercury never does any harm. If you feel restless, try bromide. If that doesnt answer, a stimulant, you know: a little phosphorus and strychnine. If you cant sleep, trional, trional, trion—

SIR PATRICK (*drily*). But no drugs, Colly, remember that.

B.B. (*firmly*). Certainly not. Quite right, Sir Patrick. As temporary expedients, of course; but as treatment, no, NO. Keep away from the chemist's shop, my dear Ridgeon, whatever you do.

RIDGEON (*going to the door with him*). I will. And thank you for the knighthood. Good-bye.

B.B. (*stopping at the door, with the beam in his eye twinkling a little*). By the way, who's your patient?

RIDGEON. Who?

B.B. Downstairs. Charming woman. Tuberculous husband.

RIDGEON. Is she there still?

EMMY (*looking in*). Come on, Sir Ralph: your wife's waiting in the carriage.

B.B. (*suddenly sobered*). Oh! Good-bye. (*He goes out almost precipitately.*)

RIDGEON. Emmy: is that woman there still? If so, tell her once for all that I cant and wont see her. Do you hear?

EMMY. Oh, she aint in a hurry: she doesnt mind how long she waits. (*She goes out.*)

BLENKINSOP. I must be off, too: every half-hour I spend away from my work costs me eighteenpence. Good-bye, Sir Patrick.

SIR PATRICK. Good-bye. Good-bye.

RIDGEON. Come to lunch with me some day this week.

BLENKINSOP. I cant afford it, dear boy; and it would put me off my own food for a week. Thank you all the same.

RIDGEON (*uneasy at Blenkinsop's poverty*). Can I do nothing for you?

BLENKINSOP. Well, if you have an old frock-coat to spare? you see what would be an old one for you would be a new one for me; so remember the next time you turn out your wardrobe. Good-bye. (*He hurries out.*)

RIDGEON (*looking after him*). Poor chap! (*Turning to Sir Patrick*) So thats why they made me a knight! And thats the medical profession!

SIR PATRICK. And a very good profession, too, my lad. When you know as much as I know of the ignorance and superstition of the patients, youll wonder that we're half as good as we are.

RIDGEON. We're not a profession: we're a conspiracy.

SIR PATRICK. All professions are conspiracies against the laity. And we cant all be geniuses like you. Every fool can get ill; but every fool cant be a good doctor: there are not enough good ones to go round. And for all you know, Bloomfield Bonington kills less people than you do.

RIDGEON. Oh, very likely. But he really ought to know the difference between a vaccine and an anti-toxin. Stimulate the phagocytes! The vaccine doesnt affect the phagocytes at all. He's all wrong: hopelessly, dangerously wrong. To put a tube of serum into his hands is murder: simple murder.

EMMY (*returning*). Now, Sir Patrick. How long more are you going to keep them horses standing in the draught?

SIR PATRICK. Whats that to you, you old catamaran?

EMMY. Come, come, now! none of your temper to me. And it's time for Colly to get to his work.

RIDGEON. Behave yourself, Emmy. Get out.

EMMY. Oh, I learnt how to behave myself before I learnt you to do it. I know what doctors are: sitting talking together about themselves when they ought to be with their poor patients. And I know what horses are, Sir Patrick. I was brought up in the country. Now be good; and come along.

SIR PATRICK (*rising*). Very well, very well, very well. Goodbye, Colly. (*He pats Ridgeon on the shoulder and goes out, turning for a moment at the door to look meditatively at Emmy and say, with grave conviction*) You a r e an ugly old devil, and no mistake.

EMMY (*highly indignant, calling after him*). You're no beauty yourself. (*To Ridgeon, much flustered*) Theyve no manners: they think they can say what they like to me; and you set them on, you do. I'll teach them their places. Here now: are you going to see that poor thing or are you not?

RIDGEON. I tell you for the fiftieth time I wont see anybody. Send her away.

EMMY. Oh, I'm tired of being told to send her away. What good will that do her?

RIDGEON. Must I get angry with you, Emmy?

EMMY (*coaxing*). Come now: just see her for a minute to please me: theres a good boy. She's given me half-a-crown. She thinks it's life and death to her husband for her to see you.

RIDGEON. Values her husband's life at half-a-crown!

EMMY. Well, it's all she can afford, poor lamb. Them others think nothing of half-a-sovereign just to talk about themselves to you, the sluts! Besides, she'll put you in a good temper for the day, because it's a good deed to see her; and she's the sort that gets round you.

RIDGEON. Well, she hasnt done so badly. For half-a-crown she's had a consultation with Sir Ralph Bloomfield Bonington and Cutler Walpole. Thats six guineas' worth to start with. I dare say she's consulted Blenkinsop too: thats another eighteenpence.

EMMY. Then youll see her for me, wont you?

RIDGEON. Oh, send her up and be hanged. (*Emmy trots out, satisfied. Ridgeon calls*) Redpenny!

REDPENNY (*appearing at the door*). What is it?

RIDGEON. Theres a patient coming up. If she hasnt gone in five minutes, come in with an urgent call from the hospital for me. You understand: she's to have a strong hint to go.

REDPENNY. Right O! (*He vanishes.*)

Ridgeon goes to the glass, and arranges his tie a little.

EMMY (*announcing*). Mrs. Doobidad. (*Ridgeon leaves the glass and goes to the writing-table.*)

The lady comes in. Emmy goes out and shuts the door. Ridgeon, who has put on an impenetrable and rather distant professional manner, turns to the lady, and invites her, by a gesture, to sit down on the couch.

Mrs. Dubedat is beyond all demur an arrestingly good-looking young woman. She has something of the grace and romance of a mild creature, with a good deal of the elegance and dignity of a fine lady. Ridgeon, who is extremely susceptible to the beauty of women, instinctively assumes the defensive at once, and hardens his manner still more. He has an impression that she is very well dressed; but she has a figure on which any dress would look well, and carries herself with the unaffected distinction of a woman who has never in her life suffered from those doubts and fears as to her social position which spoil the manners of most middling people. She is tall, slender, and strong; has dark hair, dressed so as to look like hair and not like a bird's nest or a pantaloon's wig (fashion wavering just then between these two models); has unexpectedly narrow, subtle, dark-fringed eyes that alter her expression disturbingly when she is excited and flashes them wide open; is softly impetuous in her speech and swift in her movements; and is just now in mortal anxiety. She carries a portfolio.

MRS. DUBEDAT (*in low urgent tones*). Doctor—

RIDGEON (*curtly*). Wait. Before you begin, let me tell you at once that I can do nothing for you. My hands are full. I sent you that message by my old servant. You would not take that answer.

MRS. DUBEDAT. How could I?

RIDGEON. You bribed her.

MRS. DUBEDAT. I—

RIDGEON. That doesnt matter. She coaxed me to see you.

Well, you must take it from me now that with all the good will in the world, I cannot undertake another case.

MRS. DUBEDAT. Doctor: you must save my husband. You must. When I explain to you, you will see that you must. It is not an ordinary case, not like any other case. He is not like anybody else in the world: oh, believe me, he is not. I can prove it to you: (*fingering her portfolio*) I have brought some things to shew you. And you can save him: the papers say you can.

RIDGEON. Whats the matter? Tuberculosis?

MRS. DUBEDAT. Yes. His left lung—

RIDGEON. Yes: you neednt tell me about that.

MRS. DUBEDAT. You c a n cure him, if only you will. It is true that you can, isnt it? (*In great distress*) Oh, tell me, please.

RIDGEON (*warningly*). You are going to be quiet and self-possessed, arnt you?

MRS. DUBEDAT. Yes. I beg your pardon. I know I shouldnt— (*Giving way again*) Oh, please, say that you c a n; and then I shall be all right.

RIDGEON (*huffily*). I am not a curemonger: if you want cures, you must go to the people who sell them. (*Recovering himself, ashamed of the tone of his own voice*) But I have at the hospital ten tuberculosis patients whose lives I believe I can save.

MRS. DUBEDAT. Thank God!

RIDGEON. Wait a moment. Try to think of those ten patients as ten shipwrecked men on a raft—a raft that is barely large enough to save them—that will not support one more. Another head bobs up through the waves at the side. Another man begs to be taken aboard. He implores the captain of the raft to save him. But the captain can only do that by pushing one of his ten off the raft and drowning him to make room for the new comer. That is what you are asking me to do.

MRS. DUBEDAT. But how can that be? I dont understand. Surely—

RIDGEON. You must take my word for it that it is so. My laboratory, my staff, and myself are working at full pressure. We are doing our utmost. The treatment is a new one. It takes time, means, and skill; and there is not enough for another case. Our ten cases are already chosen cases. Do you understand what I mean by chosen?

MRS. DUBEDAT. Chosen. No: I cant understand.

RIDGEON (*sternly*). You must understand. Youve got to understand and to face it. In every single one of those ten cases I have had to consider, not only whether the man could be saved, but whether he was worth saving. There were fifty cases to choose from; and forty had to be condemned to death. Some of the forty had young wives and helpless children. If the hardness of their cases could have saved them they would have been saved ten times over. Ive no doubt your case is a hard one: I can see the tears in your eyes: (*She hastily wipes her eyes.*) I know that you have a torrent of entreaties ready for me the moment I stop speaking; but it's no use. You must go to another doctor.

MRS. DUBEDAT. But can you give me the name of another doctor who understands your secret?

RIDGEON. I have no secret: I am not a quack.

MRS. DUBEDAT. I beg your pardon: I didnt mean to say anything wrong. I dont understand how to speak to you. Oh, pray dont be offended.

RIDGEON (*again a little ashamed*). There! there! never mind. (*He relaxes and sits down.*) After all, I'm talking nonsense: I daresay I a m a quack, a quack with a qualification. But my discovery is not patented.

MRS. DUBEDAT. Then can any doctor cure my husband? Oh, why dont they do it? I have tried so many: I have spent so much. If only you would give me the name of another doctor.

RIDGEON. Every man in this street is a doctor. But outside myself and the handful of men I am training at St. Anne's, there is nobody as yet who has mastered the opsonin treatment. And we are f u l l up? I'm sorry; but that is all I can say. (*Rising*) Good morning.

MRS. DUBEDAT (*suddenly and desperately taking some drawings from her portfolio*). Doctor: look at these. You understand drawings: you have good ones in your waiting-room. Look at them. They are his work.

RIDGEON. It's no use my looking. (*He looks, all the same.*) Hallo! (*He takes one to the window and studies it.*) Yes: this is the real thing. Yes, yes. (*He looks at another and returns to her.*) These are very clever. Theyre unfinished, arnt they?

MRS. DUBEDAT. He gets tired so soon. But you see, dont you, what a genius he is? You see that he is worth saving. Oh, doctor, I married him just to help him to begin: I had money enough to tide him over the hard years at the beginning—to enable him to follow his inspiration until his genius was recognized. And I was useful to him as a model: his drawings of me sold quite quickly.

RIDGEON. Have you got one?

MRS. DUBEDAT (*producing another*). Only this one. It was the first.

RIDGEON (*devouring it with his eyes*). Thats a wonderful drawing. Why is it called Jennifer?

MRS. DUBEDAT. My name is Jennifer.

RIDGEON. A strange name.

MRS. DUBEDAT. Not in Cornwall. I am Cornish. It's only what you call Guinevere.

RIDGEON (*repeating the names with a certain pleasure in them*). Guinevere. Jennifer. (*Looking again at the drawing*) Yes: it's really a wonderful drawing. Excuse me; but may I ask is it for sale? I'll buy it.

MRS. DUBEDAT. Oh, take it. It's my own: he gave it to me. Take it. Take them all. Take everything; ask anything; but save him. You can: you will: you must.

REDPENNY (*entering with every sign of alarm*). Theyve just telephoned from the hospital that youre to come instantly—a patient on the point of death. The carriage is waiting.

RIDGEON (*intolerantly*). Oh, nonsense: get out. (*annoyed*) What do you mean by interrupting me like this?

REDPENNY. But—

RIDGEON. Chut! cant you see I'm engaged? Be off.

Redpenny, bewildered, vanishes.

MRS. DUBEDAT (*rising*). Doctor: one instant only before you go—

RIDGEON. Sit down. It's nothing.

MRS. DUBEDAT. But the patient. He said he was dying.

RIDGEON. Oh, he's dead by this time. Never mind. Sit down.

MRS. DUBEDAT (*sitting down and breaking down*). Oh, you none of you care. You see people die every day.

RIDGEON (*petting her*). Nonsense! it's nothing: I told him to come in and say that. I thought I should want to get rid of you.

MRS. DUBEDAT (*shocked at the falsehood*). Oh!

RIDGEON (*continuing*). Dont look so bewildered: theres nobody dying.

MRS. DUBEDAT. My husband is.

RIDGEON (*pulling himself together*). Ah, yes: I had forgotten your husband. Mrs. Dubedat: you are asking me to do a very serious thing?

MRS. DUBEDAT. I am asking you to save the life of a great man.

RIDGEON. You are asking me to kill another man for his sake; for as surely as I undertake another case, I shall have to hand back one of the old ones to the ordinary treatment. Well, I dont shrink from that. I have had to do it before; and I will do it again if you can convince me that his life is more important than the worst life I am now saving. But you must convince me first.

MRS. DUBEDAT. He made those drawings; and they are not the best—nothing like the best; only I did not bring the really best: so few people like them. He is twenty-three: his whole life is before him. Wont you let me bring him to you? wont you speak to him? wont you see for yourself?

RIDGEON. Is he well enough to come to a dinner at the Star and Garter at Richmond?

MRS. DUBEDAT. Oh yes. Why?

RIDGEON. I'll tell you. I am inviting all my old friends to a dinner to celebrate my knighthood—youve seen about it in the papers, havnt you?

MRS. DUBEDAT. Yes, oh yes. That was how I found out about you.

RIDGEON. It will be a doctors' dinner; and it was to have been a bachelors' dinner. I'm a bachelor. Now if you will entertain for me, and bring your husband, he will meet me; and he will meet some of the most eminent men in my profession: Sir Patrick Cullen, Sir Ralph Bloomfield Bonington, Cutler Walpole, and others. I can put the case to them; and your husband will have to stand or fall by what we think of him. Will you come?

MRS. DUBEDAT. Yes, of course I will come. Oh, thank you, thank you. And may I bring some of his drawings—the really good ones?

RIDGEON. Yes. I will let you know the date in the course of to-morrow. Leave me your address.

MRS. DUBEDAT. Thank you again and again. You have made me so happy: I know you will admire him and like him. This is my address. (*She gives him her card.*)

RIDGEON. Thank you. (*He rings.*)

MRS. DUBEDAT (*embarrassed*). May I—is there—should I—I mean—(*She blushes and stops in confusion.*)

RIDGEON. Whats the matter?

MRS. DUBEDAT. Your fee for this consultation?

RIDGEON. Oh, I forgot that. Shall we say a beautiful drawing of his favorite model for the whole treatment, including the cure?

MRS. DUBEDAT. You are very generous. Thank you. I know you will cure him. Good-bye.

RIDGEON. I will. Good-bye. (*They shake hands.*) By the way, you know, dont you, that tuberculosis is catching. You take every precaution, I hope.

MRS. DUBEDAT. I am not likely to forget it. They treat us like lepers at the hotels.

EMMY (*at the door*). Well, deary: have you got round him?

RIDGEON. Yes. Attend to the door and hold your tongue.

EMMY. Thats a good boy. (*She goes out with Mrs. Dubedat.*)

RIDGEON (*alone*). Consultation free. Cure guaranteed. (*He heaves a great sigh.*)

END OF ACT I

ACT II

After dinner on the terrace at the Star and Garter, Richmond. Cloudless summer night; nothing disturbs the stillness except from time to time the long trajectory of a distant train and the measured clucking of oars coming up from the Thames in the valley below. The dinner is over; and three of the eight chairs are empty. Sir Patrick, with his back to the view, is at the head of the square table with Ridgeon. The two chairs opposite them are empty. On their right come, first, a vacant chair, and then one very fully occupied by B.B., who basks blissfully in the moonbeams. On their left, Schutzmacher and Walpole. The entrance to the hotel is on their right, behind B.B. The five men are silently enjoying their coffee and cigarets, full of food, and not altogether void of wine.

Mrs. Dubedat, wrapped up for departure, comes in. They rise, except Sir Patrick; but she takes one of the vacant places at the foot of the table, next B.B.; and they sit down again.

MRS. DUBEDAT (*as she enters*). Louis will be here presently. He is shewing Dr. Blenkinsop how to work the telephone. (*She sits.*) Oh, I am so sorry we have to go. It seems such a shame, this beautiful night. And we have enjoyed ourselves so much.

RIDGEON. I dont believe another half-hour would do Mr. Dubedat a bit of harm.

SIR PATRICK. Come now, Colly, come! come! none of that. You take your man home, Mrs. Dubedat; and get him to bed before eleven.

B.B. Yes, yes. Bed before eleven. Quite right, quite right. Sorry to lose you, my dear lady; but Sir Patrick's orders are the laws of—er—of Tyre and Sidon.

WALPOLE. Let me take you home in my motor.

SIR PATRICK. No. You ought to be ashamed of yourself, Walpole. Your motor will take Mr. and Mrs. Dubedat to the station, and quite far enough too for an open carriage at night.

MRS. DUBEDAT. Oh, I am sure the train is best.

RIDGEON. Well, Mrs. Dubedat, we have had a most enjoyable evening.

WALPOLE. } { Most enjoyable.
B.B. } { Delightful. Charming. Unforgettable.

MRS. DUBEDAT. (*with a touch of shy anxiety*). What did you think of Louis? Or am I wrong to ask?

RIDGEON. Wrong! Why, we are all charmed with him.

WALPOLE. Delighted.

B.B. Most happy to have met him. A privilege, a real privilege.

SIR PATRICK (*grunts*)!

MRS. DUBEDAT (*quickly*). Sir Patrick: are you uneasy about him?

SIR PATRICK (*discreetly*). I admire his drawings greatly, maam.

MRS. DUBEDAT. Yes; but I meant—

RIDGEON. You shall go away quite happy. He's worth saving. He must and shall be saved.

Mrs. Dubedat rises and gasps with delight, relief, and gratitude. They all rise except Sir Patrick and Schutzmacher, and come reassuringly to her.

B.B. Certainly, c e r—tainly.

WALPOLE. Theres no real difficulty, if only you know what to do.

MRS. DUBEDAT. Oh, how can I ever thank you! From this night I can begin to be happy at last. You dont know what I feel.

She sits down in tears. They crowd about her to console her.

B.B. My dear lady: come come! come come! (*very persuasively*) c o m e come!

WALPOLE. Dont mind us. Have a good cry.

RIDGEON. No: dont cry. Your husband had better not know that weve been talking about him.

MRS. DUBEDAT (*quickly pulling herself together*). No, of course not. Please dont mind me. What a glorious thing it must be to be a doctor! (*They laugh.*) Dont laugh. You dont know what youve done for me. I never knew until now how deadly afraid I was—how I had come to dread the worst. I never dared let myself know. But now the relief has come: now I know.

Louis Dubedat comes from the hotel, in his overcoat, his throat wrapped in a shawl. He is a slim young man of 23, physically still a stripling, and pretty, though not effeminate. He has turquoise blue eyes, and a trick of looking you straight in the face with them, which, combined with a frank smile, is very engaging. Although he is all nerves, and very observant and quick of apprehension, he is not in the least shy. He is younger than Jennifer; but he patronizes her as a matter of course. The doctors do not put him out in the least: neither Sir Patrick's years nor Bloomfield Bonington's majesty have the smallest apparent effect on him: he is as natural as a cat: he moves among men as most men move among things, though he is intentionally making himself agreeable to them on this occasion. Like all people who can be depended on to take care of themselves, he is welcome company; and his artist's power of appealing to the imagination gains him credit for all sorts of qualities and powers, whether he possesses them or not.

LOUIS (*pulling on his gloves behind Ridgeon's chair*). Now, Jinny-Gwinny: the motor has come round.

RIDGEON. Why do you let him spoil your beautiful name like that, Mrs. Dubedat?

MRS. DUBEDAT. Oh, on grand occasions I am Jennifer.

B.B. You are a bachelor: you do not understand these things, Ridgeon. Look at me (*They look.*) I also have two names. In moments of domestic worry, I am simple Ralph.

When the sun shines in the home, I am Beedle-Deedle-Dumkins. Such is married life! Mr. Dubedat: may I ask you to do me a favor before you go. Will you sign your name to this menu card, under the sketch you have made of me?

WALPOLE. Yes; and mine too, if you will be so good.

LOUIS. Certainly. (*He sits down and signs the cards.*)

MRS. DUBEDAT. Wont you sign Dr. Schutzmacher's for him, Louis?

LOUIS. I dont think Dr. Schutzmacher is pleased with his portrait. I'll tear it up. (*He reaches across the table for Schutzmacher's menu card, and is about to tear it. Schutzmacher makes no sign.*)

RIDGEON. No, no: if Loony doesnt want it, I do.

LOUIS. I'll sign it for you with pleasure. (*He signs and hands it to Ridgeon.*) Ive just been making a little note of the river to-night: it will work up into something good. (*He shews a pocket sketch-book.*) I think I'll call it the Silver Danube.

B.B. Ah, charming, charming.

WALPOLE. Very sweet. Youre a nailer at pastel.

Louis coughs, first out of modesty, then from tuberculosis.

SIR PATRICK. Now then, Mr. Dubedat: youve had enough of the night air. Take him home, maam.

MRS. DUBEDAT. Yes. Come, Louis.

RIDGEON. Never fear. Never mind. I'll make that cough all right.

B.B. We will stimulate the phagocytes. (*With tender effusion, shaking her head*) G o o d-night, Mrs. Dubedat. Good-night. Good-night.

WALPOLE. If the phagocytes fail, come to me. I'll put you right.

LOUIS. Good-night, Sir Patrick. Happy to have met you.

SIR PATRICK. 'Night (*half a grunt*).

MRS. DUBEDAT. Good-night, Sir Patrick.

SIR PATRICK. Cover yourself well up. Dont think your lungs are made of iron because theyre better than his. Good-night.

MRS. DUBEDAT. Thank you. Thank you. Nothing hurts me. Good-night.

Louis goes out through the hotel without noticing Schutzmacher. Mrs. Dubedat hesitates, then bows to him. Schutz-

macher rises and bows formally, German fashion. She goes out, attended by Ridgeon. The rest resume their seats, ruminating or smoking quietly.

B.B. (*harmoniously*). Dee-lightful couple! Charming woman! Gifted lad! Remarkable talent! Graceful outlines! Perfect evening! Great success! Interesting case! Glorious night! Exquisite scenery! Capital dinner! Stimulating conversation! Restful outing! Good wine! Happy ending! Touching gratitude! Lucky Ridgeon—

RIDGEON (*returning*). Whats that? Calling me, B.B.? (*He goes back to his seat next Sir Patrick.*)

B.B. No, no. Only congratulating you on a most successful evening! Enchanting woman! Thorough breeding! Gentle nature! Refined—

Blenkinsop comes from the hotel and takes the empty chair next Ridgeon.

BLENKINSOP. I'm so sorry to have left you like this, Ridgeon; but it was a telephone message from the police. Theyve found half a milkman at our level crossing with a prescription of mine in its pocket. Wheres Mr. Dubedat?

RIDGEON. Gone.

BLENKINSOP (*rising, very pale*). Gone!

RIDGEON. Just this moment—

BLENKINSOP. Perhaps I could overtake him—(*He rushes into the hotel.*)

WALPOLE (*calling after him*). He's in the motor, man, miles off. You can—(*giving it up*). No use.

RIDGEON. Theyre really very nice people. I confess I was afraid the husband would turn out an appalling bounder. But he's almost as charming in his way as she is in hers. And theres no mistake about his being a genius. It's something to have got a case really worth saving. Somebody else will have to go; but at all events it will be easy to find a worse man.

SIR PATRICK. How do you know?

RIDGEON. Come now, Sir Paddy, no growling. Have something more to drink.

SIR PATRICK. No, thank you.

WALPOLE. Do y o u see anything wrong with Dubedat, B.B.?

B.B. Oh, a charming young fellow. Besides, after all, what

c o u l d be wrong with him? L o o k at him. What c o u l d be wrong with him?

SIR PATRICK. There are two things that can be wrong with any man. One of them is a cheque. The other is a woman. Until you know that a man's sound on these two points, you know nothing about him.

B.B. Ah, cynic, cynic!

WALPOLE. He's all right as to the cheque, for a while at all events. He talked to me quite frankly before dinner as to the pressure of money difficulties on an artist. He says he has no vices and is very economical, but that theres one extravagance he cant afford and yet cant resist; and that is dressing his wife prettily. So I said, bang plump out, "Let me lend you twenty pounds, and pay me when your ship comes home." He was really very nice about it. He took it like a man; and it was a pleasure to see how happy it made him, poor chap.

B.B. (*who has listened to Walpole with growing perturbation*). But—but—but—when was this, may I ask?

WALPOLE. When I joined you that time down by the river.

B.B. But, my dear Walpole, he had just borrowed ten pounds from me.

WALPOLE. What!

SIR PATRICK (*grunts*)!

B.B. (*indulgently*). Well, well, it was really hardly borrowing; for he said heaven only knew when he could pay me. I couldnt refuse. It appears that Mrs. Dubedat has taken a sort of fancy to me—

WALPOLE (*quickly*). No: it was to me.

B.B. Certainly not. Your name was never mentioned between us. He is so wrapped up in his work that he has to leave her a good deal alone; and the poor innocent young fellow—he has of course no idea of my position or how busy I am—actually wanted me to call occasionally and talk to her.

WALPOLE. Exactly what he said to me!

B.B. Pooh! Pooh pooh! Really, I must say. (*Much disturbed, he rises and goes up to the balustrade, contemplating the landscape vexedly.*)

WALPOLE. Look here, Ridgeon! this is beginning to look serious.

Blenkinsop, very anxious and wretched, but trying to look unconcerned, comes back.

RIDGEON. Well, did you catch him?

BLENKINSOP. No. Excuse my running away like that. (*He sits down at the foot of the table, next Bloomfield Bonington's chair.*)

WALPOLE. Anything the matter?

BLENKINSOP. Oh no. A trifle—something ridiculous. It cant be helped. Never mind.

RIDGEON. Was it anything about Dubedat?

BLENKINSOP (*almost breaking down*). I ought to keep it to myself, I know. I cant tell you, Ridgeon, how ashamed I am of dragging my miserable poverty to your dinner after all your kindness. It's not that you wont ask me again; but it's so humiliating. And I did so look forward to one evening in my dress clothes (t h e y r e still presentable, you see) with all my troubles left behind, just like old times.

RIDGEON. But what has happened?

BLENKINSOP. Oh, nothing. It's too ridiculous. I had just scraped up four shillings for this little outing; and it cost me one-and-fourpence to get here. Well, Dubedat asked me to lend him half-a-crown to tip the chambermaid of the room his wife left her wraps in, and for the cloak-room. He said he only wanted it for five minutes, as she had his purse. So of course I lent it to him. And he's forgotten to pay me. I've just tuppence to get back with.

RIDGEON. Oh, never mind that—

BLENKINSOP (*stopping him resolutely*). No: I know what youre going to say; but I wont take it. Ive never borrowed a penny; and I never will. Ive nothing left but my friends; and I wont sell them. If none of you were to be able to meet me without being afraid that my civility was leading up to the loan of five shillings, there would be an end of everything for me. I'll take your old clothes, Colly, sooner than disgrace you by talking to you in the street in my own; but I wont borrow money. I'll train it as far as the twopence will take me; and I'll tramp the rest.

WALPOLE. Youll do the whole distance in my motor. (*They are all greatly relieved; and Walpole hastens to get away from the painful subject by adding*) Did he get anything out of y o u, Mr. Schutzmacher?

SCHUTZMACHER (*shakes his head in a most expressive negative*).

WALPOLE. You didnt appreciate his drawing, I think.

SCHUTZMACHER. Oh yes I did. I should have liked very much to have kept the sketch and got it autographed.

B.B. But why didnt you?

SCHUTZMACHER. Well, the fact is, when I joined Dubedat after his conversation with Mr. Walpole, he said the Jews were the only people who knew anything about art, and that though he had to put up with your Philistine twaddle, as he called it, it was what I said about the drawings that really pleased him. He also said that his wife was greatly struck with my knowledge, and that she always admired Jews. Then he asked me to advance him £50 on the security of the drawings.

B.B.		No, no. Positively! Seriously!
WALPOLE	(*All*	What! Another fifty!
BLENKINSOP	*exclaiming*	Think of that!
SIR PATRICK	*together*)	(*grunts*)!

SCHUTZMACHER. Of course I couldnt lend money to a stranger like that.

B.B. I envy you the power to say No, Mr. Schutzmacher. Of course, I knew I oughtnt to lend money to a young fellow in that way; but I simply hadnt the nerve to refuse. I couldnt very well, you know, could I?

SCHUTZMACHER. I dont understand that. *I* felt that I couldnt very well lend it.

WALPOLE. What did he say?

SCHUTZMACHER. Well, he made a very uncalled-for remark about a Jew not understanding the feelings of a gentleman. I must say you Gentiles are very hard to please. You say we are no gentlemen when we lend money; and when we refuse to lend it you say just the same. I didnt mean to behave badly. As I told him, I might have lent it to him if he had been a Jew himself.

SIR PATRICK (*with a grunt*). And what did he say to that?

SCHUTZMACHER. Oh, he began trying to persuade me that he was one of the chosen people—that his artistic faculty shewed it, and that his name was as foreign as my own. He said he didnt really want £50; that he was only joking; that all he wanted was a couple of sovereigns.

B.B. No, no, Mr. Schutzmacher. You invented that last touch. Seriously, now?

SCHUTZMACHER. No. You cant improve on Nature in telling stories about gentlemen like Mr. Dubedat.

BLENKINSOP. You certainly do stand by one another, you chosen people, Mr. Schutzmacher.

SCHUTZMACHER. Not at all. Personally, I like Englishmen better than Jews, and always associate with them. Thats only natural, because, as I am a Jew, theres nothing interesting in a Jew to me, whereas there is always something interesting and foreign in an Englishman. But in money matters it's quite different. You see, when an Englishman borrows, all he knows or cares is that he wants money; and he'll sign anything to get it, without in the least understanding it, or intending to carry out the agreement if it turns out badly for him. In fact, he thinks you a cad if you ask him to carry it out under such circumstances. Just like the Merchant of Venice, you know. But if a Jew makes an agreement, he means to keep it and expects you to keep it. If he wants money for a time, he borrows it and knows he must pay it at the end of the time. If he knows he cant pay, he begs it as a gift.

RIDGEON. Come, Loony! do you mean to say that Jews are never rogues and thieves?

SCHUTZMACHER. Oh, not at all. But I was not talking of criminals. I was comparing honest Englishmen with honest Jews.

One of the hotel maids, a pretty, fair-haired woman of about 25, comes from the hotel, rather furtively. She accosts Ridgeon.

THE MAID. I beg your pardon, sir—

RIDGEON. Eh?

THE MAID. I beg pardon, sir. It's not about the hotel. I'm not allowed to be on the terrace; and I should be discharged if I were seen speaking to you, unless you were kind enough to say you called me to ask whether the motor has come back from the station yet.

WALPOLE. Has it?

THE MAID. Yes, sir.

RIDGEON. Well, what do you want?

THE MAID. Would you mind, sir, giving me the address of the gentleman that was with you at dinner?

RIDGEON (*sharply*). Yes, of course I should mind very much. You have no right to ask.

THE MAID. Yes, sir, I know it looks like that. But what am I to do?

SIR PATRICK. Whats the matter with you?

THE MAID. Nothing, sir. I want the address: thats all.

B.B. You mean the young gentleman?

THE MAID. Yes, sir: that went to catch the train with the woman he brought with him.

RIDGEON. The woman! Do you mean the lady who dined here? the gentleman's wife?

THE MAID. Dont believe them, sir. She cant be his wife. I'm his wife.

B.B. } (*in amazed remonstrance*). My good girl!
RIDGEON } You his wife!
WALPOLE } What! whats that? Oh, this is getting perfectly fascinating, Ridgeon.

THE MAID. I could run upstairs and get you my marriage lines in a minute, sir, if you doubt my word. He's Mr. Louis Dubedat, isnt he?

RIDGEON. Yes.

THE MAID. Well, sir, you may believe me or not; but I'm the lawful Mrs. Dubedat.

SIR PATRICK. And why arnt you living with your husband?

THE MAID. We couldnt afford it, sir. I had thirty pounds saved; and we spent it all on our honeymoon in three weeks, and a lot more that he borrowed. Then I had to go back into service, and he went to London to get work at his drawing; and he never wrote me a line or sent me an address. I never saw nor heard of him again until I caught sight of him from the window going off in the motor with that woman.

SIR PATRICK. Well, thats two wives to start with.

B.B. Now upon my soul I dont want to be uncharitable; but

really I'm beginning to suspect that our young friend is rather careless.

SIR PATRICK. Beginning to think! How long will it take you, man, to find out that he's a damned young blackguard?

BLENKINSOP. Oh, thats severe, Sir Patrick, very severe. Of course it's bigamy; but still he's very young; and she's very pretty. Mr. Walpole: may I sponge on you for another of those nice cigarets of yours? (*He changes his seat for the one next Walpole.*)

WALPOLE. Certainly. (*He feels in his pockets.*) Oh bother! Where—? (*Suddenly remembering*) I say: I recollect now: I passed my cigaret case to Dubedat and he didnt return it. It was a gold one.

THE MAID. He didnt mean any harm: he never thinks about things like that, sir. I'll get it back for you, sir, if youll tell me where to find him.

RIDGEON. What am I to do? Shall I give her the address or not?

SIR PATRICK. Give her your own address; and then we'll see. (*To the maid*) Youll have to be content with that for the present, my girl. (*Ridgeon gives her his card.*) Whats your name?

THE MAID. Minnie Tinwell, sir.

SIR PATRICK. Well, you write him a letter to care of this gentleman; and it will be sent on. Now be off with you.

THE MAID. Thank you, sir. I'm sure you wouldnt see me wronged. Thank you all, gentlemen; and excuse the liberty.

She goes into the hotel. They watch her in silence.

RIDGEON (*when she is gone*). Do you realize, you chaps, that we have promised Mrs. Dubedat to save this fellow's life?

BLENKINSOP. Whats the matter with him?

RIDGEON. Tuberculosis.

BLENKINSOP (*interested*). And can you cure that?

RIDGEON. I believe so.

BLENKINSOP. Then I wish youd cure me. My right lung is touched, I'm sorry to say.

RIDGEON } (*all together*). What! your lung is going!
B.B. } (*all together*). My dear Blenkinsop, what do you tell me? (*full of concern for Blenkinsop, he comes back from the balustrade.*)
SIR PATRICK } (*all together*). Eh? Eh? whats that?
WALPOLE } (*all together*). Hullo! you mustnt neglect this, you know.

BLENKINSOP (*putting his fingers in his ears*). No, no: it's no use. I know what youre going to say: Ive said it often to others. I cant afford to take care of myself; and theres an end of it. If a fortnight's holiday would save my life, I'd have to die. I shall get on as others have to get on. We cant all go to St. Moritz or to Egypt, you know, Sir Ralph. Dont talk about it.

Embarrassed silence.

SIR PATRICK (*grunts and looks hard at Ridgeon*)!

SCHUTZMACHER (*looking at his watch and rising*). I must go. It's been a very pleasant evening, Colly. You might let me have my portrait if you dont mind. I'll send Mr. Dubedat that couple of sovereigns for it.

RIDGEON (*giving him the menu card*). Oh dont do that, Loony. I dont think he'd like that.

SCHUTZMACHER. Well, of course I shant if you feel that way about it. But I dont think you understand Dubedat. However, perhaps thats because I'm a Jew. Good-night, Dr. Blenkinsop (*shaking hands*).

BLENKINSOP. Good-night, sir—I mean—Good-night.

SCHUTZMACHER (*waving his hand to the rest*). Good-night, everybody.

WALPOLE
B.B.
SIR PATRICK
RIDGEON } Good-night.

B.B. repeats the salutation several times, in varied musical tones. Schutzmacher goes out.

SIR PATRICK. It's time for us all to move. (*He rises and comes between Blenkinsop and Walpole. Ridgeon also rises.*) Mr. Walpole: take Blenkinsop home: he's had enough of the open air cure for to-night. Have you a thick overcoat to wear in the motor, Dr. Blenkinsop?

BLENKINSOP. Oh, theyll give me some brown paper in the hotel; and a few thicknesses of brown paper across the chest are better than any fur coat.

WALPOLE. Well, come along. Good-night, Colly. Youre coming with us, arnt you, B.B.?

B.B. Yes: I'm coming. (*Walpole and Blenkinsop go into the hotel.*) Good-night, my dear Ridgeon (*shaking hands affectionately*). Dont let us lose sight of your interesting patient and his very charming wife. We must not judge him too hastily, you know. (*With unction*) G o o o o o o o o o d-night, Paddy. Bless you, dear old chap. (*Sir Patrick utters a formidable grunt. B.B. laughs and pats him indulgently on the shoulder.*) Good-night. Good-night. Good-night. Good-night. (*He good-nights himself into the hotel.*)

The others have meanwhile gone without ceremony. Ridgeon and Sir Patrick are left alone together. Ridgeon, deep in thought, comes down to Sir Patrick.

SIR PATRICK. Well, Mr. Savior of Lives: which is it to be? that honest decent man Blenkinsop, or that rotten blackguard of an artist, eh?

RIDGEON. It's not an easy case to judge, is it? Blenkinsop's an honest decent man; but is he any use? Dubedat's a rotten blackguard; but he's a genuine source of pretty and pleasant and good things.

SIR PATRICK. What will he be a source of for that poor innocent wife of his, when she finds him out?

RIDGEON. Thats true. Her life will be a hell.

SIR PATRICK. And tell me this. Suppose you had this choice put before you: either to go through life and find all the pictures bad but all the men and women good, or to go through life and find all the pictures good and all the men and women rotten. Which would you choose?

RIDGEON. Thats a devilishly difficult question, Paddy. The pictures are so agreeable, and the good people so infernally disagreeable and mischievous, that I really cant undertake to say offhand which I should prefer to do without.

SIR PATRICK. Come come! none of your cleverness with me: I'm too old for it. Blenkinsop isnt that sort of good man; and you know it.

RIDGEON. It would be simpler if Blenkinsop could paint Dubedat's pictures.

SIR PATRICK. It would be simpler still if Dubedat had some of Blenkinsop's honesty. The world isnt going to be made simple for you, my lad: you must take it as it is. Youve to hold the scales between Blenkinsop and Dubedat. Hold them fairly.

RIDGEON. Well, I'll be as fair as I can. I'll put into one scale all the pounds Dubedat has borrowed, and into the other all the half-crowns that Blenkinsop hasnt borrowed.

SIR PATRICK. And youll take out of Dubedat's scale all the faith he has destroyed and the honor he has lost, and youll put into Blenkinsop's scale all the faith he has justified and the honor he has created.

RIDGEON. Come come, Paddy! none of your claptrap with me: I'm too sceptical for it. I'm not at all convinced that the world wouldnt be a better world if everybody behaved as Dubedat does than it is now that everybody behaves as Blenkinsop does.

SIR PATRICK. Then why dont y o u behave as Dubedat does?

RIDGEON. Ah, that beats me. Thats the experimental test. Still, it's a dilemma. It's a dilemma. You see theres a complication we havnt mentioned.

SIR PATRICK. Whats that?

RIDGEON. Well, if I let Blenkinsop die, at least nobody can say I did it because I wanted to marry his widow.

SIR PATRICK. Eh? Whats that?

RIDGEON. Now if I let Dubedat die, I'll marry his widow.

SIR PATRICK. Perhaps she wont have you, you know.

RIDGEON (*with a self-assured shake of the head*). Ive a pretty good flair for that sort of thing. I know when a woman is interested in me. She is.

SIR PATRICK. Well, sometimes a man knows best; and sometimes he knows worst. Youd much better cure them both.

RIDGEON. I cant. I'm at my limit. I can squeeze in one more case, but not two. I must choose.

SIR PATRICK. Well, you must choose as if she didn't exist: thats clear.

RIDGEON. Is that clear to you? Mind: it's not clear to me. She troubles my judgment.

SIR PATRICK. To me, it's a plain choice between a man and a lot of pictures.

RIDGEON. It's easier to replace a dead man than a good picture.

SIR PATRICK. Colly: when you live in an age that runs to pictures and statues and plays and brass bands because its men and women are not good enough to comfort its poor aching soul, you should thank Providence that you belong to a profession which is a high and great profession because its business is to heal and mend men and women.

RIDGEON. In short, as a member of a high and great profession, I'm to kill my patient.

SIR PATRICK. Dont talk wicked nonsense. You cant kill him. But you can leave him in other hands.

RIDGEON. In B.B.'s, for instance: eh? (*looking at him significantly*).

SIR PATRICK (*demurely facing his look*). Sir Ralph Bloomfield Bonington is a very eminent physician.

RIDGEON. He is.

SIR PATRICK. I'm going for my hat.

Ridgeon strikes the bell as Sir Patrick makes for the hotel. A waiter comes.

RIDGEON (*to the waiter*). My bill, please.

WAITER. Yes, sir.

He goes for it.

END OF ACT II

ACT III

In Dubedat's studio. Viewed from the large window the outer door is in the wall on the left at the near end. The door leading to the inner rooms is in the opposite wall, at the far end. The facing wall has neither window nor door. The plaster on all the walls is uncovered and undecorated, except by scrawlings of charcoal sketches and memoranda. There is a studio throne (a chair on a dais) a little to the left, opposite the inner door, and an easel to the right, opposite the outer door, with a dilapidated chair at it. Near the easel and against the wall is a bare wooden table with bottles and jars of oil and medium, paint-smudged rags, tubes of color, brushes, charcoal, a small lay figure, a kettle and spirit-lamp, and other odds and ends. By the table is a sofa, littered with drawing blocks, sketch-books, loose sheets of paper, news-papers, books, and more smudged rags. Next the outer door is an umbrella and hat stand, occupied partly by Louis' hats and cloak and muffler, and partly by odds and ends of costumes. There is an old piano stool on the near side of this door. In the corner near the inner door is a little tea-table. A lay figure, in a cardinal's robe and hat, with an hour-glass in one hand and a scythe slung on its back, smiles with inane malice at Louis, who, in a milkman's smock much smudged with colors, is painting a piece of brocade which he has draped about his wife. She is sitting on the throne, not interested in the painting, and appealing to him very anxiously about another matter.

MRS. DUBEDAT. Promise.

LOUIS (*putting on a touch of paint with notable skill and care and answering quite perfunctorily*). I promise, my darling.

MRS. DUBEDAT. When you want money, you will always come to me.

LOUIS. But it's so sordid, dearest. I hate money. I cant keep always bothering you for money, money, money. Thats what drives me sometimes to ask other people, though I hate doing it.

MRS. DUBEDAT. It is far better to ask me, dear. It gives people a wrong idea of you.

LOUIS. But I want to spare your little fortune, and raise money on my own work. Dont be unhappy, love: I can easily earn enough to pay it all back. I shall have a one-man-show next season; and then there will be no more money troubles. (*Putting down his palette*) There! I mustnt do any more on that until it's bone-dry; so you may come down.

MRS. DUBEDAT (*throwing off the drapery as she steps down, and revealing a plain frock of tussore silk*). But you have promised, remember, seriously and faithfully, never to borrow again until you have first asked me.

LOUIS. Seriously and faithfully. (*Embracing her*) Ah, my love, how right you are! how much it means to me to have you by me to guard me against living too much in the skies. On my solemn oath, from this moment forth I will never borrow another penny.

MRS. DUBEDAT (*delighted*). Ah, thats right. Does his wicked worrying wife torment him and drag him down from the clouds. (*She kisses him.*) And now, dear, wont you finish those drawings for Maclean?

LOUIS. Oh, they dont matter. Ive got nearly all the money from him in advance.

MRS. DUBEDAT. But, dearest, that is just the reason why you should finish them. He asked me the other day whether you really intended to finish them.

LOUIS. Confound his impudence! What the devil does he take me for? Now that just destroys all my interest in the beastly job. Ive a good mind to throw up the commission, and pay him back his money.

MRS. DUBEDAT. We cant afford that, dear. You had better finish the drawings and have done with them. I think it is a mistake to accept money in advance.

LOUIS. But how are we to live?

MRS. DUBEDAT. Well, Louis, it is getting hard enough as it is, now that they are all refusing to pay except on delivery.

LOUIS. Damn those fellows! they think of nothing and care for nothing but their wretched money.

MRS. DUBEDAT. Still, if they pay us, they ought to have what they pay for.

LOUIS (*coaxing*). There now: thats enough lecturing for to-day. Ive promised to be good, havnt I?

MRS. DUBEDAT (*putting her arms round his neck*). You know that I hate lecturing, and that I dont for a moment misunderstand you, dear, dont you?

LOUIS (*fondly*). I know. I know. I'm a wretch; and youre an angel. Oh, if only I were strong enough to work steadily, I'd make my darling's house a temple, and her shrine a chapel more beautiful than was ever imagined. I cant pass the shops without wrestling with the temptation to go in and order all the really good things they have for you.

MRS. DUBEDAT. I want nothing but you, dear. (*She gives him a caress, to which he responds so passionately that she disengages herself.*) There! be good now: remember that the doctors are coming this morning. Isnt it extraordinarily kind of them, Louis, to insist on coming? all of them, to consult about you?

LOUIS (*coolly*). Oh, I daresay they think it will be a feather in their cap to cure a rising artist. They wouldnt come if it didnt amuse them, anyhow. (*Someone knocks at the door.*) I say: it's not time yet, is it?

MRS. DUBEDAT. No, not quite yet.

LOUIS (*opening the door and finding Ridgeon there*). Hello, Ridgeon. Delighted to see you. Come in.

MRS. DUBEDAT (*shaking hands*). It's so good of you to come, doctor.

LOUIS. Excuse this place, wont you? It's only a studio, you

know: theres no real convenience for living here. But we pig along somehow, thanks to Jennifer.

MRS. DUBEDAT. Now I'll run away. Perhaps later on, when youre finished with Louis, I may come in and hear the verdict. (*Ridgeon bows rather constrainedly.*) Would you rather I didnt?

RIDGEON. Not at all. Not at all.

Mrs. Dubedat looks at him, a little puzzled by his formal manner; then goes into the inner room.

LOUIS (*flippantly*). I say: dont look so grave. Theres nothing awful going to happen, is there?

RIDGEON. No.

LOUIS. Thats all right. Poor Jennifer has been looking forward to your visit more than you can imagine. Shes taken quite a fancy to you, Ridgeon. The poor girl has nobody to talk to: I'm always painting. (*Taking up a sketch*) Theres a little sketch I made of her yesterday.

RIDGEON. She shewed it to me a fortnight ago when she first called on me.

LOUIS (*quite unabashed*). Oh! did she? Good Lord! how time does fly! I could have sworn I'd only finished it. It's hard for her here, seeing me piling up drawings and nothing coming in for them. Of course I shall sell them next year fast enough, after my one-man-show; but while the grass grows the steed starves. I hate to have her coming to me for money, and having none to give her. But what can I do?

RIDGEON. I understood that Mrs. Dubedat had some property of her own.

LOUIS. Oh yes, a little; but how could a man with any decency of feeling touch that? Suppose I did, what would she have to live on if I died? I'm not insured: cant afford the premiums. (*Picking out another drawing*) How do you like that?

RIDGEON (*putting it aside*). I have not come here today to look at your drawings. I have more serious and pressing business with you.

LOUIS. You want to sound my wretched lung. (*With impulsive candor*) My dear Ridgeon: I'll be frank with you. Whats the matter in this house isnt lungs but bills. It doesnt matter about me; but Jennifer has actually to economize in the matter of food. Youve made us feel that we can treat you as a friend. Will you lend us a hundred and fifty pounds?

RIDGEON. No.

LOUIS (*surprised*). Why not?

RIDGEON. I am not a rich man; and I want every penny I can spare and more for my researches.

LOUIS. You mean youd want the money back again.

RIDGEON. I presume people sometimes have that in view when they lend money.

LOUIS (*after a moment's reflection*). Well, I can manage that for you. I'll give you a cheque—or see here: theres no reason why you shouldnt have your bit too: I'll give you a cheque for two hundred.

RIDGEON. Why not cash the cheque at once without troubling me?

LOUIS. Bless you! they wouldnt cash it: I'm overdrawn as it is. No: the way to work it is this. I'll post-date the cheque next October. In October Jennifer's dividends come in. Well, you present the cheque. It will be returned marked "refer to drawer" or some rubbish of that sort. Then you can take it to Jennifer, and hint that if the cheque isnt taken up at once I shall be put in prison. She'll pay you like a shot. Youll clear £50; and youll do me a real service; for I do want the money very badly, old chap, I assure you.

RIDGEON (*staring at him*). You see no objection to the transaction; and you anticipate none from me!

LOUIS. Well, what objection can there be? It's quite safe. I can convince you about the dividends.

RIDGEON. I mean on the score of its being—shall I say dishonorable?

LOUIS. Well, of course I shouldnt suggest it if I didnt want the money.

RIDGEON. Indeed! Well, you will have to find some other means of getting it.

LOUIS. Do you mean that you refuse?

RIDGEON. Do I mean—! (*letting his indignation loose*) Of course I refuse, man. What do you take me for? How dare you make such a proposal to me?

LOUIS. Why not?

RIDGEON. Faugh! You would not understand me if I tried to

explain. Now, once for all, I will not lend you a farthing. I should be glad to help your wife; but lending you money is no service to her.

LOUIS. Oh well, if youre in earnest about helping her, I'll tell you what you might do. You might get your patients to buy some of my things, or to give me a few portrait commissions.

RIDGEON. My patients call me in as a physician, not as a commercial traveller.

A knock at the door. Louis goes unconcernedly to open it, pursuing the subject as he goes.

LOUIS. But you must have great influence with them. You must know such lots of things about them—private things that they wouldnt like to have known. They wouldnt dare to refuse you.

RIDGEON (*exploding*). Well, upon my—

Louis opens the door, and admits Sir Patrick, Sir Ralph, and Walpole.

RIDGEON (*proceeding furiously*). Walpole: Ive been here hardly ten minutes; and already he's tried to borrow £150 from me. Then he proposed that I should get the money for him by blackmailing his wife; and youve just interrupted him in the act of suggesting that I should blackmail my patients into sitting to him for their portraits.

LOUIS. Well, Ridgeon, if this is what you call being an honorable man! I spoke to you in confidence.

SIR PATRICK. We're all going to speak to you in confidence, young man.

WALPOLE (*hanging his hat on the only peg left vacant on the hat-stand*). We shall make ourselves at home for half an hour, Dubedat. Dont be alarmed: youre a most fascinating chap; and we love you.

LOUIS. Oh, all right, all right. Sit down—anywhere you can. Take this chair, Sir Patrick (*indicating the one on the throne*). Up-z-z-z! (*helping him up: Sir Patrick grunts and enthrones himself*). Here you are, B.B. (*Sir Ralph glares at the familiarity; but Louis, quite undisturbed, puts a big book and a sofa cushion on the dais, on Sir Patrick's right; and B.B. sits down, under protest.*) Let me take your hat. (*He takes B.B.'s hat unceremoniously, and substitutes it for the cardinal's hat on the head of the lay figure, thereby ingeniously destroying the dignity of the conclave. He then draws the piano stool from the wall and offers it to Walpole.*) You dont mind this, Walpole, do you? (*Walpole accepts the stool, and puts his hand into his pocket for his cigaret case. Missing it, he is reminded of his loss.*)

WALPOLE. By the way, I'll trouble you for my cigaret case, if you dont mind?

LOUIS. What cigaret case?

WALPOLE. The gold one I lent you at the Star and Garter.

LOUIS (*surprised*). Was that yours?

WALPOLE. Yes.

LOUIS. I'm awfully sorry, old chap. I wondered whose it was. I'm sorry to say this is all thats left of it. (*He hitches up his smock; produces a card from his waistcoat pocket; and hands it to Walpole.*)

WALPOLE. A pawn ticket!

LOUIS (*reassuringly*). It's quite safe: he cant sell it for a year, you know. I say, my dear Walpole, I am sorry. (*He places his hand ingenuously on Walpole's shoulder and looks frankly at him.*)

WALPOLE (*sinking on the stool with a gasp*). Dont mention it. It adds to your fascination.

RIDGEON (*who has been standing near the easel*). Before we go any further, you have a debt to pay, Mr. Dubedat.

LOUIS. I have a precious lot of debts to pay, Ridgeon. I'll fetch you a chair. (*He makes for the inner door.*)

RIDGEON (*stopping him*). You shall not leave the room until you pay it. It's a small one; and pay it you must and shall. I dont so much mind your borrowing £10 from one of my guests and £20 from the other—

WALPOLE. I walked into it, you know. I offered it.

RIDGEON. —they could afford it. But to clean poor Blenkinsop out of his last half-crown was damnable. I intend to give him that half-crown and to be in a position to pledge him my word that you paid it. I'll have that out of you, at all events.

B.B. Quite right, Ridgeon. Quite right. Come, young man! down with the dust. Pay up.

LOUIS. Oh, you neednt make such a fuss about it. Of course I'll pay it. I had no idea the poor fellow was hard up. I'm as shocked as any of you about it. (*Putting his hand into his pocket*) Here you are. (*Finding his pocket empty*) Oh, I say, I havnt any money on me just at present. Walpole: would you mind lending me half-a-crown just to settle this.

WALPOLE. Lend you half—(*His voice faints away.*)

LOUIS. Well, if you dont, Blenkinsop wont get it; for I havnt a rap: you may search my pockets if you like.

WALPOLE. Thats conclusive. (*He produces half-a-crown.*)

LOUIS (*passing it to Ridgeon*). There! I'm really glad thats settled: it was the only thing that was on my conscience. Now I hope youre all satisfied.

SIR PATRICK. Not quite, Mr. Dubedat. Do you happen to know a young woman named Minnie Tinwell?

LOUIS. Minnie! I should think I do; and Minnie knows me too. She's a really nice good girl, considering her station. Whats become of her?

WALPOLE. It's no use b l u f f i n g, Dubedat. Weve seen Minnie's marriage lines.

LOUIS (*coolly*). Indeed? Have you seen Jennifer's?

RIDGEON (*rising in irrepressible rage*). Do you dare insinuate that Mrs. Dubedat is living with you without being married to you?

LOUIS. Why not?

B.B.	(*echoing him in*	Why not!
SIR PATRICK	*various tones of*	Why not!
RIDGEON	*scandalized*	Why not!
WALPOLE	*amazement*).	Why not!

LOUIS. Yes, why not? Lots of people do it: just as good people as you. Why dont you learn to think, instead of bleating and baahing like a lot of sheep when you come up against anything youre not accustomed to? (*Contemplating their amazed faces with a chuckle*) I say: I should like to draw the lot of you now: you do look jolly foolish. Especially you, Ridgeon. I had you that time, you know.

RIDGEON. How, pray?

LOUIS. Well, you set up to appreciate Jennifer, you know. And you despise me, dont you?

RIDGEON (*curtly*). I loathe you. (*He sits down again on the sofa.*)

LOUIS. Just so. And yet you believe that Jennifer is a bad lot because you think I told you so.

RIDGEON. Were you lying?

LOUIS. No; but you were smelling out a scandal instead of keeping your mind clean and wholesome. I can just play with people like you. I only asked you had you seen Jennifer's marriage lines; and you concluded straight away that she hadnt got any. You dont know a lady when you see one.

B.B. (*majestically*). What do you mean by that, may I ask?

LOUIS. Now, I'm only an immoral artist; but if youd told me that Jennifer wasnt married, I'd have had the gentlemanly feeling and artistic instinct to say that she carried her marriage certificate in her face and in her character. But y o u are all moral men; and Jennifer is only an artist's wife—probably a model; and morality consists in suspecting other people of not being legally married. Arnt you ashamed of yourselves? Can one of you look me in the face after it?

WALPOLE. It's very hard to look you in the face, Dubedat; you have such a dazzling cheek. What about Minnie Tinwell, eh?

LOUIS. Minnie Tinwell is a young woman who has had three weeks of glorious happiness in her poor little life, which is more than most girls in her position get, I can tell you. Ask her whether she'd take it back if she could. She's got her name into history, that girl. My little sketches of her will be bought by collectors at Christie's. She'll have a page in my biography. Pretty good, that, for a still-room maid at a seaside hotel, I think. What have you fellows done for her to compare with that?

RIDGEON. We havnt trapped her into a mock marriage and deserted her.

LOUIS. No: you wouldnt have the pluck. But dont fuss yourselves. *I* didn't desert little Minnie. We spent all our money—

WALPOLE. All h e r money. Thirty pounds.

LOUIS. I said all o u r money: hers and mine too. Her thirty pounds didnt last three days. I had to borrow four times as much to spend on her. But I didnt grudge it; and she didnt grudge her few pounds either, the brave little lassie. When we were cleaned out, we'd had enough of it: you can hardly suppose that we were fit company for longer than that: I an artist, and she quite out of art and literature and refined living and everything else. There was no desertion, no misunderstanding, no police court or divorce court sensation for you moral chaps to lick your lips over at breakfast. We just said, Well, the money's gone: weve had a good time that can never be taken from us; so kiss; part good friends; and she back to service, and I back to my studio and my Jennifer, both the better and happier for our holiday.

WALPOLE. Quite a little poem, by George!

B.B. If you had been scientifically trained, Mr. Dubedat, you would know how very seldom an actual case bears out a principle. In medical practice a man may die when, scientifically speaking, he ought to have lived. I have actually known a man die of a disease from which he was scientifically speaking, immune. But that does not affect the fundamental truth of science. In just the same way, in moral cases, a man's behavior may be quite harmless and even beneficial, when he is morally behaving like a scoundrel. And he may do great harm when he is morally acting on the highest principles. But that does not affect the fundamental truth of morality.

SIR PATRICK. And it doesn't affect the criminal law on the subject of bigamy.

LOUIS. Oh bigamy! bigamy! bigamy! What a fascination anything connected with the police has for you all, you moralists! Ive proved to you that you were utterly wrong on the moral point: now I'm going to shew you that youre utterly wrong on the legal point; and I hope it will be a lesson to you not to be so jolly cocksure next time.

WALPOLE. Rot! You were married already when you married her; and that settles it.

LOUIS. Does it! Why cant you think? How do you know she wasnt married already too?

<table>
<tr><td>B.B.</td><td rowspan="4">(all crying out together).</td><td>Walpole! Ridgeon!</td></tr>
<tr><td>RIDGEON</td><td>his is beyond everything!</td></tr>
<tr><td>WALPOLE</td><td>Well, damn me!</td></tr>
<tr><td>SIR PATRICK</td><td>You young rascal.</td></tr>
</table>

LOUIS (*ignoring their outcry*). She was married to the steward of a liner. He cleared out and left her; and she thought, poor girl, that it was the law that if you hadnt heard of your husband for three years you might marry again. So as she was a thoroughly respectable girl and refused to have anything to say to me unless we were married I went through the ceremony to please her and to preserve her self-respect.

RIDGEON. Did you tell her you were already married?

LOUIS. Of course not. Dont you see that if she had known, she wouldnt have considered herself my wife? You dont seem to understand, somehow.

SIR PATRICK. You let her risk imprisonment in her ignorance of the law?

LOUIS. Well, *I* risked imprisonment for her sake. I could have been had up for it just as much as she. But when a man makes a sacrifice of that sort for a woman, he doesnt go and brag about it to her; at least, not if he's a gentleman.

WALPOLE. What a r e we to do with this daisy?

LOUIS (*impatiently*). Oh, go and do whatever the devil you please. Put Minnie in prison. Put me in prison. Kill Jennifer with the disgrace of it all. And then, when youve done all the mischief you can, go to church and feel good about it. (*He sits down pettishly on the old chair at the easel, and takes up a sketching block, on which he begins to draw.*)

WALPOLE. He's got us.

SIR PATRICK (*grimly*). He has.

B.B. But is he to be allowed to defy the criminal law of the land?

SIR PATRICK. The criminal law is no use to decent people. It only helps blackguards to blackmail their families. What are we family doctors doing half our time but conspiring with the family solicitor to keep some rascal out of jail and some family out of disgrace?

B.B. But at least it will punish him.

SIR PATRICK. Oh, yes: itll punish him. Itll punish not only him but everybody connected with him, innocent and guilty alike. Itll throw his board and lodging on our rates and taxes for a couple of years, and then turn him loose on us a more dangerous blackguard than ever. Itll put the girl in prison and ruin her: itll lay his wife's life waste. You may put the criminal law out of your head once for all: it's only fit for fools and savages.

LOUIS. Would you mind turning your face a little more this

way, Sir Patrick. (*Sir Patrick turns indignantly and glares at him.*) Oh, thats too much.

SIR PATRICK. Put down your foolish pencil, man; and think of your position. You can defy the laws made by men; but there are other laws to reckon with. Do you know that youre going to die?

LOUIS. We're all going to die, arnt we?

WALPOLE. We're not all going to die in six months.

LOUIS. How do you know?

This for B.B. is the last straw. He completely loses his temper and begins to walk excitedly about.

B.B. Upon my soul, I will not stand this. It is in questionable taste under any circumstances or in any company to harp on the subject of death; but it is a dastardly advantage to take of a medical man. (*Thundering at Dubedat*) I will not allow it, do you hear?

LOUIS. Well, I didn't begin it: you chaps did. It's always the way with the inartistic professions: when theyre beaten in argument they fall back on intimidation. I never knew a lawyer who didnt threaten to put me in prison sooner or later. I never knew a parson who didnt threaten me with damnation. And now you threaten me with death. With all your talk youve only one real trump in your hand, and thats Intimidation. Well, I'm not a coward; so it's no use with me.

B.B. (*advancing upon him*). I'll tell you what you are, sir. Youre a scoundrel.

LOUIS. Oh, I don't mind you calling me a scoundrel a bit. It's only a word: a word that you dont know the meaning of. What is a scoundrel?

B.B. You are a scoundrel, sir.

LOUIS. Just so. What is a scoundrel? I am. What am I? A scoundrel. It's just arguing in a circle. And you imagine youre a man of science!

B.B. I—I—I—I have a good mind to take you by the scruff of your neck, you infamous rascal, and give you a sound thrashing.

LOUIS. I wish you would. Youd pay me something handsome to keep it out of court afterwards. (*B.B., baffled, flings away from him with a snort.*) Have you any more civilities to address to me in my own house? I should like to get them over before my wife comes back. (*He resumes his sketching.*)

RIDGEON. My mind's made up. When the law breaks down, honest men must find a remedy for themselves. I will not lift a finger to save this reptile.

B.B. That is the word I was trying to remember. Reptile.

WALPOLE. I cant help rather liking you, Dubedat. But you certainly are a thoroughgoing specimen.

SIR PATRICK. You know our opinion of you now, at all events.

LOUIS (*patiently putting down his pencil*). Look here. All this is no good. You dont understand. You imagine that I'm simply an ordinary criminal.

WALPOLE. Not an ordinary one, Dubedat. Do yourself justice.

LOUIS. Well youre on the wrong tack altogether. I'm not a criminal. All your moralizings have no value for me. I don't believe in morality. I'm a disciple of Bernard Shaw.

SIR PATRICK (*puzzled*). Eh?
B.B. (*waving his hand as if the subject were now disposed of*). Thats enough: I wish to hear no more.

LOUIS. Of course I havnt the ridiculous vanity to set up to be exactly a Superman; but still, it's an ideal that I strive towards just as any other man strives towards his ideal.

B.B. (*intolerant*). Dont trouble to explain. I now understand you perfectly. Say no more, please. When a man pretends to discuss science, morals, and religion, and then avows himself a follower of a notorious and avowed anti-vaccinationist, there is nothing more to be said. (*Suddenly putting in an effusive saving clause in parenthesis to Ridgeon*) Not, my dear Ridgeon, that I believe in vaccination in the popular sense any more than you do: I neednt tell you that. But there are things that place a man socially; and anti-vaccination is one of them. (*He resumes his seat on the dais.*)

SIR PATRICK. Bernard Shaw? I never heard of him. He's a Methodist preacher, I suppose.

LOUIS (*scandalized*). No, no. He's the most advanced man now living: he isn't anything.

SIR PATRICK. I assure you, young man, my father learnt the

doctrine of deliverance from sin from John Wesley's own lips before you or Mr. Shaw were born. It used to be very popular as an excuse for putting sand in sugar and water in milk. Youre a sound Methodist, my lad; only you don't know it.

LOUIS (*seriously annoyed for the first time*). It's an intellectual insult. I don't believe theres such a thing as sin.

SIR PATRICK. Well, sir, there are people who dont believe theres such a thing as disease either. They call themselves Christian Scientists, I believe. Theyll just suit your complaint. We can do nothing for you. (*He rises.*) Good afternoon to you.

LOUIS (*running to him piteously*). Oh dont get up, Sir Patrick. Don't go. Please dont. I didnt mean to shock you, on my word. Do sit down again. Give me another chance. Two minutes more: thats all I ask.

SIR PATRICK (*surprised by this sign of grace, and a little touched*). Well—(*He sits down.*)

LOUIS (*gratefully*). Thanks awfully.

SIR PATRICK (*continuing*).—I don't mind giving you two minutes more. But dont address yourself to me; for Ive retired from practice; and I dont pretend to be able to cure your complaint. Your life is in the hands of these gentlemen.

RIDGEON. Not in mine. My hands are full. I have no time and no means available for this case.

SIR PATRICK. What do you say, Mr. Walpole?

WALPOLE. Oh, I'll take him in hand: I dont mind. I feel perfectly convinced that this is not a moral case at all: it's a physical one. Theres something abnormal about his brain. That means, probably, some morbid condition affecting the spinal cord. And that means the circulation. In short, it's clear to me that he's suffering from an obscure form of blood-poisoning, which is almost certainly due to an accumulation of ptomaines in the nuciform sac. I'll remove the sac—

LOUIS (*changing color*). Do you mean, operate on me? Ugh! No, thank you.

WALPOLE. Never fear: you wont feel anything. Youll be under an anæsthetic, of course. And it will be extraordinarily interesting.

LOUIS. Oh, well, if it would interest you, and if it wont

hurt, thats another matter. How much will you give me to let you do it?

WALPOLE (*rising indignantly*). How much! What do you mean?

LOUIS. Well, you don't expect me to let you cut me up for nothing, do you?

WALPOLE. Will you paint my portrait for nothing?

LOUIS. No; but I'll give you the portrait when it's painted; and you can sell it afterwards for perhaps double the money. But I cant sell my nuciform sac when youve cut it out.

WALPOLE. Ridgeon: did you ever hear anything like this! (*To Louis*) Well, you can keep your nuciform sac, and your tubercular lung, and your diseased brain: Ive done with you. One would think I was not conferring a favor on the fellow! (*He returns to his stool in high dudgeon.*)

SIR PATRICK. That leaves only one medical man who has not withdrawn from your case, Mr. Dubedat. You have nobody left to appeal to now but Sir Ralph Bloomfield Bonington.

WALPOLE. If I were you, B.B., I shouldnt touch him with a pair of tongs. Let him take his lungs to the Brompton Hospital. They wont cure him; but theyll teach him manners.

B.B. My weakness is that I have never been able to say No, even to the most thoroughly undeserving people. Besides, I am bound to say that I dont think it is possible in medical practice to go into the question of the value of the lives we save. Just consider, Ridgeon. Let me put it to you, Paddy. Clear your mind of cant, Walpole.

WALPOLE (*indignantly*). My mind is clear of cant.

B.B. Quite so. Well now, look at my practice. It is what I suppose you would call a fashionable practice, a smart practice, a practice among the best people. You ask me to go into the question of whether my patients are of any use either to themselves or anyone else. Well, if you apply any scientific test known to me, you will achieve a reductio ad absurdum. You will be driven to the conclusion that the majority of them would be, as my friend Mr. J.M. Barrie has tersely phrased it, better dead. Better dead. There are exceptions, no doubt. For instance, there is the court, an essentially social-democratic institution, supported out of public funds by the public because the public wants it and likes it. My court patients are hard-working people who give satisfaction, undoubtedly. Then I have a duke or two whose estates are probably better managed than they would be in public hands. But as to most of the rest, if I once began to argue about them, unquestionably the verdict would be, Better dead. When they actually do die, I sometimes have to offer that consolation, thinly disguised, to the family. (*Lulled by the cadences of his own voice, he becomes drowsier and drowsier.*) The fact that they spend money so extravagantly on medical attendance really would not justify me in wasting my talents—such as they are—in keeping them alive. After all, if my fees are high, I have to spend heavily. My own tastes are simple: a camp bed, a couple of rooms, a crust, a bottle of wine; and I am happy and contented. My wife's tastes are perhaps more luxurious; but even she deplores an expenditure the sole object of which is to maintain the state my patients require from their medical attendant. The—er—er—er—(*suddenly waking up*) I have lost the thread of these remarks. What was I talking about, Ridgeon?

RIDGEON. About Dubedat.

B.B. Ah yes. Precisely. Thank you. Dubedat, of course. Well, what is our friend Dubedat? A vicious and ignorant young man with a talent for drawing.

LOUIS. Thank you. Dont mind me.

B.B. But then, what are many of my patients? Vicious and ignorant young men without a talent for anything. If I were to stop to argue about their merits I should have to give up three-quarters of my practice. Therefore I have made it a rule not so to argue. Now, as an honorable man, having made that rule as to paying patients, can I make an exception as to a patient who, far from being a paying patient, may more fitly be described as a borrowing patient? No. I say No. Mr. Dubedat: your moral character is nothing to me. I look at you from a purely scientific point of view. To me you are simply a field of battle in which an invading army of tubercle bacilli struggles with a patriotic force of phagocytes. Having made a promise to your wife, which my principles will not allow me to break, to stimulate those phagocytes, I will stimulate them. And I take no further responsibility. (*He flings himself back in his seat exhausted.*)

SIR PATRICK. Well, Mr. Dubedat, as Sir Ralph has very kindly offered to take charge of your case, and as the two minutes I promised you are up, I must ask you to excuse me. (*He rises.*)

LOUIS. Oh, certainly. Ive quite done with you. (*Rising and holding up the sketch block*) There! While youve been talking, Ive been doing. What is there left of your moralizing? Only a little carbonic acid gas which makes the room unhealthy. What is there left of my work? That. Look at it (*Ridgeon rises to look at it.*)

SIR PATRICK (*who has come down to him from the throne*). You young rascal, was it drawing me you were?

LOUIS. Of course. What else?

SIR PATRICK (*takes the drawing from him and grunts approvingly*). Thats rather good. Dont you think so, Colly?

RIDGEON. Yes. So good that I should like to have it.

SIR PATRICK. Thank you; but I should like to have it myself. What d'ye think, Walpole?

WALPOLE (*rising and coming over to look*). No, by Jove: *I* must have this.

LOUIS. I wish I could afford to give it to you, Sir Patrick. But I'd pay five guineas sooner than part with it.

RIDGEON. Oh, for that matter, I will give you six for it.

WALPOLE. Ten.

LOUIS. I think Sir Patrick is morally entitled to it, as he sat for it. May I send it to your house, Sir Patrick, for twelve guineas?

SIR PATRICK. Twelve guineas! Not if you were President of the Royal Academy, young man. (*He gives him back the drawing decisively and turns away, taking up his hat.*)

LOUIS (*to B.B.*). Would you like to take it at twelve, Sir Ralph?

B.B. (*coming between Louis and Walpole*). Twelve guineas? Thank you: I'll take it at that. (*He takes it and presents it to Sir Patrick.*) Accept it from me, Paddy; and may you long be spared to contemplate it.

SIR PATRICK. Thank you. (*He puts the drawing into his hat.*)

B.B. I neednt settle with you now, Mr. Dubedat: my fees will come to more than that. (*He also retrieves his hat.*)

LOUIS (*indignantly*). Well, of all the mean!—(*Words fail*

him.) I'd let myself be shot sooner than do a thing like that. I consider youve stolen that drawing.

SIR PATRICK (*drily*). So weve converted you to a belief in morality after all, eh?

LOUIS. Yah! (*To Walpole*) I'll do another one for you, Walpole, if youll let me have the ten you promised.

WALPOLE. Very good. I'll pay on delivery.

LOUIS. Oh! What do you take me for? Have you no confidence in my honor?

WALPOLE. None whatever.

LOUIS. Oh well, of course if you feel that way, you cant help it. Before you go, Sir Patrick, let me fetch Jennifer. I know she'd like to see you, if you dont mind. (*He goes to the inner door.*) And now, before she comes in, one word. Youve all been talking here pretty freely about me—in my own house too. *I* dont mind that: I'm a man and can take care of myself. But when Jennifer comes in, please remember that she's a lady, and that you are supposed to be gentlemen. (*He goes out.*)

WALPOLE. Well!!! (*He gives the situation up as indescribable, and goes for his hat.*)

RIDGEON. Damn his impudence!

B.B. I shouldnt be at all surprised to learn that he's well connected. Whenever I meet dignity and self-possession without any discoverable basis, I diagnose good family.

RIDGEON. Diagnose artistic genius, B.B. Thats what saves his self-respect.

SIR PATRICK. The world is made like that. The decent fellows are always being lectured and put out of countenance by the snobs.

B.B. (*altogether refusing to accept this*). *I* am not out of countenance. I should like, by Jupiter, to see the man who could put me out of countenance. (*Jennifer comes in.*) Ah, Mrs. Dubedat! And how are we to-day?

MRS. DUBEDAT (*shaking hands with him*). Thank you all so much for coming. (*She shakes Walpole's hand.*) Thank you, Sir Patrick (*She shakes Sir Patrick's.*) Oh, life has been worth living since I have known you. Since Richmond I have not known a moment's fear. And it used to be nothing but fear. Wont you sit down and tell me the result of the consultation?

WALPOLE. I'll go, if you dont mind, Mrs. Dubedat. I have an appointment. Before I go, let me say that I am quite agreed with my colleagues here as to the character of the case. As to the cause and the remedy, thats not my business: I'm only a surgeon; and these gentlemen are physicians and will advise you. I may have my own views: in fact I have them; and they are perfectly well known to my colleagues. If I am needed—and needed I shall be finally—they know where to find me; and I am always at your service. So for to-day, good-bye. (*He goes out, leaving Jennifer much puzzled by his unexpected withdrawal and formal manner.*)

SIR PATRICK. I also will ask you to excuse me, Mrs. Dubedat.

RIDGEON (*anxiously*). Are you going?

SIR PATRICK. Yes: I can be of no use here; and I must be getting back. As you know, maam, I'm not in practice now; and I shall not be in charge of the case. It rests between Sir Colenso Ridgeon and Sir Ralph Bloomfield Bonington. They know my opinion. Good afternoon to you, maam. (*He bows and makes for the door.*)

MRS. DUBEDAT (*detaining him*). Theres nothing wrong, is there? You dont think Louis is worse, do you?

SIR PATRICK. No: he's not worse. Just the same as at Richmond.

MRS. DUBEDAT. Oh, thank you: you frightened me. Excuse me.

SIR PATRICK. Dont mention it, maam. (*He goes out.*)

B.B. Now, Mrs. Dubedat, if I am to take the patient in hand—

MRS. DUBEDAT (*apprehensively, with a glance at Ridgeon*). You! But I thought that Sir Colenso—

B.B. (*beaming with the conviction that he is giving her a most gratifying surprise*). My dear lady, your husband shall have Me.

MRS. DUBEDAT. But—

B.B. Not a word: it is a pleasure to me, for your sake. Sir Colenso Ridgeon will be in his proper place, in the bacteriological laboratory. *I* shall be in my proper place, at the bedside. Your husband shall be treated exactly as if he were a member of the royal family. (*Mrs. Dubedat uneasy, again is about to protest*) No gratitude: it would embarrass me, I assure you. Now, may I ask whether you are particularly tied to these apartments. Of course, the motor has annihilated distance; but I confess that if you were rather nearer to me, it would be a little more convenient.

MRS. DUBEDAT. You see, this studio and flat are self-contained. I have suffered so much in lodgings. The servants are so frightfully dishonest.

B.B. Ah! Are they? Are they? Dear me!

MRS. DUBEDAT. I was never accustomed to lock things up. And I missed so many small sums. At last a dreadful thing happened. I missed a five-pound note. It was traced to the housemaid; and she actually said Louis had given it to her. And he wouldnt let me do anything: he is so sensitive that these things drive him mad.

B.B. Ah—hm—ha—yes—say no more, Mrs. Dubedat: you shall not move. If the mountain will not come to Mahomet, Mahomet must come to the mountain. Now I must be off. I will write and make an appointment. We shall begin stimulating the phagocytes on—on—probably on Tuesday next; but I will let you know. Depend on me; dont fret; eat regularly; sleep well; keep your spirits up; keep the patient cheerful; hope for the best; no tonic like a charming woman; no medicine like cheerfulness; no resource like science; good-bye, good-bye, good-bye. (*Having shaken hands—she being too overwhelmed to speak—he goes out, stopping to say to Ridgeon*) On Tuesday morning send me down a tube of some really stiff anti-toxin. Any kind will do. Dont forget. Good-bye, Colly. (*He goes out.*)

RIDGEON. You look quite discouraged again. (*She is almost in tears.*) What's the matter? Are you disappointed?

MRS. DUBEDAT. I know I ought to be very grateful. Believe me, I am very grateful. But—but—

RIDGEON. Well?

MRS. DUBEDAT. I had set my heart on y o u r curing Louis.

RIDGEON. Well, Sir Ralph Bloomfield Bonington—

MRS. DUBEDAT. Yes, I know, I know. It is a great privilege to have him. But oh, I wish it had been you. I know it's unreasonable; I cant explain; but I had such a strong instinct that you would cure him. I dont—I cant feel the same about Sir Ralph. You promised me. Why did you give Louis up?

RIDGEON. I explained to you. I cannot take another case.

MRS. DUBEDAT. But at Richmond?

RIDGEON. At Richmond I thought I could make room for one more case. But my old friend Dr. Blenkinsop claimed that place. His lung is attacked.

MRS. DUBEDAT (*attaching no importance whatever to Blenkinsop*). Do you mean that elderly man—that rather silly—

RIDGEON (*sternly*). I mean the gentleman that dined with us: an excellent and honest man, whose life is as valuable as anyone else's. I have arranged that I shall take his case, and that Sir Ralph Bloomfield Bonington shall take Mr. Dubedat's.

MRS. DUBEDAT (*turning indignantly on him*). I see what it is. Oh! it is envious, mean, cruel. And I thought that you would be above such a thing.

RIDGEON. What do you mean?

MRS. DUBEDAT. Oh, do you think I dont know? do you think it has never happened before? Why does everybody turn against him? Can you not forgive him for being superior to you? for being cleverer? for being braver? for being a great artist?

RIDGEON. Yes: I can forgive him for all that.

MRS. DUBEDAT. Well, have you anything to say against him? I have challenged everyone who has turned against him—challenged them face to face to tell me any wrong thing he has done, any ignoble thought he has uttered. They have always confessed that they could not tell me one. I challenge you now. What do you accuse him of?

RIDGEON. I am like all the rest. Face to face, I cannot tell you one thing against him.

MRS. DUBEDAT (*not satisfied*). But your manner is changed. And you have broken your promise to me to make room for him as your patient.

RIDGEON. I think you are a little unreasonable. You have had the very best medical advice in London for him; and his case has been taken in hand by a leader of the profession. Surely—

MRS. DUBEDAT. Oh, it is so cruel to keep telling me that. It seems all right; and it puts me in the wrong. But I am not in the wrong. I have faith in you; and I have no faith in the others. We have seen so many doctors: I have come to know at last when they are only talking and can do nothing. It is different with you. I feel that you know. You must listen to me, doctor. (*With sudden misgiving*) Am I offending you by calling you doctor instead of remembering your title?

RIDGEON. Nonsense. I a m a doctor. But mind you, dont call Walpole one.

MRS. DUBEDAT. I dont care about Mr. Walpole: it is you who must befriend me. Oh, will you please sit down and listen to me just for a few minutes. (*He assents with a grave inclination, and sits on the sofa. She sits on the easel chair.*) Thank you. I wont keep you long; but I must tell you the whole truth. Listen. I know Louis as nobody else in the world knows him or ever can know him. I am his wife. I know he has little faults: impatiences, sensitivenesses, even little selfishnesses that are too trivial for him to notice. I know that he sometimes shocks people about money because he is so utterly above it, and cant understand the value ordinary people set on it. Tell me: did he—did he borrow any money from you?

RIDGEON. He asked me for some—once.

MRS. DUBEDAT (*tears again in her eyes*). Oh, I am so sorry—so sorry. But he will never do it again: I pledge you my word for that. He has given me his promise: here in this room just before you came; and he is incapable of breaking his word. That was his only real weakness; and now it is conquered and done with for ever.

RIDGEON. Was that really his only weakness?

MRS. DUBEDAT. He is perhaps sometimes weak about women, because they adore him so, and are always laying traps for him. And of course when he says he doesnt believe in morality, ordinary pious people think he must be wicked. You can understand, cant you, how all this starts a great deal of gossip about him, and gets repeated until even good friends get set against him?

RIDGEON. Yes: I understand.

MRS. DUBEDAT. Oh, if you only knew the other side of him as I do! Do you know, doctor, that if Louis dishonored himself by a really bad action, I should kill myself.

RIDGEON. Come! don't exaggerate.

MRS. DUBEDAT. I should. You dont understand that, you east country people.

RIDGEON. You did not see much of the world in Cornwall, did you?

MRS. DUBEDAT (*naïvely*). Oh yes. I saw a great deal every day of the beauty of the world—more than you ever see here in London. But I saw very few people, if that is what you mean. I was an only child.

RIDGEON. That explains a good deal.

MRS. DUBEDAT. I had a great many dreams; but at last they all come to one dream.

RIDGEON (*with half a sigh*). Yes, the usual dream.

MRS. DUBEDAT (*surprised*). Is it usual?

RIDGEON. As I guess. You havnt yet told me what it was.

MRS. DUBEDAT. I didn't want to waste myself. I could do nothing myself; but I had a little property and I could help with it. I had even a little beauty: dont think me vain for knowing it. I knew that men of genius always had a terrible struggle with poverty and neglect at first. My dream was to save one of them from that, and bring some charm and happiness into his life. I prayed Heaven to send me one. I firmly believe that Louis was guided to me in answer to my prayer. He was no more like the other men I had met than the Thames Embankment is like our Cornish coasts. He saw everything that I saw, and drew it for me. He understood everything. He came to me like a child. Only fancy, doctor: he never even wanted to marry me: he never thought of the things other men think of! I had to propose it myself. Then he said he had no money. When I told him I had some, he said, "Oh, all right," just like a boy. He is still like that, quite unspoiled, a man in his thoughts, a great poet and artist in his dreams, and a child in his ways. I gave him myself and all I had that he might grow to his full height with plenty of sunshine. If I lost faith in him, it would mean the wreck and failure of my life. I should go back to Cornwall and die. I could show you the very cliff I should jump off. You must cure him: you must make him quite well again for me. I know that you can do it and that nobody else can. I implore you not to refuse what I am going to ask you to do. Take Louis yourself; and let Sir Ralph cure Dr. Blenkinsop.

RIDGEON (*slowly*). Mrs. Dubedat: do you really believe in my knowledge and skill as you say you do?

MRS. DUBEDAT. Absolutely. I do not give my trust by halves.

RIDGEON. I know that. Well, I am going to test you—hard. Will you believe me when I tell you that I understand what you have just told me; that I have no desire but to serve you in the most faithful friendship; and that your hero must be preserved to you.

MRS. DUBEDAT. Oh forgive me. Forgive what I said. You will preserve him to me.

RIDGEON. At all hazards. (*She kisses his hand. He rises hastily.*) N o: you have not heard the rest. (*She rises too.*) You must believe me when I tell you that the one chance of preserving the hero lies in Louis being in the care of Sir Ralph.

MRS. DUBEDAT (*firmly*). You say so: I have no more doubt: I believe you. Thank you.

RIDGEON. Good-bye. (*She takes his hand.*) I hope this will be a lasting friendship.

MRS. DUBEDAT. It will. My friendships end only with death.

RIDGEON. Death ends everything, doesnt it? Good-bye.

With a sigh and a look of pity at her which she does not understand, he goes.

END OF ACT III

ACT IV

The studio. The easel is pushed back to the wall. Cardinal Death, holding his scythe and hour-glass like a sceptre and globe, sits on the throne. On the hat-stand hang the hats of Sir Patrick and Bloomfield Bonington. Walpole, just come in, is hanging up his beside them. There is a knock. He opens the door and finds Ridgeon there.

WALPOLE. Hallo, Ridgeon!

They come into the middle of the room together, taking off their gloves.

RIDGEON. Whats the matter! Have you been sent for, too?

WALPOLE. Weve all been sent for. Ive only just come: I havnt seen him yet. The charwoman says that old Paddy Cullen has been here with B.B. for the last half-hour. (*Sir Patrick, with bad news in his face, enters from the inner room.*) Well: whats up?

SIR PATRICK. Go in and see. B.B. is in there with him.

Walpole goes. Ridgeon is about to follow him; but Sir Patrick stops him with a look.

RIDGEON. What has happened?

SIR PATRICK. Do you remember Jane Marsh's arm?

RIDGEON. Is that whats happened?

SIR PATRICK. Thats whats happened. His lung has gone like Jane's arm. I never saw such a case. He has got through three months galloping consumption in three days.

RIDGEON. B.B. got in on the negative phase.

SIR PATRICK. Negative or positive, the lad's done for. He wont last out the afternoon. He'll go suddenly: Ive often seen it.

RIDGEON. So long as he goes before his wife finds him out, *I* don't care. I fully expected this.

SIR PATRICK (*drily*). It's a little hard on a lad to be killed because his wife has too high an opinion of him. Fortunately few of us are in any danger of that.

Sir Ralph comes from the inner room and hastens between them, humanely concerned, but professionally elate and communicative.

B.B. Ah, here you are, Ridgeon. Paddy's told you, of course.

RIDGEON. Yes.

B.B. It's an enormously interesting case. You know, Colly, by Jupiter, if I didnt know as a matter of scientific fact that I'd been stimulating the phagocytes, I should say I'd been stimulating the other things. What is the explanation of it, Sir Patrick? How do you account for it, Ridgeon? Have we over-stimulated the phagocytes? Have they not only eaten up the bacilli, but attacked and destroyed the red corpuscles as well? a possibility suggested by the patient's pallor. Nay, have they finally begun to prey on the lungs themselves? Or on one another? I shall write a paper about this case.

Walpole comes back, very serious, even shocked. He comes between B.B. and Ridgeon.

WALPOLE. Whew! B.B.: youve done it this time.

B.B. What do you mean?

WALPOLE. Killed him. The worst case of neglected blood-poisoning I ever saw. It's too late now to do anything. He'd die under the anæsthetic.

B.B. (*offended*). Killed! Really, Walpole, if your monomania were not well known, I should take such an expression very seriously.

SIR PATRICK. Come come! When youve both killed as many people as I have in my time youll feel humble enough about it. Come and look at him, Colly.

Ridgeon and Sir Patrick go into the inner room.

WALPOLE. I apologize, B.B. But it's blood-poisoning.

B.B. (*recovering his irresistible good nature*). My dear

Walpole, e v e r y t h i n g is blood-poisoning. But upon my soul, I shall not use any of that stuff of Ridgeon's again. What made me so sensitive about what you said just now is that, strictly between ourselves, Ridgeon has cooked our young friend's goose.

Jennifer, worried and distressed, but always gentle, comes between them from the inner room. She wears a nurse's apron.

MRS. DUBEDAT. Sir Ralph: what am I to do? That man who insisted on seeing me, and sent in word that his business was important to Louis, is a newspaper man. A paragraph appeared in the paper this morning saying that Louis is seriously ill; and this man wants to interview him about it. How can people be so brutally callous?

WALPOLE (*moving vengefully towards the door*). You just leave me to deal with him!

MRS. DUBEDAT (*stopping him*). But Louis insists on seeing him: he almost began to cry about it. And he says he cant bear his room any longer. He says he wants to (*She struggles with a sob.*)—to die in his studio. Sir Patrick says let him have his way: it can do no harm. What shall we do?

B.B. (*encouragingly*). Why, follow Sir Patrick's excellent advice, of course. As he says, it can do him no harm; and it will no doubt do him good—a great deal of good. He will be much the better for it.

MRS. DUBEDAT (*a little cheered*). Will you bring the man up here, Mr. Walpole, and tell him that he may see Louis, but that he mustnt exhaust him by talking? (*Walpole nods and goes out by the outer door.*) Sir Ralph, dont be angry with me; but Louis will die if he stays here. I must take him to Cornwall. He will recover there.

B.B. (*brightening wonderfully, as if Dubedat were already saved*). Cornwall! The very place for him! Wonderful for the lungs. Stupid of me not to think of it before. You are his best physician after all, dear lady. An inspiration! Cornwall: of course, yes, yes, yes.

MRS. DUBEDAT (*comforted and touched*). You are so kind, Sir Ralph. But dont give me m u c h or I shall cry; and Louis cant bear that.

B.B. (*gently putting his protecting arm round her shoul-*

ders). Then let us come back to him and help to carry him in. Cornwall! of course, of course. The very thing! (*They go together into the bedroom.*)

Walpole returns with The Newspaper Man, a cheerful, affable young man who is disabled for ordinary business pursuits by a congenital erroneousness which renders him incapable of describing accurately anything he sees or understanding or reporting accurately anything he hears. As the only employment in which these defects do not matter is journalism (for a newspaper, not having to act on its description and reports, but only to sell them to idly curious people, has nothing but honor to lose by inaccuracy and unveracity), he has perforce become a journalist, and has to keep up an air of high spirits through a daily struggle with his own illiteracy and the precariousness of his employment. He has a note-book, and occasionally attempts to make a note; but as he cannot write shorthand, and does not write with ease in any hand, he generally gives it up as a bad job before he succeeds in finishing a sentence.

THE NEWSPAPER MAN (*looking round and making indecisive attempts at notes*). This is the studio, I suppose.

WALPOLE. Yes.

THE NEWSPAPER MAN (*wittily*). Where he has his models, eh?

WALPOLE (*grimly irresponsive*). No doubt.

THE NEWSPAPER MAN. Cubicle, you said it was?

WALPOLE. Yes, tubercle.

THE NEWSPAPER MAN. Which way do you spell it: is it c-u-b-i-c-a-l or c-l-e?

WALPOLE. Tubercle, man, not cubical. (*Spelling it for him*) T-u-b-e-r-c-l-e.

THE NEWSPAPER MAN. O! tubercle. Some disease, I suppose. I thought he had consumption. Are you one of the family or the doctor?

WALPOLE. I'm neither one nor the other. I am M i s t e r Cutler Walpole. Put that down. Then put down Sir Colenso Ridgeon.

THE NEWSPAPER MAN. Pigeon?

WALPOLE. Ridgeon. (*Contemptuously snatching his book*) Here: youd better let me write the names down for you: youre sure to get them wrong. That comes of belonging to an illiterate profession, with no qualifications and no public register. (*He writes the particulars.*)

THE NEWSPAPER MAN. Oh, I say: you h a v e got your knife into us, havnt you?

WALPOLE (*vindictively*). I wish I had: I'd make a better man of you. Now attend. (*Shewing him the book*) These are the names of the three doctors. This is the patient. This is the address. This is the name of the disease. (*He shuts the book with a snap which makes the journalist blink, and returns it to him.*) Mr. Dubedat will be brought in here presently. He wants to see you because he doesnt know how bad he is. We'll allow you to wait a few minutes to humor him; but if you talk to him, out you go. He may die at any moment.

THE NEWSPAPER MAN (*interested*). Is he as bad as that? I say: I a m in luck to-day. Would you mind letting me photograph you? (*He produces a camera.*) Could you have a lancet or something in your hand?

WALPOLE. Put it up. If you want my photograph you can get it in Baker Street in any of the series of celebrities.

THE NEWSPAPER MAN. But theyll want to be paid. If you wouldnt mind (*fingering the camera*)—?

WALPOLE. I would. Put it up, I tell you. Sit down there and be quiet.

The Newspaper Man quickly sits down on the piano stool as Dubedat, in an invalid's chair, is wheeled in by Mrs. Dubedat and Sir Ralph. They place the chair between the dais and the sofa, where the easel stood before. Louis is not changed as a robust man would be; and he is not scared. His eyes look larger; and he is so weak physically that he can hardly move, lying on his cushions with complete languor; but his mind is active; it is making the most of his condition, finding voluptuousness in languor and drama in death. They are all impressed, in spite of themselves, except Ridgeon, who is implacable. B.B. is entirely sympathetic and forgiving. Ridgeon follows the chair with a tray of milk and stimulants. Sir Patrick, who accompanies him, takes the tea-table from the corner and places it behind the chair for the tray. B.B. takes the easel chair and places it for Jennifer at Dubedat's side, next the dais, from which the lay figure ogles the dying artist. B.B. then returns to Dubedat's left. Jennifer sits. Walpole sits down on the edge of the dais. Ridgeon stands near him.

LOUIS (*blissfully*). Thats happiness. To be in a studio! Happiness!

MRS. DUBEDAT. Yes, dear. Sir Patrick says you may stay here as long as you like.

LOUIS. Jennifer.

MRS. DUBEDAT. Yes, my darling.

LOUIS. Is the newspaper man here?

THE NEWSPAPER MAN (*glibly*). Yes, Mr. Dubedat: I'm here, at your service. I represent the press. I thought you might like to let us have a few words about—about—er—well, a few words on your illness, and your plans for the season.

LOUIS. My plans for the season are very simple. I'm going to die.

MRS. DUBEDAT (*tortured*). Louis—dearest—

LOUIS. My darling: I'm very weak and tired. Dont put on me the horrible strain of pretending that I dont know. Ive been lying there listening to the doctors—laughing to myself. They know. Dearest: dont cry. It makes you ugly; and I cant bear that. (*She dries her eyes and recovers herself with a proud effort.*) I want you to promise me something.

MRS. DUBEDAT. Yes, yes: you know I will. (*Imploringly*) Only, my love, my love, dont talk: it will waste your strength.

LOUIS. No: it will only use it up. Ridgeon: give me something to keep me going for a few minutes—not one of your confounded anti-toxins, if you dont mind. I have some things to say before I go.

RIDGEON (*looking at Sir Patrick*). I suppose it can do no harm? (*He pours out some spirit, and is about to add soda water when Sir Patrick corrects him.*)

SIR PATRICK. In milk. Dont set him coughing.

LOUIS (*after drinking*). Jennifer.

MRS. DUBEDAT. Yes, dear.

LOUIS. If theres one thing I hate more than another, it's a widow. Promise me that youll never be a widow.

MRS. DUBEDAT. My dear, what do you mean?

LOUIS. I want you to look beautiful. I want people to see in your eyes that you were married to me. The people in Italy used to point at Dante and say, "There goes the man who has been in hell." I want them to point at you and say, "There goes a woman who has been in heaven." It h a s been heaven, darling, hasnt it—sometimes?

MRS. DUBEDAT. Oh yes, yes. Always, always.

LOUIS. If you wear black and cry, people will say, "Look at that miserable woman: her husband made her miserable."

MRS. DUBEDAT. No, never. You are the light and the blessing of my life. I never lived until I knew you.

LOUIS (*his eyes glistening*). Then you must always wear beautiful dresses and splendid magic jewels. Think of all the wonderful pictures I shall never paint. (*She wins a terrible victory over a sob.*) Well, you must be transfigured with all the beauty of those pictures. Men must get such dreams from seeing you as they never could get from any daubing with paints and brushes. Painters must paint you as they never painted any mortal woman before. There must be a great tradition of beauty, a great atmosphere of wonder and romance. That is what men must always think of when they think of me. That is the sort of immortality I want. You can make that for me, Jennifer. There are lots of things you dont understand that every woman in the street understands; but you can understand that and do it as nobody else can. Promise me that immortality. Promise me you will not make a little hell of crape and crying and undertaker's horrors and withering flowers and all that vulgar rubbish.

MRS. DUBEDAT. I promise. But all that is far off, dear. You are to come to Cornwall with me and get well. Sir Ralph says so.

LOUIS. Poor old B.B.

B.B. (*affected to tears, turns away and whispers to Sir Patrick*). Poor fellow! Brain going.

LOUIS. Sir Patrick's there, isnt he?

SIR PATRICK. Yes, yes. I'm here.

LOUIS. Sit down, wont you? It's a shame to keep you standing about.

SIR PATRICK. Yes, yes. Thank you. All right.

LOUIS. Jennifer.

MRS. DUBEDAT. Yes, dear.

LOUIS (*with a strange look of delight*). Do you remember the burning bush?

MRS. DUBEDAT. Yes, yes. Oh, my dear, how it strains my heart to remember it now!

LOUIS. Does it? It fills me with joy. Tell them about it.

MRS. DUBEDAT. It was nothing—only that once in my old Cornish home we lit the first fire of the winter; and when we looked through the window we saw the flames dancing in a bush in the garden.

LOUIS. Such a color! Garnet color. Waving like silk. Liquid lovely flame flowing up through the bay leaves, and not burning them. Well, I shall be a flame like that. I'm sorry to disappoint the poor little worms; but the last of me shall be the flame in the burning bush. Whenever you see the flame, Jennifer, that will be me. Promise me that I shall be burnt.

MRS. DUBEDAT. Oh, if I might be with you, Louis!

LOUIS. No: you must always be in the garden when the bush flames. You are my hold on the world: you are my immortality. Promise.

MRS. DUBEDAT. I'm listening. I shall not forget. You know that I promise.

LOUIS. Well, thats about all; except that you are to hang my pictures at the one-man-show. I can trust your eye. You wont let anyone else touch them.

MRS. DUBEDAT. You can trust me.

LOUIS. Then theres nothing more to worry about, is there? Give me some more of that milk. I'm fearfully tired; but if I stop talking I shant begin again. (*Sir Ralph gives him a drink. He takes it and looks up quaintly.*) I say, B.B., do you think anything would stop y o u talking?

B.B. (*almost unmanned*). He confuses me with you, Paddy. Poor fellow! Poor fellow!

LOUIS (*musing*). I used to be awfully afraid of death; but now it's come I have no fear; and I'm perfectly happy. Jennifer.

MRS. DUBEDAT. Yes, dear?

LOUIS. I'll tell you a secret. I used to think that our marriage was all an affectation, and that I'd break loose and run away some day. But now that I'm going to be broken loose whether I like it or not, I'm perfectly fond of you, and perfectly satisfied because I'm going to live as part of you and not as my troublesome self.

MRS. DUBEDAT (*heartbroken*). Stay with me, Louis. Oh, dont leave me, dearest.

LOUIS. Not that I'm selfish. With all my faults I dont think Ive ever been really selfish. No artist can: Art is too large for that. You will marry again, Jennifer.

MRS. DUBEDAT. Oh, how c a n you, Louis?

LOUIS (*insisting childishly*). Yes, because people who have found marriage happy always marry again. Ah, *I* shant be jealous. (*Slyly*) But dont talk to the other fellow too much about me: he wont like it. (*Almost chuckling*) I shall be your lover all the time; but it will be a secret from him, poor devil!

SIR PATRICK. Come! youve talked enough. Try to rest awhile.

LOUIS (*wearily*). Yes: I'm fearfully tired; but I shall have a long rest presently. I have something to say to you fellows. Youre all there, arnt you? I'm too weak to see anything but Jennifer's bosom. That promises rest.

RIDGEON. We are all here.

LOUIS (*startled*). That voice sounded devilish. Take care, Ridgeon: my ears hear things that other people's ears cant. Ive been thinking—thinking. I'm cleverer than you imagine.

SIR PATRICK (*whispering to Ridgeon*). Youve got on his nerves, Colly. Slip out quietly.

RIDGEON (*apart to Sir Patrick*). Would you deprive the dying actor of his audience?

LOUIS (*his face lighting up faintly with mischievous glee*). I heard that, Ridgeon. That was good. Jennifer, dear: be kind to Ridgeon always; because he was the last man who amused me.

RIDGEON (*relentless*). Was I?

LOUIS. But it's not true. It's you who are still on the stage. I'm half way home already.

MRS. DUBEDAT (*to Ridgeon*). What did you say?

LOUIS (*answering for him*). Nothing, dear. Only one of those little secrets that men keep among themselves. Well, all you chaps have thought pretty hard things of me, and said them.

B.B. (*quite overcome*). No, no, Dubedat. Not at all.

LOUIS. Yes, you have. I know what you all think of me. Dont imagine I'm sore about it. I forgive you.

WALPOLE (*involuntarily*). Well, damn me! (*Ashamed*) I beg your pardon.

LOUIS. That was old Walpole, I know. Dont grieve, Walpole. I'm perfectly happy. I'm not in pain. I dont want to live. I've escaped from myself. I'm in heaven, immortal in the heart of my beautiful Jennifer. I'm not afraid, and not ashamed. (*Reflectively, puzzling it out for himself weakly*) I know that in an accidental sort of way, struggling through the unreal part of life, I havnt always been able to live up to my ideal. But in my own real world I have never done anything wrong, never denied my faith, never been untrue to myself. Ive been threatened and blackmailed and insulted and starved. But Ive played the game. Ive fought the good fight. And now it's all over, theres an indescribable peace. (*He feebly folds his hands and utters his creed.*) I believe in Michael Angelo, Velasquez, and Rembrandt; in the might of design, the mystery of color, the redemption of all things by Beauty everlasting, and the message of Art that has made these hands blessed. Amen. Amen. (*He closes his eyes and lies still.*)

MRS. DUBEDAT (*breathless*). Louis: are you—

Walpole rises and comes quickly to see whether he is dead.

LOUIS. Not yet, dear. Very nearly, but not yet. I should like to rest my head on your bosom; only it would tire you.

MRS. DUBEDAT. No, no, no, darling: how could you tire me? (*She lifts him so that he lies on her bosom.*)

LOUIS. Thats good. Thats real.

MRS. DUBEDAT. Dont spare me, dear. Indeed, i n d e e d you will not tire me. Lean on me with all your weight.

LOUIS (*with a sudden half return of his normal strength and comfort*). Jinny Gwinny: I think I shall recover after all. (*Sir Patrick looks significantly at Ridgeon, mutely warning him that this is the end.*)

MRS. DUBEDAT (*hopefully*). Yes, yes: you shall.

LOUIS. Because I suddenly want to sleep. Just an ordinary sleep.

MRS. DUBEDAT (*rocking him*). Yes, dear. Sleep. (*He seems to go to sleep. Walpole makes another movement. She protests.*) Sh-sh: please dont disturb him. (*His lips move.*) What did you say, dear? (*In great distress*) I cant listen without moving him. (*His lips move again: Walpole bends down and listens.*)

WALPOLE. He wants to know is the newspaper man here.

THE NEWSPAPER MAN (*excited; for he has been enjoying himself enormously*). Yes, Mr. Dubedat. Here I am.

Walpole raises his hand warningly to silence him. Sir Ralph sits down quietly on the sofa and frankly buries his face in his handkerchief.

MRS. DUBEDAT (*with great relief*). Oh thats right, dear: dont spare me: lean with all your weight on me. Now you are really resting.

Sir Patrick quickly comes forward and feels Louis' pulse; then takes him by the shoulders.

SIR PATRICK. Let me put him back on the pillow, maam. He will be better so.

MRS. DUBEDAT (*piteously*). Oh no, please, p l e a s e, doctor. He is not tiring me; and he will be so hurt when he wakes if he finds I have put him away.

SIR PATRICK. He will never wake again. (*He takes the body from her and replaces it in the chair. Ridgeon, unmoved, lets down the back and makes a bier of it.*)

MRS. DUBEDAT (*who has unexpectedly sprung to her feet, and stands dry-eyed and stately*). Was that death?

WALPOLE. Yes.

MRS. DUBEDAT (*with complete dignity*). Will you wait for me a moment? I will come back. (*She goes out.*)

WALPOLE. Ought we to follow her? Is she in her right senses?

SIR PATRICK (*with quiet conviction*). Yes. Shes all right. Leave her alone. She'll come back.

RIDGEON (*callously*). Let us get this thing out of the way before she comes.

B.B. (*rising, shocked*). My dear Colly! The poor lad! He died splendidly.

SIR PATRICK. Aye! that is how the wicked die.

For there are no bands in their death;
But their strength is firm:
They are not in trouble as other men.

No matter: it's not for us to judge. He's in another world now.

WALPOLE. Borrowing his first five-pound note there, probably.

RIDGEON. I said the other day that the most tragic thing in the world is a sick doctor. I was wrong. The most tragic thing in the world is a man of genius who is not also a man of honor.

Ridgeon and Walpole wheel the chair into the recess.

THE NEWSPAPER MAN (*to Sir Ralph*). I thought it shewed a very nice feeling, his being so particular about his wife going into proper mourning for him and making her promise never to marry again.

B.B. (*impressively*). Mrs. Dubedat is not in a position to carry the interview any further. Neither are we.

SIR PATRICK. Good afternoon to you.

THE NEWSPAPER MAN. Mrs. Dubedat said she was coming back.

B.B. After you have gone.

THE NEWSPAPER MAN. Do you think she would give me a few words on How It Feels to be a Widow? Rather a good title for an article, isnt it?

B.B. Young man: if you wait until Mrs. Dubedat comes back, you will be able to write an article on How It Feels to be Turned Out of the House.

THE NEWSPAPER MAN (*unconvinced*). You think she'd rather not—

B.B. (*cutting him short*). Good day to you. (*Giving him a visiting-card*) Mind you get my name correctly. Good day.

THE NEWSPAPER MAN. Good day. Thank you. (*Vaguely trying to read the card*) Mr.—

B.B. No, not Mister. This is your hat, I think (*giving it to him*). Gloves? No, of course: no gloves. Good day to you. (*He edges him out at last; shuts the door on him; and returns to Sir Patrick as Ridgeon and Walpole come back from the recess, Walpole crossing the room to the hat-stand, and Ridgeon coming between Sir Ralph and Sir Patrick.*) Poor fellow! Poor young fellow! How well he died! I feel a better man, really.

SIR PATRICK. When youre as old as I am, youll know that it matters very little how a man dies. What matters is, how he lives. Every fool that runs his nose against a bullet is a hero nowadays, because he dies for his country. Why dont he live for it to some purpose?

B.B. No, please, Paddy: dont be hard on the poor lad. Not now, not now. After all, was he so bad? He had only two failings: money and women. Well, let us be honest. Tell the truth, Paddy. Dont be hypocritical, Ridgeon. Throw off the mask, Walpole. Are these two matters so well arranged at present that a disregard of the usual arrangements indicates real depravity?

WALPOLE. I dont mind his disregarding the usual arrangments. Confound the usual arrangements! To a man of science theyre beneath contempt both as to money and women. What I mind is his disregarding everything except his own pocket and his own fancy. He didnt disregard the usual arrangements when they paid him. Did he give us his pictures for nothing? Do you suppose he'd have hesitated to blackmail me if I'd compromised myself with his wife? Not he.

SIR PATRICK. Dont waste your time wrangling over him. A blackguard's a blackguard; an honest man's an honest man; and neither of them will ever be at a loss for a religion or a morality to prove that their ways are the right ways. It's the same with nations, the same with professions, the same all the world over and always will be.

B.B. Ah, well, perhaps, perhaps, perhaps. Still d e m o r t u i s n i l n i s i b o n u m. He died extremely well, remarkably well. He has set us an example: let us endeavor to follow it rather than harp on the weaknesses that have perished with him. I think it is Shakespear who says that the good that most men do lives after them: the evil lies interréd with their bones. Yes: interréd with their bones. Believe me, Paddy, we are all mortal. It is the common lot, Ridgeon. Say what you will, Walpole, Nature's debt must be paid. If tis not to-day, twill be to-morrow.

To-morrow and to-morrow and to-morrow
After life's fitful fever they sleep well
And like this insubstantial bourne from which
No traveller returns
Leave not a wrack behind.

Walpole is about to speak, but B.B., suddenly and vehemently proceeding, extinguishes him.

Out, out, brief candle:
For nothing canst thou to damnation add
The readiness is all.

WALPOLE (*gently; for B.B.'s feeling, absurdly expressed as it is, is too sincere and humane to be ridiculed*). Yes, B.B. Death makes people go on like that. I dont know why it should; but it does. By the way, what are we going to do? Ought we to clear out; or had we better wait and see whether Mrs. Dubedat will come back?

SIR PATRICK. I think we'd better go. We can tell the charwoman what to do.

They take their hats and go to the door.

MRS. DUBEDAT (*coming from the inner door wonderfully and beautifully dressed, and radiant, carrying a great piece of purple silk, handsomely embroidered, over her arm*). I'm so sorry to have kept you waiting.

SIR PATRICK.	(*amazed, all together in a confused murmur*).	Dont mention it, madam.
B.B.		Not at all, not at all.
RIDGEON.		By no means.
WALPOLE.		It doesnt matter in the least.

MRS. DUBEDAT (*coming to them*). I felt that I must shake hands with his friends once before we part to-day. We have shared together a great privilege and a great happiness. I dont think we can ever think of ourselves as ordinary people again. We have had a wonderful experience; and that gives us a common faith, a common ideal, that nobody else can quite have. Life will always be beautiful to us: death will always be beautiful to us. May we shake hands on that?

SIR PATRICK (*shaking hands*). Remember: all letters had better be left to your solicitor. Let him open everything and settle everything. Thats the law, you know.

MRS. DUBEDAT. Oh, thank you: I didnt know. (*Sir Patrick goes.*)

WALPOLE. Good-bye. I blame myself: I should have insisted on operating. (*He goes.*)

B.B. I will send the proper people: they will know what to

do: you shall have no trouble. Good-bye, my dear lady. (*He goes.*)

RIDGEON. Good-bye. (*He offers his hand.*)

MRS. DUBEDAT (*drawing back with gentle majesty*). I said his f r i e n d s, Sir Colenso. (*He bows and goes.*)

She unfolds the great piece of silk, and goes into the recess to cover her dead.

END OF ACT IV

ACT V

One of the smaller Bond Street Picture Galleries. The entrance is from a picture shop. Nearly in the middle of the gallery there is a writing-table, at which the Secretary, fashionably dressed, sits with his back to the entrance, correcting catalogue proofs. Some copies of a new book are on the desk, also the Secretary's shining hat and a couple of magnifying glasses. At the side, on his left, a little behind him, is a small door marked PRIVATE. *Near the same side is a cushioned bench parallel to the walls, which are covered with Dubedat's works. Two screens, also covered with drawings, stand near the corners right and left of the entrance.*

Jennifer, beautifully dressed and apparently very happy and prosperous, comes into the gallery through the private door.

JENNIFER. Have the catalogues come yet, Mr. Danby?

THE SECRETARY. Not yet.

JENNIFER. What a shame! It's a quarter past: the private view will begin in less than half an hour.

THE SECRETARY. I think I'd better run over to the printers to hurry them up.

JENNIFER. Oh, if you would be so good, Mr. Danby. I'll take your place while youre away.

THE SECRETARY. If anyone should come before the time dont take any notice. The commissionaire wont let anyone through unless he knows him. We have a few people who like to come before the crowd—people who really buy; and of course we're glad to see them. Have you seen the notices in Brush and Crayon and in The Easel?

JENNIFER (*indignantly*). Yes: most disgraceful. They write quite patronizingly, as if they were Mr. Dubedat's superiors. After all the cigars and sandwiches they had from us on the press day, and all they drank, I really think it is infamous that they should write like that. I hope you have not sent them tickets for to-day.

THE SECRETARY. Oh, they wont come again: theres no lunch to-day. The advance copies of your book have come. (*He indicates the new books.*)

JENNIFER (*pouncing on a copy, wildly excited*). Give it to me. Oh! excuse me a moment. (*She runs away with it through the private door.*)

The Secretary takes a mirror from his drawer and smartens himself before going out. Ridgeon comes in.

RIDGEON. Good morning. May I look round, as usual, before the doors open?

THE SECRETARY. Certainly, Sir Colenso. I'm sorry the catalogues have not come: I'm just going to see about them. Heres my own list, if you dont mind.

RIDGEON. Thanks. Whats this? (*He takes up one of the new books.*)

THE SECRETARY. Thats just come in. An advance copy of Mrs. Dubedat's Life of her late husband.

RIDGEON (*reading the title*). The Story of a King of Men. By His Wife. (*He looks at the portrait frontispiece.*) Ay: there he is. You knew him here, I suppose.

THE SECRETARY. Oh, we knew him. Better than she did, Sir Colenso, in some ways, perhaps.

RIDGEON. So did I. (*They look significantly at one another.*) I'll take a look round.

The Secretary puts on the shining hat and goes out. Ridgeon begins looking at the pictures. Presently he comes back to the table for a magnifying glass, and scrutinizes a drawing very closely. He sighs; shakes his head, as if constrained to admit the extraordinary fascination and merit of the work; then marks the Secretary's list. Proceeding with his survey, he disappears behind the screen. Jennifer comes back with her book. A look round satisfies her that she is alone. She seats herself at the table and admires the memoir—her first printed book—to her heart's content. Ridgeon re-appears, face to the wall, scrutinizing the drawings. After using his glass again, he steps back to get a more distant view of one of the larger pictures. She hastily closes the book at the sound; looks round; recognizes him; and stares, petrified. He takes a further step back which brings him nearer to her.

RIDGEON (*shaking his head as before, ejaculates*). Clever brute! (*She flushes as though he had struck her. He turns to put the glass down on the desk, and finds himself face to face with her intent gaze.*) I beg your pardon. I thought I was alone.

JENNIFER (*controlling herself, and speaking steadily and meaningly*). I am glad we have met, Sir Colenso Ridgeon. I met Dr. Blenkinsop yesterday. I congratulate you on a wonderful cure.

RIDGEON (*can find no words; makes an embarrassed gesture of assent after a moment's silence, and puts down the glass and the Secretary's list on the table*).

JENNIFER. He looked the picture of health and strength and prosperity. (*She looks for a moment at the walls, contrasting Blenkinsop's fortune with the artist's fate.*)

RIDGEON (*in low tones, still embarrassed*). He has been fortunate.

JENNIFER. V e r y fortunate. His life has been spared.

RIDGEON. I mean that he has been made a Medical Officer of Health. He cured the Chairman of the Borough Council very successfully.

JENNIFER. With y o u r medicines?

RIDGEON. No. I believe it was with a pound of ripe greengages.

JENNIFER (*with deep gravity*). Funny!

RIDGEON. Yes. Life does not cease to be funny when people die any more than it ceases to be serious when people laugh.

JENNIFER. Dr. Blenkinsop said one very strange thing to me.

RIDGEON. What was that?

JENNIFER. He said that private practice in medicine ought to be put down by law. When I asked him why, he said that private doctors were ignorant licensed murderers.

RIDGEON. That is what the public doctor always thinks of the private doctor. Well, Blenkinsop ought to know. He was a private doctor long enough himself. Come! you have talked at me long enough. Talk to me. You have something to reproach me with. There is reproach in your face, in your voice: you are full of it. Out with it.

JENNIFER. It is too late for reproaches now. When I turned and saw you just now, I wondered how you could come here coolly to look at his pictures. You answered the question. To you, he was only a clever brute.

RIDGEON (*quivering*). Oh, dont. You know I did not know you were here.

JENNIFER (*raising her head a little with a quite gentle impulse of pride*). You think it only mattered because I heard it. As if it could touch me, or touch him! Dont you see that what is really wonderful is that to you living things have no souls.

RIDGEON (*with a sceptical shrug*). The soul is an organ I have not come across in the course of my anatomical work.

JENNIFER. You know you would not dare to say such a silly thing as that to anybody but a woman whose mind you despise. If you dissected me you could not find my conscience. Do you think I have got none?

RIDGEON. I have met people who had none.

JENNIFER. Clever brutes? Do you know, doctor, that some of the dearest and most faithful friends I ever had were only brutes! You would have vivisected them. The dearest and greatest of all my friends had a sort of beauty and affectionateness that only animals can have. I hope you may never feel what I felt when I had to put him into the hands of men who defend the torture of animals because they are only brutes.

RIDGEON. Well, did you find us so very cruel, after all? They tell me that though you have dropped me, you stay for weeks with the Bloomfield Boningtons and the Walpoles. I think it must be true, because they never mention you to me now.

JENNIFER. The animals in Sir Ralph's house are like spoiled

children. When Mr. Walpole had to take a splinter out of the mastiff's paw, I had to hold the poor dog myself; and Mr. Walpole had to turn Sir Ralph out of the room. And Mrs. Walpole has to tell the gardener not to kill wasps when Mr. Walpole is looking. But there are doctors who are naturally cruel; and there are others who get used to cruelty and are callous about it. They blind themselves to the souls of animals; and that blinds them to the souls of men and women. You made a dreadful mistake about Louis; but you would not have made it if you had not trained yourself to make the same mistake about dogs. You saw nothing in them but dumb brutes; and so you could see nothing in him but a clever brute.

RIDGEON (*with sudden resolution*). I made no mistake whatever about him.

JENNIFER. Oh, doctor!

RIDGEON (*obstinately*). I made no mistake whatever about him.

JENNIFER. Have you forgotten that he died?

RIDGEON (*with a sweep of his hand towards the pictures*). He is not dead. He is there. (*Taking up the book*) And there.

JENNIFER (*springing up with blazing eyes*). Put that down. How dare you touch it?

Ridgeon, amazed at the fierceness of the outburst, puts it down with a deprecatory shrug. She takes it up and looks as it as if he had profaned a relic.

RIDGEON. I am very sorry. I see I had better go.

JENNIFER (*putting the book down*). I beg your pardon. I—I forgot myself. But it is not yet—it is a private copy.

RIDGEON. But for me it would have been a very different book.

JENNIFER. But for you it would have been a longer one.

RIDGEON. You know then that I killed him?

JENNIFER (*suddenly moved and softened*). Oh, doctor, if you acknowledge that—if you have confessed it to yourself—if you realize what you have done, then there is forgiveness. I trusted in your strength instinctively at first; then I thought I had mistaken callousness for strength. Can you blame me? But if it was really strength—if it was only such a mistake as we all make sometimes—it will make me so happy to be friends with you again.

RIDGEON. I tell you I made no mistake. I cured Blenkinsop: was there any mistake there?

JENNIFER. He recovered. Oh, dont be foolishly proud, doctor. Confess to a failure, and save our friendship. Remember, Sir Ralph gave Louis your medicine; and it made him worse.

RIDGEON. I cant be your friend on false pretences. Something has got me by the throat: the truth must come out. I used that medicine myself on Blenkinsop. It did not make him worse. It is a dangerous medicine: it cured Blenkinsop: it killed Louis Dubedat. When I handle it, it cures. When another man handles it, it kills—sometimes.

JENNIFER (*naïvely: not yet taking it all in*). Then why did you let Sir Ralph give it to Louis?

RIDGEON. I'm going to tell you. I did it because I was in love with you.

JENNIFER (*innocently surprised*). In lo— You! an elderly man!

RIDGEON (*thunderstruck, raising his fists to heaven*). Dubedat: thou art avenged! (*He drops his hands and collapses on the bench.*) I never thought of that. I suppose I appear to you a ridiculous old fogey.

JENNIFER. But surely—I did not mean to offend you, indeed—but you must be at least twenty years older than I am.

RIDGEON. Oh, quite. More, perhaps. In twenty years you will understand how little difference that makes.

JENNIFER. But even so, how could you think that I—his wife—could ever think of y o u—

RIDGEON (*stopping her with a nervous waving of his fingers*). Yes, yes, yes, yes: I quite understand: you neednt rub it in.

JENNIFER. But—oh, it is only dawning on me now—I was so surprised at first—do you dare to tell me that it was to gratify a miserable jealousy that you deliberately—oh! oh! you murdered him.

RIDGEON. I think I did. It really comes to that.

Thou shalt not kill, but needst not strive
Officiously to keep alive.

I suppose—yes: I killed him.

JENNIFER. And you tell me that! to my face! callously! You are not afraid!

RIDGEON. I am a doctor: I have nothing to fear. It is not an indictable offence to call in B.B. Perhaps it ought to be; but it isnt.

JENNIFER. I did not mean that. I meant afraid of my taking the law into my own hands, and killing you.

RIDGEON. I am so hopelessly idiotic about you that I should not mind it a bit. You would always remember me if you did that.

JENNIFER. I shall remember you always as a little man who tried to kill a great one.

RIDGEON. Pardon me. I succeeded.

JENNIFER (*with quiet conviction*). No. Doctors think they hold the keys of life and death; but it is not their will that is fulfilled. I dont believe you made any difference at all.

RIDGEON. Perhaps not. But I intended to.

JENNIFER (*looking at him amazedly: not without pity*). And you tried to destroy that wonderful and beautiful life merely because you grudged him a woman whom you could never have expected to care for you!

RIDGEON. Who kissed my hands. Who believed in me. Who told me her friendship lasted until death.

JENNIFER. And whom you were betraying.

RIDGEON. No. Whom I was saving.

JENNIFER (*gently*). Pray, doctor, from what?

RIDGEON. From making a terrible discovery. From having your life laid waste.

JENNIFER. How?

RIDGEON. No matter. I h a v e saved you. I have been the best friend you ever had. You are happy. You are well. His works are an imperishable joy and pride for you.

JENNIFER. And you think that is y o u r doing. Oh doctor, doctor! Sir Patrick is right: you do think you are a little god. How can you be so silly? Y o u did not paint those pictures which are my imperishable joy and pride: y o u did not speak the words that will always be heavenly music in my ears. I listen to them now whenever I am tired or sad. That is why I am always happy.

RIDGEON. Yes, now that he is dead. Were you always happy when he was alive?

JENNIFER (*wounded*). Oh, you are cruel, cruel. When he was alive I did not know the greatness of my blessing. I worried meanly about little things. I was unkind to him. I was unworthy of him.

RIDGEON (*laughing bitterly*). Ha!

JENNIFER. Dont insult me: dont blaspheme. (*She snatches up the book and presses it to her heart in a paroxysm of remorse, exclaiming*) Oh, my King of Men!

RIDGEON. King of Men! Oh, this is too monstrous, too grotesque. We cruel doctors have kept the secret from you faithfully; but it is like all secrets: it will not keep itself. The buried truth germinates and breaks through to the light.

JENNIFER. What truth?

RIDGEON. What truth! Why, that Louis Dubedat, King of Men, was the most entire and perfect scoundrel, the most miraculously mean rascal, the most callously selfish blackguard that ever made a wife miserable.

JENNIFER (*unshaken: calm and lovely*). He made his wife the happiest woman in the world, doctor.

RIDGEON. No: by all thats true on earth, he made his w i d o w the happiest woman in the world; but it was I who made her a widow. And her happiness is my justification and my reward. Now you know what I did and what I thought of him. Be as angry with me as you like: at least you know me as I really am. If you ever come to care for an elderly man, you will know what you are caring for.

JENNIFER (*kind and quiet*). I am not angry with you any more, Sir Colenso. I knew quite well that you did not like Louis; but it is not your fault: you dont understand: that is all. You never could have believed in him. It is just like your not believing in my religion: it is a sort of sixth sense that you have not got. And (*with a gentle reassuring movement towards him*) don't think that you have shocked me so dreadfully. I know quite well what you mean by his selfishness. He sacrificed everything for his art. In a certain sense he had even to sacrifice everybody—

RIDGEON. Everybody except himself. By keeping that back

he lost the right to sacrifice you, and gave me the right to sacrifice him. Which I did.

JENNIFER (*shaking her head, pitying his error*). He was one of the men who know what women know: that self-sacrifice is vain and cowardly.

RIDGEON. Yes, when the sacrifice is rejected and thrown away. Not when it becomes the food of godhead.

JENNIFER. I dont understand that. And I cant argue with you: you are clever enough to puzzle me, but not to shake me. You are so utterly, so wildly wrong; so incapable of appreciating Louis—

RIDGEON. Oh! (*taking up the Secretary's list*) I have marked five pictures as sold to me.

JENNIFER. They will not be sold to you. Louis' creditors insisted on selling them; but this is my birthday; and they were all brought in for me this morning by my husband.

RIDGEON. By whom?!!!

JENNIFER. By my husband.

RIDGEON (*gabbling and stuttering*). What husband? Whose husband? Which husband? Whom? how? what? Do you mean to say that you have married again?

JENNIFER. Do you forget that Louis disliked widows, and that people who have married happily once always marry again?

RIDGEON. Then I have committed a purely disinterested murder!

The Secretary returns with a pile of catalogues.

THE SECRETARY. Just got the first batch of catalogues in time. The doors are open.

JENNIFER (*to Ridgeon, politely*). So glad you like the pictures, Sir Colenso. Good morning.

RIDGEON. Good morning. (*He goes towards the door; hesitates; turns to say something more; gives it up as a bad job; and goes.*)

THE END